November Road

November Road

A Novel

Lou Berney

HARPER LUXE

An Imprint of HarperCollins*Publishers*

NOVEMBER ROAD. Copyright © 2018 by Lou Berney. All rights reserved. Printed in the United States of America. No part of this book may be used or reproduced in any manner whatsoever without written permission except in the case of brief quotations embodied in critical articles and reviews. For information address HarperCollins Publishers, 195 Broadway, New York, NY 10007.

HarperCollins books may be purchased for educational, business, or sales promotional use. For information please e-mail the Special Markets Department at SPsales@harpercollins.com.

FIRST HARPERLUXE EDITION

ISBN: 978-0-06-285956-3

HarperLuxe™ is a trademark of HarperCollins Publishers.

Library of Congress Cataloging-in-Publication Data is available upon request.

18 19 20 21 22   ID/LSC   10 9 8 7 6 5 4 3 2 1

For Adam, Jake, and Sam

November Road

1963

1

ehold! The Big Easy in all its wicked splendor!
Frank Guidry paused at the corner of Toulouse
to bask in the neon furnace glow. He'd lived in New
Orleans the better part of his thirty-seven years on
earth, but the dirty glitter and sizzle of the French
Quarter still hit his bloodstream like a drug. Yokels and
locals, muggers and hustlers, fire-eaters and magicians.
A go-go girl was draped over the wrought-iron rail of
a second-floor balcony, one boob sprung free from her
sequined negligee and swaying like a metronome to the
beat of the jazz trio inside. Bass, drums, piano, tearing
through "Night and Day." But that was New Orleans
for you. Even the worst band in the crummiest clip
joint in the city could swing, man, swing.

A guy came whipping up the street, screaming bloody murder. Hot on his heels—a woman waving a butcher knife, screaming, too.

Guidry soft-shoed out of their way. The beat cop on the corner yawned. The juggler outside the 500 Club didn't drop a ball. Just another Wednesday night on Bourbon Street.

"Come on, fellas!" The go-go girl on the balcony wagged her boob at a pair of drunken sailors. They stood swaying on the curb, watching their pal puke into the gutter. "Be a gent and buy a lady a drink!"

The sailors leered up at her. "How much?"

"How much you got?"

Guidry smiled. And so the world spins round. The go-go girl had black velvet kitten ears pinned to her bouffant and false eyelashes so long that Guidry didn't know how she could see through them. Maybe that was the point.

He turned onto Bienville, easing through the crowd. He wore a gray-on-gray nailhead suit the color of wet asphalt, cut from a lightweight wool-silk blend that his tailor ordered in special from Italy. White shirt, crimson tie. No hat. If the president of the United States didn't need a hat, then neither did Guidry.

A right on Royal. The bellhop at the Monteleone

scrambled to open the door for him. "How's tricks, Mr. Guidry?"

"Well, Tommy, I'll tell you," Guidry said. "I'm too old to learn any new ones, but the old ones still work just fine."

The Carousel Bar was popping, as usual. Guidry said *hello hello hello how're you how're you* as he worked his way across the room. He shook hands and slapped backs and asked Fat Phil Lorenzo if he'd eaten dinner or just the waiter who brought it. That got a laugh. One of the boys who worked for Sam Saia hooked an arm around Guidry's neck and whispered in his ear.

"I need to talk to you."

"Then talk we shall," Guidry said.

The table in the back corner. Guidry liked the view. One of life's enduring truths: If something was after you, you wanted to see it coming first.

A waitress brought him a double Macallan, rocks on the side. Sam Saia's boy started talking. Guidry sipped his drink and watched the action in the room. The men working the girls, the girls working the men. Smiles and lies and glances veiled by smoke. A hand sliding up under the hem of a dress, lips brushing against an ear. Guidry loved it. Everyone here looking for an angle to work, a tender spot.

"We already have the place, Frank, it's perfect. The guy owns the building, the bar downstairs, he'll front for peanuts. He might as well be giving it to us for free."

"Table games," Guidry said.

"High class all the way. A real carpet joint. But the cops won't talk to us. We need you to smooth the way with that asshole cop Dorsey. You know how he likes his coffee."

The art of the payoff. Guidry understood each man's price, the right kicker to close the deal. A girl? A boy? A girl and a boy? Lieutenant Dorsey of the Eighth District, as Guidry recalled, had a wife who would appreciate a pair of diamond pendant earrings from Adler's.

"You understand that Carlos will have to go along with it," Guidry said.

"Carlos will go along with it if you tell him it's a good play, Frank. We'll give you five points for your piece."

A redhead at the bar had her eye on Guidry. She liked his dark hair and olive skin, his lean build and dimpled chin, the Cajun slant to his green eyes. The slant was how the guineas could tell that Guidry wasn't one of them.

"Five?" Guidry said.

"C'mon, Frank. We're doing all the work here."

"Then you don't need me, do you?"

"Be reasonable."

Guidry could see the redhead working up her nerve with every slow revolution of the merry-go-round. Her girlfriend egged her on. The padded silk back of each seat at the Carousel Bar featured a hand-painted jungle beast. Tiger, elephant, hyena.

"Oh, 'Nature, red in tooth and claw,'" Guidry said.

"What?" Saia's boy said.

"That's Lord Tennyson I'm quoting, you uncultured barbarian."

"Ten points, Frank. Best we can do."

"Fifteen. And a look at the books whenever the mood strikes. Now, skedaddle."

Saia's boy glowered and seethed, but such were the rude realities of supply and demand. Lieutenant Dorsey was the hardest-headed cop in New Orleans. Only Guidry had the skill to soften him up.

He ordered another scotch. The redhead crushed out her cigarette and strolled over. She had Cleopatra eyes—the latest look—and a golden tan. She was a stewardess, maybe, home from a layover in Miami or Vegas. She sat down without asking, impressed with her own boldness.

"My girlfriend over there told me to stay away from you," she said.

Guidry wondered how many openers she'd rehearsed in her mind before she picked the winner. "But here you are."

"My girlfriend says you have some very interesting friends."

"Well, I've plenty of dull ones, too," Guidry said.

"She says you work for you-know-who," she said.

"The notorious Carlos Marcello?"

"Is it true?"

"Never heard of him."

She toyed with the cherry in her drink, making a show of it. She was nineteen, twenty years old. In a couple of years, she'd marry the biggest Uptown bank account she could find and settle down. Now, though, she wanted an adventure. Guidry was delighted to oblige.

"So aren't you curious?" the redhead said. "Why I didn't listen to my girlfriend and stay away from you?"

"Because you don't like it when people tell you that you can't have something you want," he said.

She narrowed her eyes, as if he'd snuck a peek in her purse while she wasn't looking. "I don't."

"Neither do I," Guidry said. "We only get one ride in this life, one time around. If we don't enjoy every minute of it, if we don't embrace pleasure with open arms, who's to blame for that?"

"I like to enjoy life," she said.

"I like to hear that."

"My name is Eileen."

Guidry saw that Mackey Pagano had entered the bar. Gaunt and gray and unshaven, Mackey looked like he'd been living under a rock. He spotted Guidry and jerked his chin at him.

Oh, Mackey. His timing was poor. But he had an eye for opportunity and never brought in a deal that didn't pay.

Guidry stood. "Wait here, Eileen."

"Where are you going?" she said, surprised.

He crossed the room and gave Mackey a hug. Ye gods. Mackey smelled as bad he looked. He needed a shower and a fresh suit, without delay.

"Must have been one helluva party, Mack," Guidry said. "Regale me."

"I've got a proposition for you," Mackey said.

"I thought you might."

"Let's take a walk."

He grabbed Guidry's elbow and steered him back out into the lobby. Past the cigar stand, down a deserted corridor, down another one.

"Are we going all the way to Cuba, Mack?" Guidry said. "I won't look as good with a beard."

They finally stopped, in front of the doors to the back service entrance.

"So what do you have for me?" Guidry said.

"I don't have anything," Mackey said.

"What?"

"I just needed to talk to you."

"You've noted that I have better things to do at the moment," Guidry said.

"I'm sorry. I'm in a bind, Frankie. I might be in a real bind."

Guidry had a smile for every occasion. This occasion: to hide the uneasiness that began to creep over him. He gave Mackey's shoulder a squeeze. *You'll be all right, old buddy, old pal. How bad can it be?* But Guidry didn't like the shake in Mackey's voice, the way Mackey kept his grip tight on the sleeve of Guidry's suit coat.

Had anyone noticed the two of them leaving the Carousel together? What if someone happened to come round that corner right now and caught them skulking? Trouble in this business had a way of spreading, just like a cold or the clap. Guidry knew you could catch it from the wrong handshake, an unlucky glance.

"I'll come by your pad this weekend," Guidry said. "I'll help you sort it out."

"I need to get it sorted out now."

Guidry tried to ease away. "I've got to split. Tomorrow, Mack. Cross my heart."

"I haven't been back to my place in a week," Mackey said.

"Name the spot. I'll meet you wherever you want."

Mackey watched him. Those hooded eyes, they seemed almost gentle in a certain light. Mackey knew that Guidry was lying about meeting tomorrow. Of course he did. Guidry came by his talent for deception naturally, but Mackey had taught him the nuances, had helped him hone and perfect his craft.

"How long have we known each other, Frankie?" Mackey said.

"I see," Guidry said. "The sentimental approach."

"You were sixteen years old."

Fifteen. Guidry just off the turnip truck from Ascension Parish, Louisiana, and tumbling around the Faubourg Marigny. Living hand to mouth, stealing cans of pork and beans off the shelves of the A&P. Mackey saw promise in him and gave Guidry his first real job. Every morning for a year, Guidry had picked up the cut from the girls on St. Peter and hurried it over to Snake Gonzalez, the legendary pimp. Five dollars a day and the quick end to any romantic notions Guidry might have still had about the human species.

"Please, Frankie," Mackey said.

"What do you want?"

"Talk to Seraphine. Get the lay of the land for me. Maybe I'm crazy."

"What happened? Never mind. I don't care." Guidry wasn't interested in the details of Mackey's predicament. He was only interested in the details of *his* predicament, the one that Mackey had just created for him.

"You remember about a year ago," Mackey said, "when I went out to 'Frisco to talk to a guy about that thing with the judge. Carlos called it all off, you remember, but—"

"Stop," Guidry said. "I don't care. Damn it, Mack."

"I'm sorry, Frankie. You're the only one I can trust. I wouldn't ask otherwise."

Mackey waited. Guidry tugged the knot of his tie loose. What was life but this? A series of rapid calculations: the shifting of weights, the balancing of scales. The only poor decision was a decision you allowed someone else to make for you.

"All right, all right," Guidry said. "But I can't put a word in for you, Mack. It's my hide then, too. You understand that?"

"I understand," Mackey said. "Just find out if I need to blow town. I'll blow tonight."

"Stay put till you hear from me."

"I'm over on Frenchmen Street, at Darlene Monette's place. Come by afterward. Don't leave a message."

"Darlene Monette?"

"She owes me one," Mackey said. He watched Guidry with those hooded eyes. Begging. Telling Guidry, You *owe me one.*

"Stay put until you hear from me," Guidry said.

"Thank you, Frankie."

Guidry called Seraphine from a pay phone in the lobby. She didn't answer at home, so he tried Carlos's private office out on Airline Highway in Metairie. How many people had that number? It couldn't have been more than a dozen. Look at me now, Ma!

"Are we not still meeting Friday, *mon cher?*" Seraphine said.

"We are," Guidry said. "Can't a fella just call to shoot the breeze?"

"My favorite pastime."

"I caught a rumor that Uncle Carlos is looking for a penny he dropped. Our friend Mackey. Or do I have that wrong?"

Guidry heard a silky rustle. When Seraphine stretched, she arched her back like a cat. He heard the *tink* of a single ice cube in a glass.

"You don't have that wrong," she said.

Goddamn it. So Mackey's fears were not unfounded. Carlos wanted him dead.

"Are you still there, *mon cher?*"

Goddamn it. Mackey had cooked Guidry dinner a thousand times. He'd introduced Guidry to the Marcello brothers. He'd vouched for Guidry when no one else in the world knew that Guidry existed.

But all that was yesterday. Guidry cared only about today, about tomorrow.

"Tell Carlos to have a look on Frenchmen Street," Guidry said. "There's a house with green shutters on the corner of Rampart. Darlene Monette's place. Top floor, the flat in back."

"Thank you, *mon cher*," Seraphine said.

Guidry strolled back to the Carousel. The redhead had waited for him. He watched her for a minute from the doorway. Yea or nay, ladies and gentlemen of the jury? He liked how she'd started to wilt a bit, her Cleopatra eyeliner blurring and the flip in her hair going flat. She shook off a mope who tried to make time with her and ran a finger along the rim of her empty highball glass. Deciding to give Guidry five more minutes, that was it, no more, and this time she meant it.

He wished that it had played out differently with Mackey. He wished that Seraphine had said, *You've heard wrong,* mon cher, *Carlos has no quarrel with*

Mackey. But now all Guidry could do was shrug. Weights and measures, simple arithmetic. Someone might have seen him with Mackey tonight. Guidry couldn't risk it. Why would he want to?

He took the redhead back to his place. He lived fifteen floors above Canal Street, in a modern high-rise that was a sleek spike of steel and concrete, sealed off and cooled from the inside out. In the summer, when the rest of the city sweltered, Guidry didn't break a sweat.

"Ooh," the redhead said, "I dig it."

The floor-to-ceiling view, the black leather sofa, the glass-and-chromium bar cart, the expensive hi-fi. She positioned herself by the window, a hand on her hip, weight on one leg to show off her curves, glancing over her shoulder the way she'd seen the models in magazines do it.

"I'm wild to live high up like this someday," she said. "All the lights. All the stars. It's like being in a rocket ship."

Guidry didn't want her to get the wrong idea, that he intended to have a conversation, so he pushed her up against the window. The glass flexed and the stars shimmied. He kissed her. The neck, the tender joint between her jaw and ear. She smelled like a cigarette butt floating in a puddle of Lanvin perfume.

Her fingers raked his hair. He grabbed her hand and pinned it behind her. With his other hand, he reached up under her skirt.

"Oh," she said.

Satin panties. He left them on her for now and lightly, lightly traced the contours beneath, two fingers gliding over every subtle swell and crease. At the same time kissing her neck harder, letting her feel his teeth.

"Oh." She meant it this time.

He pushed the elastic band out of the way and slid his fingers inside her. In and out, the pad of his thumb on her clit, searching for the rhythm she liked, the right amount of pressure. When he felt her breathing shift, her hips rotate, he eased off. The muscles in her neck tightened with surprise. He waited for a few seconds and then started again. Her relief was a shiver of electricity running through her body. When he eased off a second time, she gasped like she'd been kicked.

"Don't stop," she said.

He leaned back so he could look at her. Her eyes were glazed, her face a smear of bliss and need. "Say please."

"Please," she said.

"Say pretty please."

"Please."

He finished her. Every woman came in a different way. Eyes slitted or chin thrust out, lips parted or nostrils flared, a sigh or a snarl. Always, though, there was that one instant when the world around her ceased to exist, a white atomic flash.

"Oh, my God." The redhead's world pieced itself back together. "My legs are shaking."

Weights and measures, simple arithmetic. Mackey would have made the same calculation if his and Guidry's roles had been reversed. Mackey would have picked up the phone and made the same call that Guidry made, without question. And Guidry would have respected him for it. *C'est la vie.* Such was this particular life, at least.

He flipped the redhead around, hiked up her skirt, yanked down her panties. The glass flexed again when he thrust into her. Guidry's landlord claimed the windows in the building could withstand a hurricane, but that remained to be seen.

2

Charlotte imagined herself alone on the bridge of a ship, a storm raging and the sea flinging itself over the deck. Sailcloth ripped, lines snapped. And toss in a few splintering planks for good measure, why don't we? The sun bled a cold, colorless light that made Charlotte feel as if she had already drowned.

"Mommy," Rosemary called from the living room, "Joan and I have a question."

"I told you to come eat breakfast, chickadees," Charlotte said.

"September is your favorite month of autumn, isn't it, Mommy? And November is your least favorite?"

"Come eat breakfast."

The bacon was burning. Charlotte tripped on the dog, sprawled in the middle of the floor, and lost her shoe. On the way back across the kitchen—the toaster had begun to smoke now, too—she tripped on the shoe. The dog twitched and grimaced, a seizure approaching. Charlotte prayed for a false alarm.

Plates. Forks. Charlotte put on lipstick with one hand as she poured juice with the other. It was already half past seven. Where did the time go? Anywhere but here, apparently.

"Girls!" she called.

Dooley shuffled into the kitchen, still in his pajamas, with the greenish tint and martyred posture of an El Greco saint.

"You're going to be late for work again, honey," Charlotte said.

He sagged into a chair. "I feel awful puny this morning."

Charlotte supposed that he did. It had been after one in the morning when she heard the front door finally bang open, when she heard him come bumping and weaving down the hallway. He'd taken off his pants before he came to bed but had been too drunk to remember his sport coat. As drunk as usual, in other words.

"Would you like some coffee?" Charlotte said. "I'll make you some toast."

"Might be the flu, I'm thinking."

She admired her husband's ability to keep a straight face. Or maybe he really believed his own lies? He was a trusting soul, after all.

He took a sip of the coffee and then shuffled back out of the kitchen, into the bathroom. She heard him retch, then rinse.

The girls climbed into their seats at the table. Rosemary, seven, and Joan, eight. To look at them, you'd never guess that they were sisters. Joan's little blond head was always as sleek and shiny as the head of a pin. Meanwhile several tendrils of Rosemary's unruly chestnut hair had already sprung free from the tortoiseshell band. An hour from now, she'd look as if she'd been raised by wolves.

"But I like November," Joan said.

"No, Joan, see, September is best because that's the one month every year when we're the same age," Rosemary said. "And October has Halloween. Halloween is better than Thanksgiving, of course. So November has to be your least favorite month of autumn."

"Okay," Joan said. She was ever agreeable. A good thing, with a little sister like Rosemary.

Charlotte searched for her purse. She'd had it in her hand a moment ago. Hadn't she? She heard Dooley retch again, rinse again. The dog had flopped over and then settled. According to the veterinarian, the new medicine might reduce the frequency of the seizures or it might not. They would have to wait and see.

She found her lost shoe beneath the dog. She had to pry it out from beneath the thick, heavy folds of him.

"Poor Daddy," Rosemary said. "Is he under the weather again?"

"You could certainly say that," Charlotte conceded. "Yes."

Dooley returned from the bathroom, looking less green but more martyred.

"Daddy!" the girls said.

He winced. "Shhh. My head."

"Daddy, Joan and I agree that September is our favorite month of autumn and November is our least favorite month. Do you want us to explain why?"

"Unless it snows in November," Joan said.

"Oh, yes!" Rosemary said. "If it snows, then it's the best month. Joan, let's pretend it's snowing now. Let's pretend the wind is howling and the snow is melting down our necks."

"Okay," Joan said.

Charlotte set the toast in front of Dooley and gave each girl a kiss on the top of the head. Her love for her daughters defied understanding. Sometimes the sudden, unexpected detonation of it shook Charlotte from head to toe.

"Charlie, I wouldn't mind a fried egg," Dooley said.

"You don't want to be late for work again, honey."

"Oh, hell. Pete doesn't mind when I come in. I might call in sick today anyway."

Pete Winemiller owned the hardware store in town. A friend of Dooley's father, Pete was the latest in a long line of friends and clients who'd done the old man a favor and hired his wayward son. And the latest in a long line of employers whose patience with Dooley had been quickly exhausted.

But Charlotte had to proceed with caution. She'd learned early in the marriage that the wrong word or tone of voice or poorly timed frown could send Dooley into a wounded sulk that might last for hours.

"Didn't Pete say last week that he needed you bright and early every day?" she said.

"Oh, don't worry about Pete. He's full of gas."

"But I bet he's counting on you. Maybe if you just—"

"Lord Almighty, Charlie," Dooley said. "I'm a sick man. Can't you see that? You're trying to wring blood from a stone."

If only dealing with Dooley were so simple or so easy as that. Charlotte hesitated and then turned away. "All right," she said. "I'll fry you an egg."

"I'm going to lie down on the couch for a minute. Holler at me when it's ready."

She watched him exit. Where *did* the time go? Only a moment ago, Charlotte had been eleven years old, not twenty-eight. Only a moment ago, she'd been barefoot and baked brown by the long prairie summer, racing through swishing bluestem and switchgrass as tall as her waist, leaping from the high bank of the Redbud River, cannonballing into the water. Parents always warned their children to stay in the shallows, on the town side of the river, but Charlotte had been the strongest swimmer of any her friends, undaunted by the current, and she could make it to the far shore, to parts unknown, with hardly any trouble at all.

Charlotte remembered lying sprawled in the sun afterward, daydreaming about skyscrapers in New York City and movie premieres in Hollywood and jeeps on the African savanna, wondering which of many delightful and exotic futures awaited her. Anything was possible. Everything was possible.

She reached for Joan's plate and knocked over her juice. The glass hit the floor and shattered. The dog began to jerk and grimace again, more forcefully this time.

"Mommy?" Rosemary said. "Are you crying or laughing?"

Charlotte knelt to stroke the dog's head. With her

other hand, she collected the sharp, sparkling shards of the juice glass.

"Well, sweetie," she said, "I think maybe both."

She finally made it downtown at a quarter past eight. "Downtown" was far too grand a designation. Three blocks square, a handful of redbrick buildings with Victorian cupolas and rough-faced limestone trim, not one of them more than three stories tall. A diner, a dress shop, a hardware store, a bakery. The First (and only) Bank of Woodrow, Oklahoma.

The photography studio was on the corner of Main and Oklahoma, next to the bakery. Charlotte had worked there for almost five years now. Mr. Hotchkiss specialized in formal portraits. Beaming brides-to-be, toddlers in starched sailor suits, freshly delivered infants. Charlotte mixed the darkroom chemicals, processed the film, printed the contact sheets, and tinted the black-and-white portraits. For hour after tedious hour, she sat at her table, using linseed oil and paint to add a golden glow to hair, a blue gleam to irises.

She lit a cigarette and started in on the Richardson toddlers, a pair of identical twins with matching Santa hats and stunned expressions.

Mr. Hotchkiss puttered over and bent down to examine her work. A widower in his sixties, he smelled of apple-flavored pipe tobacco and photochemical fixative. He tended, as preface to any important pronouncement, to hitch up his pants.

He hitched up his pants. "Well, all right."

"Thank you," Charlotte said. "I couldn't decide on the shade of red for the hats. The debate with myself grew heated."

Mr. Hotchkiss glanced at her transistor radio on the shelf. The AM station that she liked broadcast from Kansas City, so by the time the signal reached Woodrow, it had gone fuzzy and ragged. Even after Charlotte had done much fiddling with the dial and the antenna, Bob Dylan still sounded as if he was singing "Don't Think Twice, It's All Right" from the bottom of a well.

"I'll tell you what, Charlie," Mr. Hotchkiss said. "That old boy's no Bobby Vinton."

"I fully agree," Charlotte said.

"Mumble, mumble, mumble. I don't understand a thing he's saying."

"The world is changing, Mr. Hotchkiss. It's speaking a new language."

"Not here in Logan County it's not," he said, "thank goodness."

No, not here in Logan County. On that fact Charlotte stood corrected.

"Mr. Hotchkiss," she said, "have you had a chance yet to look at that new photo I gave you?"

In addition to his duties at the studio, Mr. Hotchkiss served as photo editor for the local newspaper, the *Woodrow Trumpet*. Charlotte coveted one of the freelance assignments. Several months ago she'd persuaded Mr. Hotchkiss to loan her one of his lesser cameras.

Her early attempts at photography had been woeful. She'd kept at it, though. She practiced on her lunch hour, if she had a few minutes between errands, and early in the morning before the girls woke. When she took the girls to the library on Saturday, she studied magazines and art books. Taking pictures, thinking about the world from a perspective she otherwise wouldn't have considered, made her feel the way she did when she listened to Bob Dylan and Ruth Brown—bright and vital, as if her small life were, just for a moment, part of something larger.

"Mr. Hotchkiss?" she said.

He'd been distracted by the morning mail. "Hmm?" he said.

"I asked if you'd had a chance yet to look at my new photo."

He hitched up his pants and cleared his throat. "Ah, yes. Well. Yes."

The photo she'd given him was of Alice Hibbard and

Christine Kuriger, waiting to cross Oklahoma Avenue at the end of the day. The backlight, the contrast . . . what had caught Charlotte's eye was how their shadows seemed more substantial, almost more real, than the two women themselves.

"And what did you think?" Charlotte said.

"Well. Have I explained the rule of thirds?"

Only a few dozen times. "Yes, I understand," she said. "But in this case I was trying to capture the—"

"Charlotte," he said. "Dear. You're a lovely, smart girl, and I'm lucky to have you. The girl I had before you . . . well. All thumbs and not a brain in her head, bless her heart. I don't know what I'd do without you, Charlie."

He patted her shoulder. She was tempted to present an ultimatum. Either he gave her a chance with the *Trumpet*—she'd take any assignment, no matter how lowly—or he'd find out *exactly* what he would do without her.

Did she have any talent as a photographer? Charlotte wasn't sure but thought she might. She knew the difference between an interesting picture and a dull one at least. She knew the difference between the photos in *Life* and *National Geographic* that seemed to leap off the page and the ones in the *Trumpet* that sprawled like corpses on a slab.

"Mr. Hotchkiss," she said.

He'd turned and started to putter away. "Hmm?"

But of course she couldn't afford to quit the studio. The money she brought home every week kept the ship afloat. And perhaps Mr. Hotchkiss was right and Charlotte was all thumbs when it came to photography. He was a professional, after all, with a framed certificate of merit from the Oklahoma Society of Professional Journalists. He might be doing Charlotte a favor. *Thank goodness,* she might say years from now, looking back. *Thank goodness I didn't waste any more time on* that.

"Nothing," she told Mr. Hotchkiss. "Never mind."

She returned to work on the Richardson toddlers. Their parents were Harold and Virginia. Harold's sister Beanie had been Charlotte's best friend in grade school. His father had been Charlotte's choir director in junior high. His mother loved pineapple upside-down cake, and every year Charlotte made sure to bake one for her birthday.

Virginia Richardson (née Norton) had worked with Charlotte on the high-school yearbook. She'd insisted that Charlotte double-check the spelling of every caption she wrote. Bob, Virginia's older brother, had been a dashingly handsome varsity star in track, baseball, and football. He was married now to Hope Kirby, who a year after graduation had blossomed from ugly duckling to beautiful swan. Hope Kirby's mother, Irene, had been Charlotte's mother's maid of honor.

Charlotte had known them all her life, the Richardsons and the Nortons and the Kirbys. She'd known *everyone* in town all her life, she realized. And everyone in town had known her. Always would.

Was it selfish of her, she wondered, to want more from her life? To want more for Rosemary and Joan? Woodrow was idyllic in many ways. Quaint, safe, friendly. But it was also interminably dull, as locked in its stubborn, small-minded ways, as resistant to new things and ideas, as Mr. Hotchkiss. Charlotte longed to live in a place where it wasn't so hard to tell the past from the future.

A few months ago, she'd suggested to Dooley that they consider moving away—to Kansas City, maybe, or to Chicago. Dooley had stared at her dumbfounded, as if she'd suggested that they strip off their clothes and run screaming through the streets.

Today, on her lunch hour, Charlotte had no time for photography. She wolfed her sandwich, picked up the dog's medicine at the vet, and then hurried down the street to the bank. Dooley had promised to talk to Jim

Feeney this time, but no one was more adept at evading unpleasant tasks than her husband. Charlotte, unfortunately, couldn't afford the luxury.

"Oh, darn, did I forget?" Dooley would say, his smile bashful without being apologetic, a little boy who'd gotten away with much in his life and become accustomed to it.

At the bank Charlotte had to sit and wait until Jim Feeney finished a phone call.

Little Jimmy Feeney. He and Charlotte had been in the same class since kindergarten. In grade school he'd been held back a year because arithmetic eluded him. In high school he'd broken his arm while attempting to tip a cow. Yet there he sat, behind the assistant manager's desk, because he was a man. And here she sat, on the other side of the desk, because she was not.

"Hello, Charlie," he said. "What may I help you with today?"

What indeed? Charlotte wondered if Jim relished her mortification or was just oblivious to it.

"Hello, Jim," she said. "I'm afraid I have to ask for an extension on our mortgage payment this month."

"I see."

Bonnie Bublitz observed them from the teller cage. So did Vernon Phipps, cashing a check. Hope Norton (née Kirby) fluttered past and then fluttered back to hand Jim a folder.

I won't beg, Charlotte thought, as she prepared to do just that.

"We just need a short extension, Jim," she said. "A week or two."

"This puts me in a spot, Charlie," he said.

"I'm sorry."

"It'd be the third extension this year, you know."

"I do know. Things have been a bit tight lately. But they're looking up."

Jim drummed his fountain pen against the edge of his ledger. Thinking, or coming as near to it as he was able.

"You have to pinch every penny, Charlie," he said, even though he knew Dooley, even though he knew full well the real source of their financial difficulties. "A detailed budget can be very useful. Household expenses and such."

"Just an extra two weeks," Charlotte said. "Please, Jim."

His drumming trailed away. *Da-da-da, da-da, da.* Like a fading heartbeat. "Well, I suppose I can give you one more. . . ."

Earl Grindle stepped out of the manager's office. He looked wildly around, as if he couldn't fathom why everyone else in the bank continued to sit or stand calmly.

He took off his glasses and then put them back on. "Someone shot him. Someone shot President Kennedy."

Charlotte walked back to the photography studio. Mr. Hotchkiss had not learned the news about the president yet. She peeked into the darkroom and saw him tinkering, blissfully ignorant, with the lamphouse of the Beseler enlarger.

She sat down at her table and started tinting a new portrait. The Moore baby, three months old. He was propped on a carnation-shaped swirl of satin that, Charlotte decided, required a subtle shade of ivory.

The president had been shot. Charlotte wasn't sure if she'd truly grasped that yet. At the bank she'd watched as Hope Norton dropped her armful of folders. As Bonnie Bublitz in the teller cage burst into tears. As Vernon Phipps had walked out of the bank in a trance, leaving behind on the counter a stack of five-dollar bills. Jimmy Feeney kept asking, "Is this a joke? Earl, is this some kind of a joke?"

The smell of linseed oil and apple-flavored pipe tobacco. The hum and chuckle of the radiator. Charlotte worked. She continued to remain curiously unmoved, curiously removed, by the news from Dallas. For a moment she couldn't remember what day of the week it was, or what year. It could have been any day, any year.

The phone rang. She heard Mr. Hotchkiss walk to his office and answer it.

"What's that?" he said. "What? Oh, no! Oh, no!"

The parents of the Moore baby, their third, were Tim and Ann Moore. Charlotte's first babysitting job had been for Tim's pack of younger brothers. Ann's sister was none other than Hope Norton, who was married to Virginia Richardson's older brother, Bob. And yes, yet another link in the chain: Ann's cousin on her mother's side was Dooley's boss at the hardware store, Pete Winemiller.

"Oh, no," she heard Mr. Hotchkiss say. "I don't believe it."

The president had been shot. Charlotte could understand why people were shocked and upset. They feared an uncertain future. They worried that their lives would never be the same.

And maybe their lives wouldn't be the same. But Charlotte knew that *her* life would remain undisturbed, her future—and the future of her daughters—certain. A bullet fired hundreds of miles away didn't change that.

She dipped her brush and stroked rosy pink life into the Moore baby's black-and-white cheek. Her favorite movie, as a child, had been *The Wizard of Oz,* her favorite moment when Dorothy opened the door of her black-and-white farmhouse and stepped into a strange and wonderful land.

Lucky Dorothy. Charlotte dipped her brush again and not for the first time imagined a tornado dropping from the sky and blowing her far away, into a world full of color.

3

S unlight slid over Guidry, and the dream he'd been having jerked and blurred like film jumping off the sprockets of a movie projector. Five seconds later he couldn't remember much about the dream. A bridge. A house in the middle of the bridge, where no house should be. Guidry had been standing at a window of the house, or maybe he was on a balcony, peering down at the water and trying to spot a ripple.

He flopped out of bed, his head as huge and tender as a rotten pumpkin. Aspirin. Two glasses of water. He was prepared, now, to pull on his pants and negotiate the hallway. Art Pepper. That was Guidry's favorite cure for a hangover. He slid *Smack Up* from the cardboard sleeve and placed it on the turntable. "How Can

You Lose" was his favorite tune on the album. He felt better already.

It was two o'clock in the afternoon, or what residents of the French Quarter called the crack of dawn. Guidry made a pot of scalding-hot coffee and filled two mugs, topping off his with a healthy shot of Macallan. Scotch was his other favorite cure for a hangover. He took a swallow and listened to Pepper's saxophone weaving in and out of the melody like a dog dodging traffic.

The redhead was still knocked out, the sheet on her side of the bed kicked away and one arm flung over her head. But wait a second. She was a brunette now, no longer a redhead. Fuller lips, no freckles. How had that happened? He remained perplexed—was he still dreaming?—until he remembered that today was Friday, not Thursday, and the redhead had been the night before last.

Too bad. He could've dined out on that story for weeks, how he was so good in the sack that he'd banged the freckles right off a girl.

Jane? Jennifer? Guidry had forgotten the brunette's name. She worked for TWA. Or maybe that had been the redhead before her. Julia?

"Rise and shine, sunshine," he said.

She turned to him with a sleepy smile, her lipstick flaking off. "What time is it?"

He handed her a mug. "Time for you to beat it."

In the shower he lathered up and planned his day. Seraphine first, find out what she had for him. After that he'd get started on the deal that Sam Saia's boy had brought him at the Carousel the other night. Was Saia's boy steady? Everything Guidry had heard about him said so, but better to ask around and make sure before he committed himself.

What else? Pop into the bar across from the courthouse to buy a few rounds and soak up the scuttlebutt. Dinner with Al LaBruzzo, God help us all. LaBruzzo had his heart set on buying a go-go joint. Guidry would have to handle him delicately—he was Sam's brother, and Sam was Carlos's driver. By the end of dinner, Guidry would have to convince Al to convince himself that no, no, he didn't want Guidry's money after all, would refuse even if Guidry got down on his knees and begged him to take it.

Guidry shaved, trimmed his nails, browsed the closet. He picked a brown windowpane suit with slim notched lapels and a Continental cut. Cream-colored shirt, green tie. Green tie? No. Thanksgiving was less than a week away, and he wanted to get into the spirit of the season. He swapped the green tie for one the deep, dusty orange of an autumn sunset.

When he stepped into the living room, he saw that

the brunette was still there. She was curled up on the sofa—not even dressed yet, ye gods—watching the television.

He went over to the window and found her skirt and her blouse on the floor where they'd fallen the night before, her bra hanging on the bar cart. He tossed the clothes at her.

"One Mississippi," he said. "Two Mississippi. I'll give you till five."

"He's gone." She didn't even look at Guidry. "I can't believe it."

Guidry realized that she was crying. "Who?"

"They shot him," she said.

"Shot who?"

He looked over at the TV. On the screen a news-caster sat behind a desk, taking a deep drag off his cigarette. He looked limp and dazed, as if someone had just dumped a bucket of cold water on him.

"The motorcade had just passed the Texas School Book Depository in downtown Dallas," the newscaster said. "Senator Ralph Yarborough told our reporter that he was riding three cars behind the president's car when he heard the three distinct rifle shots."

The president of what? That was Guidry's first thought. The president of some oil company? Of some jungle republic that no one had ever heard of? He didn't understand why the brunette was so broken up about it.

And then it clicked. He lowered himself next to her and watched the newscaster read from a sheet of paper. A sniper had fired from the sixth floor of a building in Dealey Plaza. Kennedy, riding in the backseat of a Lincoln Continental convertible, had been hit. They'd taken him to Parkland Hospital. A priest had administered last rites. At 1:30 P.M., an hour and a half ago, the doctors had pronounced the president dead.

The sniper, the newscaster said, was in custody. Some mope who worked at the School Book Depository.

"I can't believe it," the brunette said. "I can't believe he's gone."

For a second, Guidry didn't move. Didn't breathe. The brunette reached for his hand and squeezed. She thought he couldn't believe it either, that a bullet had blown the top off Jack Kennedy's head.

"Get dressed." Guidry stood, pulled her to her feet. "Get dressed and get out."

She just stared at him, so he wrestled her arm into the sleeve of the blouse. Forget the bra. He would have tossed her naked out the front door if he weren't worried she'd make a scene or go bawling to the cops.

Her other arm now, dead and rubbery. She'd begun to sob. He told himself to cool it, cool it. Guidry had a reputation around town: the man who never rattled, no matter how hard you shook him. So don't start now, brother.

"Sunshine." He stroked her cheek with the back of his hand. "I'm sorry. I can't believe it either. I can't believe he's gone."

"I know," she said. "I know."

She didn't know anything. The newscaster on TV was explaining that Dealey Plaza in Dallas was between Houston, Elm, and Commerce Streets. Guidry knew where the fuck it was. He'd been there a week ago, dropping a sky-blue '59 Cadillac Eldorado in a parking garage two blocks away on Commerce.

Seraphine didn't usually ask him to do that sort of work. It was below his current exalted station, as it were. But since Guidry was already in town, to wine and dine and soothe the nerves of a jittery deputy chief who Carlos needed to keep on the pad . . . why not? Sure, I don't mind, all for one and one for all.

Oh, by the way, mon cher, *I have a small errand for you when you're in Dallas. . . .*

Oh, shit, oh, shit. A getaway switch car was standard procedure for a lot of Carlos's high-profile hits. After the gunman finished the job, he would beeline it to the car stashed nearby and hit the road in a clean set of wheels.

When Guidry parked the sky-blue Eldorado two blocks from Dealey Plaza, he'd assumed a dark future for some unlucky soul—a lay-off bookie whose numbers didn't tally or the jittery deputy chief if Guidry's soothing didn't work.

But the president of the United States . . .

"Go home," he told the brunette. "All right? Freshen up, and then let's . . . What do you want to do? Neither of us, we shouldn't be alone right now."

"No," she agreed. "I want to . . . I don't know. We could just . . ."

"Go home and freshen up, and then we'll have a nice lunch," he said. "All right? What's your address? I'll pick you up in an hour. After lunch we'll find a church and light a candle for his soul."

Guidry nodding at her until she nodded back. Helping her step into her skirt, looking around for her shoes.

Maybe it was just a coincidence, he told himself, that he'd stashed a getaway car two blocks from Dealey Plaza. Maybe it was just a coincidence that Carlos despised the Kennedy brothers more than any other two human beings on earth. Jack and Bobby had dragged Carlos in front of the Senate and pissed on his leg in front of the whole country. A couple of years after that, they'd tried to deport him to Guatemala.

Maybe Carlos had forgiven and forgotten. Sure. And

maybe some mope who lugged boxes of books around a warehouse for a living could make a rifle shot like that—six floors up, a moving target, a breeze, trees in the way.

Guidry eased the brunette onto the elevator, off the elevator, through the lobby of his building, into the back of a cab. He had to snap his fingers at the hack, who was bent over his radio listening to the news and hadn't even noticed them.

"Go home and freshen up." Guidry gave the brunette a kiss on the cheek. "I'll pick you up in an hour."

In the Quarter, grown men stood on the sidewalk and wept. Women wandered down the street as if they'd been struck blind. A Lucky Dog vendor shared his radio with a shoeshine boy. When in the history of civilization had that happened before? They shall beat their swords into plowshares. The leopard will lie down with the goat.

Guidry had fifteen minutes to spare, so he ducked into Gaspar's. He'd never been inside during the day. With the house lights on, it was a gloomy joint. You could see the stains on the floor, the stains on the ceiling, the velvet stage curtain patched with electrical tape.

A group was huddled by the bar, people like Guidry who'd been drawn inside by the blue throb of the

TV. A newscaster—a different one than before, just as dazed—read a statement from Johnson. President Johnson now.

"I know that the world shares the sorrow that Mrs. Kennedy and her family bear," Johnson said. "I will do my best. That is all I can do. I ask for your help—and God's."

The bartender poured shots of whiskey, on the house. The lady next to Guidry, a proper little Garden District widow, ancient as time and frail as a snowflake, picked up a drink and knocked it back.

On TV they cut to the Dallas police station. Cops in suits and white cowboy hats, reporters, gawkers, everybody pushing and shoving. There was the mope, in the middle of it all, getting bounced around. A little guy, rat-faced, one of his eyes swollen shut. Lee Harvey Oswald, the announcer said his name was. He looked groggy and bewildered, like a kid who'd been dragged out of bed in the dead of night and hoped that all this might be just a nightmare.

A reporter shouted a question that Guidry couldn't make out as the cops shoved Oswald into a room. Another reporter moved into the frame, speaking to the camera.

"He says he has nothing against anybody," the reporter said, "and has not committed any act of violence."

The Garden District widow downed a second shot of whiskey. She looked furious enough to spit. "How could this happen?" she kept muttering to herself. "How could this happen?"

Guidry couldn't say for sure, but he had an educated opinion. A professional sharpshooter, an independent contractor brought in by Carlos. Positioned on the sixth floor of the Texas School Book Depository, or on the floor below to put a frame on Oswald, or maybe set up on the other side of the plaza, an elevated spot away from the crowds. After the real sniper made his shot, he wrapped up his rifle and strolled down Commerce Street to the sky-blue Eldorado waiting for him.

Guidry left Gaspar's and headed to Jackson Square. A priest comforted his flock on the steps of the cathedral. A time to plant, a time to pluck up what has been planted. The usual jive.

Guidry was walking too fast. *Cool it, brother.*

If the cops hooked Carlos's sharpshooter and connected him to the Eldorado, they'd be able to connect the Eldorado to Guidry. Guidry had picked up the car from a supermarket parking lot in the colored part of Dallas. Door left unlocked for him, keys under the visor. Guidry's prints weren't on the car—he wasn't stupid, he'd worn his driving gloves—but someone might remember him. A sky-blue Cadillac Eldorado, a white man in the colored part of town. Someone would remember him.

Because this wasn't just another ho-hum murder, some shoe-leather wiseguy popped in a back alley, the detectives and the prosecutor already snug in Carlos's pocket. This was the president of the United States. Bobby Kennedy and the FBI wouldn't stop until they'd turned over every goddamn rock.

A sticky drizzle blew away, and the sun poked through the clouds. Seraphine stood next to the statue of Old Hickory. The horse rearing, Andrew Jackson tipping his hat. The shadow from the statue split Seraphine in half. She smiled at Guidry, one eye bright and liquid and playful, the other a dark green stone.

He wanted to grab her and shove her up against the base of the statue and demand to know why she'd stuck him right in the middle of this, the crime of the century. Instead, wisely, he smiled back. With Seraphine you had to proceed with caution, or else you didn't proceed for long.

"Hello, little boy," she said. "The forest is dark and the wolves howl. Hold my hand and I'll help you find your way home."

"I'll take my chances with the wolves, thanks," Guidry said.

She pouted. *Is that what you think of me?* And then

she laughed. Of course it was what he thought of her. Guidry would be a fool if he didn't.

"I adore autumn," she said. "Don't you? The air so crisp. The scent of melancholy. Autumn tells us the truth about the world."

You wouldn't call Seraphine pretty. Regal. With a high, broad forehead and a dramatic arch to her nose, dark hair marcelled and parted on the side. Skin just a shade darker than Guidry's own. Anywhere but New Orleans, she might have passed for white.

She dressed as primly as a schoolteacher. Today she wore a mohair sweater set and a slim-fitting skirt, pristine white gloves. Her own private joke, maybe. She always seemed to be smiling at one.

"Cut the bullshit," Guidry said. With the right smile, he could say things like that to her. To Carlos, even.

She smiled and smoked. One of the skeletal carriage horses on Decatur Street whinnied, shrill and disconsolate, almost a scream. A sound you wanted to forget the minute you heard it.

"So you've seen the news about the president," she said.

"Imagine my alarm," he said.

"Don't worry, *mon cher.* Come, I'll buy you a drink."

"Just one?"

"Come."

They walked over to Chartres. The Napoleon House didn't open for another hour. The bartender let them in, poured their drinks, disappeared.

"Goddamn it, Seraphine," Guidry said.

"I understand your concern," she said.

"I hope you're planning to visit me in prison."

"Don't worry."

"Say it again and maybe I'll start to believe you."

She flicked the ash from her cigarette with a languid sweep of a gloved hand.

"My father used to work here," she said. "Did you know? Mopping the floors, cleaning the toilets. When I was a little girl, he brought me with him occasionally. Do you see those?"

The walls of the Napoleon House hadn't been replastered in a century, and every one of the antique oil portraits hung just a little bit crooked. Mean, haughty faces, glaring down from the shadows.

"When I was a little girl," she said, "I was convinced that the people in the paintings were watching me. Waiting until I blinked so that they could pounce."

"Maybe they were," Guidry said. "Maybe they worked for J. Edgar Hoover."

"I'll say it once more, because we're such old friends. Don't worry. The authorities have their man, don't they?"

"It's just the cops in Dallas, and they only think they have their man."

Guidry knew that the FBI would never buy Oswald, not for a minute. C'mon. They'd start digging, and he'd start gabbing. No. Check that. The feds were already digging, and Oswald was already gabbing.

"He won't be a problem," Seraphine said.

Oswald. That little rat face, vaguely familiar. Guidry thought he might have seen him around town at some point. "So you can tell the future now?" he said.

"His."

"Where's the Eldorado?" Guidry said. Seraphine could reassure him till she was blue in the face, but he wouldn't be safe from the feds until that car disappeared forever. The Eldorado was the one piece of physical evidence that linked him to the assassination.

"On its way to Houston," she said, "as we speak."

"If your fella with the eagle eye gets pulled over by the cops . . ."

"He won't." Her smile a bit less serene this time. The Eldorado was also the one piece of physical evidence that linked *Carlos* to the assassination.

"And once the car's in Houston?" Guidry said.

"Someone trustworthy will send it to the bottom of the sea."

Guidry reached over the bar for the bottle of scotch.

He felt better, a little. "Is that true?" he said. "About your father working here?"

She shrugged. The shrug meant, *Yes, of course.* Or it meant, *No, don't be absurd.*

"Who's dumping the car in Houston?" Guidry said. "Your fella who's driving it down?"

"No. He's needed elsewhere."

"So who, then?" Guidry, from his elevated perch in the organization, just a branch or two below Seraphine, knew most of Carlos's guys. Some were more reliable than others. "Whoever dumps it, you better be damn sure you can count on him."

"But of course," she said. "Uncle Carlos has complete faith in this man. Never once has he failed us."

Who? Guidry started to ask again. Instead he turned to stare at her. "Me?" he said. "No. I'm not going near that fucking car."

"No?"

"I'm not going near that fucking car, Seraphine." Guidry remembered to smile this time. "Not now, not a hundred years from now."

She shrugged again. "But, *mon cher,*" she said, "in this matter who can we trust more than you? Who can *you* trust more?"

Only now did Guidry complete the arduous climb to the summit and, panting with exertion, realize just where Seraphine had led him. It had been her plan all along, he realized. Have Guidry stash the getaway Eldorado before the hit so that he'd be thoroughly motivated—his own ass on the line now—to get rid of the car afterward.

"Goddamn it," he said. But you had to admire the dazzling footwork, the elegance of the maneuver. Who needed to tell the future when you could create it yourself?

Out on the street, Seraphine handed him a plane ticket.

"Your flight to Houston leaves tomorrow," she said. "You'll have to miss your Saturday-morning cartoons, I'm afraid. The car will be left for you downtown, in a pay lot across the street from the Rice Hotel."

"What then?" he said.

"There's a decommissioned-tank terminal on the ship channel. Take La Porte Road east. Keep going after you pass the Humble Oil refinery. You'll see an unmarked road about a mile on."

What if the feds had already found the Eldorado? They'd sit on it, of course. They'd wait for some poor idiot to show up and claim it.

"In the evening you'll have all the privacy you need," she said. "The ship channel is forty feet deep.

Afterward walk half a mile up La Porte. There's a filling station with a phone. You can call a cab from there. And me."

She kissed him on the cheek. Her expensive scent, over the years, had never changed: fresh jasmine and what smelled like the scorched spices at the bottom of a cast-iron pan. She and Guidry had been lovers once, but so briefly and so long ago that he remembered that period only occasionally, and without much feeling about it one way or another. He doubted that Seraphine remembered it at all.

"You and Carlos never miss a button, do you?" Guidry said.

"So you see now, *mon cher?* Don't worry."

As Guidry walked back through the Quarter, Seraphine's scent faded and his mind worked. It was true that Seraphine and Carlos never missed a button. But what if *Guidry* was one of those buttons? What if he was worried about the feds when in fact the real danger— Carlos, Seraphine—stood smiling right behind him?

Get rid of the Eldorado.

And then get rid of the man who got rid of the Eldorado. Get rid of the man who knows about Dallas.

The priest on the steps of St. Louis was still going strong. He was just a kid, barely out of the seminary, pudgy and apple-cheeked. He clasped his hands in front of him, like he was about to blow on the dice in hopes of a lucky roll.

"When we pass through the waters, God will be with us," the priest was assuring his congregation. "When we walk through the fire, we shall not be burned."

That wasn't Guidry's experience. He listened to the priest for another minute and then turned away.

4

Barone got the call at nine. He was ready for it. Seraphine told him to meet her at Kolb's for dinner in half an hour, don't be late.

Bitch. "When have I ever been late?" Barone said.

"I'm teasing, *mon cher*," Seraphine said.

"Tell me. When have I ever been late?"

Kolb's was the German restaurant on St. Charles Avenue, just off Canal Street. Dark-paneled walls and beer steins and platters of schnitzel with pickled beets. Carlos was Italian, but he loved German food. He loved every kind of food. Barone had never seen anyone in New Orleans pack it away like Carlos.

"Sit down," Carlos said. "You want something to eat?"

The place was almost deserted, everyone at home watching the big news. "No," Barone said.

"Have something to eat," Carlos said.

The ceiling at Kolb's was fitted with a system of fans connected by squeaking, creaking leather belts. A little wooden man in lederhosen turned a crank to keep the belts and the fans moving.

"His name is Ludwig," Seraphine said. "Tireless and reliable, just like you."

She smiled at Barone. She liked to make you think that she could read your mind, that she could predict your every move. Maybe she could.

"It's a compliment, *mon cher*," she said. "Don't look so grumpy."

"Try a bite of this," Carlos said.

"No."

"C'mon. You don't like German food? Let bygones be bygones."

"I'm not hungry." Barone didn't have anything against the Germans. The war had happened a long time ago.

Seraphine wasn't eating either. She lit a cigarette and then set the matchbook on the table in front of her. She positioned it this way and that, observing it from various angles.

"It's time for you to proceed," she told Barone. As if he were too dumb to figure it out by himself. "The matters we discussed."

"Houston?" he said.

"Yes."

"What about Mackey Pagano? I don't have time for that, too."

"Don't worry," Seraphine said. "That's already been taken care of."

"Did I say I was worried?" Barone said.

"Your appointment in Houston is tomorrow evening," she said. "As we discussed. You'll need to go see Armand first, though. Tonight."

Carlos still eating, not saying a word, letting Seraphine handle everything. Most people thought that Carlos kept her around—the well-dressed, well-spoken colored girl—for blow jobs and dictation. Barone knew better. For every problem that Carlos could think up, Seraphine had a solution.

"All right," Barone said.

His Impala was parked on Dumaine, a block off Bourbon. Friday night and hardly a handful of people around. Down on the corner, an old colored man was blowing "'Round Midnight" on the alto sax for a few tourists. Barone walked over to listen. He had a minute.

The old colored man knew how to play. He hit a D-sharp and held it, the note rising and spreading like water over a levee.

The guy next to Barone jostled him a little. Barone

felt a hand brush against his pocket. He reached down and grabbed the hand. It belonged to a scrawny punk with pitted cheeks. Needle marks up and down the pale belly of his arm.

"What's the big idea, pal?" the dope fiend said, playing innocent. "You wanna hold hands with somebody, go find a—"

Barone bent his hand backward. The human wrist was fragile, a bird's nest of twigs and tendons. He watched the dope fiend's face change.

"Oh," the dope fiend said.

"Shhh," Barone said. "Let the man finish his tune."

Barone couldn't remember the first time he'd heard "'Round Midnight." On the piano, probably. Over the years he'd listened to fifty, maybe a hundred different versions. Piano, sax, guitar, even trombone a time or two. The old colored man tonight made the song feel brand-new.

The music ended. The dope fiend's knees sagged, and Barone turned him loose. The dope fiend stumbled away, not looking back, hunched over his hand like it was a flame he worried might flicker out.

Barone dropped a dollar bill in the sax case. The old man might have been fifty years old or he might have been eighty. The whites of his eyes were as yellow as an old cue ball, and there were needle marks running the length of his arms, too. Maybe the old man and the dope fiend were partners, one drawing the crowd so the other could rob it. Probably.

The old man looked down at the dollar bill and then looked back up. He adjusted the mouthpiece of his alto. He didn't have anything to say to Barone.

Barone didn't have anything to say to him. He walked over to his Impala and slid behind the wheel.

The west bank of the Mississippi, just across the river from New Orleans, was a dirty strip of scrapyards, body shops, and lopsided tenement buildings, the wood rotting off them. The Wank, people called it. Barone understood why. The smell was something else. A couple of refineries fired night and day, a burning funk that stuck to your clothes and skin. Ships dumped their garbage on the New Orleans side, and it washed up here. Dead fish, too, the ones even the gulls wouldn't touch.

He pulled off the main road and guided the Impala down a narrow track of oyster-shell gravel that ran parallel to the train tracks. Tires crunching, headlights bouncing over rows of busted windshields and caved-in grills. A stack of chrome bumpers ten feet high.

It was after midnight, but the lights in the office were still on. Barone knew they would be. A man gets in a certain habit, he stays there.

Armand's office was just a shack, four walls and a corrugated tin roof. The front room had a desk, a sofa with one arm sawed off so it would fit, and a camp stove that Armand used to boil coffee. The back room was behind a door that looked like any other door. Solid steel. Try to kick that in and walk with a limp for the rest of your life.

Armand gave Barone a big smile. He was happy to see Barone. Why not? Barone shopped the top-shelf merchandise and never dickered too much.

"What's doing, baby?" Armand said. "Where you been at? How long since the last time you come round to see me? Three months?"

"Two," Barone said.

"You want something to drink? Look at you. Nice and trim. That ain't me, baby. Man, I just peek round the corner at a plate of beans and rice, I get fatter." He grabbed his belly with both hands and jiggled it for Barone. "See that? So where you staying at these days? Still over there by Burgundy Street?"

"No."

"What you think 'bout all that business up there in Dallas? Awful shame, ain't it? You ask me, it was the Russians behind it. One hundred percent. You just wait and see. The Russians."

"I've got a new piece of work," Barone said.

Armand laughed. "Down to business. Every time."

"I need something tonight."

"What you looking for?"

"Tell me what you have."

Armand took out his ring of keys. "Well, snubbies, take your pick, two-inch or four-inch. Clean, guaranteed. Or you want something with a little more gris-gris, I got another .22 Magnum, cut down to the stock."

"How much for the .22?" Barone said.

"Cost me a nickel more than the last one did."

Barone doubted it. "Clean?"

"Guaranteed."

"I'm not paying an extra nickel."

"Oh, baby, you gonna put me outta business."

"Let's see it," Barone said.

Armand unlocked the door to the back room. It was half the size of the front room, just enough space for a few boxes and a steamer trunk. He squatted down to unlock the steamer trunk. The effort made him groan.

"How's LaBruzzo and them?" Armand said. "You know who I run across the other day? That big ugly rumpkin from Curley's Gym. You remember him, muscles all over. I know you remember him. Guess who he works for now. I'll tell you who. He . . ."

Armand glanced over and saw the gun in Barone's hand. A .357 Blackhawk.

It took a beat for the gun to register. Then Armand's face went flat, like a mask coming off. He stood back up.

"I sold you that," Armand said. "Didn't I? Threw in a box of .38 Short Colts."

"A couple of years ago," Barone said.

There were no cars on the road this time of night, and the shack was a long way from the next yard over. But Barone never took chances, not if he could help it. He decided to wait for a barge to pass and blow its horn.

"Just listen to me now, baby," Armand said. "You barking up the wrong tree. Carlos is. I ain't have no idea what this all about."

He had one hand at his side and the other one on his belly, making slow circles. Barone wasn't worried. Armand never carried a gun. The guns in the trunk were never loaded.

"Please," Armand said. "I ain't sold nothing to nobody. Whatever happened up there in Dallas, I ain't got the first idea. Put me in front of Jesus Christ himself and I'll swear it."

So Armand did have an idea what this was about after all. Barone wasn't surprised.

"Please, baby, you know I know how to keep my mouth shut," Armand said. "Always have, always will. Let me talk to Carlos. Let me straighten him out."

"You remember that big Christmas party at Mandina's?" Barone said. "A couple of years after the war."

"Yeah, sure," Armand said. He couldn't figure out why Barone was asking about a long-ago Christmas party. He couldn't figure out why Barone hadn't shot him yet. He was starting to think that he might have a chance. "Sure. Sure, I remember that party."

Winter of '46 or '47. Barone had just gone to work for Carlos. He was living in a cold-water flat down the street from the Roosevelt Hotel.

"There was a piano player," Barone said. He wondered if that Christmas party at Mandina's was when he heard "'Round Midnight" the first time. "A piano player with a top hat."

"And there was a Christmas tree," Armand said. Nodding and grinning and finally giving in to hope, the sweet embrace of it. "That's right. A big old Christmas tree with an angel on top."

Barone thought about the old colored man playing "'Round Midnight" on his alto sax earlier, his fingers flying over the keys. Some people were born with a gift.

Finally a barge blew its horn, so loud and low that

Barone felt the throb in his back teeth. He pulled the trigger.

A quarter of a mile east of Armand's scrapyard, driving back to the bridge, Barone saw a car coming on, headed in the opposite direction. An old Hudson Commodore with a sunshade like the brim of a base-ball cap.

Behind the wheel a woman. Barone's headlights lit up her face as they passed. Her headlights lit up his.

He tapped the brakes and swung around. When he caught the Commodore, he flashed his headlights. The Commodore pulled onto the shoulder. Barone parked behind it. On his way to the driver's window, he popped his switchblade and gave the back tire a quick jab.

"Damn it to hell, you scared me to death." The woman had her hair up in curlers. Who was she? Why was she out here this time of night? Barone supposed it didn't matter, the who or the why. "I thought you was the damn cops."

"No," he said.

She was missing a piece of a front tooth. Her smile was friendly. "The cops is the last thing in the damn world I need right now."

"You've got a flat," Barone said.

"Damn it. That's the next-to-the-last thing in the world I need."

"Come look."

She climbed out of the car and came around to the back. She wore an old housecoat the color of dirty dishwater. When she heard the back tire hissing, she laughed.

"Well, if that ain't the cherry on top of my sundae." She laughed again. She had a nice laugh, like the cheerful jingle of coins in a pocket. "After the day I had, it's the damn cat's pajamas."

"Open the trunk," Barone said. "I'll change it out for you."

"My hero," she said.

He checked to make sure the road was empty and then cut her throat, turning her a little so that she didn't spill blood on his suit. After a minute she relaxed, like a silk dress slipping off a hanger. Barone just had to let her slide into the trunk of the car, no effort at all.

5

While everyone else gathered around the television in the living room, Charlotte inspected the dining table to see what she might have forgotten. She'd been awake since five-thirty that morning, baking and basting and grating and mincing. And last night she'd stayed up until almost midnight, polishing the silverware and ironing the Irish-lace tablecloth that Dooley's parents had given them for their wedding.

Had she slept at all? She wasn't entirely sure. At one point, lying on her back in the darkest hollow of the night, she'd felt the dog's whiskery muzzle twitching close to her mouth, making sure she was still breathing.

Dooley's mother, Martha, popped into the kitchen. "Need any help, Charlie?" she said.

"No thank you," Charlotte said. "I'm just about ready."

"You're sure?"

"Yes."

Both Martha and Dooley's father, Arthur, were lovely people, gracious and unfailingly kind. If Charlotte had left the silver unpolished, the tablecloth unironed, if she'd forgotten the rolls or the cranberry sauce, they would have made a point not to notice.

Which made it worse somehow. Charlotte wished that her in-laws were less gracious, less lovely. Better a pair of cruel snippers, icy snubbers, implacable adversaries she could never hope to appease. The searchingly earnest way Dooley's father studied Charlotte, the way his mother would reach out, unprompted, to pat Charlotte's hand—their pity, at times, was agonizing.

In the living room, the mood was hushed and grim. The television report showed a horse-drawn caisson bearing the president's casket from the White House to the Capitol. A reporter broke in to confirm that Lee Harvey Oswald, who had been shot earlier that morning, was dead.

Charlotte saw that Joan and Rosemary had snuck back inside to watch the TV.

"Rosemary," she said. "Joan."

Rosemary prepared to deliver arguments for the defense. "But, Mommy—"

"But nothing," Charlotte said. "I told you to go play outside with your cousins."

The girls had already been exposed to far too many hours of disturbing television news for which they were far too young. They understood that a bad man had killed the president of the United States. They didn't need to know all the gruesome details.

"But they're playing fort," Rosemary said.

"So?" Charlotte said.

"They said we can't play fort with them because we're just girls."

Before Charlotte could answer, Dooley's brother, Bill, handed Charlotte his empty beer bottle. "I sure could use another one of these, Charlie," he said.

During grace, her eyes closed and head bowed, Charlotte's thoughts returned to that eleven-year-old girl knifing her way fearlessly across the river seventeen years ago. The following winter Charlotte's father—just turned thirty-two, the very picture of ruddy health—had suffered a heart attack and died. His death devastated her. For the first time, Charlotte learned that life's currents were more treacherous than she'd thought, that she was not as strong a swimmer.

After that . . . what happened? Charlotte's mother, a distant and timid woman, grew even more so. She discouraged Charlotte from taking risks, from stand-

ing out, from expecting too much. Before too long
Charlotte proved quite adept at discouraging herself.
She'd enrolled at the University of Oklahoma instead
of at one of the smaller colleges closer to home (though
her mother discouraged it), but the moment Charlotte
stepped foot on campus, she was overwhelmed. She'd
just turned seventeen, she'd never been away from
Woodrow before, she knew not a soul. In October, only
six weeks into the semester, she packed her things and
fled back home.

She found a job at the bakery, which is where one
afternoon she struck up a conversation with a handsome customer. Dooley was three years older than
Charlotte, so she hadn't known him well in school. But
he was friendly, fun, and he didn't take himself as se-
riously as the other boys in town. He asked her out,
and soon after that they started going together. Soon
after that she married him and they moved into a house
three blocks from the one she'd grown up in. Soon
after that she was pregnant with Joan. Soon after that
she was pregnant with Rosemary. Soon after that was
right now.

"Mommy," Rosemary whispered. "It's your turn."

"My turn?" Charlotte said.

Her turn. If only life were like that, Charlotte
thought, a game where every round you were allowed

to spin the wheel again, to pluck a fresh card from the pile. Though who was to say that a new spin or a fresh card would improve your position on the board?

There's always a bumpier road than the one you're driving on, Charlotte's mother had always cautioned her. Be content with what you have, in other words, because the alternative is probably even worse. Her mother shared this philosophy when, for example, Charlotte complained that the math teacher in eighth grade refused to let any of the girls in class ask questions. When her boss at the bakery followed Charlotte into the back room and pressed her up against the wall. When Charlotte began to worry that Dooley, her fiancé at the time, was drinking too much.

"It's your turn to say what you're thankful for, Mommy," Rosemary said.

"Well, let me see," Charlotte said. "I'm thankful for my two beautiful daughters. I'm thankful for the family that could be with us today. I'm thankful for this wonderful Sunday dinner."

Dooley carved the roast. The knife in his hand was steady. Each slice of the meat flopped onto the platter perfect and glistening. Whenever his parents came over for dinner, Dooley limited himself to a single beer or glass of wine. Even though his parents knew, everyone knew, that five minutes after the last guest was gone, Dooley would be out the door, too. Claiming that he had to pick up cigarettes or mail a letter or put gas in the car, back in a jiffy.

Early afternoon, the light from the dining-room window stern and wintry and uncompromising. Interesting light. Rosemary reached for the salt, and Dooley's father reached for the rolls, and Dooley passed the gravy boat across to his mother. The arms overlapped and interlocked, creating frames within the frame, each a perfect miniature still life. An eye, a pearl in a necklace, the stripe of a tie. Charlotte wished that she had her camera handy. She'd get down low, shoot up from the surface of the table.

"The world is going to hell," Dooley's brother was saying. "Pardon my language, ladies, but it's the truth. Kennedy, Oswald, Ruby, civil rights. Women thinking that they can do anything a man can do."

"But shouldn't they be allowed to try at least?" Charlotte said. "What's the harm?"

Bill didn't hear her and charged ahead, lifting his fork higher and higher with each point he made.

"It's a battle for civilization, just like in the movies," Bill said. "Fort Apache. That's what a place like Woodrow is like. We're the only ones left to fight off the Indians. We've got to circle the wagons, protect what this country stands for before it gets turned upside down by people who are all turned inside out. The Negro, for example. What most people don't realize, the Negro prefers a separation of the races just as much as you or I do!"

Dooley and his father nodded along. Charlotte was curious to know when exactly the Negro had confided this preference to Bill, but she lacked the energy—or was it the courage?—to ask him. Bill was the second-most successful lawyer in Logan County and had never lost a case. Dooley's father was the most successful lawyer in Logan County. If Charlotte dared dip a toe in a discussion about politics, the men would genially and implacably expose the various flaws in her logic, the way one might pick every last bone from a fish.

Charlotte's sister-in-law touched her arm and gushed about a new pattern—a free-line overblouse on a pleated stem—that she'd discovered.

"It's a terrible tragedy, what happened," Dooley's father said, "but the silver lining is that Johnson is an improvement on Kennedy. Johnson isn't nearly so liberal. He's from the South and understands the importance of moderation."

"I can't decide between a thin plaid wool or a whisper-check cotton," Charlotte's sister-in-law told her. "What's your vote?"

Charlotte glanced over and noticed that Joan was

watching her. Seeing what? Charlotte wondered. Learning what?

After dinner the men retired to the living room, the children went outside to play, and Charlotte started on the dishes. Dooley's mother followed her into the kitchen. Charlotte tried to shoo her away from the dirty plates, but Martha ignored her and began to scrape.

"How have you been, dear?" Which meant, Charlotte knew, *How has* he *been?*

"Just fine," Charlotte said.

"Those girls are little angels."

"Well. Accounts vary."

Martha placed a plate on top of the stack. "We spoiled him terribly," she said after a moment. "The youngest, you know."

Charlotte shook her head. "No, Martha," she said. If anyone was to blame for the man Dooley had become, it was Charlotte. As his girlfriend she'd been stupidly blind to his flaws. As his wife she'd indulged him because the alternative was too difficult to contemplate.

"We'd like to pitch in, Arthur and I," Martha said.

Charlotte shook her head again, the familiar ritual. "You've done too much already, Martha."

"We know how hard it can be for a young couple."

Charlotte's eyes welled without warning, a hot, stinging shame. She turned to wipe down the stove so that Martha wouldn't see. So that Martha could slip the folded bills into the pocket of her apron.

"Really," Charlotte said. "It's not necessary."

"We insist," Martha said. "We just wish it was more."

Thirty minutes later they were gone, Dooley's parents and his brother and sister-in-law, their three boys, all of them headed home. Five minutes after that, Charlotte was filling the roasting pan with hot water and dish soap when Dooley strolled into the kitchen, his coat and hat and gloves already on.

"We'll need some milk for tomorrow morning, won't we?" He gave her a kiss on the cheek. "I better run up there before the store closes."

"Your mother gave us another three hundred dollars," Charlotte said.

He rubbed the back of his neck. Dooley preferred to enjoy the fruits of charity without having to acknowledge the tree or the picking.

"Well, dang it, Charlie," he said. "I don't want their money. We don't need it."

She wanted to laugh. Instead she turned off the hot water and stepped away from the cloud of steam. "She insisted."

"Well, next time you tell her no, Charlie. You understand?" He started edging toward the door. "Anyway, I better run up and get that milk."

"And you'll be back in a jiffy," she said, "right after you have just one drink."

That stopped him in his tracks. His expression reminded her of the picture that had been on TV all afternoon: Lee Harvey Oswald bent double, his mouth a startled O as Jack Ruby fired a bullet into his stomach.

Charlotte had surprised herself, too. But in for a penny, in for a pound. "We can't keep on like this," she said.

"Keep on like what?" he said.

"Let's sit down and talk about it, honey. Really talk, for once."

"Talk about what?"

"You know what."

His face darkened, a gathering storm of righteous indignation. When he was drunk, he swore that he would never in his life touch another drop of liquor. When he was sober, he swore that he had never in his life touched a drop.

"What I know," he said, "I know the girls are going to need some milk for their cereal in the morning."

"Dooley . . ."

"What's the matter with you, Charlie? Why do you want to ruin Sunday for everybody?"

She felt her energy drain away. He would keep at

this, keep at her, for as long as it took. When you stood between Dooley and a bottle, he was the surf pounding the cliffs to sand. Surrender was the only sensible course of action.

"Go ahead," she said.

"Don't you want the girls to have milk for their cereal in the morning?"

"Go ahead. I'm sorry."

He left, and she folded the tablecloth. She swept up the crumbs under the dining-room table and checked on the girls in their room. Rosemary had no fewer than three different Disney True-Life Adventures books open before her. *Prowlers of the Everglades, The Vanishing Prairie,* and *Nature's Half Acre.* Joan was carefully clipping squares from sheets of colored construction paper. The dog lay curled between them on the bottom bunk, his usual spot.

"What are you doing, sweetie?" Charlotte asked Joan.

"She invented a game," Rosemary said. "She's going to teach me how to play when she's finished inventing it. Where's Daddy?"

"He ran up to the store," Charlotte said.

Joan lifted her head. A look flashed between her and Rosemary. Or did Charlotte just imagine it? They were still too young, surely, to understand.

"What are the rules of the game, Joan?" Charlotte said.

"They're very complicated," Rosemary said. "Aren't they, Joan?"

"Yes," Joan said.

"Mommy?" Rosemary said. "Is Mrs. Kennedy very, very sad because the president died?"

"I would think so, yes," Charlotte said.

"What will she do now?"

"What will she do? I'm not sure. Do you mean—"

"Who will she live with?" Rosemary said. "Who will take care of her?"

The question surprised Charlotte. "Why, I imagine that she'll take care of herself."

Rosemary looked doubtful. Another look flashed between her and Joan. "Mommy?" Rosemary said.

"One more question," Charlotte said. "And then I have to get the clothes off the line before it's dark."

"You'd be very, very sad if Daddy died," Rosemary said, "wouldn't you?"

"Daddy's not going to die. I promise."

"But you'd be very, very sad."

"Of course I would," Charlotte said, and she meant it. Dooley wasn't a bad person—far from it. He loved Charlotte and loved the girls, and he'd never once lifted a hand to any of them in anger. And the drinking . . .

Deep down, she knew, he genuinely wanted to quit. One day, perhaps, he'd manage to do it.

But suppose he did quit drinking. What then? Charlotte's life would be easier, certainly, but would it be happier? The seconds and minutes and hours would continue to tick past. The weeks, the months, the years. The futures she might have had, the women she might have become, those ghosts would grow fainter and fainter in the distance until they disappeared altogether. If Charlotte was lucky, she'd forget that they'd ever haunted her.

And the girls. It pained Charlotte that one day Rosemary and Joan might ask the same questions of themselves: *What will we do? Who will take care of us?*

Rosemary had turned back to her books, Joan to her squares of construction paper. Charlotte lingered in the doorway. She thought about her initial reaction to the assassination, how permanently *fixed* in her life the news had made her feel. But maybe that idea needed amendment. No, her world would never change—not unless *she* did something to change it.

The tornado might have blown Dorothy from Kansas to Oz, but Dorothy was the one who'd had to open the front door of the farmhouse and step outside.

Charlotte's fingers touched the money in the pocket

of her apron. Three hundred dollars. She had perhaps twice as much in the girls' college savings account, money that Dooley didn't know about and couldn't squander.

Nine hundred dollars. It wasn't nearly enough. But Charlotte didn't let herself stop and think.

"Girls," she said. "Go pack your suitcases."

"Are we going somewhere?" Rosemary said, excited. "When are we leaving?"

Every now and then, Charlotte dreamed that she could fly. She'd be skipping to school, a child again, and then suddenly she'd find herself gliding weightlessly over cars, over trees, over entire houses. The secret was to not think about what was happening to you, what you were doing. Pretend it was just an ordinary day or the spell would be broken and down you'd come crashing.

"Mommy," Rosemary said, "when are we leaving?"

"Now. In five minutes."

"Is Daddy coming?" Joan said.

"No. It's just us girls."

"What about Lucky?" Rosemary said.

The dog. Oh, good Lord. But Charlotte couldn't just leave the poor thing here. Dooley might forget to feed him or to give him his medicine. He might forget that the dog even existed.

"Lucky can come with us," Charlotte said. "Now, hurry, go pack your suitcases."

"Can I bring one doll or two dolls?" Rosemary said.

"One."

"Are two small dolls the same as one big doll?"

"No."

"But Joan can bring one doll, too. And we can each bring one book."

"Yes. Now, go."

Rosemary bounded away. Joan considered Charlotte solemnly.

"Where are we going, Mommy?" Joan said.

Charlotte reached out to smooth the golden hair that never needed it. "Let's find out."

6

Guidry's Friday-night dinner with Al LaBruzzo dragged on. Guidry was his usual sparkling self, thank you very much, but it took some effort. He couldn't chase the idea from his head that maybe, just maybe, Seraphine and Carlos planned to kill him.

No, don't be ridiculous.

Yes, the math made sense. Guidry knew about the getaway Eldorado and its connection to the assassination. That made him a risk.

But he was one of Carlos's most trusted associates, Seraphine's friend and confidant. He'd proved his loyalty time and time again. Just count the times! Al LaBruzzo didn't have enough fingers.

And look at it, too, from a more practical perspective. Guidry did important work for the organization. He opened doors through which flowed cash and influence. Carlos—a penny-pincher, so tight he squeaked when he walked—wouldn't throw away as valuable an asset as Guidry. Waste not, want not, Carlos always said.

After dinner Guidry took a cab up Canal to the Orpheum and slipped into the middle of the picture, a comedy western with John Wayne and Maureen O'Hara horsing around on a ranch. The theater was almost empty.

Get rid of the Eldorado.

And then get rid of the man who got rid of the Eldorado. Get rid of the man who knows about Dallas.

The projector clattered. Cigarette smoke rose and bloomed in the beam of light from the booth. Three scattered couples in the theater, plus two other solo acts like Guidry. No one had come in since he'd plopped down. He was pretty sure no one had followed his cab up Canal.

Guidry was letting his imagination get the best of him. Could be. He'd seen it happen to guys who'd been around too long. The stress of the life worked away at them like salt spray on soft wood, and they started to fall apart.

Maybe I'm crazy. That was what Mackey Pagano had said to Guidry when he begged Guidry to find out if Carlos wanted him dead. *Maybe I'm crazy.*

But Mackey hadn't been crazy, had he? Carlos *had* wanted Mackey dead, and now, almost certainly, dead Mackey was.

What else had Mackey said Wednesday night at the Monteleone? Guidry tried to remember. Something about a guy from San Francisco, the hit on the judge a year ago that Carlos had eventually decided against.

That was the kind of work Mackey had been doing the last few years, arranging for out-of-town specialists when Carlos didn't have someone at hand, local, to do the work he needed.

Specialists, independent contractors. Such as, perhaps, a sniper who could pick off the president of the United States and then afterward drive away in a sky-blue Eldorado.

Guidry could no longer stomach the high jinks on the screen. He left the theater before the movie ended and walked back to his apartment building. Nobody following him, he was ninety-nine percent sure.

The canceled hit on the judge last year. Maybe it had been one of Seraphine's elaborate smoke screens. Guidry knew how she operated. She'd used the cover of darkness to line up the sniper that Carlos had sent to Dealey Plaza today.

Mackey must have figured out some corner of the

puzzle a few days ago. He must have recognized that he possessed dangerous information.

And now Guidry had figured out the same corner of the puzzle. Now he possessed that same dangerous information. Throw another log on the fire, shall we? Ye gods. Guidry's day was just getting shittier and shittier.

But there was still hope. It was still possible that what had happened to Mackey was a coincidence, that Carlos had bumped him for reasons entirely unrelated to the assassination.

Guidry knew a source who might be able to shed light. When he reached his apartment building, he bypassed the lobby and went straight to the garage. Chick was sitting crumpled in the booth and staring at the radio like it was his own sweet mother who'd been shot in Dallas. The Negroes thought that Jack Kennedy loved them. Hate to break the news, Chick, but Jack Kennedy was like every smart cat: He loved himself and himself only.

"Bring my car around for me, Chick, will you?" Guidry said.

"Yes, sir, Mr. Guidry," Chick said. "You been listening to the news? Good Lord, Good Lord."

"You know what the Good Book says, Chick. 'When thou walkest through the fire, thou shalt not be burned.'"

"Yeah you right." Chick blew his nose into a hand-kerchief. "Yeah you right."

Guidry drove over the bridge to the west bank. He tried the scrapyard first. Armand wasn't in his little shack of an office, a surprise. Guidry knocked and knocked till his knuckles were numb. It was fine. He knew where Armand lived. Not too far up the road, a tidy little neighborhood of shotguns in Algiers Point.

Armand's wife answered the door. Esmeralda, faded Cajun beauty, the crumbling ruins of a once-glorious civilization. Guidry wished he'd known her when. How a tubby motormouth gun peddler like Armand had landed such a prize, it was an enigma to unravel.

But another enigma had priority right now. Guidry crossed his fingers that Armand could help with the unraveling. Armand had known Mackey for almost half a century. The two of them had grown up together. Armand would know what Mackey had been up to.

"Sorry to trouble you, Esme, I know it's late," Guidry said. Late, but the lights in the house blazed and the smell of fresh-brewed coffee drifted out from the kitchen. Strange.

"Hello, Frank," Esme said.

"I'm looking for Armand. He's not at the office."

"He's not home."

"I wish I could steal you away from him, Esme,"

Guidry said. "I know you've been married a while, but give me the blueprints and I'll do what it takes."

"He's not home," she said again.

"No? Do you know where he is?"

Strange, too, that Esme hadn't invited Guidry in yet, hadn't offered him a cup of coffee. Every other time that Guidry had come round, now and then over the years, she'd dragged him through the door and pinned him to the sofa and flirted like she was seventeen years old. Usually Guidry had to make like Houdini just to wriggle free.

And why, if she was still up this late, wasn't the television or the radio playing? Esme would throw herself in front of the St. Charles streetcar for Jackie Kennedy.

"He's gone fishing," Esme said. "Out to the Atchafalaya for a few days. You know how he loves it out there."

In the spring, sure, when the bass were biting. But in November? "When's he coming home?" Guidry said.

"I don't know."

She smiled, no strain showing. But Guidry could *feel* it. Something. Fear? He looked past her, into the house, and saw a suitcase by the kitchen door.

"My sister in Shreveport." Esme answered the question before Guidry could ask it. "I'm taking the bus up to visit her this weekend."

"How can I get hold of Armand?" Guidry said.

"I don't know. Good-bye, Frank."

She shut the front door. Guidry walked slowly back to his car. Armand was dead. Guidry resisted the conclusion, but it was the only one he could draw. Armand had been bumped, like Mackey, and Esme knew it. She was scared out of her wits that Carlos would come after her if she breathed a word. Smart lady.

Mackey had been bumped because he'd arranged for the sniper.

Armand had been bumped because . . . That was easy. Because he was Carlos's most discreet and reliable source of weapons. You wouldn't know to look at Armand, at the scrapyard shack, but he could get any kind of gun and move it anywhere.

The evidence mounted. Carlos was clipping the threads that connected him to the assassination. Who next but Guidry?

No, don't be ridiculous. Guidry was a valuable asset, et cetera, his perch in the organization only a branch or two beneath Seraphine's, et cetera. Though that wasn't as encouraging a notion, Guidry realized, as he'd first assumed. From up here he could see it all, he could see too much, he could put all the pieces together.

And what about that jittery deputy chief in Dallas, the reason Seraphine had sent Guidry to Dallas in the first place? Did that count as another strike against Guidry?

As he crossed the bridge back over the Mississippi, the black water below reminded him of the dream he'd had last night. Omens and portents.

Carlos and Seraphine could have used anyone in the organization to stash the getaway Eldorado in Dallas, someone disposable. Why did they use Guidry? Because, maybe, they'd already decided that his time was up.

He rented a room at a cheap motel out in Kenner. He didn't think that Seraphine would make a move before he dumped the Eldorado in Houston, but just to be safe. Guidry always kept a suitcase in the car. A toothbrush, a change of clothes, a couple grand in cash. Saturday morning he stood in the terminal at Moisant and studied the departure board. The flight to Houston that Seraphine had booked for him left at ten. A flight to Miami left at half past.

Guidry could take the flight to Miami and try to disappear. Suppose, though, he wasn't on Carlos's list after all. If Guidry ran now, he'd shoot straight to the top of the charts, congratulations.

If he ran, he would have to leave behind everything. His life. The smiles and the nods and the bellboys at the Monteleone scrambling to open the door for him, the beautiful redheads and brunettes eyeing him from across the room.

His nest egg was back in the nest. How the fuck was he supposed to disappear forever with only a couple thousand bucks in his wallet?

Seraphine might have someone at the airport watching him. Guidry didn't overlook the possibility. So he moseyed over to the bar and ordered a Bloody Mary and chatted up the cocktail waitress. Not a care in the world, had Frank Guidry.

After the last call from the gate, he boarded the plane to Houston. Carlos wouldn't bump him. Seraphine wouldn't let him. Armand and Mackey—they were beasts of burden, spare parts. Guidry was the right hand of the right hand of the king himself, untouchable. Or so he hoped.

The Rice, at the corner of Main and Texas, was the swankiest hotel in Houston, with a pool in the basement and a dance pavilion on the roof. The Thanksgiving decorations were out—a papier-mâché turkey in a Pilgrim hat, a horn of plenty overflowing with wax apples and squash. But the lobby felt like a funeral, every step soft, every voice hushed. Kennedy had spent the night before his assassination in a suite here. Probably an enjoyable night, given the stories Guidry had heard about him.

Guidry's room on the ninth floor of the Rice looked down on the pay lot across the street. The sky-blue Cadillac Eldorado sat in the back corner, the sun winking off the chrome. Guidry watched the Eldorado for a while. Watched the lot. He counted his money again. Two thousand one hundred and seventy-four bucks. He called down and had room service bring up a club sandwich, a bottle of Macallan, a bucket of ice. Don't think of it as a last supper. Don't. He hung his suit coat on the back of the bathroom door and ran the shower, hot, to steam the creases from the wool.

At four-thirty he walked across the street and tugged on his Italian calfskin driving gloves and slid behind the wheel of the Eldorado. South toward La Porte, window rolled down to flush out the lingering ghost of sweat and Camels and hair oil. Where was he now? The specialist from San Francisco who took the shot and then drove the Eldorado down from Dallas? Long gone, Guidry supposed, one way or another.

He stuck to the speed limit, watched for a tail. A few blocks before he reached La Porte, he pulled in to the crowded parking lot of a Mexican restaurant.

The backseat was clean. He popped the lid of the trunk. Why? Guidry couldn't say for sure. He just wanted to know everything he could know. He'd been that way since he was running around in diapers.

An old army barracks bag, olive-drab canvas with a drawstring neck. Guidry opened it. Inside, wrapped in a denim work shirt, was a bolt-action rifle with a four-power scope. A box of 6.5 millimeter shells, a couple of brass casings. Binoculars. The embroidered patch on the work shirt said DALLAS MUNICIPAL TRANSIT AUTHORITY.

Guidry cinched the duffel back up and shut the trunk. East on La Porte, past a few miles of new prefab tract houses that would collapse if you sneezed on them. The houses gave way to the refineries and chemical plants and shipyards. After the Humble Oil refinery, last on the row, a long stretch of virgin swamp and pine. *There is a pleasure in the pathless woods.* Which doped-up English dandy had written that? Guidry couldn't remember. Coleridge or Keats, Byron or Shelley. One of them. *I love not Man the less, but Nature more.*

The sun sank behind him. It wasn't much of a sun to start with, just a patch of shiny gray in the darker gray of the sky, like the worn elbow of a cheap blazer.

No other cars, coming or going, not since he'd passed the Humble refinery. The unmarked road was a single narrow lane of broken asphalt and black mud gouged through the trees.

Guidry turned onto it and then stopped. Go on? Or back up? He idled, thinking. His father used to play a game when he was a little drunk or a lot drunk or not drunk and just bored. He'd hold his hands in front of him and order Guidry or his little sister to pick a hand, right or left. You didn't win the game. One hand was a punch, the other hand was a slap. Lose your nerve and fail to pick in time, you'd get one of each, good old Pop busting a gut he laughed so hard.

The road led to a sagging chain-link fence. Gate open. The bottom half of the wooden sign clipped to the gate had splintered off. All that remained was a big red NO.

Omens and portents. Guidry drove on, between the two rows of corroded metal drums, each one as big as a house. When he reached the dock, he put the Eldorado in park and climbed out. Something, the weedy muck at the base of the tanks, made his eyes burn—a rich, earthy shit-rot, a poisonous chemical tang.

Guidry, once he turned seven or eight years, had refused to play his father's game—he'd refused to pick left hand or right. A small act of rebellion that he paid dearly for, but Guidry didn't like surprises. He'd rather take the punch *and* the slap than not know which one was coming.

He looked around. He didn't see a glint of metal,

didn't hear a rustle of movement. But he wouldn't, would he?

A heavy chain was looped between a pair of iron cleats, but the key was in the padlock. Seraphine had made this simple for Guidry. Or she'd made it simple for the man sent to kill him. Put Guidry in the trunk when you're done. Put the car in the channel.

He dragged the chain to the side and rolled the Eldorado to the end of the dock. The big car hung on the edge for a second—nose down, like it was sniffing the water—and then slid in and under, barely a ripple.

Walking through the trees back to La Porte. Breathing deeply, in and out. With each step he took, Guidry's heart thudded a little slower, a little slower, a little slower. He needed a drink and a steak and a girl. And he needed to move his bowels all of a sudden, to beat the goddamn band.

He was alive. He was all right.

At the filling station on La Porte, the pump jockey squinted at Guidry. "Where's your car at, mister?"

"About a mile up the road, headed due west at forty miles an hour, my wife behind the wheel," Guidry said. "I hope you're not married, friend. It's a carnival ride."

"I ain't married," the pump jockey said. "Wouldn't mind to be, though."

"Stand up straight."

"What?"

"If you want to have luck with the ladies," Guidry said. He was in a generous mood. "Head up, shoulders back. Carry yourself with confidence. Give the lady your full attention. You have a phone I can use?"

A pay phone on the side of the building. Guidry used his first dime to call a cab. He used his second dime to call Seraphine.

"No problems," he said.

"But of course not, *mon cher.*"

"All right, then."

"You'll spend the night at the Rice?" she said.

"Uncle Carlos better cover my tab."

"He will. Enjoy."

Back inside, Guidry caught the pump jockey practicing his posture in the reflection off the front glass. Head up, shoulders back. Maybe he'd get the hang of it. Guidry asked about the men's room, and the pump jockey sent him outside again, to the back of the building this time.

WHITES ONLY. Guidry entered the single stall and sat down and with great relief released the acid churn he'd been carrying around in his belly for the past twenty-four hours. On the cinder-block wall next to the toilet, someone had used the tip of a knife to scratch a few words.

HERE I SIT ALL BROKEN HEARTED

TRIED TO

That was it. Inspiration had flagged or the poet had finished his business.

When Guidry came out of the men's room, his cab had arrived. It dropped him at the Rice, and he headed straight to the Capital Club. A few promising Texas bluebonnets were scattered about, but first things first. Guidry sat at the bar and ordered a double Macallan neat, another double Macallan neat, a rib eye with creamed spinach.

One of the bartenders, blond hair so pale it was almost white, sidled over and asked out of the corner of his mouth if Guidry wanted to buy some grass. Don't mind if I do. Seraphine had instructed him to enjoy his evening, had she not? The bartender told Guidry to meet him in ten minutes, the alley behind the hotel.

Guidry had lifted the last sip of Macallan to his lips. *You'll spend the night at the Rice?* That's what Seraphine had asked him on the phone. Why would she need to ask that? She'd booked his hotel room and knew that his return flight departed tomorrow morning. Why would she need to ask that, and why had Guidry not wondered about it until now?

"I'm a dumb-ass," he said.

The bartender watched him. "What?"

"I left my wallet upstairs." Guidry gave him a wink. "See you in five minutes."

He left the bar and crossed the hotel lobby, past the elevators and out through the revolving door. The bell-hop in the porte cochere said he'd whistle up a cab for Guidry, it'd only take a minute. Guidry didn't have a minute. He walked to the end of the block, turned the corner, and started running.

7

Saturday afternoon Barone caught his flight to Houston. On the plane he flipped through last month's *Life*. NASA had picked fourteen new astronauts. Buzz cuts, bright eyes, square jaws. Barone couldn't tell them apart. God and Mom and country. If they wanted to strap themselves to a bomb and go flying through space, Barone wasn't going to stop them.

The guy sitting next to him was from Dallas. He told Barone that everyone in his office cheered when they heard the news about Kennedy. Good riddance. The guy said he didn't know what was worse about Kennedy, that he was a Catholic or a liberal or loved the Negroes so much. Dollars to doughnuts, Kennedy probably had some Jew blood, too. The guy had it on good authority that the Oval Office had a special phone line direct to the Vatican. Jack and Bobby took their orders straight from the pope. The newspapers covered it up because they were owned by Jews. How did Barone like that?

"I'm Catholic," Barone said. It wasn't true, or not any longer, but he wanted to see the guy's face.

"Well . . ." the guy said. "Well . . ."

"And I'm married to a colored girl. She's meeting me at the airport if you want to say hello."

The guy stiffened. His lips disappeared. "There's no need to get smart with me, friend," he said. "I'm not trying to start any trouble."

"It's all right with me," Barone said. "I don't mind trouble."

The guy looked around for a stewardess to witness Barone's poor manners. When one didn't appear, he harrumphed and flapped open his newspaper. He ignored Barone the rest of the way to Houston.

A quarter to six, the plane landed at Municipal. Barone stepped out of the terminal in time to catch the last light of day burning on the horizon. Or maybe just a refinery flaring off gas. The air in Houston was even wetter and heavier than it was in New Orleans.

One of Carlos's elves had left a car for him in the airport parking lot. Barone tossed the briefcase in back. Under the seat was a .22 Browning Challenger.

Barone didn't think he'd need a piece, but no one ever ended up in a morgue drawer by being too careful. He removed the screw-on can and checked the barrel for crud. He checked the magazine, the slide. The Browning was accurate up close and fairly quiet.

The guy from the plane walked across the lot. Barone put the front sight on him and followed along until the guy found his car, got in, drove off. Maybe some other time, friend.

Traffic. Barone inched along. It took him twenty minutes to get to Old Spanish Trail. The Bali Hai Motor Court was an L-shaped cinder-block building, two stories high, canted around a pool. Every few seconds the glow in the pool shifted from green to purple, from purple to yellow, from yellow to green again.

Barone parked across the street, in front of a bull-dozed barbecue joint. Most of this side of Highway 90 was already a construction site, the roadhouses and filling stations and motor courts torn down to make room for a new stadium and parking lot. When it was finished, the stadium would have a roof, a giant dome you'd be able to see from miles away. Astronauts and an Astrodome, the future. So far only a few curved steel girders had been raised. They looked like the fingers of a hand trying to claw up through the crust of the earth.

The Bali Hai had two separate sets of stairs that led up to the breezeway on the second floor. Barone had been out last week to look the place over. One set of stairs at the far north end of the building. One set in the middle, crook of the L, in back. Only the maid used those stairs. You couldn't see them from the pool or the highway or the office.

The mark had the room on the second floor that was closest to the middle stairs. Number 207. Seraphine said that the mark would check in around five. Barone couldn't tell for sure if he was in the room yet or not. A light in the room was on, but the curtains were drawn.

Barone settled in. If he was lucky, the mark would step outside for a breath of fresh air. Some guys didn't mind doing a hit on the cuff. Barone, no. He liked to be as prepared as possible. Seraphine said the mark was a big boy. Barone wanted to see how big, with his own two eyes.

The mark was an independent contractor from San Francisco, going by the name of Fisk. That was all Barone knew about him. That, and he was good with a scope. Long-range shooters tended to be oddballs. Barone had known one guy, years ago, who could barely tie his shoelaces by himself. But point out a German in the bushes three hundred yards away and pow.

Thirty minutes passed. An hour. Barone yawned,

still thinking about the war. In Belgium once he fell asleep in his foxhole while his company waited for the Germans to come out of the woods at them. The sergeant shook Barone awake and asked if he had a screw loose, how calm he was all the time.

Maybe Barone did have a screw loose. He'd considered the possibility. But what if he did? There was nothing he could do about it. You're born a certain way. You stay that way. Everyone got what they deserved.

It started to rain. The sign for the Bali Hai featured a hula girl with a neon grass skirt that shimmied back and forth. The rain and the light from the sign and the headlights from the cars driving past formed strange shapes on Barone's windshield, slow, sinuous dancers. He hummed along, Coltrane's solo from "Cherokee."

At a quarter till nine, the rain stopped. A minute later the door to 207 opened and the mark, Fisk, stepped out onto the breezeway. A big boy, all right. Seraphine hadn't exaggerated. Six foot two or three, with a barrel chest and a thick slab of gut that made his arms and legs look spindly. Around fifty years old. He was playing tourist, dressed in a short-sleeved Ban-Lon shirt the color of brown mustard, a pair of checkered slacks.

He lit a cigarette and leaned against the wooden balcony rail. The deep end of the pool was right beneath his room. The reflection rippled over him, the glow shifting. Purple, yellow, green. When he finished the cigarette, he flicked it away and took out a comb. He ran the comb through his thinning hair. A lefty. See? Seraphine hadn't mentioned that. That was why Barone liked to take his time, gather his own information.

He couldn't read the mark's expression from this distance. Fisk didn't seem jumpy. A strong gust rattled the fronds of the palm tree by the pool, and Fisk barely glanced over. He had a good forty pounds on Barone. Or look at it a different way: Barone had a good forty pounds on him.

Fisk finished combing his hair, inspected the teeth of the comb, and then went back inside.

The pool deserted, the breezeway empty. The hula girl on the sign shimmied. Room 207 had the only second-floor light on down the long leg of the L. No lights on down the short leg. A couple of lights were on below, on the first floor, but those rooms had the curtains pulled.

The motel office faced Old Spanish Trail. From behind the reception desk, the night clerk could see the street, the pool, the short leg of the L, the parking lot. *Most* of the parking lot. His blind spot was the turn-in from Old Spanish Trail and the northeast corner of the lot.

The dashboard clock ticked. Let Fisk start to worry.

Let him get steamed. At a quarter past nine, fifteen minutes late, Barone pulled onto Old Spanish Trail, looped back around, and parked in the northeast corner of the Bali Hai lot. He grabbed the briefcase from the backseat, put the burned-out bulb in the pocket of his suit coat, and climbed the middle stairs. Knock-knock.

The door cracked open. The thinning hair on Fisk's scalp like the whorls of a thumbprint. He took a long look at Barone. "You have it?"

"What do you think?" Barone said.

Fisk let Barone inside and shut the door behind him. He motioned to the bed with the Police Positive .38 in his hand. "Sit down while I make sure," Fisk said.

"You have anything to drink?"

"No."

"Nothing?" Barone said. "Or nothing you want to share with me?"

Fisk popped open the briefcase. He took out the first envelope, ripped it open. Passport. He went over the passport inch by inch, using his thumbnail to pick at the corners.

"How long is this going to take?" Barone said. "I was just supposed to drop the case and fly."

"Shut the fuck up," Fisk said.

He set the passport on the nightstand and ripped open the second envelope. Plane ticket. He went over that inch by inch, too, and then reached for the cash. Two fat stacks.

"That was some nice shooting yesterday in Dallas," Barone said. "How far away were you? Couple hundred yards?"

Fisk stopped counting. He looked up at Barone, a dead, empty stare. "I don't know what you're talking about."

"Sure," Barone said. "My mistake."

Fisk held the stare for a while. He had to start the count over again.

Barone waited until Fisk was almost done with the second stack of cash and then stood. "All right, then."

"Hang on," Fisk said.

"Happy trails, pardner."

"You're light a grand."

"I don't know anything about that," Barone said.

"Ten up front, fifteen when the job was done," Fisk said. "That was the deal."

"I'm just the delivery boy." Barone, out the door and onto the breezeway. "Take it up with management."

"I said hang on, asshole."

Barone kept walking. He felt Fisk coming after him, light on his feet for such a big boy. At the top of the stairs, Fisk grabbed for Barone's shoulder. Barone, ready for the first touch, slipped away and under, two steps to the left, and hit Fisk beneath the chin with the heel of his hand. If Fisk had been a smaller guy, the shot would have knocked his block off. Barone didn't need to knock his block off. Fisk's head snapped back and smacked against the wall of the breezeway.

The impact dazed Fisk, his hands floating in front of him. Barone cinched his belt around Fisk's wrists and kicked his feet out from under him. Down the stairs Fisk tumbled. All that beef, nothing to slow it. Barone had played through every move in his head a hundred times. It was like watching something from the grandstand. Like watching a replay of something that had already happened.

Fisk hit bottom hard. Barone moved down the stairs and retrieved his belt. Fisk lay sprawled on his back. The top half of him looked like he was running left, the bottom half like he was running right. Breathing, just barely. One eye open, the other filled with blood. Barone crouched over him. Careful now. Make sure it looks right, one good pop. Lift the head and crack it like an egg on the edge of a skillet. Barone grabbed Fisk's ears.

He sensed the knife. Luck, or maybe his guardian angel. Barone just managed to get a hand up, between the knife and his ribs. The blade slid through his palm and out the other side.

No pain yet, just surprise. Barone fought the impulse to jerk his hand away. Jerk your hand away and you give your pal his knife back, you give him a mulligan, another shot. Fisk tried to pull the switchblade free. Barone held on. Now the pain came, building and building, like a band warming up before a show, one instrument at first and then the others joining in. Barone held on. With his good hand, he grabbed Fisk by the hair. Fisk watched him with his blood-filled eye. Barone lifted Fisk's head and drove it back down. The lights went out.

Barone's concern now was blood. Yank the blade out of his hand, he'd bleed everywhere. So he left the knife in his hand and went back upstairs. Over the sink in Fisk's bathroom, he inched the knife out. He rinsed his hand with cold water and wrapped it up in a towel, best he could. He didn't have time to get too cute.

Everything went into the briefcase. The passport, the plane ticket, the cash, Fisk's .38, his switchblade. Take your time. You always have more time than your body thinks you do.

Barone locked the door behind him. He checked the spot in the breezeway where Fisk had smacked his head against the wall. No blood. Good.

He swapped his burned-out bulb for the one in the socket overhead, at the top of the stairs. Whoever found

Fisk's body would think the poor unlucky bastard had tripped in the dark. No one would ever guess how he'd really died, or why.

No blood from Barone's hand at the bottom of the stairs. Good. He tossed the briefcase in the backseat of the car. He pulled onto Old Spanish Trail. He had to drive with only his left hand, reaching across the steering wheel to work the gearshift and the turn signal. He kept his right hand, wrapped in the towel, pressed between his thighs.

The pain played on, the whole band. Barone ignored it. Carlos had a guy here in Houston, a hophead doctor in the Mexican part of town. A shot, a pill, a proper bandage. That was all Barone needed, and then he'd be ready for the next job.

8

For almost an hour, Charlotte soared. Light-headed, almost giddy. I'm leaving. *I have left.* The girls picked up on her mood. The three of them sang songs— "On Top of Spaghetti (All Covered with Cheese)," "The Ballad of Davy Crockett"—and counted pumpjacks, horses, cars with out-of-state license plates. The dog, his head in Rosemary's lap, sighed contentedly and smacked his lips in his sleep.

But then, as they neared Oklahoma City, the full weight of what Charlotte had done dragged her back to earth. *I have left.* Wax wings melted, Icarus plunged.

Divorce. Until today she'd never really even imagined the possibility of it. Who, in a place like Woodrow, did? You met a man, you married the man, you stayed by his side until one of you died. The kind of women who abandoned their husbands and ran off to Reno or Mexico—those woman lived in seedy big cities, in the pages of a scandal magazine.

When Charlotte's friends found out what she'd done, they would be appalled. Every single person Charlotte knew would be appalled. Every single person in Wood-row, in other words.

And the sheer number of questions overwhelmed her. Did she need to go to Reno or Mexico to file for divorce? Would she need a lawyer? How much would a lawyer cost? Where would she and the girls live? What would she do to support them?

They'd reached the intersection with Highway 66. It wasn't too late to turn around. If she turned around now, here, she'd be home well before Dooley stumbled in for the night. She'd be tucked back into her bed, into her life, as if none of this had ever happened.

"Mommy?" Rosemary said. "The light's green."

"I know," Charlotte said. "I just need a minute to think."

The car behind her honked. The man driving flapped an arm at her, annoyed. Charlotte turned right on 66 and headed west.

"We're going to visit Aunt Marguerite," she said, the name popping out of her mouth almost before it had popped into her head. "In California."

"Who?" said both Rosemary and Joan.

"My aunt," Charlotte said. "Your great-aunt. My mother's sister."

In the rearview mirror, she saw the girls look at each other. The dog lifted his big head, to measure the sudden silence, and then thudded back to sleep.

"You have an *aunt*," Rosemary said.

"Yes, of course," Charlotte said. "I'm sure I've mentioned her. Aunt Marguerite. She lives in Los Angeles. In Santa Monica, right by the ocean."

Or Marguerite *had* lived there at one point. She'd moved away to California when Charlotte was only six or seven years old and never returned to Oklahoma, not even for a visit. Whenever Charlotte asked her mother why not, her mother would scowl. "I don't know and I don't care," Charlotte's mother would say. And refuse to discuss the matter further.

Every year Marguerite had sent Charlotte a perfunctory birthday card—no salutation, no message, just Marguerite's full formal name in a rushed scribble, as if she had a stack of such cards to get through as quickly as possible.

When Charlotte's mother passed away, five years ago, Marguerite didn't attend the funeral. The birthday cards had trickled to a stop long before then. The last time Charlotte heard from Marguerite had been . . . she couldn't recall exactly. Before she'd married Dooley.

She couldn't recall Marguerite exactly either. It had been so long ago that Charlotte's memories were shards of shards that didn't fit together into any sort of whole. Marguerite wore black. She had very cold hands and never smiled. She was thin as a blade and frighteningly tall, a head taller than Charlotte's mother. She wore eyeglasses with black cat-eye frames. She said once, to Charlotte's mother, "Oh, for God's sake, Dolores."

Was Marguerite still at the same address? Was she still in California? Was she even still alive? If so, how would she feel when a niece she'd long ago forgotten showed up on her doorstep with two little girls and an epileptic dog?

More questions. Too many questions.

"Let's sing another song, shall we?" Charlotte said.

"Mommy?" Rosemary said. "How long does it take to get to California?"

"I'm not sure, chickadee."

"One day?"

"It's like *The Wizard of Oz*," Charlotte said. "We just have to follow the Yellow Brick Road."

Charlotte didn't dwell on the irony. The moral of

The Wizard of Oz, of course, the lesson that Dorothy finally learned, was that there's no place like home.

"I want to be the Scarecrow," Rosemary said. "Joan can be the Tin Man or the Cowardly Lion."

"Maybe Joan wants to be the Scarecrow," Charlotte said.

"Joan. Do you want to be the Scarecrow? Or wouldn't you much rather be the Tin Man or the Cowardly Lion?"

"I can be the Tin Man or the Cowardly Lion," Joan said.

"See, Mommy?" Rosemary said.

At nine o'clock they stopped for the night in McLean, Texas. Charlotte didn't want to be out on the road any later than that, and the girls were exhausted. By now Charlotte had begun to fear that she'd made the most rash and disastrous decision of her life. *I have left.* She needed a kind face, an encouraging word.

Instead she found a sour Baptist pickle behind the motel reception desk. The woman eyed Charlotte. She eyed the girls. She eyed the dog. Charlotte could not be sure which among them the woman found most unwelcome.

"We do not allow dogs," the woman said. "Under any circumstances."

"I understand," Charlotte said.

"You'll have to leave the dog in the car or find somewhere else to stay."

"He can sleep in the car," Charlotte said. "That's fine."

"Or find somewhere else to stay," the woman said. "It's all the same to me. And we do not allow male visitors. Under any circumstances."

Really, Charlotte thought. She'd been up since five-thirty that morning and had just driven three and a half hours. Did she look as if she were expecting a male visitor?

"I understand," Charlotte said.

The woman handed over the room key but kept her grip on the fob. She eyed Charlotte even more sourly than before. "If you lie down with dogs," she said, "you get up with fleas."

Their room was cramped and dreary and smelled as if someone had boiled cabbage in the bathroom. Rosemary and Joan had never stayed in a motel before, though, and found every detail of the experience—the tiny bars of soap, the promotional brochure for Indian war dances in Tucumcari—fascinating.

Charlotte showered and then unwrapped the leftover roast-beef sandwiches she'd brought from home. They ate sitting cross-legged on one of the beds.

"Mommy?" Rosemary said. "Lucky doesn't have fleas."

"It's just an expression," Charlotte said.

"What does it mean?"

"It means . . . well, I suppose it means that you should choose your friends wisely."

"Because they might have fleas?" Rosemary said. "And the fleas might jump on you and now you have fleas?"

"Something like that," Charlotte said. "Yes."

While the girls took their baths, Charlotte buttoned her coat back up, tucked her damp hair down under the collar, and carried the bedspread outside to shake off the crumbs. She fed the dog the other half of her sandwich and walked him in the rutted field behind the motel. She hated the thought of leaving him in the car all night, in the dark and cold and lonely.

The light was off in the motel office, the sour Baptist pickle nowhere to be seen. Charlotte wasn't in the habit of breaking the rules, but neither was she in the habit of leaving her husband, taking the children, and driving to California. In for a penny, she decided, in for a pound.

"Come on," she told the dog. "Hurry."

The dog regarded her dubiously.

"Last chance," Charlotte warned him.

The girls said their prayers, and Charlotte tucked them in and kissed their foreheads, their noses, their chins. The dog claimed the center of the other bed. Charlotte had to shove him over before she could climb in.

She gave the Esso road map one more quick look, measuring the distances with her thumb. It was more than a thousand miles from McLean to Los Angeles. If they got an early start tomorrow morning and didn't stop too often along the way, they should reach Gallup, New Mexico, by nightfall. Spend the night there, call Aunt Marguerite. Tuesday would be another long day, another long drive. If all went smoothly, though, they might make it to Santa Monica in time to see the sun sink into the Pacific Ocean.

Charlotte turned off the bedside lamp. Rosemary had begun to snore, but in the darkness Charlotte could hear Joan thinking.

"What is it, sweetie?" Charlotte whispered.

"Are we going to call Daddy?" Joan whispered back.

"I told him we'd call him tomorrow. I left him a note."

Joan considered. "What if he doesn't see it?"

"I put it right where he'll see it," Charlotte said.

On the bathroom counter, next to the big box of Alka-Seltzer. Dooley might overlook the note when he came home tonight, too drunk to brush his teeth, but Charlotte was confident that he'd head straight for the Alka-Seltzer tomorrow morning.

That seemed to satisfy Joan. Her breathing slowed. Charlotte tried to imagine Dooley's reaction when he read the note, when he grasped that she and the girls were gone. She tried to imagine what *her* reaction would be if she came home one day and the girls were gone. She would be . . . obliterated. With nothing left of her for the crows to peck at, as the Bible said, not even the palms of her hands or the soles of her feet.

Dooley wasn't the most attentive father, but he *was* the girls' father. What right did Charlotte have to take Rosemary and Joan from him? What right did she have to snatch them away from everybody and everything they knew, home and school, father and friends? She wanted to give them opportunities they'd never have in Woodrow. But was she destroying their lives instead of saving them?

Charlotte heard the thunk of a car door in the parking lot, the hiss of whispers. She remembered, again, her mother's warning: *There's always a bumpier road than the one you're riding on.* She got out of bed and made sure the chain on the door was latched.

9

Guidry knew that Seraphine would expect him to scramble. She'd have someone waiting for him to step off every plane that landed in Miami or L.A., every train that steamed into Chicago and Kansas City, every Greyhound that pulled in to Little Rock, Louisville, and Albuquerque.

He had to get out of the country. Mexico. Central America, maybe. But he needed cash and he needed a passport. It was a big, big world. How hard could it be to disappear off the face of it? Oh, so hard if Carlos Marcello was the man searching for you.

Dolly Carmichael lived here in Houston. She'd have plenty of local contacts. A friend with a boat, perhaps? Seraphine might overlook Dolly, since she'd been out of the business for a few years. Dolly might be in the dark.

Was Guidry willing to bet his life on it? On Dolly? He pondered as he stood in the shadows across the street from her house.

No, he decided finally. He couldn't risk it. At some point Seraphine would remember Dolly. And Dolly would sell him out. Every human heart was rotten meat, but Dolly's was more rotten than most.

So he turned away. The last Scott Street bus of the night dropped him on Old Spanish Trail. A dozen motels to choose from. He picked one with an astronaut theme. The clerk gave him a room key attached to a miniature balsa-wood rocket. A rocket to the moon! Guidry supposed you had to keep your sense of humor at a time like this.

He slept like a baby, if the baby jerked awake every time the wind rattled the window or a fly buzzed past. In the morning he walked over to the greasy spoon next door. He ordered a plate of corned-beef hash, two fried eggs on top. Hot black coffee, please, and keep it coming. The man at the next table offered him a piece of his Sunday paper. No thanks. Guidry didn't need any more bad news right now.

Guidry knew how to make friends. That was his gift, his greatest asset. Over the years, working for

Carlos, he'd bought thousands of drinks and greased thousands of palms, laughed at thousands of bad jokes and listened with convincing sympathy to thousands of sob stories. He had a girl in every port. A girl and a busboy and a bookie and an assistant district attorney. But who among them, now that Guidry was on the wrong side of Carlos, could he ask for help? Who among them would even bat an eyelash before they sold Guidry down the river?

Picture Tantalus in hell, dying of thirst as he stood in the pool of cool water up to his neck.

No planes, no trains, no buses. Well, that made Guidry's next step a simple one.

"Is there a car lot around here?" he asked the waitress. "Used cars, not new."

"Why don't you go see for yourself?" the waitress said. "I'll keep your plate warm for you."

"You're just a golden ray of sunshine, aren't you?"

"Two stoplights up, on the left. You ain't gonna eat that?"

"I'll have some white toast. Dry." Guidry pushed the plate of hash away. His stomach hadn't recovered from yesterday. Maybe it never would.

Big Ed Zingel in Las Vegas. Guidry couldn't think of another option. Try as he might. Big Ed Zingel. Ye gods, Guidry's life had come to this. Ed liked Guidry.

He could be generous if you caught him in the right mood. And—this was the salient fact—Ed hated the Marcello brothers the same way Carlos hated the Kennedys. So give him an opportunity to screw over Carlos by helping Guidry and he'd jump at it.

Or he wouldn't.

Guidry had always taken a simple approach to life: live it loose and easy, let it roll off and over you. Well, easier said than done these days. But he couldn't let himself brood about it, just how badly fucked he was.

The man at the other table put down his newspaper. Guidry could see one of the headlines, a story about the surgeon who'd worked on Kennedy at Parkland in Dallas. "HE NEVER KNEW WHAT HIT HIM," SAYS DALLAS DOC.

The used-car lot was open on Sunday. A lanky salesman came loping over. Guidry was probably the first customer he'd had all weekend.

"How're you?" the salesman said. "Name's Bobby Joe Hunt."

"Like Bobby Joe Hunt who pitches for the Pittsburgh Pirates?" Guidry said.

"Even better," the salesman said.

"No."

"In the flesh."

Guidry had watched Bobby Joe Hunt get shellacked in the World Series a few years ago. "Did you retire?"

"No," Bobby Joe Hunt said. "I work here during the off-season."

"They don't pay you fellas enough, do they?" Guidry said.

"Not nearly. What can I help you with?"

Guidry looked around and settled on a 1957 Dodge Coronet with four bald tires and a hamster on a wheel where the engine should have been. Maybe it wasn't quite that bad. Guidry got the price down a couple hundred after some parry-and-thrust. Bobby Hunt negotiated better than he'd pitched against the Yanks. He agreed to put a set of nearly new tires on the Coronet and swap out the old belts for fresh ones.

Guidry drove back to the motel and packed his suitcase. He pictured Seraphine in her office out on Airline Highway. Curtains drawn to block the light, just the desk lamp on. She'd have been up all night, would've made all the calls she needed to make by now. She'd be smoking, thinking, picturing *him*. Wondering, *Where are you,* mon cher? *Where do you think you're going?*

Two possible routes led to Big Ed Zingel in Las Vegas, the northern and the southern. Head up 75 to

Dallas and then 287 to Amarillo and 66. Or follow 90 and the new interstate due west to San Antonio and El Paso. Flip a coin—Carlos owned every inch of Texas. The coin came up tails. Go north, young man. Why not?

Downtown Dallas on Sunday afternoon was a grave-yard. The cops still had Dealey Plaza blocked off, so Guidry looped the long way around. Forty miles east of Amarillo, he stopped to gas up the Dodge and get something for dinner. A town called Goodnight. He didn't like that name. Omens and portents.

There was a diner next to the filling station. Guidry took a seat at the counter and ordered the chicken-fried steak. It arrived as advertised, chopped steak fried like a chicken and then covered with cream gravy to hide the crime. Guidry tried not to think how he'd prob-ably never taste a real roux again, or red beans that had been simmering in a pot all day. Funny what mattered to you, the little things.

"I just cain't get over it," the waitress said when she topped his coffee. She was younger and friendlier and prettier than the waitress back in Houston.

"Kennedy?" Guidry said. "Oh, it's just awful."

The waitress eyed him. "You didn't hear?"

"Hear what?"

"This morning in Dallas," she said, "about Jack Ruby."

Jack Ruby? Who ran one of the sleaziest strip clubs in Dallas? Who, every chance he got, sidled up and tried to weasel himself into Guidry's good graces? What did Jack Ruby have to do with anything about anything?

"He shot Oswald," the waitress said.

"Jack Ruby did?" Guidry said.

"Right in the stomach," she said. "When they was bringing Oswald downstairs, at the police station. He walked right up and shot him dead."

Guidry made the appropriate noises of shock and distress to hide his genuine shock and distress. Seraphine had hinted that Oswald's days were numbered. But this . . . At the police station? With Oswald surrounded, presumably, by a mob of cops and reporters? It was just another ominous reminder Guidry didn't need: that Carlos could get to anyone, anywhere, at any time.

The door opened. A cop entered and took a seat at the counter, two stools down. He touched the brim of a cowboy hat that was the same dirty white as the cream gravy.

Guidry nodded back. "Sheriff."

The cop's big ears pinked up. He was just a lad, raw-boned and weak-chinned. "Deputy," he said.

"What's that?" Guidry said.

"I'm a deputy, not the sheriff."

"Beg your pardon. But one of these days you'll get there, just you wait."

The cop didn't know if he was allowed to smile or not. He concentrated on his knife and fork and napkin. Guidry had taken only two bites of his chicken-fried steak. First the news about Ruby, now a goddamn deputy sitting six feet away.

Guidry couldn't get up and walk out, not yet. Wait a minute, take your time, create the impression of a relaxed and happy man. The deputy had no reason to be suspicious of Guidry, none at all. He was just your typical cop, giving the stranger from out of town—the city slicker in the fancy suit—the typical cop once-over.

"Passing through?" the deputy said.

"That's right." Guidry showed him the business card. "Bobby Joe Hunt, Greenleaf Used Automobiles in Houston. I'm on my way to a car auction in Amarillo."

The waitress scowled. "On a Sunday? That don't seem right, does it? That they'd have a car auction on Sunday?"

Why, thanks for chiming in, sweetheart, Guidry thought. What would we ever do without you?

"Well, the auction's not till tomorrow," he said. "I'm

spending the night in Amarillo because I heard some advice about early birds and worms."

"It don't seem right to me, that folks should have to work on Sunday," the waitress said. "They should be at church or home with their loved ones."

"Hear, hear," Guidry said.

The deputy squinted at the business card. "Bobby Joe Hunt. He's that pitcher for the Pirates. He's from Houston too, ain't he?"

Guidry ate steadily. Not too slowly, not too quickly. He noticed he was about to strangle the handle of his coffee mug to death and loosened his grip.

"You know your baseball, Deputy," Guidry said.

"Yes he is, matter of fact. No relation to me, I'm afraid."

"I got his baseball card," the deputy said. "I got every baseball card from 1957 through to 1963. Topps cards. I don't have no interest in the Fleer. All Fleer's got is Ted Williams, and I wouldn't walk across the street for a Ted Williams card."

"Eat your supper, Fred, and stop boring the poor man to death." The waitress saw that Guidry was almost finished with his steak and brought over the tin pie stand. "Pecan pie, fresh as the day it was baked."

"Why, thank you," Guidry said.

The deputy shifted on his stool to study Guidry. "Passing through, you say?"

"He already said so, Fred." The waitress gave Guidry a clean fork for the pie. "Don't mind him, mister. Usually takes him a minute to get out of first gear."

Guidry turned to face the deputy. "You played some ball yourself, I bet."

"Yessir, I did," the deputy said.

"Any good at it?"

The deputy's ears pinked again. "All-County third base, two years in a row."

"Ask him how many high schools we got here in the county," the waitress said.

"Lord Almighty, Annabelle," the deputy said. "You wear a soul out."

Guidry had finished the slice of pie in four big bites. He put his money on the counter and stood. In no hurry at all. He'd heard a story about Art Pepper, how once he'd strolled out of a police station with a bag of dope in the pocket of his sport coat. Guidry's hero.

"Well, I better hit the road," Guidry said. "Happy Thanksgiving in advance. God bless us everyone."

The deputy studied Guidry for another few seconds and then touched the brim of his hat. "See you," he said.

The prairie, weathered and leathery and endless. Like God meant to get around to it during Creation but had run out of steam. Twenty miles outside Goodnight, the sun puddling golden and red on the horizon, Guidry started to loosen up about the deputy. He shouldn't have been worried in the first place.

Half a mile later, he saw the patrol car coming up fast in his rearview mirror, the siren wailing and the lights flashing.

10

Barone didn't get finished with Carlos's hophead Mexican doctor until almost midnight, so he had to stay and spend Saturday night in Houston. He didn't sleep much. The hand that the knife had gone through kept waking him up, throbbing, reminding him that it still hurt. Don't worry, I remember. The hophead doctor had given him some pills for the pain, but they didn't have much punch. Barone took double what the doctor instructed and could barely feel a difference. He thought that the pills might be sugar and the doctor had kept the good ones for himself.

The doctor had informed Barone that he was lucky. It didn't look as if the blade had severed tendons or sliced through anything too important. The doctor took a snort of dope before he started stitching the hand up.

He explained that the dope steadied his nerves. He said his father had been a doctor, too, and one time in Chihuahua had removed a bullet from the leg of the bandit Pancho Villa. Barone told the doctor to shut up and pay attention to what he was doing. The doctor said that Villa's notorious compadre Rodolfo Fierro stood by during the entire procedure with a gun pointed at the father's head. Rodolfo Fierro, who later would become known as "El Carnicero," the butcher.

Barone asked the doctor if he should point a gun at *his* head—would that help him pay attention? The doctor giggled. No, no, my friend, he said, and took another snort.

Sunday morning Barone drove back to the airport. His flight didn't leave until one o'clock. Barone couldn't wait to get home. In New Orleans he could go to a real doctor who wasn't just bat wings and chicken blood. Carlos's doctor in New Orleans had a fancy office on Canal Street. He lived in a Garden District mansion and rode a float on Fat Tuesday. He'd give Barone the good pills.

Barone went into the men's room and checked under the bandage. The stitches in his hand looked okay. Two sets of them, the back of the hand and the palm.

In the terminal he found a seat not far from the one television set and watched Ruby shoot Oswald.

The cops tackled Ruby afterward. Ruby never stood a chance of getting away, the middle of police head-quarters.

Ruby must have known, going in, that he didn't stand a chance of getting away. So why'd he do it? What made a guy agree to go to the electric chair for you? Carlos must have scared him with something even worse than the electric chair.

A few minutes before the plane was supposed to board, a guy sat down next to Barone. The guy didn't look over at him.

"Call her," the guy said. "Right now."

He stood and walked away. Barone stood and walked over to the pay phone.

"I asked you to call last night," Seraphine said.

"I don't call unless there's a problem," Barone said. "There wasn't a problem."

"You were supposed to stay at the Shamrock."

"Why do you need to know where I'm staying?"

He heard a match scratch and blaze. "There's been a change of plans," Seraphine said.

"Not for me. I'm coming home."

"We need you to stay in Houston."

Barone watched the stewardess for his flight come out and adjust her pillbox hat and smile at the people waiting by the gate. Tickets, please. Barone set his bum hand on top of the pay phone. The throbbing eased for a second.

"I know you've been a busy bee, *mon cher*," she said. "I know you must be weary, but duty calls."

"I'm about to get on the plane," Barone said.

"I said I was sorry."

"No you didn't. Carlos needs me to stay in Houston? Or do you?"

"He's taking a nap," Seraphine said. "Shall I wake him so that you can discuss?"

Bitch. "Who is it?"

"Frank Guidry. Do you know him?"

"I've seen him around," Barone said. "I didn't know he was on the list."

"Remy was supposed to take care of it," she said, "since you were otherwise disposed. He was supposed to collect him at the Rice last night, but our friend failed to appear. So says Remy."

It sounded like Seraphine was thinking the same thing Barone was thinking. Remy was trying to cover his ass. He was dumb as a brick and had probably spooked his mark. At least this gave Barone a place to start.

"I want to make it absolutely clear," Seraphine said. "This is now a matter of the highest priority."

Because you fucked up and used Remy instead of

me. But Barone didn't say it. Seraphine already knew it. She knew that Carlos already knew it, too. Good. Let her sweat.

"Do you understand, *mon cher*?" she said.

"Does Guidry have a wife?" Barone said.

If Guidry had a wife, Barone's job would be easy. Find the wife, wait for Guidry to call her. Guidry would call at some point—the husband always did. And then Barone would hold the phone close to the wife's mouth. He'd let Guidry imagine what had happened to her so far. Let him imagine what would happen to her if he didn't come in fast.

"He doesn't have a wife," Seraphine said.

"Ex-wife?" Barone said. "Girlfriend? Brother or sister?"

"Nobody."

"How many people do you have watching for him here at the airport?"

"Two, since last night. Plus two at the train station and two more at the bus depot downtown. And I've notified everyone in the organization."

"I'll need a new car," Barone said.

"The black Pontiac at the back of the lot."

Barone drove back downtown. The room clerk at the Rice told him that the night shift came on at four. Barone waited in the bar. He chased his last two pills with a glass of cold beer.

The night-shift bell captain with his epaulets and double row of brass buttons said yeah, he knew the man Barone was talking about. A handsome Dan, sharp dresser, dark hair and light eyes. Yeah, he'd seen him last night. Around eight o'clock or so, hotfooting it out of the lobby like the devil himself was on his tail.

Barone had been right. Remy had blown his shot at Guidry. So long, Remy, it was good to know you.

"You put him in a cab?" Barone asked the bell captain.

"He didn't want to wait for one."

"Which direction did he hotfoot it?"

Barone walked up to the corner of Fannin Street. He looked left and then right. Two blocks south down Fannin was the Texas State Hotel. That's where Barone would go if the devil was on *his* tail and he needed to catch a cab in a hurry.

The first hack he talked to outside the Texas State Hotel didn't know anything. The second hack sent him to a third hack.

"Yeah," the third hack said. "I rode him out to the airport last night."

"You're sure it was him?" Barone said.

"Sure I'm sure. I remember because he tipped me five bucks on a dollar fare. I figured he must've had a well come in."

So Guidry had taken a cab to the airport and jumped on the first flight out of Houston. Seraphine's people at the airport must have just missed him. But she'd be able to figure out which flight Guidry took, where it was headed.

"What time did you drop him at the airport?" Barone said. "What time exactly?"

"Hell, I don't know. Let me think. Eight-thirty or so."

But slow down, Barone told himself. Go back. Guidry left a five-dollar tip on a dollar fare. That was a helluva tip. Either Guidry was dumb or he was smart. Of course the hack would remember a tip that big. Maybe Guidry wanted the hack to remember it, remember him.

"Did you see him go inside?" Barone said.

The hack was confused. "Did I what?"

"See him walk through the door and go inside the terminal."

"Why wouldn't he go inside?" the hack said. "I don't know. I didn't stick around. They don't let you stick around after you drop a passenger. You gotta have a permit to wait in the pickup line."

Barone used the pay phone in the lobby of the Texas State Hotel to call Seraphine.

"Have one of your boys at the airport ask around on

the taxi line and see if he took a cab back into town last night," Barone said.

"A cab *back* from the airport?" Seraphine said.

"That's what I said."

She didn't ask any more questions. Twenty minutes later she called back.

"One driver says maybe," she said. "He's not sure."

"Where did he drop the fare?" Barone said.

"The corner of Lockwood and Sherman."

A neighborhood of crummy old Victorians southeast of downtown. Barone was getting somewhere now.

"Are you certain about this, *mon cher*?" Seraphine said. "A flight to Miami left at nine o'clock, so . . ."

"Is he smart?" Barone said. "Guidry?"

"Yes."

"Then he's still in Houston. Who here owes him a favor?"

She thought about it. "Ah."

"Who?"

"Dolly Carmichael lives in the Second Ward. She used to manage Vincent Grilli's clubs, up until a year or two ago."

Seraphine had an address for her, on Edgewood, a ten-minute stroll from where? From the corner of Lockwood and Sherman, where the driver at the airport had dropped his fare. Barone wrote down the address and hung up. He went outside and looked around. A skinny colored kid was loitering at the bus stop across the street. Barone walked over.

"Do you know how to drive?" Barone said.

"Shoot," the colored kid said. "Do I know how to drive."

If Barone kept trying to steer and shift and flip the turn signal with just his left hand, his one good hand, sooner or later he'd end up ramming the Pontiac into a wall.

"I'll give you a dollar if you drive me out to the Second Ward," Barone said. "I've got a car."

"Shoot. You'll give me a dollar."

"Two dollars. Take it or leave it."

The colored kid drew himself up to his full height and glared. He weighed all of a buck twenty and couldn't have been more than sixteen years old.

"I don't do none of that," the kid said. "I'll tell you right now. If that's what you after."

"I want you to drive me to the Second Ward," Barone said. "That's what I'm after. How old are you?"

"Eighteen."

A lie. "Let's go."

"What happened to your hand?" the colored kid said.

"I cut it shaving my palms. Let's go."

The colored kid knew how to drive, more or less. Barone made sure he stuck to the speed limit, signaled every turn, stopped for the yellow lights. They parked down the street from the address on Edgewood.

A two-story Victorian painted blue with white gingerbread trim. Flowers in the boxes and the yard not too weedy. Next door, yellow with white trim, a Mexican woman sat on her porch and rocked a baby in her arms.

"Mexicans," the colored kid said.

"What do you have against Mexicans?" Barone said.

"Shoot. What do I have against Mexicans."

"Tell me. What did a Mexican ever do to you?"

"Nothing," the kid said. "You Mexican? You don't look Mexican."

"No, I'm not Mexican," Barone said. "What's that got to do with it?"

A few minutes later, the baby on the porch fell asleep and the Mexican woman went back inside. Dolly Carmichael's house was dark except for one light on upstairs. Barone told the kid to wait for him.

A big elm screened Dolly's side door from the street. Barone picked the lock. The chain was latched, but he carried a rubber band in his wallet. He reached inside and looped one end of the rubber band over the door handle, the other end over the button at the end of the chain. Turn the handle. That easy. The chain slid down the notch and dropped free.

Dolly was in the front bedroom, taking off her earrings. She turned and saw him and didn't scream. Barone put a finger to his lips anyway and closed the door softly behind him.

"Sit," he said.

She sat down on the edge of the bed. "May I put on a robe, please?"

"No," Barone said. She was older than he'd expected. Pushing seventy, at least. A scrappy old broad with glittering eyes. "Where is he?"

"Pardon me?" she said.

"Where is he?" Barone said.

"Who?"

He walked over and sat down next to her. "Which bedroom? Left or right side of the hall?"

"There's nobody in the house but me," she said. "Go see for yourself."

"Tell me."

"I'm not scared of you."

Barone had heard that before. Only at the beginning, though, never at the end. He touched her earlobe, the spot where she'd had it pierced. She tried not to flinch. The old-timer who'd taught Barone the ropes had said, one time, "The fear of pain is more powerful than any pain itself." And then he'd winked. "Unless you know what you're doing."

On a table in the corner sat a portable phonograph and a stack of albums. The album on the top of the stack was *'Round About Midnight.* "'Round Midnight" was the first track on the album.

"You like Miles Davis?" Barone said.

"Just get it over with or get out of my house," she said.

Barone started to ask her if she believed in God. Probably she'd say no. Or ha! Barone might believe, though. Not God with a white beard. But if life was color and noise and pain, there had to be a backing for it, canvas for the paint. Friday night he'd listened to the old man in New Orleans play "'Round Midnight." Which got him onto that Christmas party at Mandina's, which now that he thought about it was when and where he saw Frank Guidry the first time. And now here was the song again, the Miles Davis version, in the old broad's bedroom.

"He was here," Barone said. "Where did he go?"

"*Who* was here, for Chrissakes?"

"Guidry."

Her confusion was genuine. He could tell. Watch the forehead, the crease between the eyebrows, the pull of the lip. That was another thing the old-timer had taught Barone.

"Frank Guidry? You mean Frank Guidry?" she said.

Barone stood. "You can put your robe on."

"Good Lord," she said. "I haven't seen Frank Guidry since I don't know when. It's been three years at least."

He checked the bedrooms, just to make sure. When he came back, she was pouring rye into a glass. Her hand shaking, the rye spilling over.

"Do you have any aspirin?" he said.

"In the bathroom. The medicine cabinet."

He chewed up four aspirin and helped himself to some of the rye. "Any guess where he might be headed? Carlos would appreciate your help."

"He'll try to get out of the country, I suppose," she said.

Barone supposed so, too. "Who owes him a favor?"

She laughed, like a rock breaking another rock. "Who's Frank Guidry ever done a favor for in his entire goddamn life?"

Barone started to leave.

"Wait," she said.

"What?"

"You ought to go see Doc Ortega about that hand. He's just over there off Navigation Boulevard."

"I've already been there," Barone said.

He called Seraphine from a phone box on Scott Street.

"Guidry didn't go for Dolly Carmichael," Barone said. "He's smart."

"That's all right, *mon cher*," Seraphine said. "I've got good news. You have a long drive ahead of you."

"Where am I going?" Barone said.

"Goodnight, Texas."

"What's the good news?"

"What once was lost," she said, "has now been found."

11

The patrol car parked behind Guidry. Out climbed an older cop in a cowboy hat. Sheriff of Godforsaken, Texas. He moved stiffly, like he'd just swung down off a horse. Fred, the deputy from the diner, took the other side of Guidry's car, a shotgun cradled in his arms.

Guidry rolled down his window. "Good evening, Sheriff."

The sheriff bent and peered in. He had a graying handlebar mustache that hid most of his mouth and some of his chin. He looked over at the deputy. "I believe you might be right on the money about this, Fred."

"Hello there, Fred." Guidry waved to the deputy, who lifted a hand off the stock of the shotgun to wave back but then decided to scratch his nose instead. "How can I help you, Sheriff? Was I driving too fast?"

Guidry prayed for a routine shakedown. City slicker comes through town—hook him, empty his wallet, send him on his way. But if the sheriff worked for a man who worked for a man who worked for Carlos, if the word had gone out to keep an eye out for *this* particular city slicker . . .

"Are you it?" the sheriff asked Guidry.

"Am I what?"

"The thorn in the flesh from Proverbs. The fly in the ointment. The fella causing all the fuss."

Exactly the words Guidry didn't want to hear. But he kept smiling. Desperately, one might say.

"My name's Bobby Joe Hunt," he said. "I sell used cars in Houston. I wish you'd tell me what this is about, Sheriff."

"Get out of the car, son," the sheriff said. "Hands where I can see 'em."

"Sure."

"Billfold. Toss it here." The sheriff flipped through Guidry's wallet. "Where's your driving license?"

Torn to bits and buried under a pile of garbage in a metal can behind the motel in Houston.

"It's not in there?" Guidry said. "Should be. And a business card. My name's Bobby Joe Hunt. Like I said,

I'm from Houston, and I'm on the way to Amarillo for a car auction. Just ask Fred over there."

The sheriff flicked the business card away and drew the pistol from his holster. "Turn around," he told Guidry. "Hands behind your back."

Guidry was livid that his end had come this quickly. Less than twenty-four hours of freedom, the best he'd been able to do. And livid that his end would come this way, in this place—at the hands of a crooked hick-town sheriff, on the bare brown plains of the Texas panhandle, a place so ugly that not even a glorious sunset could redeem it.

The sheriff cuffed him and patted him down. "Fred," he said to the deputy. "Take his car and follow us back to the station."

The sheriff whistled as he drove. Guidry didn't recognize the tune. He could try kicking the seat in front of him. Kick and hope that the sheriff swerved off the road. But then what? Even if the sheriff split his head open and Guidry didn't split his, Guidry would still be cuffed and trapped. The deputy was right behind them, a hundred feet back, with the shotgun.

"I believe it's Corinthians, Sheriff, not Proverbs," Guidry said. "The thorn in Paul's side you've referred to."

"I believe you're correct," the sheriff said.

"If memory serves, the thorn was a messenger of

Satan, sent to torment Paul when he became too conceited."

The sheriff whistled and drove.

"You've got the wrong man, Sheriff," Guidry said.

"If that turns out to be the case," the sheriff said, "you'll have my sincere apology and a hearty handshake."

The police station in Goodnight was just one room. Fake wood paneling and a linoleum floor the color of speckled green seasick. On the wall behind the desk hung a dozen framed paint-by-number paintings. Through the bars of the jail cell, Guidry could see them all. A lighthouse, a covered bridge in autumn, mallards on a pond. Two different versions of the Last Supper, one with the Holy Ghost hovering behind Jesus and one without.

"I have to go across the street and make a telephone call, Deputy," the sheriff said. "Keep the Comanches at bay."

"Yessir," the deputy said.

How long did Guidry have left? The sheriff would call whoever he reported to in Dallas. The news about Guidry would hop from lily pad to lily pad, all the way back to Seraphine in New Orleans. As soon as she found out that he was in Goodnight, she'd send someone *tout de suite.*

"Fred," Guidry said.

Nothing.

Seraphine might have someone in Dallas. But probably her cleanup hitter was in Houston right now. Eight hours away. What time was it? Seven-thirty. Suppose Seraphine got the word about Guidry at 10:00 P.M.

Six o'clock tomorrow morning. The deadline that Guidry was looking at. Tick, tock.

"Annabelle over at the diner," he told the deputy, "I think she's sweet on you. Why else would she badger you like that?"

Nothing.

"Who were you supposed to be on the lookout for, Fred? A big bad Mafia gangster from the city? I'm not even Italian, my hand to God. I'm French Cajun with a little Irish, a country boy like you, from Ascension Parish, Louisiana. Speck of a town called St. Amant. I bet you've never heard of it. I played shortstop for my high-school team."

Stretch the truth a little. Guidry had been friends with the shortstop on the high-school team.

"What else did the sheriff tell you, Fred?" Guidry said. "That I'm a wanted fugitive? That some boys from the FBI are going to come out here and haul me in?"

The deputy stood and walked over to the cooler and filled a tiny pleated paper cup with water. He drank the water, crumpled the cup in his fist, and then sat back down.

"Ask yourself a question, Fred. Why did the sheriff go across the street to make a call when there's a telephone right there on the desk in front of you? Why didn't he want you to hear what he had to say?"

The deputy put his feet up on the desk and yawned.

"I'm a federal witness, Fred," Guidry said. "It's the mob that wants me dead. The boys who show up here in a few hours won't be from the FBI. You don't have to take my word for it. Just wait and see."

"You know what?" the deputy said.

"What?"

"I don't care she's sweet on me or not," the deputy said. "I wouldn't walk across the street to stick my dick in Annabelle Ferguson."

A few minutes later, the sheriff returned from making the call. He sent the deputy home for the weekend, put a pot of coffee on to brew, and settled in behind the desk. Guidry surveyed his cell. A window, high up and not much more than a slot. He wouldn't be able to squeeze through it, even if somehow he managed to pry off the rusty wire mesh bolted to the plaster.

"I won't insult your intelligence, Sheriff," he said.

"Appreciate it."

The sheriff had lined up a dozen miniature screw-top paint pots in front of him. He unscrewed a pot and dipped his brush.

"I don't envy you," Guidry said. "You're in a fix, aren't you?"

The sheriff's gray handlebar mustache twitched with amusement, but he didn't look up from his painting. "Am I."

"You know this is about what happened to Kennedy."

Still the sheriff didn't look up, but for a moment his hand with the brush in it stopped moving. "I don't know anything of the sort."

"You know that Oswald couldn't make a shot like that," Guidry said. "Not one regular Joe in a thousand could make a shot like that. Six floors up, a moving target, trees in the way. Pow-pow, bull's-eye two times? You'd need a professional for the job."

"I advise you to get some sleep if you can," the sheriff said. "You want an extra blanket, I'll fetch you one."

"That professional," Guidry said, "right after he pulled the trigger, he stopped being a solution, though. He became a problem. Didn't he? For the people who hired him. You can understand why."

The sheriff said nothing. He balanced his brush on the lip of a paint pot so that he could massage his fingers.

"The people who hired him needed to fix the problem," Guidry said. "You're the solution. Until you hand me over at least, and guess what you are then?"

Guidry measured each breath and let the minutes crawl past. Know when to yank your line, know when to play it out. Every boy in Ascension Parish grew up fishing.

The sheriff was a smart man. Guidry hoped so anyway. Smart but not too smart. That was Guidry's only chance. The shot *he* had to make was one in a thousand, too.

An hour passed. Two. Guidry was running out of them.

"Well, doggone, I done it again." The sheriff, still painting away, dipped the corner of a napkin in his coffee mug and dabbed at his canvas. "Seems like the more careful you are, the more mistakes you make."

"They'll kill you," Guidry said. "Just tell me you understand that and I'll be quiet. You know too much, Sheriff. You're a liability, just like me."

"That's your opinion," the sheriff said.

"How long have you been in Carlos's pocket?"

"I don't see it that way."

"Of course you don't," Guidry said. "Just a little extra work on the side. Skim the cream from the jukebox take and nobody gets hurt. What's the harm?"

"You ever decide about that extra blanket?" the sheriff said. "It'll get chilly here in a bit."

"They'll kill you, and then they'll go find Fred and kill him," Guidry said. "If you have a wife, they'll kill her, too, just in case you mentioned anything to her. You can't blame them for being thorough, so much at stake. They'll probably go kill that girl who works at the diner. Annabelle? After they find out what she knows. Is your wife pretty? I hope not. Who do you think these people are, you dumb, crooked hick? What made you think you could sell them one part of your soul and not all of it?"

The sheriff's hand had stopped moving again. After a minute he set the brush down and started to screw the lids back on all the paint pots, one by one.

"There's a way out, Sheriff," Guidry said. "I can show it to you."

"Get some sleep, son," the sheriff said.

"Who do you work for in Dallas? Howie Fleck? Call Howie Fleck and tell him you made a mistake, turns out your deputy picked up the wrong man. His wife from Amarillo showed up and took him home, false alarm."

The sheriff put his boots up on the desk. He leaned back in his creaking chair and tilted his hat down over his face.

"Hold on, I've a better idea," Guidry said. "Do you

know anybody around here who looks like me? Height, coloring. It doesn't have to be perfect, just in the ballpark. Let your visitors see for themselves that you landed the wrong fish. Say, 'Sorry for the bother, boys.' Say, 'Better safe than sorry.'"

The sheriff didn't stir. Guidry stretched out on the cot. Now wait and see. That was all he could do. He'd made his play, the speech of a lifetime. The dice rolled off his fingertips and tumbled across the felt.

He tried to empty his mind. Socrates, the night before they brought the hemlock. In India, Guidry had read somewhere, certain shamans and sadhus could slow their breathing, could slow the beating of their hearts down to just a dribble. Maybe he could pull that off himself. When Seraphine's men arrived, they'd think he was already dead.

Socrates or Sophocles? Guidry could never keep their deaths straight. One was forced to drink poison, the other died when he tried to recite an impossibly long line of poetry without taking a breath. One of his buddies had dared him.

Guidry thought about what he'd do when the sheriff handed him over in the morning. He would go for the gun on the sheriff's hip. Hopeless, but he wasn't going to let Seraphine's men take him alive, not if he could help it.

The linoleum squeaked. Guidry opened his eyes. He must have fallen asleep. He wondered how long he'd been lying there. The sheriff stood on the other side of the bars.

"When do you expect they'll get here?" the sheriff said.

Guidry sat up. He looked at his watch. Five o'clock in the morning, Monday. "An hour or so."

The sheriff unlocked the cell. He handed Guidry back his wallet and car keys. "Go."

"Good luck, Sheriff," Guidry said.

"Go to hell," the sheriff said.

Guidry drove all morning. West of Tucumcari, New Mexico, the sleet hissed sideways. He passed a broken-down car by the side of the road, a woman standing drenched next to it and two children staring out the back window.

He didn't slow up. Sorry, sister. Guidry had trouble all his own and didn't need to borrow any.

12

Monday morning Charlotte and the girls left McLean just after dawn. Near Amarillo it began to rain softly and then harder and then so hard that the headlights of approaching cars fluttered like candle flames. The rain seemed to be coming from every direction at once, front and back and below, the spray off the road pounding the floor beneath her feet.

When they stopped for gas, the station attendant leered at Charlotte as he checked the oil. He unsheathed the metal wand and pretended to run his tongue along the length of it. Charlotte stared down at her hands in her lap. Thank God the girls were busy charting their journey on the map.

She handed the station attendant a five-dollar bill

for the gas. He handed back her change and continued to leer. She didn't know what to say.

"Thank you," she said.

She was shaking as they drove off. *It's fine*, she told herself. *It will be fine.*

Soon after they crossed from Texas into New Mexico, the rain turned to sleet and the asphalt shimmered like glass, and when the road curved unexpectedly, they slid into a ditch.

It happened so quickly. Charlotte felt the car floating beneath her, and then the steering wheel jerked out of her hands. Joan tumbled against Rosemary, who tumbled against the dog, who woke up and barked once, uncertainly.

The ditch was shallow, only a foot or two deep, but the nose of the car seemed to point straight up. All Charlotte could see out the windshield was the long, putty-colored hood of the car and an empty sky almost the exact same shade. The engine had died, and the silence buzzed.

"Are you all right?" Charlotte asked the girls.

"What happened?" Rosemary said.

"Girls! Are you all right?"

"Yes," Rosemary said.

"Joan?"

"Yes."

The girls climbed onto the seat so that they could look out. They were flushed and thrilled. "We've had an automobile accident!" Rosemary said.

Charlotte pushed her door open. She climbed the bank of the ditch to inspect their situation. Bad. The car appeared to be hopelessly wedged, the back tires buried in the mud and the front tires suspended a foot off the ground, rotating lazily.

Take a deep breath. It was fine. It will be fine.

"Are we stuck, Mommy?" Rosemary said.

"Wait here," Charlotte said. "Put on your coats and curl up next to Lucky. Pretend he's a friendly bear in the woods."

Cars splashed past, one after another, not even slowing. Charlotte stood by the side of the road until she was soaked to the bone and shivering. Take another deep breath. It was one o'clock in the afternoon on a main highway. Someone, eventually, would stop. According to the map, the next town, Santa Maria, New Mexico, was only a few miles away.

Finally a tow truck rumbled past, braked, and pulled onto the shoulder. Santa Maria Wreck and Repair. A stone-faced mechanic climbed out of the truck. He examined the car from various angles, grunted a few times, shook his head. He fished the chewing tobacco from his cheek and flung the dark, bristling lump onto the sleet-slick road.

"Ain't your lucky day," he said.

Charlotte was so cold that her teeth had begun to chatter. She'd always thought that was just a figure of speech, the chattering of teeth. "Can you get us out?" she said.

"Folks always take that curve too fast," he said. "Keeps me in business."

"Can you get us out?"

"Fifteen dollars."

He couldn't be serious. "Fifteen dollars?" she said.

"Let me know if you find a better price." He turned and started walking to his truck.

"Wait."

The mechanic backed up his truck and chained their car to it. He gunned his engine, and their car began to rock. Finally it came loose from the mud with a wet, sucking sound.

Charlotte saw that the rear fender had been badly dented in the crash, one taillight smashed, the exhaust pipe mangled.

The mechanic's lump of chewing tobacco sat leaking on the road like some organ torn from a body and discarded, like a heart beating one last time. The mechanic walked a slow circle around the car. He shook his head.

"Still ain't your lucky day, is it?" he said.

They crammed into the cab of the truck with him, Charlotte and the girls and the dog, too. In town he dropped them off at a motel with whitewashed adobe bungalows arranged around an empty swimming pool. He told her that he wouldn't be able to get to the car until Wednesday.

"Wednesday?" Charlotte said. "But that's two days from now. Isn't there any way . . . ?"

"Wednesday maybe," he said. "Come by in the afternoon and I'll let you know. Otherwise it'll be the Monday after, 'cause of Thanksgiving."

He drove away. It was almost two by now. The girls were starving. Charlotte bought two cartons of chocolate milk from a vending machine, and they ate the last of the roast-beef sandwiches. The clouds paled a bit, and the rain stopped. Their room was no nicer than the one in McLean, but at least it didn't smell like boiled cabbage. She waited until the girls were absorbed with their Disney True-Life Adventures books, warned them not to unlock the door for anyone but her ("*Anyone.* Do you understand, Rosemary?"), and followed the stone path back to the main building.

There was a pay phone on the porch in front of the

motel office. Charlotte paged through her address book until she found what she hoped was still Aunt Marguerite's number in Los Angeles. She lifted the handset and told the operator she wanted to make a long-distance call. The operator instructed her to insert fifty cents.

Charlotte dialed the number and waited. She counted the rings. One, two, three. Charlotte didn't worry. Four, five, six. Marguerite might be out shopping, or at lunch with friends, or outside tending to her rosebushes. It was likely. It was possible. Seven, eight, nine.

Midway through the twelfth ring, Charlotte hung up. She searched her purse for cigarettes. New Mexico, or at least this part of it, was flat and brown and empty. Apart from the whitewashed adobe bungalows, the ornamental stump-shaped cactus next to the motel drive, a faint smudge of what could be mountains on the horizon, Charlotte might as well have still been in Oklahoma.

She lifted the receiver and told the operator that she'd like to make a collect call.

"Charlie?" Dooley said.

"Hello, honey," Charlotte said.

"What in the world, Charlie! I came home last night and you were gone and the girls were gone, and I about had a heart attack."

"I know, I'm sorry. Did you see the note I left for you?"

"I went in their bedroom and their little beds were empty, and you can't even imagine how that made me feel, Charlie."

The guilt she'd managed to keep at a low simmer, deep in the pit of her stomach, began to churn and bubble and spill hissing over the lip of the cauldron. "I know, I'm sorry," she said. "Did you see the note?"

"This morning I did," he said. "Last night I could barely sleep, I was so worried sick."

"We're fine, the girls are fine," Charlotte said. "We're in New Mexico. We had a little accident, with the car, but—"

"New Mexico!" Dooley said. "What's gotten into you, Charlie?"

"I think this is for the best, honey, I do. For all of us. I think—"

"What happened to the car? Charlie, you don't want a divorce. I know you don't."

"I can't keep on this way, Dooley. This isn't what . . ." Charlotte couldn't explain it to herself. How could she ever hope to explain it to him? "I'm not . . . I'm not the person I want to be. Maybe I'll never be, but I need the chance. I need the girls to have the chance, too, to be the people they want to be. If I don't go away, I'm afraid that—"

"Go away? You mean you need a vacation?"

"No. I—"

"You can't do this to me, Charlie," Dooley said. "A divorce, just like that, out of the blue. Without even talking to me about it?"

"Dooley . . ."

"It's not right, Charlie, making a decision like that all by yourself and I don't even have a say in it. It's like you snuck up behind me out of nowhere and hit me over the head with a two-by-four. What married people do, they discuss their problems."

Over the years she'd tried to get him to discuss their problems hundreds of times. Still, though, she asked herself if his point might be a fair one. She'd been a coward, fleeing the house when he wasn't there, when he couldn't try to talk her into staying. She should at least have waited for him to come home. Or she could have proposed a trial separation. She could propose one now.

Divorce was the edge of a cliff. Once you flung yourself into the great blue yonder, there was no going back. . . .

It infuriated Charlotte, how doubt crept into her every thought, her every decision. This was it, exactly what Charlotte had meant a moment ago: *I'm not the person I want to be.*

"Dooley, I think—"

"You *think*. You *think*, Charlie. That's what I mean. You don't *know*. Tell me you know for sure. Say it out loud. Say, 'I want a divorce. I'm one hundred percent sure.' Can you say that?"

"I . . . I don't know if anything in life is one hundred percent sure," she said. "Is it?"

"Marriage is," Dooley said. "That's what we told the priest, wasn't it? Till death do us part. We made a vow to each other that . . ." She heard him opening cabinet doors. "Where's the sugar for the coffee, Charlie?"

"On the shelf next to the refrigerator," she said.

He started to cry. "Oh, God, Charlie, what would I do without you? You and the girls, you're the best thing that ever happened to me."

"You'll still get to see the girls," she said. "I'll make sure of it, I promise. I—"

"I'm just a sorry son of a bitch. I know I am."

"You're not, Dooley. You're not listening to me."

The sky had darkened again, giant stacked slabs of slate-gray clouds. Charlotte thought of collapsed fortress walls, the lids of ancient tombs. She was exhausted suddenly, too tired to think.

A few drops of rain plinked against the tin roof of the overhang, and then without further preamble a great pounding deluge swept down. A man in a suit, another guest at the hotel, made it to shelter just in time.

"I'm a sorry son of a bitch," Dooley said, "but I love you. Nobody will ever love you like I do. Why do you want to throw that away?"

"I have to go, honey," Charlotte said. "Someone else needs to use the phone."

"You don't want a divorce, Charlie, not really. You don't want to throw everything away. Just come on home. We'll discuss it. That's all I want to do."

"I'll call you soon."

"So just come on home, Charlie," Dooley said. "You know you'll come home. You know you will. I'm not mad. Just—"

Charlotte hung up before he—or she—could say anything else. The man in the suit gave her a friendly smile as they passed.

"When it rains, it pours, doesn't it?" the man said.

She nodded and managed to smile back. "Yes, it certainly does."

13

They left Houston just around eleven o'clock and drove all night. Well, the colored kid drove all night. Barone stayed awake to make sure the kid stayed awake. Theodore. That was the kid's name. Theodore, don't call me Ted, don't call me Teddy. He griped about the way the Pontiac handled and about the weather and about the road and about his high school back in Houston and about his four older sisters who still treated him like a baby even though he was a growed-up man, sixteen years old. He griped that he was hungry and he griped that he was tired. They listened to a radio station out of Dallas that played colored soul singers. Barone didn't mind Sam Cooke. He couldn't find a station that played jazz.

"Who you after anyways?" the kid said.

"A man," Barone said.

"Why you after him? He steal your woman?"

"He owes me money."

"How much?" the kid said.

"Enough," Barone said.

"I want to be a lawyer."

"A lawyer."

"There's colored lawyers," the kid said.

"I never said there weren't."

"What kind of work you do?"

"I'm a colored lawyer," Barone said.

"Shoot," the kid said. "You a salesman. What I think. Or work in a company."

"That's right."

"You like it? The kind of work you do?"

Barone had never given it much thought. Might as well ask, *You like who you are?* Nobody had a say in the matter.

"I know a colored lawyer," Barone said. "She's like a lawyer."

The kid swiveled around to goggle at him. "She? A *lady* colored lawyer?"

"I said she's *like* a lawyer."

"Hoo-wee."

They reached the town at seven o'clock, Monday morning. Goodnight, Texas. Still dark outside. Barone told the kid to park across the street from the little police station.

"I'll be back in a minute," Barone said.

"Shoot," the kid said. "Be back in a minute. What you said last time. A minute."

"And then we'll get some breakfast."

"All right," the kid said.

Barone stepped out into the cold, damp howling. The Texas panhandle in November. His stitched-up hand felt better, but he still couldn't close his fingers. It wouldn't be a problem. He could shoot left-handed if he didn't have to rush. He shifted the Browning .22 from the one side of his pants to his other, so he'd be able to get to it more cleanly.

Two cops in the police station, one old and one young. Sheriff and deputy. Sheriff at his desk, boots up. Deputy on the other side of the room, to Barone's left, filling out some kind of duty roster pinned to a corkboard. A double-barrel shotgun stood propped against the sheriff's desk, arm's reach.

The sheriff nodded. "Mornin'."

"Where is he?" Barone said.

"Over there. In the pokey."

One jail cell. A man lay on a cot, bundled under a wool blanket, his face turned to the wall. Barone walked over and watched him through the bars. The man was sleeping or pretending to sleep.

Barone pointed to the deputy. "Pour me a cup of that coffee, will you?" he said.

He wanted to move the deputy over by the sheriff, against the same wall. The wall behind the sheriff's desk displayed a dozen or more paintings of lighthouses and bridges and religious figures. Barone had been in several police stations. Until now he'd never seen a police station with even a single painting in it.

The deputy looked at the sheriff. The sheriff tilted his head at the coffeepot. The deputy took his time making his way across the room. He wanted to show Barone who was boss.

Barone whistled at the man in the cell. "Get up," he said. He saw the blanket stir.

"My deputy here stopped him yesterday for speeding," the sheriff said. "Couple miles east of town. Claims his name is Watkins, but he doesn't have a lick of ID on him. The car he was driving is registered under the name of Watkins, but my suspicion is it's stolen."

"You want cream or sugar, you can come get it for yourself," the deputy told Barone. He set the mug down on the table, full of himself.

Barone whistled again, louder. The man in the cell was just pretending to sleep. "Get up," Barone told him.

The man sat up and yawned and wrapped the blanket more snugly around him. "Let me out of here," he said. "I don't know who the hell you are, but I ain't whoever the hell these dumb sons of bitches think I am."

The man wasn't Guidry. Barone needed one look.

"Well?" the sheriff asked Barone. "Is that your boy?"

"My damn name is Melvin Watkins. I don't know who the hell you're looking for. I live in Clarendon, Texas, eighteen miles east of here. Go to Clarendon and ask the first person you meet. They'll tell you."

Barone didn't lose his temper very often. But eight hours of driving, eight hours wasted. And now another eight hours back to Houston. He took out the Browning .22 and pointed it at the man in the cell. Barone heard the sheriff's boots hit the floor, his chair scrape back as he stood.

"Now, hold on there, son," the sheriff said.

The man in the cell stared at Barone, eyes about to pop out of his head. He was the same age and height as Guidry, with close to the same hair and coloring. He even had a slight slant to his eyes. Part Indian, probably. Dark eyes, not light, but Barone supposed he could see how someone could have made an honest mistake.

Barone put the gun away. "It's not him," he said.

The man in the cell blinked. The deputy stood frozen with his mug in one hand and the coffeepot in the other. The sheriff slowly eased himself back down into his chair.

"You're sure?" the sheriff said.

Barone had been burning up a second ago. Now he felt as cold as ice. "It's not him," he said.

"We didn't have a picture of him to go by," the sheriff said. "But they told me to err on the side of caution, your people in Dallas."

"You sure it ain't him?" the deputy said, piping up. "Take another look if you need it."

The sheriff turned to glare at the deputy, and then he turned back to Barone. "I know you've come a long way," the sheriff told Barone. "I apologize for the inconvenience."

Barone walked back to the car. The kid drove a few blocks up until Barone spotted a diner. The kid ordered scrambled eggs and bacon and sausage patties and biscuits with gravy and a short stack of silver-dollar pancakes. Side-eyeing Barone the whole time like he was daring Barone to say something.

"And a big glass of chocolate milk," the kid said.

"We only got regular milk," the waitress said.

"Not even none of that chocolate powder you can mix in with it?"

"We got regular milk."

The waitress wasn't too happy to have a colored kid sitting at her counter. Barone could see the pinch to her face. More than likely she called herself a Christian and went to church every Sunday morning.

They were the only ones in the place. After the breakfast crowd, before the lunch crowd. The radio played a live report from Washington, D.C. A procession of world leaders following Kennedy's coffin from the White House to St. Matthew's Cathedral.

The kid worked through his breakfast and couldn't find anything to gripe about. Barone ate a runny fried egg and drank two cups of black coffee. He was hot all over again. The flu. A bad time to come down with it, but he'd had the flu before and it had never killed him.

The waitress came back over. "It's a National Day of Mourning. But ask me if I got to work anyway."

"You finished?" Barone asked the kid.

"Shoot," the kid said. "White man gets shot, it's National Day of Mourning. Colored man gets shot, it's Monday morning."

"Good Lord, how can you eat so much and be so skinny?" the waitress said. She gave the kid a friendly poke with her elbow as she piled up his plates. Maybe Barone had her figured wrong. "Y'all headed to Amarillo for that car auction?"

"No," Barone said.

She started to walk away.

"Wait," he said. "Come back here."

"More coffee?" the waitress said.

Barone put his hand over the top of his cup. "Why did you ask that? About the car auction?"

"That's where the other fella was headed," she said. "The one what come through yesterday. We don't get many folks from out of town, so I thought you might be headed to that car auction, too."

Maybe the man she was talking about was the man in the cell. But the sheriff said his deputy had picked up Melvin Watkins a few miles east of town. The diner was on the west side of town. Amarillo was west of town. Maybe the sheriff had made another honest mistake.

"What did he look like?" Barone said.

"The fella yesterday?" the waitress said. "I don't know. He was real friendly."

"Handsome."

She blushed. "I suppose."

Barone hadn't thought to wonder about it earlier, how the county deputy didn't recognize a man from just the next town over. Recognize his name, at least. Or how the sheriff wouldn't just call over to Clarendon and check. Barone had been too busy being mad that the man in the cell wasn't Guidry.

"He had dark brown eyes," Barone said. "Like mine."

"Brown? No. His was green as glass." She blushed again. "I don't know. Maybe they was brown. Can I get y'all anything else?"

When Barone walked back into the police station, Melvin Watkins had been released from the cell but was still hanging around, drinking coffee and having a laugh about something with the deputy. The sheriff was shrugging on his quilted jacket, about to head home.

Barone shot the deputy before the deputy could even think about reaching for the pistol on his hip. The shot yanked a piece of his head away and slapped it across the paintings on the wall. The sheriff had time to grab for his pistol but not time to draw it. Barone shot him twice in the stomach. Firing left-handed, he had to concentrate. The sheriff slid down the wall and sat with his legs splayed out in front of him, his cowboy hat bumped crooked.

Melvin Watkins had his hands high up over his head and was talking so fast that Barone could barely understand him. Barone stuffed the Browning .22 in his pants and took the gun out of the deputy's holster. A Colt Trooper revolver.

"Sheriff called me and said he needed somebody

looked like some fella," Melvin Watkins said. "I didn't want to do it, but Sheriff said he'd haul me in if I didn't, and I don't have no idea why—"

Barone shot him with the deputy's gun. He went over to the sheriff and stood over him, careful not to put a shoe in the blood pooling out. The sheriff was trying to slide his gun out of the holster but was too weak to do it, both his hand and the gun grip slick with blood.

Tough bastard. Looking up at Barone, looking him right in the eye, not about to beg.

"Did he pay you off?" Barone said.

"Go to hell," the sheriff said.

"How much?" Barone said. "It wasn't enough, whatever he paid you. Did he say where he was headed?"

"Go . . . to . . . hell." Each word was like the sheriff dragging a dead body out of the river and up onto the bank. "Every . . . damn one . . . of you."

"He got you killed. Look around, all this. Frank Guidry did it, not me. Don't you want me to find him and send your regards?"

The sheriff hissed and gurgled and finally gave up trying to draw his pistol. "Don't . . . know where," he said.

"Headed west?" Barone said.

The sheriff jerked his chin. Yes.

"What else?"

"Dodge," the sheriff said. "Blue over . . . white."

"Old one or new?"

"A '57 or . . . a '58. Dodge . . . Coronet."

"When did he leave?"

"Few . . . hours ago."

Maybe Guidry would ditch the car, but maybe he wouldn't. Guidry would think that his plan had worked, that Barone had taken the bait and was headed back to Houston right now. He'd think that Barone would get on the phone with Seraphine and tell her that Goodnight had been a wild-goose chase.

"What else?" Barone said.

The sheriff jerked his chin. Nothing else.

"Why do you have all these paintings on the wall?" Barone said.

"Go . . . to . . . hell," the sheriff said.

Barone switched over to the Browning again. He stepped back so the spray wouldn't catch him and shot the sheriff in the head. He put the Browning in Melvin Watkins's hand and the deputy's gun in the deputy's hand and then moved around the shell casings to match. No, it wouldn't fool every Texas Ranger in the state, but it might fool the ones assigned to the case. At the very least, they'd need some time to scratch their heads.

He wiped down everything in the cell that Guidry might have touched. Barone had on gloves, so he wasn't worried about his prints.

The kid had fallen asleep when Barone got back to the car. Barone elbowed him awake.

"Let's go," he said.

"You find out what you need this time?" the kid said. "Or we gonna have to turn around and come back again?"

"Let's go," Barone said.

What about the waitress? Barone thought about it. No. Lunch started soon. Customers. And he couldn't spare the time to wait around and take care of her after she got off work. He would have to let it go. Guidry was waiting for him.

14

Only now, one o'clock in the afternoon and four hundred miles from Goodnight, four hundred miles from his almost certain doom, did Guidry finally begin to breathe a little easier. He pulled off the highway in the town of Santa Maria, New Mexico. Town? The cluster of buildings on the endless grassy plain looked like a patch of stubble a man missed while shaving.

When Guidry got out of the car, his knees were still jelly. That was a close call, brother. Do you understand just how close?

Why, yes, in fact I do.

The only motel in town was the Old Mexico Motor Court. Guidry went into the office and asked for a room. The boy behind the counter didn't give him a second glance.

"We have casitas," the boy said. "That's what I'm s'posed to call 'em."

"Is a casita the same as a room?" Guidry said.

"Yes."

"Well then," Guidry said, "I'm sold."

The boy wrote down the name that Guidry gave him. *Frank Wainwright.* He still didn't give Guidry a second glance. Guidry made sure, watching the boy closely. After what had happened back in Goodnight, he would have to keep his guard up. Who could say how many people between here and Las Vegas had been instructed to keep an eye out for him? For a man traveling solo, late thirties, medium height and weight, dark hair and green eyes, a dimple in the middle of his chin that made all the chicks swoon?

Who could say how many people *in* Vegas had been instructed to keep an eye out for him? Vegas was a company town. Word would get around. Guidry would have to sweat about every busboy and showgirl who glanced at him.

Seraphine would guess that he was headed to Vegas or Miami. Maybe Los Angeles. Definitely not Chicago or New York. How to keep her guessing? That was the question.

The hot water in the shower trickled out, and the towel could have sanded the faces off Mount Rushmore.

Guidry had grown weary of shitty accommodations, of motel rooms and jail cells and casitas. He'd had enough of them these past few days to last a lifetime.

His emptied his bowels. Eighteen months in the Pacific and not a hint of dysentery. When just about every other GI in his company had succumbed.

On TV the funeral procession unspooled. There was Jackie, gaunt and wobbly, stupefied. Guidry knew just how she felt. Three days ago her world had been shipshape and right side up. The future had cast a rosy glow.

He napped for a couple of hours. The motel clerk gave him change for a dollar. He dropped the first dime in the pay phone and dialed up his old pal Klaus in Miami. Klaus, the sneakiest, squirrelliest, most reliably untrustworthy ex-Catholic ex-Commie ex-Nazi in the Western Hemisphere. He worked for Santo Trafficante but sold information to anyone who could pay for it.

"Klausie baby," Guidry said.

"*Ja*. What?" Klaus said. And then, realizing, "Oh. This is Guidry?"

"Can you talk? Are you alone?"

"*Ja*. Sure. Guidry. Hello, hello, old chum." Klaus recovered from his surprise and spotted the opportunity immediately. He unhinged his jaw and slithered toward Guidry as fast as he could. "It is a pleasure, old chum."

"Klausie, can I count on your discretion?" Guidry said.

"*Ja,* of course."

"I need a change of scenery. You understand. Somewhere warm and tropical."

You had to believe your own lie. You had to get inside it. Guidry had known a cute little actress once. She was in Hollywood now, a second-fiddle femme fatale on some third-rate TV show. She said once that you couldn't expect to fool the audience if you couldn't fool yourself. Nobody needed to tell Guidry that.

"I've got my ride lined up already," Guidry said. "A guy I served with overseas, my old staff sergeant, he runs a fishing charter out of the Keys now. He's a prick, through and through, but I think I can trust him, and he has a boat that can get me to Honduras."

Guidry could picture the guy, could picture the boat, could smell the salt breeze. "I need paper, though," he said. "And a couple of introductions once I get down south."

"You are in Miami now?" Klaus said.

"None of your beeswax where I am now, Klausie." Make him work for it, a little bit at least. "Can you help with the paper? I'll pay. And you've got some old *Kamaraden* down in the jungle, haven't you?"

Klaus could get touchy when you brought up his

wartime attachments. Not this time. He fell all over himself. "*Ja, ja,* of course, Guidry. I can help you. It is my pleasure, old chum."

Guidry told Klaus he'd be in touch soon, to set the meet in Miami, and then hung up. Seraphine would be skeptical when Klaus called her—under normal circumstances Guidry would never put his life in the hands of a man like Klaus. But these, old chum, were not normal circumstances. Guidry was a desperate man. Seraphine knew it. She would have to water this seed of possibility, watch it, see if it bloomed.

The next call, the real call. Las Vegas. Why would Seraphine believe that Guidry might put his life in the hands of a man like Klaus? Because Guidry was about to put his life in the hands of a man like Big Ed Zingel.

A man with an English accent answered the phone. "Good afternoon. The Zingel residence."

"Put Ed on," Guidry said.

"Mr. Zingel isn't in. Would you care to leave a message?"

"Tell him that Mr. Marcello from New Orleans would like to ask him for a favor," Guidry said, "for old times' sake."

He hung up. It was raining again, an Old Testament deluge. He waited out the storm in his room and then walked into town.

Santa Maria, New Mexico. Get a load of this place. A little toy town, like something a kid would play with on Christmas morning. Like a color drawing in a magazine ad selling margarine. Two teenage girls strolled along the sidewalk, their ponytails bouncing. One girl's poodle skirt was decorated with polka dots, the other's with daisies. It was 1955 all over again, and someone had failed to inform Guidry.

He counted three churches in two blocks. A couple of teenage boys in leather jackets, skulking on the corner, smiled and said hello. Even the hoods here in Our Town were well mannered.

Guidry found a "department store" that had one department: everything. The selection of men's attire was what he'd anticipated. He bought two pairs of synthetic slacks ("Dacron," ye gods) and two pairs of cheap Florsheims and a houndstooth sport coat. The sport coat was an inch short in the sleeves and too big everywhere else. And, for the topper, a gray wool fedora with a clashing houndstooth pattern.

He checked himself in the mirror and wanted to weep. He was no longer Frank Guidry. He looked like he sold life insurance and lived in a place like Santa Maria, New Mexico.

Well, he supposed, that was the point, wasn't it?

The little liquor store carried two kinds of scotch: cheap and cheaper. Guidry was in no position to complain.

Tuesday morning the clouds had vanished. The air clear and crisp, the sky a bright trembling blue. He ate a stale Danish from the vending machine and drank scotch with weak coffee and stood by the window. Two little girls perched on the edge of the empty swimming pool, swinging their legs. Their mother lounged on a chaise close by. Yesterday, on his way into town, Guidry had seen a tow truck deliver the three of them here to the Old Mexico Motor Court. He guessed that the woman was the one he'd passed on the highway, standing next to the broken-down car.

Tuesday morning. Nine o'clock. Guidry had survived another night. That was how he'd begun to measure the march of progress.

The woman by the pool wasn't bad. He'd had a look at her yesterday when they crossed paths at the pay phone. Big serious eyes, rosebud lips. She needed to let her hair down, switch to a brighter shade of lipstick, and get out of that dress—a modest high-waisted number that Donna Reed would consider square. At another time, in happier days, Guidry might have enjoyed warming her up, feeling her melt in his palm. In another life.

The bad-fitting sport coat, the fedora. Maybe he could find a pair of glasses to wear. Dye his hair? Sure, but Guidry would still be Guidry. That was the inescapable quandary. He'd still be a man traveling solo, late thirties, medium height and weight, green eyes and a dimple in the middle of his chin. He couldn't change any of that.

Or could he? An idea formed. He walked over to the motel office and bought another Danish from the machine. On the way back to his room, he paused by the pool to admire the view of the desert.

"Beautiful day, isn't it?" he said.

The woman looked over at him. She wore a wedding ring, but Guidry hadn't seen any sign of a husband. "It is," she said. "Yes."

"Hello again. Our ships passed yesterday by the pay phone. My name's Frank. Frank Wainwright."

"Yes, I remember. Charlotte Roy."

Charlotte Roy. A small-town girl, as wholesome and dull as a field of corn, with a dog-eared New Testament in her purse and uncomplicated notions about right and wrong. Guidry didn't want to spook her, so he'd have to take it nice and easy. He was capable of that. He was capable of whatever was necessary.

He tipped his hat back off his forehead and leaned

against the iron fence that bordered the pool. A chilly breeze blew, but the sun was nice and warm.

"They seem closer than they did yesterday," he said. "The mountains do. Like they've been sneaking up on us during the night."

The woman shielded her eyes with the flat of her hand and scanned the horizon. "I'm confident that we can outrun them," she said.

Guidry laughed and glanced at her, taking a fresh look. He liked a woman who could hit the ball back over the net.

The little girls, one blond and one with curly brown hair, had turned to regard him.

"I'm Rosemary, and this is Joan," the curly-haired one said. She had her mother's coloring. The blondie had the big serious eyes. "We live in Oklahoma."

"I've heard of it," Guidry said.

"We're going to Los Angeles to visit Aunt Marguerite. She lives in Santa Monica, right by the ocean."

So they were headed west, as Guidry had hoped. He tried it on for size: Frank Wainwright, insurance salesman, traveling with his wife and two daughters. If Guidry could pull this off, he'd be practically invisible.

"That's where I'm headed, too," Guidry said. "Los

Angeles. City of the Angels. Did you know that's what the ancient Spaniards called it?"

"Really?" the curly-haired girl said.

"You have my word of honor," Guidry said.

He wondered when the woman's car would be fixed. He was optimistic. The car had looked pretty beat, and Guidry had never met a mechanic who rushed to finish a job.

"Well then, I better be off," Guidry said. Nice and easy, don't push it, especially the first conversation. He tipped his hat to the ladies. "So long and a pleasure to meet you. Maybe I'll see you around."

15

At lunchtime on Tuesday, Charlotte and the girls crossed the highway and walked into Santa Maria proper. The girls had been cooped up for two days in the car, in motel rooms. They needed to sprint and skip and spin in circles until they were dizzy. So they did. Charlotte thought of the educational cartoons that the teachers had shown back in high school ("A is for Atom!"), with the excited electrons zinging around the nucleus.

"Girls, slow down, please!" she called.

With the unerring instinct possessed by all children, Rosemary and Joan led Charlotte straight to a park with a playground. The girls swarmed the monkey bars, and Charlotte found a bench.

She was in good spirits today. Or better spirits at

least. She'd had a full night's sleep, the rain had stopped and the sun had emerged, and she'd manage to negotiate a truce between the warring armies in her mind, a temporary cease-fire. The car wouldn't be repaired until tomorrow, so today she didn't have to think about the past, didn't have to think about the future. Forward to California or back to Oklahoma? No decision, at the moment, was required of her.

"Come on, Mommy!" Rosemary said.

"I'm just fine right here, thank you," Charlotte said.

"Mommy!" Joan said.

Charlotte hadn't been on a playground swing in almost twenty years. But the girls would brook no argument, and she discovered that it was just as much fun now as it had been then. The sky rushing toward you, the earth tilting away, the sense that for a split second you'd come unstuck from your own self. The girls laughed and she laughed and the dog felt left out. He rested his head on his paw and surveyed them with indignation.

At the grocery store, she bought enough provisions to last a few days: a loaf of Wonder Bread, cheese, apples, cereal, cans of Vienna sausages, and a package of chocolate-chip cookies. They ate a picnic—cheese sandwiches, apples—sitting on a bench in front of a bank even smaller than the one in Woodrow. Charlotte

watched a woman about her age hurry down the sidewalk. Late for work, perhaps, after a lunch hour spent
running errands.

On their way back to the motel, they passed a shop
window packed with a dusty, dizzy jumble of used
appliances: toasters, radios, vacuum cleaners, percola-
tors, and electric griddles. Awaiting repair or for sale?
Probably some of each, but it was impossible to tell
which was which. Charlotte noticed a camera on the
very bottom shelf, an inexpensive little Kodak Brownie
Cresta, and paused for a closer look.

The shopkeeper somehow spotted Charlotte through
the clutter and waved to her. She handed the dog's leash
to Rosemary and went inside.

"Hello," she said. "The camera in the window, there
at the bottom, is it for sale?"

"That old thing?" The shopkeeper, stooped and
bald and wizened, with a long gray tooth pointed like
a fang, reminded Charlotte of a character from a children's story. The troll under the bridge, but an amiable
one. "I don't know if it even works, but tell me what
you can spare and I'll probably take it."

Charlotte couldn't really spare anything at all. "A
dollar?" She knew the camera had to be worth more
than that. "I'm sorry. I know it's not very much."

"It's enough," the shopkeeper said. "Today only."

He threw in a roll of film for free. Charlotte welcomed the reminder that not everyone in the wide world was sour, sleazy, or mean. Some people out here—like this man, like their neighbor at the motel, Mr. Wainwright—were friendly and kind and perfectly pleasant.

While the girls and the dog napped, Charlotte inspected the Brownie. Fixed shutter, fixed aperture, and fixed focus, a prize you won when you mailed off fifteen soup labels to Campbell's. Still, it appeared to be in good shape. Charlotte went outside and snapped a picture of the motel courtyard. The curved pool without water, the curved sky without clouds, the horizon like the hinge between two halves of an empty locket.

It was remarkable what a change of light could do to a subject. The whitewashed walls of the bungalows, so stark and ashen in the rain, had turned a deep, rich cream. The red clay roof tiles, faded before, were now the life of the party.

For dinner Charlotte decided that they could splurge and eat at the diner in town. The waitress seated them in a booth by the window. At the table next to them sat their neighbor from the motel, Mr. Wainwright.

"We've got to stop meeting like this," he said.

She smiled. The girls ran off to inspect the jukebox. The song playing was "Moody River." Charlotte winced as Pat Boone crooned the big, syrupy finish.

Mr. Wainwright lifted his palms. "I'm innocent, I swear," he said. "The crime was in progress when I arrived."

"Any eyewitnesses?" she said.

"You'll have to take my word for it. Find a Bible and I'll lay my hand on it."

The waitress brought a menu for Charlotte. Mr. Wainwright had finished his meal. He pushed his empty pie plate away and took a sip of coffee.

"So I've heard on the grapevine," he said, "that you're from Oklahoma."

"Rosemary will tell you her entire life story if you give her half a chance," Charlotte said. "No. Make that a quarter of a chance."

"How do you like it? I've never been to Oklahoma."

"I'm not sure you'd remember it if you had."

"I drove through it on my way here, now that I think about it."

"Well, there you have it."

The girls returned to the table. "Mommy," Rosemary said, "can we have a nickel for the jukebox?"

"Your manners, girls," Charlotte said. "Say hello to Mr. Wainwright."

"Hello, Mr. Wainwright."

"Hello, Mr. Wainwright."

"Allow me," he said. He reached into his pocket and came up with a nickel. "Have you made your decision? What song shall we hear?"

Charlotte nodded permission, and Rosemary took the nickel from him.

"Thank you," Rosemary said. "Joan is going to pick the letter and I'm going to pick the number. I'm going to pick number seven because I'm seven. Joan is eight. We're exactly eleven months apart. For one month every year in September, we're the same age. Joan is going to pick J because her name starts with J. Aren't you, Joan?"

"Okay," Joan said.

"Rosemary and Joan," Mr. Wainwright said. "I like those names. You know, my grandmother's name was Aiglentine, which means 'rose' in French. She was a trapeze artist back in the old country, back in France. This is a true story. One night she slipped and fell. The net caught her, but she bounced out. You think they'd make nets with less bounce, wouldn't you?"

The girls listened, rapt.

"Anyway," he continued, "my grandmother bounced out of the net and collided with one of the poles that held up the circus tent. She broke every bone in her leg. But that's how she met my grandfather. He was a doctor, sitting in the stands watching the show. He came down and patched her leg back together."

Charlotte laughed. "Did she get up and finish the performance first?"

"You're dubious," he said. "I don't blame you. My grandmother was a magnificent liar. But I know for a fact that she was a trapeze artist at one point in her life. I've seen the pictures. Or maybe she just had the outfit."

Charlotte told the girls to go pick their song and wash their hands before dinner. J-7 turned out to be "Will You Love Me Tomorrow" by the Shirelles. A vast improvement on Pat Boone.

"So what takes you to Los Angeles, Mr. Wainwright?" Charlotte said. "If you don't mind me asking?"

"Frank, please," he said.

"What takes you to Los Angeles, Frank?"

"I'm on my way there to peddle insurance. My company in New York City won't rest until they conquer the world, so forth I go. But don't panic, I'm off the clock till a week from tomorrow. I won't try to sell you anything."

"Isn't that exactly what a good salesman would say?" she said.

"Now that you mention it," he said, "allow me to

explain the difference between term and whole life. If you ask nicely, I might give you a discount. I can be a soft touch."

The waitress, passing by, gave Charlotte a sly wink. Charlotte ignored it. She supposed that most women would consider Mr. Wainwright a catch, with his eyes and chin and dark hair parted just so, but Charlotte was certainly not fishing.

"So you're from New York City?" she said.

"Maryland, originally," he said. "But I've been on the Upper West Side for twenty years."

"I'm dying to see New York City. The museums, the plays."

"I hate to be the one to break the bad news," he said, "but you're headed in the wrong direction."

"Well, I'm dying to see California, too. Though as Rosemary informed you this morning, we're not headed anywhere at the moment."

"I thought that was you I saw pull in yesterday. Your car hitched to the back of a tow truck."

"It was indeed," Charlotte said.

"That's a shame," he said. "When will you be able to hit the road again?"

"Tomorrow, I hope. I'm to see the mechanic in the afternoon."

"You don't want to spend Thanksgiving in Santa Maria, New Mexico?"

"I can't say I do."

"Have you ever heard of karma?" he said.

"Karma?" Charlotte said.

"That's what the Buddhists in the Orient call it. I learned this in the service. The Buddhists believe in balance. The universe tips and tilts, the weight shifts around, but karma always sets it straight again. For every wrong there's right. Do you follow?"

"I'm not sure."

"Your car breaks down on the way to California and you're stranded here in Santa Maria, New Mexico, for a few days. A tough break. But now the universe owes you a favor."

"Oh, does it?" Charlotte cocked an eyebrow. Though the notion was an appealing one. Karma. She pictured the liquid mercury in a thermometer, rising and falling, always seeking a happy medium. "I'm flattered that I have the universe's attention. But I wonder if it might have more important matters to contemplate."

"I'm just reporting what the Buddhists say," he said.

"So you don't believe in it yourself? Karma?"

He thought about the question for a moment. She liked that he took the time to do so. Most people's ideas were so ingrained that they had every answer at the ready. Most people in Woodrow, Oklahoma, at least.

"I don't know if I believe in it or not," he said. "I know I *want* to believe it."

The girls returned. The food arrived. While they ate, Rosemary and Joan made a list of the day's highlights, in order from one to ten. The girls liked their lists. Mr. Wainwright, Frank, paid his check, left a good tip for the waitress, and stood.

"I'll see you back at the ranch," he said.

As Charlotte tucked the girls into bed, Rosemary had many questions about trapeze artists and France and broken bones and did the doctor fall in love with Mr. Wainwright's grandmother while he was watching her perform or only when he patched her up? Joan remained silent. Charlotte had seen the question building in her face at dinner.

"Why isn't Daddy coming with us to California?" Joan said. "To visit Aunt Marguerite with us?"

"Shhh," Charlotte said. "Go to sleep. We'll talk about it later."

"Daddy didn't come with us because he has to work, Joan." Rosemary propped herself up on an elbow. She never suggested tentatively when she could declare emphatically. "That's why, of course."

"Oh," Joan said.

Charlotte saw that she was unconvinced, though. So look out. Once Joan had the scent, she was patient and relentless.

After the girls nodded off, Charlotte took the dog outside for his bedtime walk. The moon waxing, more than half full, and the sky cloudless. Every surface seemed as if it had been glazed with silver.

Mr. Wainwright, Frank, was standing at his spot by the pool fence, gazing up at the moon. She felt a tickle of suspicion—that he'd been there for a while, waiting for her. But of course that was silly.

She made her way over. "I suppose it was inevitable, wasn't it?" she said.

"The Old Mexico is a small world," he said. "Not that I'm complaining."

"No?"

"Because we never did finish our conversation about term life, you realize."

She smiled. He flirted with such good nature, his warmth seemed so genuine, that she didn't mind. But she wondered if she should break the news to him, that his efforts were all for naught.

"When you live in New York, you forget what the sky looks like," he said.

"I'll have to take your word for that," she said.

"I imagine there's plenty of sky in Oklahoma."

"You can't miss it."

He reached down to rub the dog's ear, and his shoulder grazed her hip. The surge of desire took her by surprise, a dirty, crackling electricity. She imagined sliding her hand down his stomach and under the band of his slacks, holding him and squeezing him and feeling him turn hard in her palm. Her mouth pressed against his, her legs hitched around his waist, and her back against the fence, the iron picket digging between her shoulder blades. He wouldn't last long. He would beg for release. And then tomorrow she would be gone. Charlotte might remember him, she might not.

The dog closed his eyes, tilted his head, and grumbled blissfully.

"Dogs tend to like me," he said. "I can't explain it."

"Do you think people can change?" Charlotte said.

The question took him by surprise. "Change?"

"Who they are," she said. "Their character, I suppose. How they act, what they believe. After years of being one sort of person, can you just decide to become a different sort?"

He mulled. Charlotte had another tickle of suspicion. That behind his smile he was assessing her, picking among various options the answer he thought she wanted to hear.

"Most people don't change," he said.

"No," Charlotte. "I agree."

"But maybe they can. If they want it badly enough."

She thought for an instant that he might kiss her then. Instead, though, he gave the dog a final pat.

"Well. I suppose I should get back inside," he said. "Good night."

16

The woman, Charlotte, required a bit more effort than Guidry had anticipated—she was a bit tougher to read. But he did the spadework. He made sure that their paths kept crossing, he dropped himself into the middle of her life, he made himself . . . *familiar*. That was half the battle right there. And then turn on the charm, turn up the heat. But not too much. He needed her to trust him. When the opportunity arose on a romantic moonlit night—or, rather, when Guidry created the opportunity for himself—he didn't make a pass at her. Why, the thought never even crossed his mind. He was the perfect gentleman.

He slept fitfully. Every time he started to drift off, a persistent worry tapped him on the shoulder and drew him back. What if he was wrong? What if Seraphine's men hadn't been fooled in Goodnight? What if they knew he was on 66, headed west? What if they were closing in on him right this minute, slowly but surely?

Wednesday morning he filled his mug with scotch and a splash of coffee. Picked up the Albuquerque paper in the motel office—CAROLINE VISITS FATHER'S GRAVE—and told the operator to give him Las Vegas, please, Evergreen 6-1414.

The butler with the English accent answered the phone again. "Mr. Zingel's residence."

Guidry hesitated. How about this. Hang up and call Seraphine instead. And tell her what? Let's forgive and forget, water under the bridge. He knew what she would say. She would tell Guidry, *But of course,* mon cher. *Come home. My arms are open.* And then she'd have someone waiting for him to step off the plane. Seraphine was fond of Guidry, he knew, but that and a nickel would get him one song on the jukebox.

"It's me again, Jeeves," Guidry said. "I called yesterday."

"Ah, yes. Mr. Marcello," Ed's butler said. "One moment, please."

Half a second later, Big Ed picked up.

"Listen to me, you backstabbing piece of shit," Ed said. "You miserable cocksucking wop. So you want me to do a favor for you? I'll do a favor for all mankind.

I'll stick the barrel of a gun up your wop asshole and pull the trigger. I'll stick two guns up your asshole and pull both triggers."

"Hi there, Ed," Guidry said.

"A favor? For old times' sake? Is that supposed to be a joke, you fucking—" Ed stopped. Guidry could hear him pacing, breathing through his mouth. "Frank?"

"I figured that message would get your attention," Guidry said.

"Frank Guidry. Goddamn it."

Guidry didn't know why Ed hated Carlos so much. He was just relieved to confirm it.

"How've you been, Ed?"

"Goddamn you, boychick," Ed said. "You almost gave me a heart attack I was so worked up. I ought to stick the barrel of a gun up *your* ass."

"I'm just fine," Guidry said, "thanks for asking."

Guidry heard Ed tell the butler to get lost. A door clicked shut. Now began the dance. Guidry would lie. Ed would lie. They'd circle and twirl, each of them hoping to catch a flash of bare skin—the truth, or part of it. Watch your step and don't lose the beat.

"So tell me," Ed said. "What did you do to get that greasy bastard tied into such a knot? Word is, he won't stop till you're dead yesterday. You were his fair-haired boy."

"I got my hand caught in the cookie jar," Guidry said.

"Bullshit. All this fuss over a little money? Bullshit. Carlos has everyone and his monkey looking for you. What really happened?"

"Who said the cookie jar was full of money?"

Ed chewed on that for a while and then laughed. "You screwed his daughter?"

"She screwed *me*. Hand to God, Ed. I just lay there turgid with fear while she did most of the work. I tried to escape, don't think I didn't think about it."

Ed laughed so long and so hard he started to cough. Maybe he didn't buy Guidry's story. But it was an amusing one, and with Ed that counted for something.

"I wish I'd seen that bastard's face when he found out," Ed said. "Did you knock her up, too? I'll give you ten grand right now if you knocked her up. I'm getting my checkbook out of the drawer."

"I didn't knock her up," Guidry said. "No. And I'd appreciate it if you didn't spread such ugly rumors."

"He can only kill you once," Ed said.

"It's the part that comes before the killing that I'm worried about."

"Where are you?"

"Miami."

"Bullshit."

"I need to get out of the country, Ed. Will you lend me a hand or not?"

"I said I would, didn't I?"

"Did you?" Guidry said. "I must have missed that."

"I'll lend you a hand, boychick," Ed said. "Of course I will."

"What'll it cost me?"

"Don't insult me. It'll be my pleasure. On the house."

Not likely. Sure, Ed hated Carlos and he liked Guidry, but that wouldn't be enough. Guidry would have to pony up, his very last penny.

"I know about a few business ventures the Marcellos are planning," Guidry said. "The details. Carlos is expanding the empire. A fella in the know could make a killing, Ed."

"Hmm."

Hmm. In the language they both spoke, this meant, *What else you got?* The problem was that Guidry didn't have anything else to offer. "Ed . . ."

"Forget all that, boychick," Ed said. "I've got bigger plans for you."

It didn't surprise Guidry that Ed had already figured out a price, in the few short minutes that they'd been on the phone together. Or else Ed had started his figuring earlier, when Guidry left the first message for him. He'd known all along that it was Guidry calling, not Carlos. He'd guessed correctly *why* Guidry was calling.

"I'd love to hear about it, Ed," Guidry said.

"Indochina," Ed said.

"Indochina?"

"There's money pumping into Vegas today, but where's the money going tomorrow? That's the question that piques my interest. Now that he's president, LBJ will want to swing his big Texas dick around. Not Cuba, that's old news. Vietnam, boychick, that's the new hot spot. The CIA needs a real war. Hughes does, too. Military contracts don't grow on trees."

Until now Guidry had been plotting only a single move ahead. Stay alive. Get out of the country, away from Carlos. Past that, Guidry would worry about the fire once he made it out of the frying pan.

"You want me to work for you?" Guidry said.

"*With* me," Ed said. "You're clever and you're smooth, and you'd sell your own mother to the Gypsies. I want a man like that representing my interests. That dumb greaseball in New Orleans wasted your talents. You'll run the show over there. Saigon is a helluva lot of fun, I've heard. Right up your alley. You're going to beat the crowd and get us the best seat in the house. How does that sound?"

It sounded good. It sounded beautiful. It sounded like an Art Pepper saxophone solo or a woman sighing with pleasure. Ed would own him, and Guidry would be in his debt forever, but so what? He was offering to give Guidry his life back. Not the exact one he'd had in New Orleans, maybe, but one a lot like it, even brighter and better.

Sure, it sounded good. Or did it sound *too* good?

"Ed, you're a prince," Guidry said. "Thank you."

"How soon can you get to Vegas?" Ed said. "You've got a passport?"

"A couple of days. Friday. I don't have my passport."

"All right. That's not a problem. Call me the minute you get here. I'll take care of everything."

Guidry hung up. He remained in the same state of suspended uncertainty he'd been in before the call. Just suspended even higher now, staring down at a drop without a bottom.

Trust Ed. Trust Ed? Guidry confirmed that he still hadn't a better play. Las Vegas, here I come. Now all he had to do was make it from here to there without getting recognized, without getting killed.

Eight-thirty in the morning. He didn't want to accidentally cross paths with Charlotte in town, so he walked over to her casita to see if she was there. The blond daughter opened the door.

"Hello there, Joan," Guidry said.

She gravely weighed her opening remarks. "Hello."

The curly-haired daughter, Rosemary, pushed in front of her. "Hello, Mr. Wainwright. We're in New Mexico."

"Yes we are," Guidry said. "Every part of us."

Charlotte appeared behind her daughters, smiling. She noticed the car keys in Guidry's hand, and the smile, he was pleased to see, faltered. "Oh," she said. "Are you leaving?"

"Leaving?" he said. "No, not till tomorrow or Friday. I thought I'd take a drive into town and pick up a few necessaries. And bring back a sack of jelly doughnuts, if somebody here promises to help me eat them."

"Yes!" Rosemary said.

"That's very thoughtful of you," Charlotte said.

"Don't move a muscle, any of you," Guidry said. "I shall return."

He drove into Santa Maria. It didn't take him long, in a town this tiny, to find the garage. The grease monkey was working on a car in the bay, wiring up a new taillight assembly. The same car that Guidry had seen broken down by the side of the highway. The same car he'd seen attached to the tow truck that delivered Charlotte to the Old Mexico Motor Court.

The grease monkey looked over. Guidry watched

for his reaction. There wasn't much of one. Call it mild irritation, surly indifference. Good. He wasn't on the lookout for any Guidrys.

"Busy," the grease monkey grunted at him.

"I was hoping to get my Dodge tuned before I hit the highway tomorrow," Guidry said. "The belts checked, at least."

"Busy."

"You don't say? What's that you're working on there?"

Guidry took a ten out of his wallet and set it on a tool bench. That changed the temperature in the room. The grease monkey straightened up and eyed the dough.

"I believe that's the car I saw on the back of your truck day before yesterday," Guidry said. "Belongs to a lady and her two daughters?"

"That's right," the grease monkey said.

"Looked pretty beat when I saw it. What's the status?"

"Wasn't too bad. Be done with it in a few hours."

Guidry kept his wallet out. "That's wonderful news," he said.

17

For lunch Charlotte and the girls had Vienna sausages and crackers. Dessert: the remaining doughnuts Frank had delivered to their door that morning. Afterward they walked into town again. It was another gorgeous day, almost springlike. Charlotte wondered how winter in California would be. Sunshine, warm ocean breezes, emerald landscapes. Back in Woodrow, when December rolled around, the cold sucked the color from the sky, the wind stripped the trees bare.

A note taped to the door of the garage said *"Back in 5 min,"* so Charlotte told the girls to go play in the park across the street. She used the pay phone on the corner to try Aunt Marguerite's number again.

"Fifty cents, please," the operator said.

Charlotte inserted the coins. She began to count the rings, but a woman answered almost immediately.

"Hello?"

"Marguerite?" Charlotte said.

"Speaking. Who is this?"

"Aunt Marguerite, it's Charlotte."

"Charlotte."

"Your niece, Charlotte. From Oklahoma."

"Yes, of course," Marguerite said. "I know who you are. Charlotte. This is unexpected."

Marguerite's voice had a clipped, metallic ring to it, like a hammer striking the head of a chisel—Charlotte remembered that now. And she remembered now, too, what her mother had said once: that if you needed ice for your drink, you could just chip a piece or two off Marguerite.

"It's so nice to speak with you, Aunt Marguerite," Charlotte said, "after such a long time."

"Yes."

And then silence. Charlotte had hoped to ease into the conversation, to sidle up to the main point and wring every last penny's worth from her fifty cents. No such luck, apparently.

"Aunt Marguerite, I'm calling because the girls and I might be coming to California soon. My daughters and I, to Los Angeles. And I thought, if it's not too much of an imposition, I thought we might pay you a visit."

"Stay with me, you mean?" Marguerite said.

"If it's not too much of an imposition," Charlotte said.

"It's not a good idea. My house is small, and I work at home, you understand. I can't have noisy children all about and underfoot."

Charlotte had prepared for the possibility that Marguerite might say no, but the swiftness of it, the decisiveness of the ruling—like the limb of a tree snapped cleanly in half—took her by surprise.

"Hello?" Marguerite said. "Are you still there?"

"Yes, I'm sorry," Charlotte said. "I understand, of course."

"I can recommend a good hotel. How long will you be in Los Angeles?"

"How long? Actually, I . . . My husband and I, Dooley, we're . . . We might be getting a divorce."

"A divorce. I see."

"And I thought . . . California. I've always wanted to live there. What I want, what I think the girls and I need, is a fresh start, a blank page. I know that must sound silly."

Marguerite did not rush to disagree. Instead she sighed. "Los Angeles is a difficult city," she said. "It's not remotely what people imagine, all golden beaches and orange groves and movie studios."

"No, of course not." Though that was, when Charlotte stopped to consider, not very far from what she had imagined.

"Well then," Marguerite said. "As I've explained, I can recommend a good hotel when you're ready. Though if you want my advice, I'd encourage you to arrange for an apartment before you arrive. Hotels here can be quite expensive."

It took Charlotte a moment to realize that the conversation—another limb of a tree snapped cleanly in half—had ended.

"Thank you," she said.

"Good luck, Charlotte," Marguerite said.

Charlotte replaced the receiver. Staying with Aunt Marguerite had always been an uncertain prospect, she reminded herself. She'd recognized that from the beginning. So. Well. There were other possibilities, if she decided to continue on to California. There would be other possibilities.

She returned to the garage and rang the bell. She rang it again. Finally the mechanic emerged, wiping his hands on a greasy rag. Tobacco juice seeping from the corner of his mouth.

"Hello," Charlotte said. "I'm here about my car."

"Yep," he said.

"Will you be able to have it repaired today? How much will it cost?"

He shifted the lump of tobacco from one cheek to the other. He wouldn't look her in the eye. She prepared herself for the bad news. Fifty dollars? Seventy-five? Surely not a hundred.

"Front axle's broke plumb in two, the subframe all beat to hell," the mechanic said. "Worse'n that, the transmission got beat to hell, too. You must have hit that ditch like a bomb. It's a goner."

"The transmission is a goner?" Charlotte said.

"Car is. Car's a goner." The mechanic shifted the lump of tobacco to the opposite cheek. "Fixing it'd cost you more than what the whole car's worth. I won't lie to you."

Charlotte felt her fingertips tingle. A flush of heat spread across her collarbone, and the mix of smells in the cramped little office—tobacco and grease and sweat, the mechanic's sweat and her own—made her dizzy.

"Do you . . . Can I sit for a moment?" she said.

He moved a stack of parts catalogs and girlie magazines off a folding chair. He brought her a paper cup full of water and found a book of matches so that she could light her cigarette.

He still refused to look her in the eye. "Sorry, ma'am," he said.

When Charlotte stepped back outside, the girls were trying to coax the dog onto the teeter-totter across the street. She stood and watched them. She felt numb, brittle, the hollow husk of a cicada crunched beneath a shoe.

She rummaged in her purse for another cigarette. A teardrop rolled off her chin and smeared the ink on the cover of her address book. She hadn't realized that she was crying. She didn't know when she'd started.

How stupid she'd been, to think that she might actually have the nerve to see this through, that she might actually leave Oklahoma for good and leave Dooley for good and start fresh on her own. Nerve, after all, was not her strong suit. Her talent was for surrender. When Mr. Hotchkiss refused to let her take photos for the newspaper, she gave up. When Dooley refused to concede that he had a drinking problem, she gave in. When the service-station attendant back in Texas leered at her, she'd stared down at her hands and said, "Thank you."

She remembered the story about the three pigs that the girls had loved when they were younger. In the story of her life, Charlotte wasn't brick and she wasn't even sticks—she was made of straw, the house that the wolf needed but a single good breath to blow down.

Dooley knew her better than she knew herself, didn't he? *So just come on home, Charlie,* he'd said at the end of their conversation on Monday. *You know you will.*

She watched the girls. Would Rosemary and Joan remember any of this years from now? How would they remember it? How would they remember her?

The dog leaped off the seat of the teeter-totter, and the girls scrambled, laughing, to catch him. He wriggled on his back and bit happily at the dead grass.

He'd not had a seizure, Charlotte realized, since they'd left Woodrow. The new medicine was working. She could see that he felt better and livelier and more like himself than he had in a long time.

Was it a permanent state? No. The vet had cautioned her that even under the best of circumstances it was likely the dog would still experience an occasional seizure. These setbacks would be milder, though, and less frequent. The dog would be more resilient, able to more quickly bounce back up each time life knocked him down.

And just like that, Charlotte's mind was made up. She wasn't going back to Oklahoma. She wasn't going back to Dooley. Come what may. The car was a blow.

Other blows were sure to follow. But she needn't let that deter her. She would just choose, each time, to bounce back up.

She wasn't sure how they'd make it to California, but Charlotte would find a way. And once they arrived? How would they manage to get by? Charlotte would find a way. And maybe Frank was right. Maybe the universe did owe her a favor.

A moment later here he came, Frank, strolling up the street as if she'd conjured him out of thin air. When he got closer, his smile disappeared and his face creased with concern. She knew that she must have looked like a mess, her mascara running.

"What's the trouble?" he said. "And how can I help?"

18

Barone had the colored kid drive straight from the police station in Goodnight to Amarillo. Guidry would jump on 66 there. Barone would jump on it right behind him. First, though, he had to get rid of the Pontiac.

"Down there," Barone said. An alley off Amarillo's main drag. A couple of cheapskates, not wanting to pay the meter on the street, had parked there.

The kid squeezed the Pontiac in.

"Leave the keys in it," Barone said. Here, kitty, kitty. With a little luck, some punk or vagrant would boost the Pontiac and drive it to Canada.

"Do what?" the kid said.

"Do what I say. Don't ask questions."

"We just gonna walk off?"

"That's the idea."

"Shoot." But the kid didn't give him any extra lip. More than Barone could say for most of the so-called professionals that he'd worked with over the years.

They caught a bus that ran to the highway. Walked up 66 a couple of blocks to a motel the exact same layout as the Bali Hai in Houston. The cinder-block L, the stairs in the crook of the L, just like the ones the sniper from San Francisco had tumbled down. This motel didn't have a tropical theme, though, or any theme at all. It was just the Amarillo 66.

"'Bout time we stop," the kid said. "Wake me up for breakfast."

Barone was tired, too. Aching and hot. It was Monday, one o'clock in the afternoon, and he'd been awake for . . . he couldn't remember how long. He could use some rest. He might end up having to check every motel between here and California. All right. It would take Seraphine a few hours to arrange a new car for him.

On the way into the motel, Barone studied each car in the lot. He didn't see a '57 or '58 Dodge Coronet, blue over white.

He asked the clerk about Guidry. Described him. Barone explained that he was a private dick, looking for a guy who ran out on his wife and kids back home, didn't know what name the guy was using. Barone doubted that Guidry would have stopped in Amarillo, but better make sure.

The clerk said no, sorry, nobody had registered since yesterday afternoon. He gave Barone and the kid two rooms next to each other. Barone told the kid to be ready to go in three hours, and then he went to find a phone booth.

"Well?" Seraphine said.

"No," Barone said.

"No?"

"He talked his way out of it somehow."

"Ah." She didn't sound too surprised.

"The sheriff said he's headed west," Barone said. "I have the make and the model, what he's driving. I had to get a little rough."

Barone waited for her to say something. Seraphine knew exactly the wrong way to rub him.

"I couldn't have gotten there any faster," he said.

"It's not your fault, *mon cher*," she said.

"I didn't say it was."

"At least we know where he's going now. Las Vegas or Los Angeles."

Las Vegas *or* Los Angeles? It didn't sound to Barone like they knew where Guidry was going.

It was a long drive either way. Barone thought about

the move Guidry had made in Houston. How he'd tried to fool Seraphine, doubling back and not taking the first flight out of Municipal.

"Put your people on it in Vegas and L.A.," Barone said, "but maybe he'll stop for the night along the way. Maybe for a few nights. Hoping we'll hop right over him."

She was quiet again. This time because she realized that Barone might be right. "Perhaps," she said. "Yes."

"How quick can you get me a car?" he said. "And a new piece."

"I'll make a call right now."

He gave her the name of the motel and hung up and went back to his room. The fever pounded away at him. Upper cut, jab, cold, hot. He didn't worry. The flu never lasted too long, not the worst of it. A shower would help. But Barone couldn't sit up, the world spinning so fast it kept him pinned to the bed. He didn't remember lying down. He tried to unbutton his shirt. Next thing he knew, he was kneeling on the tile floor of the bathroom, the hot water from the shower steaming up the mirror.

And then he was standing on the shore of a mountain lake, the lake from one of the paintings on the wall of the police station. But the lake was on fire now, and the heat from it turned him to cinders. Barone could feel his skin bubble and pop. He knew it was just a dream. But when dreams are more real than life, what difference does it make?

An icy breeze blew him free. He was running now. The colored kid running next to him. Theodore, don't call me Ted. Theodore, don't call me Teddy. The kid was hollering. *Hurry up!* What were he and the kid running from? What were they running toward? Barone didn't have anything against the Germans. The scream of the shells as they dropped from the sky. *Jump!* the kid hollered at Barone. Now? *Jump!*

A room. A red mohair sofa. A woman with her feet up on the bolster. Barone five or six years old again. The woman smiling at him. Her bare thighs under the robe. She cocked her head at a door. *It's in there,* she said. What is? She wouldn't tell him. *Go see for yourself. Don't be afraid.*

When Barone woke up, he was back in bed, the motel in Amarillo, under the covers. A bald man with a round face and round wire-frame glasses sat in a chair next to the bed, picking at his teeth with the corner of a matchbook.

"Hello, Mr. Roberts," the man said. "And how are we feeling this morning?"

Barone couldn't see the man's eyes because of the way the light from the window flashed off the lenses. "Who are you?" Barone said.

"We are looking significantly more vigorous, I would say."

He handed Barone a glass of water. Barone could barely lift his head. He had to hold the glass with both hands. But he felt better. Just a little hot, a little dizzy. The water tasted good. He drank every drop.

"Who the hell are you?" Barone said.

"I," the man said, "am the doctor who saved your life. Lest you think I exaggerate, I assure you I do not. Boy!"

The colored kid popped out from behind the doctor and took the empty glass from Barone and carried it into the bathroom. Barone heard the water running.

"Your hand was badly infected," the doctor said. "You had a fever of one hundred and four when I first arrived."

Barone drank the second glass of water. The room no longer pitched and heaved.

"Your boy here had the good sense to badger the hotel manager until he called me. I would be honored to meet the trained capuchin monkey who put those sutures in your hand, by the way. He neglected to clean the wound first, it appears, but it's the most accomplished suturing work by a trained capuchin monkey I've ever observed."

"You was on the floor." The kid kept a wary distance, like he was afraid Barone might be mad. "All laid out, tangled up with your undershirt up over your head. Door was open. I thought you was dead."

"What time is it?" Barone said.

"Eleven o'clock in the morning," the doctor said. "Open your mouth, please, Mr. Roberts."

The doctor stuck a thermometer under Barone's tongue. Eleven o'clock in the morning. That couldn't be right. They'd reached Amarillo at one o'clock in the afternoon. Time never rolled backward, no matter how much you might want it to.

"Very good," the doctor said, inspecting the thermometer. "Just a hair over one hundred degrees. We're making progress, Mr. Roberts."

"What day is it?" Barone said.

"Tuesday."

"No. It's Monday."

"It's Tuesday, November twenty-sixth, in the year of our Lord nineteen hundred and sixty-three," the doctor said. "I administered antibiotics yesterday, and earlier this morning. I cleaned your wound and changed the dressing."

"What else you want me to do?" the kid said. He

still hung back but had gone from wary to defensive. "I thought you was dead till I poked at you. You 'bout tried to kill me before you gone down all in a heap again."

"In my medical opinion, the sutures need to be removed and the wound thoroughly irrigated and drained forthwith," the doctor said. "Culture the drainage and immobilize the hand. Fresh sutures and a cast forthwith. If you come to my office tomorrow morning, I will assist."

"Get out," Barone said.

"Adequate rest is paramount. Plenty of fluids, though of course you should avoid any fluids of the alcoholic nature. And it's absolutely essential that you take these for the next two weeks. Do you see?"

The doctor showed Barone a bottle of pills, rattled it, and then set it back on the bedside table. He picked up a second bottle and rattled it.

"Take these if you experience any pain," the doctor said. "They're quite potent, so moderation is advised. May I ask how you came by your injury?"

"He cut it shaving his palms," the kid said.

The doctor chuckled. "Wonderful."

"Come here," Barone told the kid. "Help me up."

The kid helped Barone hobble to the bathroom. Barone had to grip the kid's shoulder while he took a piss. He felt like his bones had been put in a pot and boiled until they were soft. By the time he flopped back into the bed, he was out of breath.

The doctor picked at his teeth with the corner of the matchbook.

"Get out," Barone said.

"With alacrity, Mr. Roberts. There's just the small matter of payment."

After the doctor got his money and left, Barone told the kid to help him out of bed again.

"You suppose to rest," the kid said. "Doctor just said so."

"Come here," Barone said.

Once Barone was dressed, he sent the kid off to find him cigarettes, whiskey, and a 5th Avenue candy bar. Barone walked to the door. He counted to ten, catching his breath, before he opened it and stepped outside.

Parking lot. A Ford Fairlane sat in the corner, off by itself. In the glove box, there was a Police Positive .38, like the one that Fisk had been carrying but this one with a worn wooden grip.

Barone made it back to the room. Just barely. The kid returned with the cigarettes and the candy bars but no whiskey. Barone was too weak to cuss him out about the whiskey. Barone could barely crawl into bed again.

"Told you to rest," the kid said. "Didn't I?"

"Shuuhhh," was all Barone could say.

"Didn't I tell you? Here. Take your pill."

The kid ran a washrag under the cold water and laid it across Barone's forehead. Barone ate half of the 5th Avenue candy bar and took two of the pain pills. He went to sleep. The kid woke him up in the night and made him take another one of the other pills, made him drink a glass of water.

When Barone woke up again, it was morning. A quarter past nine.

"What day is it?" Barone said.

"Wednesday," the kid said. "Day before Thanks-giving."

Wednesday. Barone had pissed away almost two full days.

Barone sat up. Gingerly. Put his feet on the floor. He shaved and showered. The kid buzzed around, grip-ing that Barone needed to keep resting, doctor said so, doctor said so.

"Nothing yet," Barone said when Seraphine an-swered. "You?"

"No," she said. Her voice flat.

"What's wrong."

"'A little rough.'"

"What?"

"That's what you said about Texas," Seraphine said. "That you had to get 'a little rough.'"

So she'd heard about the police station in Goodnight. She was right to be mad. Barone was mad at himself. He blamed the fever. He shouldn't have lost his temper. Wait for the sheriff to leave the station and follow him home. Get the number on Guidry just as quickly, a lot more quietly.

But fuck Seraphine. In her comfortable office, her comfortable life, having cocktails before dinner every evening, strolling through the park. Barone was the one who had to do all the heavy lifting. Who risked his life for Carlos. Seraphine had to worry about chipping her nail polish on the adding machine.

"So?" he said.

"I'm not sure you appreciate the urgency," she said. "I've been assured that the authorities won't rest until the responsible party is found."

"Then they won't get any rest, will they?"

"How far along are you?"

Barone shouldn't have stopped in Amarillo. He blamed the fever. He hadn't planned to stop in Amarillo for more than a few hours.

"Albuquerque," he said. He didn't know if she'd be able to tell he was lying.

224 • LOU BERNEY

"Good," she said. "Though you'll still need to be cautious. And don't return to Texas for any reason. I hope I don't have to remind you. The sooner you find our friend, the better for everyone."

Back in the room, the kid was in his stockinged feet, watching TV. Barone kicked his shoes over to him.

"We're leaving," Barone said.

"Now?" the kid said. "What about breakfast? And you got to take your pill first. Doctor said—"

"Right now."

19

Thanksgiving Day. As Guidry wheeled onto the highway, he gave thanks that he was finished forever with Santa Maria, New Mexico, and on the move again.

"Away we go," he told his audience. Charlotte in the passenger seat next to him, her daughters and their dog in the backseat.

The grease monkey had balked at first, when Guidry offered him fifty dollars to tell the woman her car was dead. He'd claimed that he could never do such an underhanded thing, not to such a nice lady and her daughters. Like hell. He just wanted to drive up the price. Guidry, bent over the barrel, had no choice. In the good old days, he never had to dicker. Yes, sir. Whatever you say, sir. Give Mr. Marcello my regards, sir.

Look on the bright side, though. If Big Ed Zingel
kept his word, Guidry wouldn't have to worry about
money once he got to Las Vegas. And if Ed didn't keep
his word? Guidry wouldn't have to worry about money
then either, except for the penny he'd have to pay
Charon to cross the river Styx into the land of the dead.

The grease monkey held up his end of the bargain.
Charlotte walked out of the garage like she'd been hit
by a bus.

Guidry timed his swoop down from the skies just
right. "How can I help?"

She told him about the car. He listened sympatheti-
cally. Guidry had to hand it to her. She might have been
crying a minute ago, but she wasn't now. She seemed
to be taking the punch like a champ: Her voice didn't
break, her gaze didn't falter.

"Well, Charlotte," he said, "it's a good thing that
you have a backup plan."

She managed a smile. "Well, Frank, I'm not sure
that I do."

"I'm going to Los Angeles, too, aren't I?" he said.
"There's plenty of room in my car. And you've seen
my way with dogs."

She studied him. Her expression more surprised
than wary, but for a second there Guidry was sure she
could see right through him.

"You're very kind," she said, "but I couldn't possibly—"

"Let's discuss the reasons why not. You go first."

"Because . . ."

"The bus will take you three days," he said. "It stops at every town between here and the Pacific Ocean. And it won't be cheap, three people and a dog."

Guidry watched her work out the next part for herself. How much would the bus cost? Would the driver even allow the dog on the bus?

He rubbed his jaw, inspiration striking. "You'll need a car in Los Angeles, won't you? Listen to this. I have a pal in Las Vegas. He's right on our way to Los Angeles. Ed owns a couple of businesses out there. One of them, as it happens, is a car dealership."

"I don't have nearly enough money to buy a car," Charlotte said.

"You have more than enough to borrow one," Guidry said. "Ed's the original Good Samaritan. He's got daughters of his own."

Guidry didn't know if Big Ed had children or not. Well, he had them now. He had daughters and a car dealership and a soft, giving heart.

"But I couldn't possibly . . ." she said. Trying to talk herself into it. Trying to talk herself out of it.

He almost had her. Now ease off and let her go. A

woman's first yes needed to be an easy one. Get her in the habit of saying it.

"I apologize," Guidry said. "I promised I wouldn't try to sell you anything, didn't I? How about this? I'm not leaving until tomorrow. Will you at least think it over before you decide? Sleep on it?"

Still she hesitated. Guidry couldn't tell if he'd blown it or not. *Had* she seen through him, right down into the depths of his dark, duplicitous soul?

No. Of course not. But she was perceptive enough to sense that all was not quite what it seemed.

"Yes," she said, "I'll sleep on it. You're very kind, Frank."

"Well, Charlotte, I'm glad you think so."

And now here they were, cruising down 66. Charlotte was tense, the fist in her lap clenching, clenching. Still not entirely convinced that accepting a ride with him had been a wise choice. But Guidry saw signs that she'd begun to relax. The occasional glance drifting out to the high desert and lingering there. A hint of a smile when a song she liked came on the radio.

"We're making a list," the curly-haired daughter said, Rosemary.

Guidry realized she was talking to him. She had her chin on the back of the seat next to his shoulder. He didn't know how long she'd been there.

"Rosemary," Charlotte said, "don't disturb Mr. Wainwright."

"That's all right," Guidry said. "I approve of lists. The sign of an organized mind."

Rosemary showed him their Disney nature book. On the front cover were an owl, a spider, what might looked like a coyote, an octopus. *Secrets of the Hidden World.*

"It's about animals and fish and birds and bugs that only sneak out at night," she said. "We're making a list of our favorite animals in the book. The coyote is first, of course, because he looks like a sweet dog. Doesn't he, Joan? We have a separate list for fish and a list for birds and a list for bugs."

Charlotte cut Guidry an amused look. "Abandon hope, all ye who enter here."

"Well," he told the girls, "you better keep an eye peeled, out there to the right. Coyotes come out during the day every now and then. You might spot one."

Both girls crowded up against the window. The small palms pressed flat against the glass. Sunlight pooling and a concentration in their faces so intent, so pure, that if ever it flagged, the earth would cease to turn. A long-lost memory floated toward Guidry. His sister Annette, four or five years old. Kneeling on a chair by the window, watching as their mother walked toward the house. Guidry would have been eight or nine. Their mother spotted the two of them in the window and smiled. Sunlight pooling. Don't blink or she'll disappear forever.

The worst part of an unhappy childhood: the occasional happy moments, when you're allowed a glimpse of the life that you might have instead.

"Do you think we'll see a coyote, Joan?" Rosemary said. "I think we will."

The little girls needed to pee in Coolidge. Another stop for lunch, at a hamburger stand in Gallup. The carhop was chatty. Guidry tried to make the right impression on her, that he was a family man. In case one of Seraphine's men showed up later and started asking after a handsome bachelor.

We're on our way to Los Angeles. The two kiddos back there have never been to Disneyland. Here you go, Rosemary, here you go, Joan. Who had the vanilla malt and who the chocolate? Shall I walk the dog before we go?

His dog-walking stratagem almost backfired. While he stood waiting for the dog to finish squeezing out a coiled turd the length of a garden hose, the carhop came over and bent down and asked the name of his cute doggy. Guidry would have loved to know that, too.

"Well," he said, "usually he thinks his name is 'Dinnertime.'"

The carhop giggled. The dog, squeezing out his turd, eyed Guidry reproachfully. *I have your number, pal.*

Rosemary needed to pee again in Lupton. Joan needed to pee again in Chambers. At this rate Guidry could have walked to Las Vegas. Though the slow pace might be to his advantage. Seraphine might be far out in front of him, swarming the cities and ports, scanning the distant horizons.

The girls sang songs, softly. Guidry learned the dog's name for future reference. Lucky. Charlotte had relaxed enough by now to reach for the radio dial.

"May I?" she said.

"Go right ahead," he said.

For a couple of miles, they listened in silence to the station she settled on. Guidry didn't recognize the singer. The voice wasn't much, scratchy and nasal, but it had a character all its own.

"What's the title?" Guidry said.

"'Don't Think Twice, It's All Right,'" Charlotte said. "It's an interesting message, isn't it?"

"He's leaving her," Guidry said. "Or she's kicked him out. I'm not clear on that part."

"But maybe the song isn't about a man and a woman. Or not really."

He glanced over at her, curious. "Illuminate me."

"Maybe it's also about all of us," she said. "As individuals, and as a nation. Having the courage of our convictions. When the president was shot, my brother-in-law said that the world was going to the dogs. But he's believed that for a long time. I don't think what happened in Dallas is what really frightens people like him."

"The Negroes, you mean," Guidry said. "Civil rights and all that. Your brother-in-law worries that the genie can't be stuffed back in the bottle."

"Not just the Negroes," she said. "Women, too. Young people. Everyone who's been pushed aside for so long that they're sick and tired of it."

"The Bible says that the meek shall inherit the earth," Guidry said. "But I've always been skeptical of that opinion."

"I agree. I think Bob Dylan agrees. The meek don't inherit the earth. You have to raise your voice. You have to take what's yours by right. You can't count on anyone just giving it to you."

It wasn't the answer that Guidry had expected. She wasn't, he was reminded again, the woman he'd expected. He wondered about her husband back in Oklahoma. Wheat farmer? Butcher, baker, candlestick maker? The man, when it came to Charlotte, had drawn an interesting hand. Maybe he didn't realize it.

Speaking of which. Why wasn't Dad along on this family jaunt? It was an odd time of the year to visit an aunt in California, wasn't it? The Christmas holidays were almost a month away. Rosemary and Joan should have been sitting in a school classroom these past three days.

"How long will you be staying in Los Angeles?" he said.

She hesitated. Guidry noted it. He'd been right. Charlotte was on the run, just like him.

"Mommy? Can we talk about it now?" Joan asking, but Rosemary paying attention, too. "How long we'll stay in California?"

"Oh, look, girls!" Charlotte said.

She pointed to a billboard advertising the Petrified Forest and Painted Desert. An Indian in a feathered headdress stood on a ridge and surveyed the bluffs and mesas spread out before him, a rumpled landscape of bright blood and molten gold the same unnaturally unhealthy orange as the Indian's skin.

The little girls pressed up against the window again. Charlotte smoothed her skirt and pretended to be just as fascinated by the billboard.

When Guidry caught her eye, he gave her an apologetic look. *Sorry, I'll keep my big trap shut from now on.*

"Mommy! Is the desert really painted?" Rosemary said. "Who painted it? Is the whole forest petrified? Can we climb the trees? Why are the trees petrified? Why is the desert painted? Will there be Indians?"

The Petrified Forest came first. Guidry stopped at the scenic pull-out. Families, plus one lone wolf sitting on the hood of his beat-up truck. Dirty chinos, a dirty flannel mackinaw, three days of salt-and-pepper stubble. When Guidry got out of the car, the man took a long look at him. Guidry ignored him. He followed Charlotte and the girls over to the rail.

The Petrified Forest disappointed. Forest? No, just blackened lumps scattered across the gravel pan like cigar stubs in an ashtray. But the little girls were delighted. Rosemary was, at least.

"Look, Joan!" Rosemary said. "A forest turned all to stone! By a magician! Because the princess he loved broke his heart. That's what I think, Joan. Do you think that, too?"

Guidry had seen the shifty-looking bastard in the flannel mackinaw before, hadn't he? Had he seen the beat-up truck back in Gallup, at the hamburger stand? Guidry wasn't sure. Could he feel the man watching him. He wasn't sure about that either.

The Painted Desert was even less impressive than the Petrified Forest. A cloudy late afternoon, everything the color of old soap. Even Rosemary couldn't make a silk purse out of it. A few miles on, though, they came upon a gigantic plaster Indian, ten feet tall. The Big Chief Trading Post and Restaurant.

The girls circled Big Chief, awestruck. Big Chief looked like he'd been through fifteen rough rounds with an Even Bigger Chief. He listed to one side, an ear and a few fingers broken off, most of the paint scoured away by the desert wind. One eye blank, blind, dazed. Now, who did that remind Guidry of? Hmm. Let me think.

Guidry watched Charlotte watch her daughters, smiling as she did, and for a moment he couldn't take her eyes off her.

This trip, her flight from Egypt, had taken its toll on her. How could it not? Two little girls, a wrecked car, a future that could be considered uncertain at best. A weight in her face, the skin beneath her eyes too delicate and translucent. Faint fine lines, new lines. She was still young, but she wouldn't be for too much longer. That didn't make her less attractive. Some smiles improved with age.

But Guidry had been attracted to plenty of women over the years. Never once had it clouded his judgment. Why would this time be any different?

The beat-up truck chugged into the parking lot. Guidry tracked it with the corner of his eye. The shifty bastard in the flannel mackinaw got out of the truck. He stretched and yawned and scratched his ass.

Relax. The man wasn't following Guidry. The Big Chief Trading Post and Restaurant was crowded, the only place to eat for miles. Can't blame a guy for being hungry.

They sat outside, at one of the picnic tables. Guidry decided to be daring and ordered the tamales for his Thanksgiving dinner. They weren't bad, mostly corn mush with a little hamburger meat inside. The hot sauce made him hiccup, but Rosemary knew a cure and guided him through it, her hand on his knee.

Close your eyes, hold your breath, count backward from ten. Look, there's a scary, scary monster! Boo! Right behind you!

It worked, how do you like that? Guidry's hiccups ceased.

The shifty bastard, a few tables down, reached for his mustard and gave Guidry an even longer, even closer look this time.

Relax. Relax? The sword above Guidry's head hung suspended, as in the myth, by a single hair from a horse's tail. It would take so little to finish him: a puff of wind, a chance encounter, a spark of recognition. One man, one phone call to New Orleans, the end.

The shifty bastard finished his dinner and went back inside. Guidry stood. He picked up his empty beer bottle.

"Shall I go see about dessert for us?" he asked Charlotte and the girls. "I believe I shall."

Inside, the man was winding his way through the tourists, past the cases of curios, the Navajo blankets and genuine arrowheads. He turned down a corridor and disappeared.

What are you doing, you shifty bastard?

Looking for a phone booth. That was what.

Guidry followed. The corridor empty. A back door open. Guidry tested the weight of the empty bottle in his hand. You could use almost anything to bash in a man's brains. Guidry had learned that in the Pacific. If you found the right seam, if you kept at it, the skull opened up like the petals of a flower.

He stepped outside, behind the building. The man turned, saw him.

"Looking for the telephone?" Guidry said.

Belt him now, he told himself, before the man saw it coming. The light fading, the two of them all alone. Drag the body over there, behind the trash barrels. With a little luck, nobody would find it for hours.

"What?" the man said.

Guidry didn't see a pay phone. But there would be

one at the next stop down the road, or the one after that, and the man would call from there. Seraphine would be able to pin Guidry right to the map. She'd guess exactly where he was headed.

"I'm looking for place to piss, you don't mind," the man said. "Pisser inside is occupied, and I gotta go bad, not that it's any of your business."

Guidry couldn't risk it. He had only one guiding principle in life. If it's between you or me, friend, I choose me. Every single time.

He took a step toward the man. The man wasn't looking at him. He was peering instead off to Guidry's left. Guidry had started to turn—what the hell was he looking at?—when he realized that the man's other eye was pointed straight at him.

Ye gods, Guidry realized, the man hadn't been staring at him earlier—he was as wall-eyed as a praying mantis.

Guidry flipped his empty beer bottle away.

"What are you laughing at?" the man said.

"Nothing," Guidry said. "I apologize."

"Laugh if you want, you son of a bitch. I'm used to it."

Guidry bought fried sweet-potato pies for Charlotte and the girls. Another beer for himself. He needed it. Back in the car, Big Chief sinking away into the twilight behind them, Guidry started to laugh again. Rosemary set her chin on the seat next to his shoulder.

"Are you thinking of a funny joke?" she said.

Guidry took a long swallow of his beer. "Why, yes," he said, "in fact I am."

20

The road climbed, the car labored. They reached Flagstaff a little after nine o'clock at night. It was too dark to see the pine trees all around, but Guidry smelled them. The air brittle and thin and cold, barely enough of it to fill your lungs. Like life on the moon, on a different planet.

Guidry stopped downtown at the first hotel he saw. A creaky old brick and knotty-pine relic that had been around since pioneer days. Probably it hadn't been dusted since then either. The wallpaper curling, the tiles chipped, one of the wagon-wheel chandeliers listing. The registration book was two feet long and a foot thick. The room clerk in his brass cage used both hands to flip the page.

The little girls were down for the count. Guidry

carried Rosemary and Joan up the creaking stairs, one on each hip. Their weight against him, their heat, the scent of sweet potato on their breath. He felt another shiver of memory, a shiver of something.

No. Stop it, stop it. Guidry didn't want to remember. He'd made a deal with himself long ago.

He said good night to Charlotte and locked the door to his room behind him. Latched the chain, wedged a chair under the knob. His new bedtime routine. The lock and the chain and the chair wouldn't stop anyone that Carlos sent for him, but Guidry might have enough time to jump out the window, drop three stories, snap his neck, and meet a quick, merciful end.

He wished he knew how close Seraphine was. Did she have all her best people in Miami? Or was somebody right behind Guidry, edging closer and closer?

The room was cold as an icebox. Guidry wrapped himself in the blanket off the bed and stood by the window. The clouds had cleared away, and the stars were smeared thick across the sky, like margarine on toast.

Midway upon the journey of our life, I found myself within a forest dark, for the straightforward pathway had been lost.

Those were the only lines from Dante that Guidry could remember. Dante had experienced a few scares along the way. Eventually he made it out of the inferno, though, up to paradise safe and sound. So, too, might Guidry, though without the shade of Virgil to point the way.

Saigon. Guidry, running his own show. Big Ed would keep his nose out of it. He'd have to, he'd be thousands of miles away. Carlos had kept Guidry in a box. Guidry would show Ed what he could do when the lid was off. Government, military, civilian contractors. The money, the hustle, the sizzle. Bourbon Street multiplied by a hundred.

He got into bed. Soon after, he heard the squeak of bedsprings. Charlotte in the room next door, right on the other side of the wall. He listened to her shift around. He heard her clear her throat.

Life wasn't complicated. Women weren't complicated. So why couldn't Guidry keep it straight, if he wanted Charlotte or not? If he wanted her or didn't want her or was just happy to lie there quietly in the darkness next to her?

Overnight the heat in the hotel waxed and waned. By morning the room was still freezing. Guidry woke shivering and followed the smell of hot coffee down to the lobby. My kingdom for a pint of scotch. The hotel bar didn't open until noon.

He took a chair by the fireplace. He noticed through

the window that Charlotte was standing outside with a camera, taking pictures of . . . what? He couldn't tell. She had the lens pointed down at the sidewalk. The wind made her hair dance and snap. When she reached up with one hand to tuck the hair back behind her ear, she kept the camera steady. She never moved her eye from the viewfinder.

He poured a cup of coffee for her and stepped outside. The morning was bright and cold. "Give me three guesses," he said. "No. Better let me have five of them."

"Move to your right, please," she said, pointing down.

"You're going to take a picture of my shadow?" he said.

"I'm bored with my own. Just a little bit more to your right. That's it."

"I'm not usually so accommodating."

"I'm not usually so demanding."

She snapped the photo and then set the camera down. Guidry handed over her coffee. She held the mug against her chin for a moment, for the warmth, before she took a sip.

"I can't explain it," she said. "Why I'm so fascinated by shadows. Look at yours. It's like it's trying to escape. Thank you for the coffee."

The morning sun still low in the sky, Guidry's

shadow straining, stretched taut across the sidewalk and folded up the brick front of the hotel. Lift a foot and away it would fly.

"Now I can't see anything but shadows everywhere," he said. "Look what you've done to me."

"You're very welcome," she said.

Guidry turned up his collar, but it wasn't as cold out as he'd thought, not with the sun full on your face. "You're up early."

"I'm the only one," she said. "Rosemary will sleep till noon if I let her."

"I'm sorry about yesterday. I should have known better."

"I should have told them already, the girls. That we're not going back to Oklahoma."

"Why haven't you?" he said.

"I don't know why, exactly. I feel guilty, I suppose."

"For what?"

He lit her cigarette. Even the smoke she exhaled, drifting away, had its own shadow.

"For everything," she said. "Leaving him. Taking the girls. I feel guilty for telling myself that I'm doing it for the girls, to make their lives better. I *am* doing it for them. But also for myself, of course. I feel guilty for not feeling more guilty, as silly as that sounds."

"Well," Guidry said, "my philosophy—"

And then he stopped himself. He'd almost forgotten for a moment that he was supposed to be Frank Wainwright, insurance salesman, not Frank Guidry, former fixer extraordinaire for the Marcello organization.

"Yes?" she said. "I'm all ears."

But maybe it was safest, Guidry decided, to speak his true mind. He didn't want to give a woman as sharp as Charlotte any extra opportunities to spot a fake.

"My philosophy is that guilt is an unhealthy habit," he said. "It's what other people try to make you feel so you'll do what they want. But one life is all we ever get, as far as I know. Why give it away?"

"My husband, when I called him from Santa Maria," she said, "he told me I was selfish."

"Of course he did. He doesn't want you to leave. And of course you are. Because you know what matters to you and you're not going to . . . What's the title of that song again? 'Don't Think Twice.'"

She smoked, thoughtful. "This has been an interesting conversation," she said.

"I concur," Guidry said.

Upstairs, ten minutes later, he was packing his suitcase and listening to the radio when a fist drummed on his door. He didn't panic. Paul Barone wouldn't knock first.

Paul Barone. It was the first time that Guidry had

allowed himself to think the name. He said a short prayer. To God or to Carlos? A distinction without a difference right now. Please, God or Carlos, don't send Paul Barone. Send somebody, anybody, else.

He opened the door. It was Charlotte. He knew right away that something was wrong.

"Frank," she said, her voice low and hoarse. "Joan's gone."

"What?" he said.

"I got back to the room and . . ." She was trying to stay calm. "Rosemary doesn't know where she went. She was asleep when Joan left. Joan's been upset about California, I think. I was only downstairs for half an hour, Frank."

"Don't worry," he said. "We'll find her. She can't have gone too far."

Joan must have slipped out the back way while they were having coffee in front of the hotel. Guidry and Charlotte split up. He went left down the alley behind the hotel, she went right. Guidry checked the doorways, behind the empty beer kegs. A man dumping potato peels and eggshells into a trash can said no, sorry, he hadn't seen any little blond girl.

Guidry poked his head into every shop and restaurant that was open. You're a kid, you're in a strange land, you want to go home. What do you do?

Well, of course. You go home. There was a bus depot two blocks over—they'd driven past it last night. Guidry beelined over, and sure enough there sat Joan—on a bench by the ticket window, so tiny, her coat buttoned up and a little purse in her lap. Not one jerk in the place stopping to see if she needed any help.

He sat down next to her. "Hello there, Joan. Where are you headed?"

"Home," she said. Solemn and inscrutable, like the stone Buddhas that Guidry had seen in the wrecked temples on Leyte.

"I thought you might be. Have you bought your ticket yet?"

She looked up at him.

"Don't worry," he said. "I'll take care of it for you."

"Thank you."

"You're a very polite young lady."

"Thank you."

"I don't know any children, so if it's all right with you, I'm just going to talk to you like I'd talk to anybody else."

Joan nodded.

"You think that if you go home," Guidry said, "to Oklahoma, everything will flip back to the way it was before. That's all you want, isn't it? You're not asking for much, just everything back the way it was before."

"Yes," she said.

"I understand that. Boy, do I. I had to leave my home, too, you know."

"Why?"

"Same as you. Circumstances beyond my control. And I'll tell you the truth that neither one of us wants to hear: The world turns. Time marches on. Life won't ever be the same. Even if you get on that bus and go back to Oklahoma. How old are you?"

"Eight," she said.

"Rosemary's younger, but she thinks she's the boss," he said.

"Yes."

"It'd be a shame if you two split up and she didn't have you to boss around. She wouldn't know what to do, would she?"

"No."

"It's all going to be new for you and me," Guidry said. "From here on out, wherever we go. Who knows? Maybe the new will be even better than the old. We won't know till we find out."

She started to cry. Guidry didn't know what to do. Put an arm around her or not? Pat her little blond head? He put an arm around her. She pressed her face against his chest. A spot spread across his shirt, hot and damp.

"Go ahead," he said. "I don't blame you."

Next to his chair was a spinning wire rack filled with tourist brochures. He reached out with his free hand and turned it. *Famous Arizona Ranches Welcome You. Saguaro National Monument. Grand Canyon and the Indian Empire.*

"Don't you want to see the Grand Canyon first?" he said. "Before you go back?"

Joan shook her head.

"Seems like a shame. To come all this way and miss it. The Grand Canyon, where once upon a time the mighty dinosaurs roamed."

Charlotte entered the depot. When she spotted Joan, Charlotte almost buckled with relief. Guidry thought for a moment that it might kill her.

"Joan," she said. "Oh, Joan."

He passed Joan over to Charlotte. "I believe this belongs to you, madam."

Joan had stopped crying, more or less. Charlotte kissed every inch of her wet, snotty face.

"We're going to see the Grand Canyon," Joan said.

Charlotte looked at Guidry. "We are?"

He'd stooped to pick up the little red vinyl purse, which had dropped to the floor. Oh, Joan, one day she'd learn never to take a man like Guidry at his word. But he couldn't afford to upset the applecart. He would need his new family in Vegas, better late than never.

"Of course we are," Guidry said. "Frank Wainwright never welches on a promise."

The Grand Canyon was ninety miles up, ninety miles back, so Guidry told the clerk at the hotel to hold their rooms for another night. They set off at just before noon. Unlike the Unpainted Desert and the Barely Petrified Forest, the Grand Canyon was truly grand. Guidry, who thought he'd seen it all, had seen nothing like it. Dusted with snow, impossible depths. Standing here on the brink, you felt smaller than small, a speck. You were forced to face the uncomfortable truth of your own existence: You did not, in the scheme of things, matter at all.

Charlotte kept the girls back a few feet from the edge, but it still made Guidry nervous, how they bounced and darted.

"Look, Joan!" Rosemary said. "I can see a river way down there!"

"So can I!" Joan said.

For a few hours, Guidry almost forgot about Carlos and Seraphine and Big Ed Zingel. About the unforeseeable fate that awaited him in Vegas. But then, driving back to Flagstaff, they heard a radio announcer report that President Johnson had created a special commission, headed by Earl Warren, to investigate the Kennedy assassination.

Here it was. The full weight of the federal government brought to bear. On Airline Highway in Metairie, Louisiana, Carlos Marcello paced and paced and paced while Seraphine tried her best to appear unruffled. Guidry could see it as if he were right there in the room with them.

Guidry had harbored a secret fantasy ever since Houston. A few weeks would pass, the FBI would pin everything on Oswald, they'd shut down the case. Carlos would breathe easy and decide that Guidry posed no real threat.

So much for that. Earl Warren was the chief justice of the Supreme Court of the United States of America. He wasn't in anybody's pocket, as far as Guidry knew. How much influence would Bobby Kennedy have? It didn't matter. Carlos wouldn't stop pacing until Guidry was dead.

"Is everything all right?" Charlotte asked.

Guidry turned to smile at her. "Of course. How about some music?"

At the hotel Charlotte tucked the girls in for the night and then she stepped back into the hallway to say good night to Guidry. She closed the door softly behind her.

"Thank you for your help this morning," she said. "With Joan."

"I think she'll be just fine," Guidry said.

"You're very good with children, you know."

"Am I? Listen, why don't you come downstairs and have a drink with me?"

"No." She reached up and brushed her thumb lightly against his cheek. The spot next to his right eye, where the bone curved. "Do you know you have a little scar here?"

"I do," he said. A waxy nick, the size and shape of a fingernail paring. Guidry couldn't remember exactly how he'd acquired it. The buckle of his father's belt, maybe? He remembered the general circumstances. "I was climbing a tree when I was a little boy. The bough broke, and down came baby, cradle and all."

"I'd like to take a photo of it sometime," she said, "if you don't mind."

"Of my scar?" he said.

She was standing close. Her hand still on his cheek, her other hand on his shoulder. "Let's go to your room," she said.

"You want to take a picture right now?" he said.

She kissed him. Sure of herself, sure of the kiss. Her thumb pressing lightly against his scar as she kissed him.

"No," she said. "Not right now."

21

He felt familiar in Charlotte's hand. A man was a man was a man, she supposed. Everything else, all the other parts of him—his fingers and his mouth and the rhythm of his breathing, the foreign flavor of his skin—that was what made it seem as if she'd fallen asleep and blundered into some other woman's dream.

Oops! Sorry! I'll show myself out.

Well, ahem, not just yet, not right away, if you don't mind.

Because it was a very nice dream. Charlotte kept her eyes open as Frank pushed against, into, and through her. She watched his face, his eyes. At the moment of connection, she felt the muscles in his stomach tighten. And then he smiled. She thought for a second that he might wink at her, but he didn't.

Who are you?

But that wasn't really what she was thinking, it wasn't really the question she wanted to have answered.

Who am I?

She was terrified and exhilarated and most of all curious. *Who am I?* Sunday dinner with Dooley's family had taken place five days ago. It seemed five centuries. That time and place were gone, "Charlotte Roy" gone, too, buried in lava and lost to posterity. The here and now was a room in an old hotel, a brass-and-cowhide light fixture overhead, a man she barely knew holding the lobe of her ear between his teeth.

He rose and fell. She arched her back and shifted to her left. More memories: her first few times with her first boyfriend, her first few times with Dooley. That period of tentative discovery and polite adaptation, of walking through the steps instead of dancing them. *Pardon me, madam. Allow me, sir.* The scrape of hair against a tender inner thigh, the unexpected clank of bone against bone. Charlotte had been with Dooley for so long that the sex between them had become effortless, a lazy glide through the motions. They could practically do it without even touching.

Frank smiled at her again. "You're thinking too much."

She knew she was. But still. "It's rather presumptuous of you to say so, isn't it?"

"Stop thinking so much," he said.

"Make me."

He eased himself out of her until almost nothing connected them, and then he eased himself even more slowly back in. She locked her legs around his waist and tried to catch her breath, but he refused to let her. Her head banged against the headboard—she heard it, didn't feel it—and now they were dancing, not thinking. She pushed him over and climbed on top. He lifted her up and threw her down. She forgot Dooley. She forgot Oklahoma. She forgot everything and concentrated on her own pleasure only. When she came, she grabbed for the cast-iron scrolls of the headboard, to keep from spinning into outer space, and accidentally punched Frank in the nose.

"I'm so sorry," she said after she'd had a minute (or was it five?) to loll like the dead on the cool sheets, to gather the various slivers of herself and reassemble them.

He laughed. "I'll get my gloves up next time."

"You're bleeding," she said.

"No I'm not." He checked, two fingers. "Yes I am."

While he was in the bathroom, Charlotte returned

to her room. The girls didn't stir. The dog padded after her and spread out on the tile, to supervise her shower.

"I'll thank you," she said, "to keep your opinion to yourself."

But the dog had already fallen back asleep. She laughed. Because he didn't give a damn about what she did or with whom she did it, and now Charlotte no longer had to give a damn either. The realization filled her with helium and sunlight. She stood in the shower for as long as she could bear it, letting the scalding water spill luxuriantly over her scalp and down the groove between her shoulders.

As she brushed her teeth, she inspected her reflection in the mirror. *Who am I?* She saw the same familiar eyes (too large, if you asked her, and set just a bit too wide apart), the same familiar mole on her neck (mortifying when she was a teenager, though she didn't mind it now), the same familiar nose and lips and chin.

But appearances could deceive. The woman who'd walked into that grimy garage back in Santa Maria was not the same woman who walked out of it. The decision Charlotte made that day—to leave Dooley and Oklahoma behind once and for all, to stop doubting herself—had caused the beginning of a shift inside her.

She'd felt it, like the branches of a tree stirring as the wind picked up.

When Frank offered to drive them to Las Vegas, Charlotte should have tossed and turned all night, she should have dithered and wavered. Well, there *had* been a fair bit of that, it was true. Because she wasn't naïve. She'd known that Frank was attracted to her, that his generosity was not entirely virtuous. And there was something about him that Charlotte still couldn't quite put her finger on, a certain intricacy of character that was at odds with what he'd told her of himself.

Deep down, though, she'd had a good feeling about him. And she'd trusted that feeling, she'd trusted herself to make the right decision.

If Charlotte was going to make the most of her one and only life, if she was going to help Rosemary and Joan do the same, she'd need to seize every opportunity, *don't think twice.*

Saturday morning she woke the girls early so that they could walk the dog with her. They grumbled, but Charlotte persisted. She'd already waited too long to tell them the truth.

A bakery a few blocks over sold sugared elephant ears. Charlotte bought one for them to share, and they found a place to sit on the sunny courthouse steps. Rosemary explained to Joan that an elephant ear was not *really* an elephant's ear, don't worry, it was just *called* that, because nobody would ever *really* eat a real elephant's ear.

Charlotte wondered when Rosemary would finally drive her sister up the wall. Joan had the patience of Job, but sooner or later—in junior high or high school or on Joan's wedding day, when Rosemary insisted on this piece of music, not that one—Joan would turn to Rosemary and say, *For God's sake, just be quiet for one . . . minute . . . please.* Or maybe she wouldn't. Maybe Rosemary was exactly the sister that Joan wanted and needed. It made Charlotte happy to think so.

"Girls," Charlotte said. "I know how much you miss Daddy."

"He's going to meet us in California," Rosemary said, "at Aunt Marguerite's house on the beach, when he's done at work. He's going to fly on an airplane to meet us there. Isn't that right, Mommy? We're going to stay two weeks in California, and we'll go to Disneyland."

Charlotte marveled at the conclusions to which Rosemary steered herself, always so detailed and convincing.

"No," Charlotte said. "Daddy isn't going to meet us in California. He's going to live in Oklahoma and we're going to live in California."

"But . . ." Rosemary said.

"Sometimes it's best for grown-ups, for parents, to live in different places. It's best for everyone. You'll still get to talk to Daddy on the telephone. And you'll still see him. He'll come visit. You'll go visit him."

"But . . ." Rosemary searched desperately for a loophole, a chink of light, the secret passage leading through castle walls that only appeared to be solid. What if . . . maybe . . . ?

When the truth finally pierced her defenses, when Rosemary's face crumpled, Charlotte felt the pain just as sharply as she did. "Come here, sweetie," she said.

Rosemary shook her head and staggered away, sobbing and hiccupping. She made it a few feet before she tripped and skinned her knee on the concrete step.

Joan reached her before Charlotte did. She sat down next to Rosemary and put her arms around her. Rosemary tried to escape, but Joan calmly, stubbornly refused to let go. She whispered something in Rosemary's ear that Charlotte couldn't hear until, finally, Rosemary caught her breath and stopped crying.

Charlotte dabbed at Rosemary's skinned knee with her handkerchief, but she knew enough to say nothing.

When they got back to hotel, Frank was in the lobby, standing by the fireplace and drinking coffee. He frowned when he saw Rosemary's knee.

"Rosemary took a tumble, I'm afraid," Charlotte said. "We were having a discussion about California."

He grasped the situation and crouched to examine the knee. "Tell me what happened, Rosemary," he said. "And don't leave out any details."

"I fell," Rosemary said.

"That's it? Rosemary, an adventure like this deserves an interesting story. Don't you agree?"

Rosemary continued to sniff and snuffle, but she liked adventures, she liked stories. "Maybe," she said. "Yes."

"'I fell.' You can do better than that," he said. "I'll give you an hour. Two if you need it. Do we have a deal?"

Up in the room, Charlotte washed the knee with soap and put a Band-Aid on it. Rosemary's face needed washing, too, after all the crying and the sugared elephant ear.

They packed their bags and carried them downstairs. Frank had already settled the bill, so Charlotte opened her wallet and took out a twenty-dollar bill.

"The room's already paid for," he said.

"No," she said. "It's not."

"Charlotte . . ." But when he saw that she wasn't going to yield, he accepted the money. "I'll bring the car around."

While she waited, she asked the room clerk if she could use his desk phone to make a collect call. Dooley picked up immediately, as if he'd been staring at the phone and just waiting for it to ring.

"Charlie?" Dooley said. "Is that you?"

"Yes, it's me," she said.

"Where the hell are you, Charlie? You said you were coming home."

She hadn't said that. She knew she hadn't. "I'm not coming home, Dooley. I'm going to get a divorce. I just wanted to let you know that we're fine. The girls are fine. I don't want you to worry."

"You don't want me to worry? Why are you doing this to me, Charlie? I can't stand it, another second away from you and the girls."

He sounded the way Rosemary's knee looked, scraped and raw. When Charlotte remained silent, he tried again, his voice softer, gentler.

"I'll stop drinking, Charlie," he said. "I know I'm not worth a damn, but I can do that. I'll stop drinking, I swear. I can do that for you."

Charlotte's old self would have wavered. Was she a terrible person for leaving her husband of nearly ten years behind? Her new self marveled at how easy it was for her to recognize now, from this fresh perspective, Dooley's various tactics.

"Do you want to say hello to the girls?" she said.

"I want you to come home, Charlie. That's what I want. Now, listen to me. If—"

"Good-bye, Dooley. Take care of yourself, will you?" she said. "I'll call you again when we get to California."

She hung up. She thought for a moment and then asked the room clerk if she could make a long-distance call and pay him for it. He agreed, and Charlotte dialed Aunt Marguerite's number.

"Aunt Marguerite," Charlotte said when she answered, "it's me again. It's Charlotte."

"Charlotte."

Clipped, curt, and followed by what Charlotte suspected might have been a sigh. Charlotte chose to ignore it. She chose to ignore the jab of panic between her ribs, the flush of embarrassment spreading over her, the voice in her ear that whispered urgently, *Sit down, be quiet, what do you think you're doing?*

You could do that, she was discovering. Experience an emotion without allowing it to determine your actions. Hear a knock on the door without feeling compelled to open it. The world didn't end, towers didn't topple. Life went on.

"Hello, Aunt Marguerite," she said. "How are you?"

"I'm quite busy at the moment," Marguerite said.

"Then I'll try not to take up too much of your time.

My husband and I are getting a divorce. It's decided. I've decided. And I'm coming to Los Angeles with the girls. I've decided that, too. We'd like to stay with you for a month or two, until I find a job and a permanent place to live."

"Charlotte—"

"I know you said that it's not a good idea," Charlotte said. "And I wholeheartedly agree. But I don't have a better idea right now, Marguerite. I'm quite new at this, and it's quite overwhelming, and my plan, such as it is, is to put one foot in front of the other, one step at a time. My daughters are very well behaved. Well, they're little girls, and I don't doubt that they'll be a disruption. I'm happy to share a room with them, of course. I'm happy to sleep in a cupboard, if it comes to that. I'm under no illusions how difficult Los Angeles will be. I don't think I am, anyway. I'll have my own car. I hope to have my own car. I'm under no illusions how difficult my life will be wherever I go, which is why I'd be so very grateful for your help. You're the only family I have left."

Charlotte took a breath. She'd intended her speech to be more succinct, less haphazardly organized, but she supposed that she'd made her point. Whatever Marguerite's answer might be, Charlotte at least felt better about herself now.

"Well." And then Marguerite laughed. A surprise in itself, but even more so because her laugh—a hearty boom and an expansive rippling—in no way resembled her clipped, chip-of-ice speaking voice. "It appears you haven't given me a choice, have you?"

"We have a dog, too, by the way," Charlotte said. "He has epilepsy."

"I have a cat with one eye," Marguerite said. "Perhaps they'll be friends."

Charlotte took another breath, and then she laughed as well. "Thank you, Marguerite."

"When will you arrive?"

"We're going to Las Vegas for a day or two first. So we should be in Los Angeles by the end of the week, I think."

"Very well. I'll prepare the cupboard for you."

Frank had returned with the car. Everyone piled in. As they drove, Rosemary related the story of her scraped knee. It involved outlaw bandits, a giant Indian with a tomahawk who badly needed a friend, a headlong chase across the desert. On and on the story went. Charlotte smiled, drowsing contentedly in the front seat. Rosemary was still adding details to her adventure when they turned north and crossed the Nevada state line.

22

"I never been nowhere but Texas before," the colored kid said.

"Congratulations," Barone said. "You're a world traveler now."

Tucumcari, New Mexico. Half a dozen motels strung along Highway 66. Barone checked them all.

I'm a private dick. I'm looking for a guy. He ran out on his wife and kids back home, and the wife hired me to find him. Might be driving a Dodge, blue over white. I don't know what name he's using. Let me tell you what he looks like.

After that: two motels in Santa Rosa, two in Clines Corners, one in Moriarty. The same spiel, the same blank look in return, the same, *Sorry, nope, nuh-uh, haven't seen him.*

Barone watched the rearview mirror. Now that they were out of Texas, he wasn't too worried about the cops. They didn't have any good way to track him down.

They spent Wednesday night in Moriarty. Barone had overdone it. He could barely make it from the car to his room. The kid walked down the street to the only restaurant in town and brought back a bowl of soup for Barone. He gave Barone his pills and crumbled saltines into the soup, the way he said his sisters did for him back in Houston whenever he was sick.

A full night's sleep did wonders for Barone. Thursday morning, Thanksgiving Day, he felt more or less right again. The swelling in his hand, when he peeked under the bandage, had gone most of the way down.

It took Barone all day to check the motels and hotels and rooming houses in Albuquerque. In between stops the kid shared his many opinions. He said he'd never go to work for a company like Barone's, one that didn't let him have a day off every now and then. He said he planned to find himself a pretty woman with a head on her shoulders and get married just as soon as he graduated high school, year after next. Or maybe he'd join the army first.

"You don't want to join the army," Barone said.

"Why don't I?" the kid said.

"Just listen to me. And why are you so hot on getting married so quick?"

"Shoot. Why am I so hot on getting married so quick."

"I don't know. That's why I asked."

"Why don't you introduce me to her?" the kid said. "That colored-lady lawyer you was talking 'bout the other day."

Friday they covered the rest of New Mexico and a good piece of Arizona. As they neared Holbrook, one radio station faded out and another faded in. The song that was playing emerged bit by bit, like bubbles rising to the water's surface.

"'Round Midnight." There it was again, the Billy Taylor piano version this time. It was like the song was following Barone. Or like he was following it.

"Do you believe in God?" Barone said.

"Why you want to know?" the kid said.

"Why don't you want to tell me?"

The kid scowled for a mile or two. He was a careful and conscientious driver. He never took his hands off the wheel or his eyes off the road. Maybe when all this was over, Barone *would* introduce him to Seraphine, put in a word and get the kid a permanent job.

"Yes and no," the kid said, "do I believe in God."

"You can't have it both ways," Barone said.

"I believe Jesus wasn't no white man."

"Where'd you hear that?"

"I heard it."

They stopped for the night in Holbrook and checked in to the Sun and Sand Motel. Tried to check in. When the manager saw the kid, he shook his head. The manager was bloodshot and fat, maybe an ex-cop gone to seed, that kind of curl to his lip.

"Nope," the manager said. "No. Nosirree."

"What?" Barone said.

The manager curled his lip. "We've experienced a sudden lack of vacancy."

Barone could have shot him. Better yet, strap him to a chair and drop him in the deep end of the swimming pool. Watch down through shifting plates of light and water as his eyes bulged out and it dawned on him—this was it, the end, curtains. The moment took a lot of people by surprise, even when it shouldn't have.

The kid had disappeared. Barone found him back outside in the car.

"What are you doing?" Barone said.

"Sleep in the car. I don't mind."

"No."

They backtracked a quarter of a mile to Lucille's Come On Inn. Lucille, if that's who she was, eyeballed the kid. She shook her head as if to mourn the sorry state of world affairs, little Negroes roaming free on the mother road. Finally, though, she surrendered a room key.

The kid soaked a cold washrag for Barone to put on his forehead. "We need us a Green Book."

"A what?"

"A Green Book. Shows you where to stop along the way if you're colored. So you don't ruffle no feathers. Colored folks take vacations, too. Shoot. You think they don't?"

Barone didn't know what the hell the kid was talking about. He was used to it by now.

"Here's a five-dollar bill," Barone said. "Bring me some whiskey or don't come back."

"Take your pill," the kid said. "Drink that water."

The next day, Saturday, Barone checked Winslow. No luck. On to Flagstaff.

At an old-timey hotel downtown, he ran through his spiel for the thirtieth, the fortieth, the fiftieth time.

I'm a private dick. I'm looking for a guy. He ran out on his wife and kids back home, and the wife hired me to find him. Might be driving a Dodge, blue over white. I don't know what name he's using.

The clerk wore an old-timey string tie made out of braided leather, with a silver-and-turquoise clasp. Probably the hotel owner made him wear the tie so that he fit with the hotel.

"No, I can't think of anybody like that." The clerk checked his big book. "No. Just families and lovebirds."

Barone had this all wrong. It was a possibility. The sheriff in Texas had lied, and Barone had been snowed. Barone didn't like to think so. Guidry could have headed east, not west. Or he'd driven twenty-four hours straight to Los Angeles, not stopping to sleep along the way. He was already in Mexico.

Half past noon. It felt like half past midnight. Barone wanted to lie down and sleep for a year or two. But he never quit a job. It was his only good quality and had been so for his entire life. Even his stepmother, who hated his guts, used to admit it. Paul Barone never quits.

And the song he'd heard again yesterday. "'Round Midnight." Maybe it didn't mean anything. Maybe it did.

So he described Guidry—for the thirtieth, the fortieth, the fiftieth time—to the clerk in the old-timey string tie. Height and weight. Dark hair, light eyes, the smile. The way Guidry tried to make you feel like the two of you were already old pals.

The clerk thought about it for a second. "Well, you know . . . No."

Barone felt a prickle. "Go ahead."

"That does sound an awful lot like Mr. Wainwright," the clerk said. "But he was *with* his wife. And his daughters."

"His wife and his daughters?" Barone said.

"They arrived together. Yes. I watched them leave together, too."

That wasn't Guidry. It couldn't be Guidry. "What else about him?"

"What else about him?" the clerk said.

"About Mr. Wainwright. Think."

"Well . . ." The clerk perked up. "He had a bit of an accent, now that I think about it. A bit like yours."

Guidry, the crafty son of a bitch. Somehow he'd managed to pick up a wife and kids along the way, like a hat and coat off the rack. The disguise had almost worked.

"When did they leave?" Barone said.

"This morning," the clerk said. "Around nine."

Barone stared. Guidry wasn't in Mexico. He was only three hours in front of Barone.

"Where were they headed?" Barone said. "Do you know?"

The clerk hesitated. Barone had to stop himself from taking out his new Police Positive .38 and sticking it in the clerk's face.

"She just wants him to call her," Barone said. "His wife does. That's all. She's torn to pieces. He's not a bad egg. He fell in love with somebody else. I'm not going to hassle him. But if I don't find him and get him to call home, I don't get paid."

The clerk relented. "They're going to Las Vegas," he said. "I heard her say so on the phone, Mrs. Wainwright did. Or Mr. Wainwright's . . . companion."

Barone went outside. There was a phone booth across the street.

"He's headed to Vegas," Barone told Seraphine. "I'm three hours behind him."

"I see." She tried to hide the relief in her voice. Barone heard it. Probably she heard the relief in his voice, too. "Carlos will be so pleased. Go see Stan Contini at the Tropicana. You'll need to tread lightly in Las Vegas. Do you understand?"

"I know what to do." He started to hang up.

"One more thing, *mon cher,*" she said.

"What is it."

"The incident at the police station in Texas? I've just heard from a reliable source that the suspect is a white man traveling with a Negro boy in his teens."

The waitress at the diner. Barone had forgotten about her. He'd made himself forget about her.

"Is this troubling news?" Seraphine said.

"Why would it be?" Barone said.

"If the police know that—"

"I'll call you from Vegas."

Barone hung up. On the way out of Flagstaff, he told the kid to stop at a supper club called the Tall Pine Inn. *Fine Atmosphere, Good Food, Beer and Wine to Go.* Barone bought two six-packs of Schlitz to go.

"I know what the doctor said," Barone said. "It's just beer. Let me celebrate."

"Gimme one," the kid said.

"You're driving. Forget it."

A couple of miles later, Barone handed the kid a can. "Put some music on."

They couldn't find anything worth listening to. Hillbilly yodelers and brimstone preachers and Lesley Gore crying at her own party. She was the worst of the bunch, her voice like getting nails hammered into your skull.

Barone turned the radio off. The kid finished his beer and reached for a second one. Not asking permission, feeling his oats.

"No more after that one," Barone said. "Better make it last."

"Shoot," the kid said. "Better make it last."

"That's what I said."

"How 'bout you?"

"What about me?"

"You believe in God?" the kid said.

"Not the one most people do," Barone said.

They'd left behind the piney mountains. The bone-dead desert stretched before them. A sign with a bullet hole punched through the sheet metal said LAS VEGAS 150 MILES.

The kid started singing the Lesley Gore song in a fractured falsetto. He'd get halfway through the opening and then crack himself up, have to start all over again. Drunk on two and a half cans of weak beer.

"Whoo!" the kid said. "I gotta take a leak."

"I'm not going to stop you," Barone said.

There was a dry wash that ran parallel to the highway, fifty feet off into the desert and deep enough that you could do your business in private.

"Up there," Barone said. "Pull off."

"Let me ask you something," the kid said.

"I thought you had to take a leak. Go on. I've got to take one, too."

"Let me ask you something."

"What?"

"I forgot."

Barone followed the kid down into the wash. He'd planned to use his belt, keep it quiet, but he liked the kid and the belt was a slow way to go. Plus, Barone wasn't feeling all the way up to snuff yet, still weak from the fever and with the bad right hand. So he shot the kid once in the back of the head with the Police Positive and then twice more between the shoulders.

He climbed out of the ravine. The highway was clear, miles in each direction. Barone got into the car, behind the wheel. The climb had taken the breath out of him, but he didn't have far to go now.

23

Big Ed Zingel. Where to begin? Guidry met him for the first time in 1955, at a shindig Moe Dalitz threw to celebrate the opening of the Dunes. Sinatra was there, Rita Hayworth and her husband, Dick Haymes. After the show in the main room, Vera-Ellen stopped by to mingle and play craps.

Then as now Ed was at the center of the spiderweb in Vegas. Moe Dalitz's associates back east preferred to make money, not spend it, so they needed someone who could line up straight investors to build and expand the casinos. Ed brought in Valley National Bank in Phoenix, schoolteacher pension funds from California, you name it. He had the touch. He'd already made one fortune during the war, buying old silver mines and stripping them for construction materials.

At the Dunes party in '55, Big Ed had handed Guidry a business card with his name, a telephone number, and two words in elegant embossed script: *"Big Ideas."*

They'd chatted. Ed had taken a shine to Guidry. "I like the cut of your jib, kid." Until Ed discovered that Guidry worked for Carlos Marcello.

"You know what I'd like to see?" Ed grabbed another glass of champagne from the waiter and mused. "I'd like to see that backstabbing cocksucker's face when he opens a package and inside it's full of pieces of you. How sore would he be, do you think?"

Big Ed, dead serious. Guidry could play this one of two ways: the right way or the wrong way. Which was which?

"It depends on the pieces," Guidry said.

Ed laughed and laughed. The kid with the well-cut jib wiped sweat from his brow, relieved. Because Big Ed Zingel was no joke. That very night he'd given a toast to his old friend and business partner Maury Schiffman that was so heartfelt not an eye remained dry. Two weeks later Maury and his wife were found dead in their vacation cabin in Tahoe, Maury strangled and the wife shot in the head. Rumor had it that Big Ed killed them himself, just for kicks. Sofa pillows had been placed around the wife's head so her brains wouldn't leak onto the expensive Oriental rug.

More recently, a year or so ago, Hoover had wanted an inside peek at Ed's operation. The FBI didn't have any female agents, so they picked a number from the typing pool to go undercover. The girl never stood a chance. Ed sniffed her out and sent Hoover a message.

"He's a real sweetheart, humble as pie," Guidry told Charlotte. She'd never have to meet Ed, so Guidry could lay it on thick. "He built a hospital in Las Vegas, every dime out of his own pocket, but he wouldn't let them put his name on it."

"And you really think he'll just . . . loan me a car?" she said.

"I do think so," Guidry said. "He's out of town for the next couple of days, but once he gets back, you can count on it."

"How do you two know each other?"

"Besides the dealerships he owns the biggest insurance agency in Nevada. That's how we met, at a convention in Minneapolis. We started jawing about policy proceeds."

Guidry made it to Vegas only once every year or so. Ed always made time for drinks or dinner. At the end of the evening, he'd give Guidry a bear hug. "Guys like us, we have to stick together."

Las Vegas approached. Too bad it was only one o'clock in the afternoon. Vegas was best at dusk. The mountains banded with different shades of purple, the lights of the Strip heating the low-hanging clouds like coals.

Guidry looked over at Charlotte. He moved his knee so that it touched hers. She smiled and pressed her knee back against his. In bed last night, he'd had the usual good time. Better than the usual. He hadn't lost interest halfway through. He hadn't wanted to be somewhere else.

"I read in a magazine that they test atomic bombs near Las Vegas," Charlotte said. The girls were asleep in the backseat. "I read that families drive out to watch, like they're watching a drive-in movie."

"Not for the last few years," Guidry said. "Before that, yes. You could see the blast from the top floor of the hotels downtown. From the roofs."

"Really?" she said.

"Kiss me."

Charlotte smiled again but didn't turn from the window. "An atomic bomb. I don't think I'd want to see something like that."

"Neither would I," Guidry said.

"I know it's supposed to be beautiful. Maybe I'd take a picture of the people watching the explosion instead."

Keep your eye on the ball, Guidry cautioned himself again. A man like Big Ed required one's complete attention. Ed enjoyed the sport of life, and Guidry could expect, in the best of circumstances, a surprise twist or two. In the worst of circumstances, Ed had lured Guidry to Vegas so that he could sell him back to Carlos. Ed was a businessman, after all, and what profiteth it a man if he made no profit?

And even if Ed fully intended to honor his promise to Guidry today, his mood might shift on a whim tomorrow. Ed's mood was notorious for doing just that.

"You take pictures of shadows," Guidry said. "You take pictures of people watching the thing, but not of the thing they're watching."

She laughed. "You're baffled."

"I'm intrigued," he said.

"I like . . . what gets missed."

"What gets missed?"

"Every morning when I step out the front door, I always look over to the left, to see if Mr. Broom is on his porch. And I always think the same thing: He's such a grouch, why do I even bother to wave? And then I look to the right, at the crepe myrtle by the fence. And I always think the same thing, that I wish it bloomed for more than just a few weeks every summer."

He liked how he didn't know which turn her mind might take next. "*Now* I'm baffled," he said.

"When I have a camera in my hand, it reminds me

to look in new places. To have new thoughts, I suppose." She laughed again, embarrassed. "Just listen to me. Or rather please don't."

"Please don't stop," Guidry said. "I beg of you."

The Hacienda suited Guidry's needs to a tee. The only casino and resort in Las Vegas aimed at squares and families, with a miniature-golf course and a go-kart track. The only casino and resort stranded at the southern end of the Strip, across from the airport and far from all the swinging joints. The only casino and resort with no mob connection. The Hacienda lost money every year, even without a rake. It wasn't worth the trouble.

Sure, never say never, Guidry might run into someone he knew at the Hacienda, but it was unlikely. And with Charlotte and the girls by his side, he'd blend right in.

The sign towered above the parking lot, a cowboy on a bucking bronco waving hello, hello, hello, to the passing motorists—or maybe good-bye, good-bye, good-bye to his money. He put old Big Chief back in Arizona to shame.

Rosemary and Joan oohed and aahed. There was a Bonnie Best dress shop in the lobby, and the theater marquee advertised a puppet show called *Les Poupées de Paris.* Guidry translated for them: The Dolls of Paris.

"Mommy," Rosemary said, her voice hushed, like she was in church. "Do you know what this is just like?"

"What, sweetie?" Charlotte said.

"It's just like the movie," Joan said, her voice hushed, too. "Like *The Wizard of Oz.*"

The desk clerk barely glanced at the dog. Las Vegas was like New Orleans in that respect: Anything goes, as long as you had the dough to pay for it. God bless America.

Too chilly to swim this time of year but warm enough to eat lunch outside by the sparkling pool. The hot dogs came with ketchup, mustard, and pickle relish, each condiment in its own dish with its own tiny spoon. Rosemary and Joan had died and gone to heaven.

Lists and more lists. Favorite colors. Favorite songs. Favorite foods. Guidry tried to add fried eggs to the list of favorite foods and was duly corrected. Favorite *lunch* foods.

He hadn't realized until now just how much the girls resembled their mother. They had the same set to the jaw, the same way of looking life right in the eye. Letting it know, *Go ahead and just try, I dare you.*

Favorite books. Favorite fairy tales. Favorite characters in fairy tales. The wind ruffled the surface of the pool.

He didn't hit the girls, the father. That was Guidry's well-educated guess, now that he'd spent a few days around them. Maybe the guy was crazy about his daughters. Guidry couldn't see any reason he wouldn't be. Did the guy, now that he'd lost his kids, feel like his heart had been torn from his chest? How did it feel to feel that way? Guidry had forgotten. He had no desire to find out again.

"Hey," he said. "Who wants to go drive the go-karts?"

But you had to be at least twelve years old to get behind the wheel. So they played miniature golf instead. Guidry discovered that he was a bad miniature golfer. Truly awful. He skipped the ball off the slope of the volcano, sank it in the drink, missed the windmill entirely. The girls remained unfailingly polite. "Don't worry, that was a very hard hole."

Before her last putt, Charlotte paused. She looked up, around. At the palm trees and the casino towers down the Strip. At Guidry.

"Where *am* I?" she said.

Guidry didn't have to ask what she meant. He understood exactly.

In bed that night, Guidry once again couldn't get

enough of Charlotte. You'd have thought that Charlotte was the first naked woman he'd ever had his hands on, his mouth.

Afterward he lifted his arm and she slipped underneath to lay her head on his chest. A perfect fit, like the tumblers of a lock clicking into place. He turned his knee, and she hooked a bare leg over. They'd left the drapes open. The moonlight hummed.

With most women Guidry would've been shot out of the cannon by now, already dressed and halfway out the door. But he had to play the part, didn't he? Frank Wainwright. The skin of her inner thigh was warm and silky and sticky. He could feel her pulse just beneath the skin, the beat of the band slowing bar by bar. So what if he happened to like the role he was acting, the part he was playing? It was still only that, a role, a part.

She ran her palm over his chest, almost touching it but not quite, like she was checking to see if a stove burner was hot.

"You're hairy," she said.

"You've just now noticed?" he said.

In the drowsy, dreamy moonlight, it wasn't hard for Guidry to imagine that this was really his life. It wasn't hard to imagine a different life for Annette, too. Where would his baby sister be right now? Not stuck in Ascension Parish, Louisiana, Guidry could promise you that.

A nurse. Yes. The cool head in a crisis, up to her elbows in blood and guts, never batting an eyelash, keeping boys alive during the war until the doctors could sew them back together.

She fell for one of those dogfaces, a big-beamed, broad-shouldered sergeant, jovial and kindhearted. Were there those sorts of men in the world? Maybe there were. Guidry came to every Christmas dinner, he spoiled his nieces and nephews rotten. Annette lectured him affectionately. She told him to find a woman as smart as him, or smarter, even better. Don't be scared, Frick, she won't bite. She still called him Frick, from when she was a fat, wobbly toddler and couldn't pronounce his name. He still called her Frack.

Someday she'd have to die, but this time in a hospital bed, surrounded by kids and grandkids and flowers in vases, her big brother holding her hand.

"Were you ever married, Frank?" Charlotte said.

"No."

Her hand had moved to his face. Her fingers traced the outline of his lips, his nose, his cheek, the scar.

"I don't want to go," she said.

He didn't want her to go either. When she left, the curtain would come down and Frank Wainwright would exit stage left. He'd already put off the call to Ed longer than was wise. He couldn't put it off any longer.

"You know you can spend the night here," he said.

"You know I can't," she said.

"The girls are just across the hall, and they're sound sleepers. You said so yourself."

She swung out of bed and got dressed. When she finished, she gathered the hair off her long, bare neck, twisted, snapped a rubber band in place. He reached for her hand, but she was already moving toward the bureau. She buttoned the last button of her blouse and gave herself a quick appraising glance in the mirror.

"I fell out of a tree once, too," she said.

Guidry lagged for a beat. And then, when she noticed, when she turned to look at him, he realized that she was talking about the scar under his eye, the lie he'd told about it. He tried to cover with a yawn and a stretch. Get your head out of your ass, he warned himself again. If he got lazy or too comfortable around Big Ed Zingel, the hammer would drop.

"Most kids do, I imagine," he said. "I just happen to have the ding to prove it."

She studied him for another moment and then put on her shoes.

"I remember lying on my back and staring up at the sky," she said. "I wasn't hurt, just the wind knocked out of me. Stunned. One second I was in the tree, the next second I was down on the ground. I remember thinking, 'Now, how did that happen?'"

"I'm impressed," he said. "I started bawling, probably."

She leaned down to kiss him good-bye. "I don't really know much about you, do I?"

Guidry, prepared now, plenty of lies at hand, started to say, *What do you want to know about me?* But as she moved toward the door, he realized that she'd been observing, not wondering.

"Shall we all have breakfast together tomorrow morning?" he said.

"It's a date," she said.

The Hacienda was only two stories tall. From his window Guidry couldn't see the Strip or the mountains or even the pool. Just the moon and the razor-cut silhouettes of a few palm trees. He stood and listened to the faint fizzing and *pop-pop-pop* from the go-kart track for a while, and then he watched old reruns of *Janet Dean, Registered Nurse.* Poor Ella Raines, that good heart of hers always landing her in hot water.

Almost midnight. Quit stalling. Pick up the phone and dial the fucking thing.

The guy with the silky British accent answered. "Good evening," he said. "The Zingel residence."

"It's Ed's old pal from New Orleans," Guidry said.

Guidry waited. Here we go. His last chance to read the tea leaves, to get a bead on Ed's true intentions, good or evil, before it was too late. In the pulp westerns that Guidry had loved as a youth, the cowboy outlaw hero would put his ear to the iron rail and try to feel the vibrations of a train barreling down the tracks.

"Where are you?" Big Ed asked. "I thought you said you'd be here yesterday."

"You're eager to see me," Guidry said.

"Why wouldn't I be?"

Guidry smiled. Some men played cards, others chased girls. Ed liked to make you sweat. "Stop toying with me, Ed. I'm already worried down to a nub."

"Stop what?" Ed said. "All right, all right. You can count on me, boychick. I haven't changed my mind. There. Does that make you feel better?"

Guidry tried to pick up the vibrations in the smooth iron rail of Ed's voice. Did Ed mean what he said? Or did he just believe that he meant it? Had he even made up his mind yet, what he was going to do about Guidry?

"You know when I'll feel better, Ed?" Guidry said.

"When you're on a plane to beautiful Indochina," Ed said.

No. When the plane had landed in Indochina and Guidry hadn't been shoved out of the cargo door somewhere over the Pacific Ocean.

"We have a lot to talk about," Ed said. "Now, tell me where you're staying. I'll send Leo to pick you up. Tomorrow at one o'clock. We'll have a nice lunch."

"I'll take a cab," Guidry said. "I don't want to put you out."

Ed laughed. "Where are you staying?"

"The Hacienda."

"The Hacienda? What, you want to die of boredom?"

"I'm lying low, Ed. Maybe it slipped your mind why I'm here."

"Who wants a life without a little snap, crackle, and pop?" Ed said.

Guidry thought about the moment, during the game of miniature golf, when Charlotte looked up and around. Where am I? How did I get here?

"Tomorrow at one," Guidry said. "I'll be ready."

24

S unday morning. Pancakes and maple syrup for breakfast. A stroll around the resort. Joan spotted a lizard, baking on the sidewalk. Blinking, blinking, and then pop, gone. A game of checkers, fetch with the dog, more miniature golf. Guidry finally started to get the hang of the golf. Rosemary and Joan cheered his every putt. I could become accustomed to this, he thought. Accustomed to what, exactly? He wasn't sure.

After the last hole, Guidry told Charlotte that he was off to meet his friend, the saintly and charitable car dealer. He made the girls promise, cross their hearts, not to have too much fun without him.

"I'll be back in a couple of hours," he said. "Wish me luck."

Out front idled a Rolls-Royce Silver Cloud. The driver opened the rear door for Guidry. He was in his early seventies, tall and slender and debonair as hell, with a pencil-line mustache and a black-on-black Savile Row suit.

"Welcome to Las Vegas," he said. The silky English accent from the phone. "I'm Leo, Mr. Zingel's assistant. I trust you had a pleasant journey?"

Guidry looked over Leo. Guidry looked over the Rolls. The car was a mile long, sleek and gleaming, painted the metallic green shade of a menacing sky.

"Ed likes to make an impression, doesn't he?" Guidry said.

Leo kept a straight face, but Guidry spotted a wry twinkle in his eye. "I'm sure I don't know what you mean," he said.

They drove north up the Strip and then turned east on Bonanza. Guidry had never been to Ed's house before. He envisioned a stone Tudor manor, gardens and manicured lawns, a secret room down in the basement with tile walls and a drain in the middle of the floor.

"Leo," Guidry said. "Tell me. How long have you worked for Ed?"

"Almost twenty years," Leo said.

"It's been quite an adventure, has it?"

The straight face, the wry twinkle. "Quite."

They drove past the old neighborhoods, past the new neighborhoods. Las Vegas was booming, sprawling, leaking like a stain into the desert. Sure, the weather in winter was pleasant. But what else? Nothing. The city had the charm of chewing gum that you scraped off the bottom of your shoe.

Guidry wished he could show Charlotte around New Orleans. The French Quarter on a quiet Sunday morning, when only the birds and the birdlike old ladies were awake. The Garden District, the river at sunset, Plum Street Snowballs. Rosemary and Joan would flip when they saw the zoo at Audubon Park.

"How much farther?" Guidry said.

They were in the desert bona fide now. Civilization, if that was what you wanted to call Las Vegas, dwindled away behind them.

"Not far," Leo said.

"Ed lives all the way out here?"

Leo lifted a finger off the wheel and gave it a flick. Was that a yes? Guidry was familiar with the mob's purity code. Dirty business in Vegas depended on legal gambling, and legal gambling depended on the precarious fiction that business in Vegas was clean. So the various factions had an agreement: no public spats, no blood spilled or brains blown in front of the tourists. If a guy in Vegas needed hitting, take him out to the lonely desert—just like this!—and hit him there.

"You're a handsome devil, Leo," Guidry said. "I bet back in the day you had the ladies lined up around the block."

That finally got a smile out of Leo.

"No?" Guidry said. He'd had his suspicions. "The lads lined up, then. Come visit New Orleans and I'll make a few introductions."

They'd been driving for twenty minutes. They were miles outside of Vegas proper.

"What am I getting myself into, Leo?" Guidry said.

"I beg your pardon?"

"Give me a hint. What awaits me? Out of the goodness of your heart. It's too late for me to do anything about it, so what's the harm?"

Leo slowed the Silver Cloud. He turned onto a rough gravel road that sawed off into the rocks. After a quarter mile or so, around a cut, the gravel yielded to a freshly paved driveway lined with cactus.

"We have arrived," Leo said.

Ed had gone space-age mod instead of Tudor. The house was a rambling split-level with entire walls made of windows and a flat white roof angled to look like the sail of a ship, like a shark fin. The grand entryway was framed by cement blocks arranged in a complexly decorative lattice.

"Well?" Ed came out of the house, wearing his usual. Billowing linen slacks, a silk shirt open at the collar, a pair of sunglasses on top of his head. He gave Guidry a rib-cracking hug. "What do you think?"

"I thought Leo was going to drive me out into the desert and shoot me," Guidry said.

"Leo? No. What do you think about the pad?" Ed turned so that they could examine the house together. "It's the latest thing, I'm told. But all that glass in the summer. You're roasting, you feel like you're going to burst into flames. Leo, who has class, thinks the house lacks class. He thinks *I* lack class, don't you, Leo?"

"Shall I take the car around to the back, Mr. Zingel?" Leo said.

"Thank you," Ed said. "Come on, boychick."

They went inside. There was a sunken living room inside the sunken living room, that's how big the place was. Fifteen-foot ceilings, a stone fireplace that could fit a small car, a curved white vinyl sofa and a zebra-skin rug.

On the rug stretched a girl, seventeen years old maybe, leafing through a magazine. She wore a man's camp shirt and denim shorts cut shorter than short. Her long legs were dirty or tan or both. There were a few other beautiful teenage loungers, too. A couple of shirtless boys watching the fish in the giant aquarium, a girl with glasses painting her toenails, a girl with a paper sack full of cherries feeding them to a boy on the marble floor at her feet.

"Don't worry about them," Ed said. "They're high as kites, most of them."

"Friends of yours?" Guidry said.

"More like family, really. The wind blows them here, from all over the country. Cindy there by the fireplace is from Maine."

"How about that."

"Stop clutching your pearls, Mamie Eisenhower. I don't touch them, I just watch. I'm too old to keep up. I don't have them do anything to each other that they're not dying to do already."

The girl on the zebra-skin rug, Cindy from Maine, rolled lazily onto her back, lifted a long, slender, dirty, bare leg, and pointed her toes at the ceiling. She regarded Guidry from behind a spill of blond hair. She had the bluest, emptiest eyes he'd ever seen. The whitest, emptiest smile.

"Far be it from me to judge, Ed," Guidry said.

Ed led Guidry through the living room, around the corner, past the kitchen.

A door.

"After you," Ed said.

Guidry took a deep breath, but behind the door was not a secret tiled room with a drain in the floor—no, just the dining room. A wall of glass that faced the pool, a table with a snowy white tablecloth, a bucket of ice next to a bottle of Black & White. Guidry headed straight to the scotch and poured himself a double. But don't relax just yet. All that this guaranteed, this and Leo coming in with a chafing dish of what smelled like lobster thermidor, was that Guidry would live to see another hour or two. Maybe.

"Dig in," Ed said. "And don't worry about Leo either. He's the soul of discretion. Aren't you, Leo?"

Guidry took a seat across the table from Ed, next to Leo. On the other side of the window, out by the pool, a pair of matched bronze teens lay glistening and motionless.

Guidry took a bite, a sip. He waited. Ed was having a ball, watching Guidry twist.

"So when do I leave, Ed?" Guidry said. "For Vietnam?"

"You're eager to know," Ed said. "The when and the how and the what-do-I-do-when-I-get-there. The pertinent details, as it were."

"Exactly that."

"I don't blame you. But let's show each other our cards first, get that out of the way. What do you say?"

So here it was. The first jolt, the first bump. Guidry knew what he had to do. Stay on his feet and not go down.

"I'd enjoy that, Ed," he said. "But you've already seen all my cards."

Ed laughed. "You're a cool customer, boychick. I've always liked that about you. You've got aplomb in spades."

Guidry was glad to hear that it appeared so, at least.

"Tell me what really happened," Ed said. "You didn't fuck Carlos's daughter. Maybe you did. But that's not why you're on the outs. That's not why he's beating the bushes for you, practically shitting himself. If we're going to be in this thing together, I need to know everything."

"*If* we're going to be in it together?" Guidry said.

"It's a figure of speech."

Tell Ed the truth. Tell Ed a lie. If Guidry admitted that he knew what happened in Dallas, that he had dirt on Carlos, Ed would be even more eager than he already was to help him. Carlos, exposed and vulnerable, Ed's dream come true—stick Carlos right in the tender parts and make him squeal.

That was the one hand. On the other hand, the president of the United States had been assassinated. The Earl Warren Commission, the FBI. Ed didn't need a headache that big, a headache like Guidry.

Maybe Ed already knew about Dallas and Carlos and this was a test. But the right answer? Guidry didn't know. Ed Zingel, his wiles legendary, his motives unknowable. He waited, patient and smiling. Tell the truth, tell a lie. Guidry decided to go with a bit of each.

"It's the Kennedy thing," Guidry said.

"I suspected."

"I don't know much," Guidry said. "I know that the real sniper drove down to Houston after the job. I heard Seraphine on a call that I wasn't supposed to hear."

"What else?" Ed said.

"That's it. That's all I've got."

As Guidry thought about Mackey and Armand and Jack Ruby. As he felt again the wet warmth of the Houston night on his skin, smelled the refineries as he popped the trunk of the Cadillac and unzipped the army duffel, as he saw before him the rifle, the brass shell casings.

"But Carlos thinks you have more," Ed said.

"Those are all my cards, Ed," Guidry said.

Ed leaned back in his chair and mused. Guidry poured himself another double. Don't let Ed see your hand shake. Finally Ed nodded and tucked into his lobster thermidor.

"See how good that feels?" Ed said. "To unburden your heart to a friend?"

"Like a breath of fresh air," Guidry said.

"I have mixed feelings about the whole thing. Jack was an arrogant son of a bitch, but he knew how to have a good time. And he knew how to play the game. Bobby was the problem."

"You're saying pop Bobby instead of Jack."

"Don't pop anybody. But sure, pop Bobby instead. Send a message, get Jack back in line. You can't let a personal grudge stand in the way of business. Even a dumb wop like Carlos should understand that."

Ed's personal grudge against Carlos was the reason Guidry was sitting there right now, sipping scotch and picking at a plate of lobster thermidor. Guidry chose not to point out the irony.

The teenagers who were spread out by the pool still hadn't moved. Guidry wasn't sure that they were even still breathing. Leo left and returned with a pot of coffee. Ed wiped his mouth and tossed the napkin onto the table.

"You want to hear something funny?" Ed said. "I was about to retire. Call it a day. But then Jack gets popped, LBJ takes over, and I start to think . . . hmm, Vietnam. So you see? For you and me both, that first bullet in Dallas turned everything around."

"Ed," Guidry said.

"What?"

"I put my cards on the table."

"And now it's my turn?" Ed said. "Okay, let's talk turkey. I'm going to get you on a flight out of Nellis. A colonel with a bomber wing is a friend of mine. He—"

Ed stopped. The empty-eyed girl with the legs, Cindy from Maine, had wandered into the room. She slid onto Ed's lap and smiled her white, empty smile at Guidry. When Leo cleared his throat, she bared her teeth and snapped at him, like a dog biting at a fly. Leo ignored her. He tipped a spoonful of sugar into his coffee.

"When is it, Ed?" Guidry said. "The flight out of Nellis?"

Cindy tugged at Ed's jowls. "Daddy. Are we going to play today?"

"Is it time?" Ed said. "Boychick, you're going to get a kick out of this."

No. Whatever it might be that Ed had in mind, no, no, no. And definitely not now, not yet. Guidry smiled. Aplomb in spades, sure.

"I'd love to finish our conversation first," Guidry said.

"We'll have plenty of time to talk," Ed said. "Trust me, you've never seen anything like this in your life."

Guidry caught Leo's eye. Leo's Clark Gable mustache twitched.

"Leo doesn't approve of our shenanigans," Ed said. "Do you, Leo?"

"C'mon, Daddy," Cindy said. "We want to play."

Leo stood. "I'll gather the equipment."

"Ed," Guidry said. "I don't want to be a drag, but maybe—"

"You're not a drag, boychick," Ed said. "If I wanted a drag working for me in Saigon, I'd send Leo."

A good-natured warning. Guidry guessed there wouldn't be a second one. "Let the games begin," he said.

On the way outside, Guidry stopped in the bathroom. A signed Picasso over the toilet, authentic as far as Guidry could tell, probably worth a fortune. A charcoal sketch of a catlike creature with wings and fangs, devouring itself. He took a leak and combed his hair. From far away in the house, he heard a faint bang, like a door or the lid of a coffin slamming shut. He heard a shriek of laughter or terror. Get me out of here, he thought.

Out back, on a half acre of lush emerald grass that Ed must have kept watered around the clock, the teenagers had gathered. Eight of them, stripped down to their underwear, the four boys in their Fruit of the Loom whities, the four girls in bras and panties. Leo went down the line with a carton of raw eggs. Each of the boys selected an egg.

"Come here. I'll explain the rules to you." Ed sat on the flagstone patio, smoking a cigar. "The egg goes on top of the guy's head. The nylon stocking holds the egg so that it doesn't fall off."

"Naturally," Guidry said.

The boys already had their nylons. The girls helped the boys get the eggs fixed in place. The sheer, flesh-colored nylons, when pulled all the way down to the chin, flattened and blurred the faces of the boys, as if a thumb had tried to rub out a mistake. The egg protruding from the top of the skull . . . Guidry didn't know what the hell that looked like. A tumor, a rudimentary horn?

Leo went back down the line with a Coleman cooler box. What was in the cooler? Fish, naturally. Each fish was more than a foot long and frozen stiff. One fish for each of the girls. Guidry wished that Picasso could get a load of this. He'd throw up his hands, throw in the towel.

"We played this when I was a kid," Ed said, "the camp where my parents used to send me in the summer."

Ye gods. "What in the hell kind of camp was that, Ed?" Guidry said.

"See, the girl rides on the guy's shoulders. She has the fish. The object of the game, it's simple. Use your fish to break the other eggs. Don't let anyone break your egg."

Leo came over to sit with them. "Ready when you are, Mr. Zingel."

"Mount up, ladies and gentlemen!" Ed said. "A hundred bucks to the last team standing, winner takes all!"

He opened a drawer in the side table next to him and took out a gun and fired into the air. Guidry didn't have time to brace himself. The crack zinged off the canyon walls, zinged back around and around. Guidry felt like he was being shot at from every direction at once.

"Giddyup!" Ed said.

At first there was just a lot of stumbling, a lot of giggling. Eight teenage kids high as kites, the boys half blind because of the nylons over their heads, the fish so slippery that the girls could barely keep a grip.

Guidry glanced over at Leo. This wasn't so bad. Leo looked away.

The girls began to swing the fish hard, harder. One boy took a vicious smack to the face. He staggered, dazed. Cindy from Maine maneuvered into position, white smile gleaming, and blindsided the girl on the boy's shoulders, a blow that almost took her head off.

A fish frozen solid—it must have been like getting hit with a two-by-four.

A girl with pigtails smashed the egg on top of a boy's head, smashed and smashed, driving him to his knees. Guidry, who'd seen rough action, who'd been on the beach at Leyte, remember, winced. Cindy broke the second egg and then just for the hell of it grabbed the girl's hair and yanked her backward off her partner's shoulders. The girl hit the ground with a crunch that made Guidry wince again. When the girl sat back up, her mouth full of blood, Cindy laughed.

"Ed," Guidry said.

Ed grinned. "Did I tell you? The almighty id. Nature's most beautiful creation. Give it sunshine, watch it blossom."

"Someone's going to get hurt."

"Maybe not," Ed said.

Here was the savior, Guidry reminded himself once again, into whose hands he had delivered himself. Get me out of here now.

One egg left. Cindy went in for the kill. The two girls hammered savagely at each other. Their partners went down. The girl with the pigtails tried to crawl away. Cindy chased her, caught her, pinned her, beat her until the girl's screams turned to whimpers and Cindy's fish, softening in the heat, flew apart in her hands.

Two of the boys dragged the girl with the pigtails into the house. Cindy came over to collect her prize. She knelt in front of Ed. She had a smear of blood on her cheek, what might have been part of a handprint, and glittering silver fish scales caught in her eyelashes. Ed tucked a hundred-dollar bill beneath her bra strap.

"And you get to be queen for the day," he said.

"I like to win, Daddy," Cindy said.

"Watch this," Ed told Guidry. He lifted the gun and pressed the barrel against her forehead. "Do you want me to blow your brains out, Cindy?"

She smiled her white, empty smile. "I don't care."

Ed put the gun away. He leaned down and kissed her forehead. "Go get cleaned up. Have some candy."

Ed drove Guidry back to the Hacienda himself. He told stories most of the way. How he and Norman Biltz had raised millions of dollars for Jack in '60. How Sam Giancana wanted to put pressure on Bobby, so he had Marilyn Monroe drugged and passed around at the Cal-Neva in Reno. Ed owned copies of the pictures, if Guidry ever wanted to see them.

Guidry listened and smiled. He had a headache, and his stomach was starting to cramp again. He tried delicately to edge the conversation back to that flight out of

Nellis. Ed ignored him. He told more stories about the good old days.

Guidry listened and smiled. He thought about Charlotte. Her eyes, her smell, the taste of her sweat. All the usual dumb clichés. Guidry was disappointed in himself. Her laugh and her frown. Ye gods, what was wrong with him? If a thought puzzled or enticed her, if she found a notion dubious or tempting, she squinted one eye shut the way she did when she looked through the viewfinder of her camera.

"We did a few deals," Ed was saying, "but he never succumbed to my charms."

Guidry listened and smiled. Did a few deals with who? "I can't imagine that, Ed."

It wasn't real, Guidry knew, what he felt for Charlotte. It was puppy love, a trick of the light, a temporary infatuation brought on by the novelty of the situation (his first Oklahoma housewife!), by the burden of stress under which he'd been laboring.

Then why did it feel so real? Why the wrench of joy in his gut when he pictured himself getting back to the hotel and strolling out to the pool and seeing Charlotte and the girls again, seeing them look up, light up. The force of that desire—to be right there, right this minute—unnerved him.

They pulled up to the Hacienda. Guidry started to get out of the car, but Ed shut off the engine.

"You fly out of Nellis on Tuesday," Ed said. "That colonel I mentioned. It's all arranged."

"The day after tomorrow?" Guidry said.

"I told you I'd take care of everything, didn't I?" Ed said. "Ye of little faith. Once you get to Vietnam, Nguyen will take care of you. He's your man on the ground. That's spelled N-g-u-y-e-n. He does work for the Company, but don't worry, we're all going to hold hands and dance around the maypole together. Another guy has connections to the Vietnamese government, the military. He'll be in touch. His name's Nguyen, too. Nguyen and Nguyen, get it?"

"A win-win situation."

"Now, go get your suitcase. Come back to the house with me. I have plenty of room. The Hacienda. Hayseed heaven. I can't bear to think of you rotting away in there."

"I appreciate the offer," Guidry said.

"Fine," Ed said. "You like your freedom. You like to roam like the buffalo."

Guidry got out of the car. Ed got out, too, and came around—arms spread wide, prepared to crack another few of Guidry's ribs. But before he could move in for the hug, Ed's attention drifted to the lobby doors.

Guidry turned as Charlotte and the girls emerged from the lobby. Charlotte smiled at him.

"You're just in time," she said. "We're going to get a closer look at the airplanes."

Ed looked at Guidry. He looked at Charlotte and the girls. He smiled, too.

"Why," Ed said, "what have we here?"

25

Charlotte had one last shot left on the roll, so she
brought the Brownie out to the miniature-golf
course. The frame: Joan preparing to putt, Frank
crouched behind her, Rosemary staring up at the sky,
distracted by a plane or a cloud or a bird.

The rule of thirds. Mr. Hotchkiss would approve.
Though of course he'd be horrified by Las Vegas in
general. Too much noise, too much flash, too much
raw, raucous emotion. Too much, too much, oh, dear.

Charlotte found it all fascinating. Yesterday evening
they'd taken a drive up the Strip, to downtown and
back. The people! Men and women from every imag-
inable walk of life. They strode along, they stumbled
along, they cuddled and shoved and ducked furtively
into cars. A man stripped off his tuxedo jacket and

waved it like a flag. Why? A woman sat on the curb, head in her hands but smiling. Why? Charlotte loved how every person they passed, every single person in the wide world, had his or her own story.

A chorus girl strutted across the intersection. Who was she? What purpose so propelled her that she'd not had time to change out of her costume? The costume was made from opalescent beads and flamboyant feathers and very little, if any, actual fabric. Mr. Hotchkiss would not have survived the shock.

Los Angeles was far bigger than Las Vegas. Charlotte reeled at the thought. If Las Vegas was this much, so much, too much, what awaited her in Los Angeles? She remembered what she'd told the girls right before they left Oklahoma: *Let's find out.*

Joan concentrated on her putt. Rosemary gaped at the sky above. Charlotte waited, waited, waited, the blades of the windmill turning, turning, turning. She wanted to freeze the moment in the perfect grid of shadows.

Now. She pressed the shutter. Time stopped.

And then the windmill resumed its slow, creaking sweep. The head of Joan's putter clicked against the ball. Frank murmured encouragement as the ball dipped and curved. "Get in there," he said. Rosemary twirled, attempting to duplicate the dancer's pirouette she'd seen on a poster for the *Jewel Box Revue*.

Charlotte wouldn't know if she'd snapped the picture a split second too early or a split second too late until she saw the prints. That was what made photography so nerve-racking, so thrilling. You couldn't really judge the result of what you were doing until it was already done.

"I'll be back in a couple of hours," Frank said. "Wish me luck."

After Frank left to meet his friend, the car dealer, Charlotte and the girls ate lunch, walked the dog, and from across the street observed a memorial ceremony for President Kennedy. A troop of Cub Scouts in front of McCarran Air Field raised a flag, saluted, and then lowered the flag to half-mast.

The dog required a nap, but the girls were still full of energy. So off they set in search of a darkroom. The hotel had everything else under the sun, Charlotte reasoned, why not that, too?

The clerk at the gift shop, a gruff émigré named Otto, sold her a new roll of film, but he knew of no darkroom or lab at the Hacienda. He was an aspiring magician, though, and demonstrated several tricks with a pack of souvenir cards. Rosemary tugged Charlotte's sleeve. Charlotte bent down.

"Mommy," Rosemary whispered, "will you ask him if he'll teach us a trick?"

"*You* ask him," Charlotte said.

So Rosemary summoned her courage, and Otto obliged. Patiently, he walked the girls through a trick called Who's the Magician? While they practiced, he described for them the salt mines near his hometown in Austria, the cave walls sparkling with crystal and a vast underground lake across which you could row a boat.

Otto sent them off to see Gigi, the photographer at the Jewel Box, who recorded all the champagne toasts, the anniversary smooches. Otto offered to have a bellboy show them the way, but where was the fun in that?

They got lost, of course, and ended up outside, in a serene little cactus garden. A Mexican man raking the sand, Luis, asked the girls did they know that a cactus could live three hundred years and weigh five thousand pounds? No! He invited them to touch the different prickly spines, some soft and straight, others hard and curved. The spines discouraged animals that might eat the cactus and also prevented the water inside the cactus from turning to vapor and escaping into the air.

And to think: Charlotte had been worried about the girls missing school, about them falling behind in their education.

They located Gigi, finally, tweezing her eyebrows in the staff break room. It turned out that she used a Polaroid Highlander instant camera, so she had no need of a darkroom. There was a lab downtown, though, near Gigi's apartment, and she offered to drop off Charlotte's roll of film.

"What's your room number?" Gigi said.

"We're in 216," Charlotte said. "But I'm not sure how long we'll be staying."

"I'll give them a kick in the pants. Don't worry."

The girls were fascinated with the Highlander. It was Joan who piped up, to Charlotte's surprise, without needing any encouragement from her at all.

"May we try it, please?" Joan asked Gigi.

"Why, sure you may," Gigi said.

She let Joan take a photo of Rosemary. She let Rosemary take a photo of Joan. She showed them how to fan the prints gently until the fixative dried and the phantom of the image began to appear. Charlotte, curious, asked Gigi if she liked her job at the hotel.

"It's a hoot," Gigi said. "Oh, the things I see. You wouldn't believe half of them."

Exactly the kind of job, Charlotte decided, that she'd like to find in Los Angeles. And why not? What was to stop her?

They decided to walk over to the airport. Frank, right as they exited the hotel, was climbing out of a limousine.

"You're just in time," Charlotte said. "We're going to get a closer look at the airplanes."

Another man had climbed out of the limousine, too. He came around to the other side and smiled at Charlotte. He was tall, broad as a barn, and not just larger than life but also somehow more vivid than it—the deep, rich tan, the tonsure of downy white hair that circled his bald dome, a smile so forceful that it practically wrestled you to the ground and pinned you there.

He had a story, Charlotte guessed. Oh, yes.

"Why, what have we here?" he said.

"You must be Ed." Charlotte smiled back at him. "It's a pleasure to meet you."

Frank had to struggle to make his way over to them. The girls had him in their clutches—Rosemary hanging on to one hand, Joan the other.

"Ed, here she is," Frank said. "Charlotte. The damsel in distress I've been telling you about."

"I feel horribly presumptuous about all this," Charlotte said. "I hope Frank hasn't put you in a difficult position because of me. I don't usually go around asking perfect strangers to borrow one of their cars."

Ed lifted his sunglasses to better examine her. His eyes, as Charlotte had expected, were a sparkling Kodachrome blue. "Borrow one of my cars?" he said.

She didn't know how to respond. He had absolutely no idea, it slowly dawned on Charlotte, what she was talking about.

And then, as her mind began to race—why hadn't Frank mentioned the car yet?—Ed laughed. He bent down, lifted Charlotte's hand to his lips, and kissed it. His breath was warm, his palm soft, his fingernails perfectly manicured.

"I'm pulling your leg," he said. "Of course you can borrow one of my cars, Charlotte dear. I told Frank you could have the pick of the fleet. Didn't I, Frank?"

"You did," Frank said.

"Any friend of Frank's is a friend of mine. Why, he's like a son to me. What's mine is his and what's his is mine. Isn't that right, Frank?"

Charlotte relaxed. "Thank you so much. I can't tell you how grateful I am."

Ed turned to the girls. "And these must be the lovely daughters I've heard so much about. I'm your Uncle Ed. How do you do? Are you enjoying Las Vegas so far?"

"How do you do," Rosemary said. "Yes. There's cactus and miniature golf and a man who taught us tricks with cards. It's just like in *The Wizard of Oz*. Isn't it, Joan?"

"Yes," Joan said.

Frank nudged the girls toward Charlotte. "We won't keep you, Ed," he said. "Let's talk tomorrow, shall we?"

Ed snapped his fingers three times, three loose flicks of the wrist, like a jazz singer tossing off the band's beat.

"Do you know who's playing a gig in town this week, up at the Stardust?" he said. "You won't believe it. Ray Bolger, the Scarecrow himself."

"You know the Scarecrow?" Rosemary said.

Even Joan, whose poker face slipped only once every century or so, gaped up at Ed, too.

"Know him?" Ed said. "Ray and I are old pals. Listen, I've got a little boat at Lake Mead. Have you been to Lake Mead yet? Why don't we go out tomorrow, a family outing. I'll see if Ray wants to tag along."

"That's generous of you, Ed, but . . ." Frank tried to keep nudging the girls forward, but he'd run up against the immovable object of their astonishment.

Charlotte looked over at him. Why not? It would be an adventure. Ed captivated her. He was, like Las Vegas, too much.

Frank continued to smile his easy smile, but she glimpsed a pinch between his eyebrows, an almost invisible pucker of hesitation, a trace of dismay. Or did she? Here and gone, vanished in the blink of an eye. Charlotte wasn't sure.

Frank gave Ed a hearty slap on the back. "I think that's a first-rate idea, Ed. When do we sail?"

The girls ate an early dinner in the Garden Room. Afterward Charlotte and Frank left them for the evening with the hotel babysitter. Rosemary bristled at the name of the Hansel and Gretel Nursery—"We're not *babies*"—but then discovered that the "nursery" catered to children of all ages and was stocked with board games, building blocks, and jigsaw puzzles.

The hotel's formal dining room was just across the lobby. Frank escorted Charlotte to a table by the pianist. Their first proper date. That realization, as they sipped champagne, made Charlotte laugh.

"What's so funny?" Frank said.

"This," she said. "Don't you agree?"

He smiled. "I do."

He knew exactly what she meant. How was that possible? How could two people know each other so well and yet not at all?

"You don't want to go to Lake Mead with Ed tomorrow," Charlotte said.

He pulled the bottle of champagne from the bucket and refilled her glass. "Why do you say that?"

"Just a feeling, I suppose," she said.

"You're right," he said. "I don't want to go."

"Why not?"

"I want you all to myself," he said. "You and the girls. I don't want to share you with anyone else, not even for an afternoon."

She believed him. He leaned across the table to kiss her. It was a lovely moment. The champagne, the candlelight, the music. Only when Frank had folded his napkin neatly and left to visit the men's room did Charlotte stop to wonder why the question had occurred to her in the first place, whether she believed him or not.

26

Barone dropped the Fairlane downtown, by the train station. He wiped it clean and emptied it out. The kid had left behind his Windbreaker and a brown paper sack with the toothbrush and the toothpaste and the pimple cream he'd picked up along the way. Barone wadded up the Windbreaker and stuffed it into a trash can across from the Golden Nugget. He stuffed the brown paper sack into a trash can a block farther on.

He took a cab out to the Tropicana. Carlos's joint in Vegas. Or maybe he just owned a big piece of it, Barone wasn't sure which.

Dandy Stan Contini was the whole nine yards. Rings, diamond stickpin, a walking stick with a carved ivory handle. Underneath, though, he was nothing but sagging gray skin and bone, already a skeleton, every breath a rattle. He took Barone up to his office.

"You want a drink?" Contini said. "Something to eat?"

"No."

"Cancer, in case you're wondering. Stomach and lung, the daily double. So you're the infamous Paul Barone. You don't look all that hot yourself, if you don't mind me saying."

"What do you know about Guidry?" Barone said.

Contini started coughing and couldn't stop. He stabbed his walking stick into the carpet and held on, as if the coughing might shake him to pieces if he didn't. The ivory handle of his walking stick was carved to look like a girl's leg in a fishnet stocking.

Finally he hacked himself dry. He wiped his forehead with a hankie that matched the cravat. "My apologies."

"What do you know about Guidry?" Barone said.

"Nothing so far," Contini said. "My boys are sniffing around. If he's in Vegas, I'll know something soon."

"I'm going to do my own sniffing around, too."

"Do what you want. I don't mind."

Barone hadn't asked if he minded or not. "Anything else?"

"Be discreet," Contini said. "This is Vegas. Did Seraphine explain that to you?"

Shoot. Did she explain that to me. Barone could hear the kid's voice. He almost smiled. Instead he stood. "If you hear anything," Barone said, "I need to know it right away."

Contini scribbled something on a pad. He peeled off the page. "Take this down to the desk. Slim will fix you up with a room. You can call in for your messages. What else?"

"I need a car."

"Just tell Slim," Contini said. "He'll fix you up. If you want—"

He started coughing again. Barone paused on his way out the door. "How long did they give you?" he said. "The doctors?"

Contini kept coughing. He waved a hand. Too long, that's how long.

Barone's room at the Tropicana had a view of the Strip. Room service brought him a steak. He ate a few bites. He went easy on the rye, just a splash over ice. He took one of the pain pills. The other bottle of pills . . . where was it? Oh. Still in the kid's pocket, that's where. It wasn't a problem. Barone felt all right, and his appetite had started to return, a good sign. He called Seraphine and gave her his number at the Tropicana.

The Dunes. He started there, just up the street.

The casino floor was crowded, hardly any room to move, suburban squares on the loose for the weekend, wild-eyed and dressed to the nines and laughing too loudly, holding their cigarettes above their heads as they moved around so that nobody got burned.

I'm a private dick. I'm looking for a guy. He ran out with the company's payroll, his boss hired me to find him. He's with his wife and kids, two little girls.

Stickmen, bartenders, cocktail waitresses, bellhops. A house dick came over and asked Barone who the fuck he was and what the fuck did he think he was doing.

"I'm a private dick." Et cetera.

"Beat it, pal," the house dick said.

Barone beat it. He was done with the Dunes anyway.

The Stardust, the Sands.

Nothing. Barone called to check his messages at the Tropicana every half hour.

Sunday he checked the rest of the Strip. The Sahara. The New Frontier. The Flamingo. The house dick at the Desert Inn played it tough. Barone restrained himself. He tried the hotels downtown. The Mint. He could feel the fever creeping back. Paul Barone doesn't quit. Binion's Horseshoe.

Nothing, nothing, nothing.

Where the hell was Guidry? Sunday evening, eight

o'clock, he went up to his room to rest. A quick break. He called down and told the desk to wake him in an hour.

But he couldn't sleep. Lying in bed, the room an oven, light from the Strip bleeding through the crack in the curtains. Barone realized that he'd been driving in the wrong lane, the wrong direction. Guidry wouldn't stay at one of the big fancy joints. Too many people, too many eyes, someone might recognize him. He was at one of the dozens of little motels in town. The Del Rey, the Monie Marie, the Sunrise, the Royal Vegas. But no, that didn't feel right either. Not enough people, Guidry would feel too conspicuous.

Barone got out of bed and went downstairs and found Dandy Stan Contini in the showroom. Contini was tap-dancing, twirling his cane. "Look at me!" Contini sang. "I'm dead, and I feel like a million bucks!"

No. That wasn't real. The fever. The colored kid turning around and looking at him. *Theodore, don't call me Ted, don't call me Teddy.* That was the fever, too. The kid with the hole in his head, looking at Barone before he even pulled the trigger.

Barone woke at eight in the morning. Monday. He opened the curtains, and the blast of white desert light was like getting slugged in the face. His bad hand hurt like hell again. Go see a doctor. All right, but first he needed to follow a hunch. He told the switchboard to put him through to Dandy Stan Contini.

"I still haven't heard anything," Contini said.

"Where do families stay?" Barone said.

"What do you mean?"

"You come to Vegas with your family. Is there a joint like that?"

"Who comes to Vegas with their family? But the Hacienda. That's where."

The Hacienda was about a mile south of the Tropicana, stuck off by itself in the no-man's-land across from the airport. Barone sat in the parking lot and watched the people come and go. Some of the usual crowd, the wolves and the sheep that you'd see anywhere on the Strip, but lots of families, too. A father and his two teenage boys in matching madras golf slacks. A little girl in a red velvet dress hop-hop-hopping on one foot. The doorman wore a Santa hat and handed out candy canes to all the kiddies who passed by.

Guidry was here. Barone didn't know how he knew it, but he did.

He went inside and paid for a room. Two dollars extra for a view of the pool. Sure, why not.

The coffee shop had a clean line on the lobby doors. Barone took a seat at the counter. He ordered chops and black coffee. He set the room key next to his plate so the waitress could see it. He had a long wait, most likely, and didn't want any hassle.

He wasn't worried that Guidry might make him. Guidry knew the name, but he didn't know Barone. And they'd only been in the same room a couple of times, years ago. Guidry grinning and greasing the big wheels at the party, Barone just another forgettable face in the crowd. Watching Guidry, watching everybody.

"Top off that java for you, hon?" the waitress said.

"Yeah," Barone said. "And some ice water."

"Any luck at the tables today?"

"Not yet."

A couple of hours later, just before noon, Barone saw Guidry emerge from the elevator. He was with the woman, the one he was using, and the two little girls. Guidry said something to the woman, and she smiled. The doorman in the Santa hat held the doors open for them.

Barone took his time and gave Guidry plenty of room. He paid his ticket and took a toothpick from the tray and strolled out of the coffee shop. Through the big glass lobby doors, he watched Guidry and the woman and the two little girls get into a green Rolls. No suitcases. He watched the Rolls drive off. They'd be back.

He stepped outside and looked around.

"Help you, sir?" the doorman said.

"Oh, hell," Barone said. "I must have missed them."

"Who's that, sir?"

"My pal and his wife. You didn't see anybody get in a Rolls-Royce just now, did you?"

"Mr. and Mrs. Wainwright. Sure."

So Guidry hadn't switched up the names. He was cutting corners, starting to breathe easy. Good. Or he had to keep the name to keep the woman in the dark.

"Don't mention it to them that you saw me, will you?" Barone told the doorman. "It's a surprise. I'm here for the anniversary party. That's a surprise, too."

The bar. Barone ordered rye on the rocks and took two more of the pain pills. Now what? This was the part of the job he enjoyed the most. All the pieces spread out on the table in front of him, the cogs and the springs and the screws. Try this, try that. Fit every-thing together just right, wind it up, watch the clock start ticking.

The woman and the two girls made it interesting. Barone preferred to take care of them separately. Maybe he could find a way to lure Guidry downstairs, alone. Get him in the car, drive somewhere nice and quiet, and then go back afterward for the others.

Hello, Frank. Let's go for a ride.

But Guidry might cause a fuss. He'd already bolted once, in Houston. Most guys saw the light and accepted the inevitable. A few guys kept kicking until the bitter end. Good for them, as long as it wasn't Barone who got kicked. He remembered his old buddy Fisk in Houston. Barone's aching hand remembered the son of a bitch's switchblade.

He asked for more ice in his drink. The bartender chopped up a chunk. Barone watched the steel pick flash, the glitter fly.

Let's go for a ride, Frank. Be polite and I won't touch the woman and her kids.

No. Guidry wouldn't buy. He wasn't stupid. And he wouldn't give a shit anyway, what happened to the woman and her kids.

Don't give Guidry an opening. Find his room, jimmy the lock, knock him cold when he walked in the door. Barone had his jawbreaker with him, always, a leather sap filled with lead shot.

Were the woman and her daughters staying in the same room as Guidry? Barone would make them wait in the bathroom while he finished Guidry with the belt. Stan Contini could send a crew to tidy up. Just the one stiff left for him at the hotel. That wasn't too much of a mess. Barone would take care of the woman and her kids somewhere private.

Let's go for a ride, lady. You and your daughters. Don't worry. I'm not going to hurt you.

She'd buy. *I'm not going to hurt you.* She'd buy because she'd want to buy, with all her heart.

Barone held the glass of ice to his forehead and closed his eyes. When he opened them again, a guy was sitting on the stool to his right. Another guy slid in on his left. Barone looked at them in the mirror. Heavyweights, both of them, all smiles.

The meat on the right held a .45 in his lap, down low so that the bartender couldn't see it. "Mr. Barone," he said. "Welcome to Las Vegas."

"I'm on a job," Barone said.

"No fooling. That's why the man wants a word."

Barone was too hot, too tired, to smile at the twist. "Let's go for a ride?"

The meat on the right glanced at his partner. They'd been warned, but up close Barone didn't seem like such a bad brass boy, did he?

"That's right, Mr. Barone. No trouble, okay? We're all friends here."

"Sure we are," Barone said.

They took Barone's Police Positive and drove him up to the Desert Inn. Barone in the backseat, his thoughts drifting. Not memories as such. His mouth filled with the flavor of strawberries. A song playing faintly, in the corner of his mind.

Past the cages, down a corridor, elevator up. The door to the office, carved wood and a truss of black iron, looked like it had been pried off a cathedral in Germany.

"After you, Mr. Barone," the meat who did the talking said.

The man sitting behind the desk had a world-class schnoz and friendly eyebrows. Thick glasses with black plastic frames.

"You know who I am?" he said.

"Moe Dalitz," Barone said.

"So you know I run this town."

"For the boys back east."

The meat behind Barone tensed and shifted. Barone could feel it. But Moe Dalitz just grinned. He tapped a finger against his schnoz.

"Exactly," he said. "Like you, Mr. Barone, I serve the greater good. The community, as it were."

"Who tipped you?" Barone couldn't figure it. Only Stan Contini knew he was at the Hacienda. Stan Contini had no reason to bring Moe Dalitz into the mix. He had every reason not to do it.

"Who tipped me?" Dalitz said. "Nobody tipped me.

You've made enough noise to wake the dead. Asking around, yanking on pant legs."

He was lying. If Dalitz put a tail on him Saturday or Sunday, Barone would have picked it up. Though Barone hadn't spotted his boys just now, had he? Not until they walked into the bar and sat down right next to him.

Barone knew he was slipping. The fever. But Dalitz had been tipped.

"I have enormous regard for you, Mr. Barone," Dalitz said. "I have enormous regard for your employer. But we have a certain way of doing business in Las Vegas."

"It's an open city," Barone said.

"You're right again. Because everyone agrees it's an open city. Because everyone agrees to follow the rules."

What fucking rules? While Barone stood here with Moe Dalitz's dick in his hand, wasting time, Frank Guidry was on his way back to the Hacienda. He was packing his suitcase, heading to the airport, disappearing forever. All this, this whole last week, the kid dead in a ditch, all of it for nothing.

"Something like this," Dalitz said, "the committee has to look it over. All the particulars, you understand. And then we give the green light or we don't."

"Call Carlos," Barone said.

"I will. I'll discuss everything with the committee. In the meantime take a load off. Relax."

"Call him now."

"I know you're in a rush. I appreciate that." Moe Dalitz shrugged but stopped halfway, with his shoulders up around his ears. *What can I do?*

Who tipped him? Why? Someone who wanted to gum up the works and keep Guidry alive for another five minutes. Or was Barone slipping and Moe Dalitz telling the truth? Had Barone missed the tail?

"The boys here will look after you," Dalitz said. "Anything you want, just bark. I've got a little place down in Searchlight. The El Condor. You'll like it. Craps, girls, whatever you want, everything on the house until you get your green light. You'll get your green light, be patient. All right?"

The eyebrows friendly and innocent, but not his eyes. Dalitz didn't care if Barone thought it was all right or not. Don't force my hand. That's what Dalitz was telling Barone. You're pain enough in my ass alive, I don't need you dead. I don't want to have to kill you.

"My mark," Barone said. "What about him?"

"We'll make sure he doesn't go anywhere," Dalitz said. "Don't you worry. Who is he anyway? This Wainwright cat you're so hot for?"

"Call Carlos."

"If he wants me to know, yeah, he'll tell me. Good man. I could use a guy like you around here."

Barone could keep pushing. A waste of time. But he had one more question.

"Who do you know in town owns a green Rolls?" he said.

"A green Rolls?" Dalitz said. "Doesn't ring a bell."

Dalitz's face was blank on top of blank, a study in smooth nothing. Barone didn't know if he was lying about being tipped, if he was lying about the Rolls. Stick to what you do best, *mon cher,* Seraphine told Barone once when she caught him trying to read her.

Barone gave Moe Dalitz a nod, respectful. Fuck you. Seraphine's advice was good. Barone would stick to what he did best.

He turned to the meat. "Let's go. Lead the way."

27

Monday morning Charlotte woke before the girls, as usual. She got dressed and took the dog downstairs to the cactus garden. They watched the sunrise from there, watched the mountains drink in the color and light, every last drop of it. And oh, the shadows.

The limousine arrived for them at noon. The chauffeur gave Charlotte a bow. He bowed to each of the girls, too.

"My name is Leo," he said, "Mr. Zingel's assistant. I'm delighted to meet you. Mr. Zingel awaits us at the marina."

With his English accent and amused smile, the checkered waistcoat and brilliantined mustache, he was as much of a character as Ed—though Charlotte suspected that Leo had stepped from the pages of a different book, a novel by Dickens or one of the Brontë sisters.

Lake Mead was something of a shock, a rude and beautiful slash of iridescent blue in the middle of the dry desert, ringed by chocolate and cinnamon canyons. Charlotte rolled down her window and took a photo as the limousine wound around the shoreline. She would have to be thrifty with her film. She had only one roll for the day and guessed that much was still to come.

When they reached the marina, she discovered that Ed's "little boat," the *Miss Adventure,* was an enormous yacht, spacious enough to accommodate half the population of Woodrow, Oklahoma. She wasn't surprised. Ed waved to them from the bridge, his captain's hat cocked at a jaunty angle. In which novel did he belong? That was the question. Perhaps *Gatsby,* Charlotte decided. Or perhaps his width and breadth required more room to maneuver, so an epic poem like the *Odyssey.*

They boarded. As the *Miss Adventure* slid away from the dock, Leo showed Charlotte and Frank and the girls to the vast teak sundeck. He introduced them to the other passengers, two teenage boys and a teenage girl. Ed's nephews, Dennis and Tim, and his niece, Cindy.

"Very nice to meet you, ma'am," Dennis told Charlotte.

"Have you had a nice time in Las Vegas, ma'am?" Tim said.

Cindy, a pretty girl with her blond hair plaited into Heidi-of-the-Alps braids, lifted a heel and bent one knee, a little curtsy.

Charlotte couldn't decide if Ed's nephews and niece were the most extravagantly well-mannered high-schoolers she'd ever encountered or if they were just putting her on.

"Did you come straight from class?" she asked.

All three of them wore Catholic-school uniforms: the boys in dress shirts, ties, and pressed navy slacks, Cindy in a white blouse with Peter Pan collar, a plaid skirt, knee socks. Charlotte could imagine Ed blowing like a gale wind through their high school, charming and terrifying the nuns, liberating his nephews and niece from Algebra II so they could spend the afternoon with him.

"What?" Tim said. He and Dennis and Cindy regarded Charlotte blankly.

"I just assumed," Charlotte said. "Your uniforms . . ."

"Yes," Cindy said. "We came from class."

"Yes," Dennis and Tim agreed.

Before Charlotte could wonder about their odd reaction, Frank put a hand on her shoulder and pointed across the deck. An unshaven man in dark glasses lazed in a canvas deck chair, swaddled in blankets. He looked vaguely familiar, but Charlotte couldn't quite place him.

"Is that who I think it is?" Frank said. "I think it might be."

The man noticed them staring. He lifted his bottle of beer in greeting and, without any sort of preliminary, began to sing "If I Only Had a Brain" from *The Wizard of Oz.*

Charlotte saw Joan squeeze Rosemary's hand. That's *him.*

"I *know,*" Rosemary whispered. But she seemed uncertain. Where was the floppy hat? Where were the tufts of straw? Why did his voice sound as if it had been dragged through gravel?

Still, though, what a voice. So distinctive that it could never be confused for any other.

"It looks as if Ray had a late night," Frank murmured to Charlotte. "I think his head really is full of stuffing."

Halfway through the last verse of the song, Ray Bolger lost steam. But he took a swig of beer and managed to finish. He threw off the blanket, as everyone applauded, and made his way unsteadily toward them. Frank stepped forward to take his elbow, to keep him from toppling over the railing.

"Thank you very much, ladies and gentlemen," he said. "Most kind, most kind. For my next number . . ."

A look passed over his face. Charlotte knew that look, from long experience with Dooley. So did the girls.

"Are you feeling under the weather?" Rosemary asked.

"Not at all," Ray Bolger said. He eyed the railing, but then the nausea seemed to pass. "I'm fit as a fiddle. In tip-top shape. Never better."

"It's such an honor to meet you, Mr. Bolger," Charlotte said.

"It's an honor to be here," he said. "On a lake, apparently."

Charlotte could see the girls conferring telepathically. *You* ask him. No, *you*. Finally Joan took the plunge.

"Are you really the Scarecrow?" she said.

"Every single day for the past twenty-five years," he said. "Now, if you'll excuse me, I shall retire below for a short intermission. You've been a most delightful audience."

The surface of the lake was as flat as glass, the wind barely a whisper, but the journey across the deck almost defeated him. He rolled, he pitched. But then, just before he reached the hatch, he kicked a leg and shrugged a shoulder and flapped the opposite arm.

Wrist, elbow, hip, and knee—he came gracefully un-hinged, the dance that Charlotte had seen him perform on the movie screen so many times.

"It really *is* him, Joan," Rosemary said.

"I *know*," Joan said.

Charlotte turned to smile at Frank, but he was watching Ed's niece, Cindy, who had reached out to stroke Joan's head.

"So smooth," Cindy said.

"Let's go up front," Frank said. He took Joan's hand in his. "Ed! Do you have anything to eat on this rust bucket?"

Of course Ed had *everything* to eat. He exchanged his captain's hat for a chef's toque and cooked ham-burgers and red-hots on a portable charcoal grill. Leo set up a buffet of deviled eggs, German potato salad, corn on the cob, succotash. For dessert there were chocolate-chip cookies, fudge brownies, fruit cocktail in strawberry Jell-O with whipped cream on top.

They ate and ate and yet barely made a dent. Char-lotte climbed onto a locker so that she could take a photo of the spread from above. Which fairy tale was it, where the hero encountered a table that magically replenished itself? Had the enchanted table been a reward or a dangerous temptation? She couldn't recall.

They anchored in what appeared to be the very center of the lake, far from shore. Charlotte considered how deep the water must be. Compared to Lake Mead, Oklahoma reservoirs and ranch ponds were just boot prints filled with muddy rainwater. She kept a close eye on the girls. The pair of cork life preservers tied to the railing looked more decorative than practical.

Ed beckoned to her. Charlotte left Frank and Leo to fend for themselves—Rosemary and Joan were teaching them how to play Down Down Baby—and pulled over a chair.

"Are you enjoying yourself?" Ed said.

"Very much," Charlotte said. "We're having a wonderful time."

"Good. Now, let's get to know each other. Tell me a juicy secret about yourself. I promise not to breathe a word."

She laughed. "I'm afraid I don't have any secrets, juicy or otherwise."

"Of course you do. Everybody has a secret or two."

"Then shall you go first?"

He grinned with approval. "I can see why Frank likes you. All right. Let me think. Once upon a time, there was a boy. He had nothing. He wanted everything. So he worked hard. He made certain sacrifices. He held on for dear life. That's the best way I can describe it. Now the boy has everything he ever wanted."

"But?" Charlotte said.

"But?"

"There's not a moral to the story?"

"Sure there is," Ed said. "Decide what you want and let nothing stand in your way. Come, see, conquer. That's the moral to the story. It's what I like about Frank."

About Frank? The assessment surprised Charlotte. And then she remembered what she'd said to Frank the other night, after they'd made love. *I don't really know much about you, do I?* She remembered the thought that had nagged at her from the beginning, how she might know even less about him than she thought.

And what, really, did she know about Ed? The limousine, the yacht. Frank said that the two of them had become friends at an insurance convention in Minneapolis, that they'd discussed policy proceeds. Now that she'd actually met Ed, Charlotte found every individual part of that account difficult to grasp.

She looked over at Frank, who was obediently following Rosemary's instructions. *Clap clap shimmy clap, down down baby.* Frank was watching her and

Ed, too, Charlotte realized, from the corner of his eye.

"Ed?" Charlotte said. "How did you and Frank meet?"

"Oh, no," he said. "Do I look like a sucker to you? It's your turn. How did *you* and Frank meet?"

"Frank didn't say?"

"I want to hear your account."

She told him about the accident with the car, the motel, the mechanic.

Ed grinned again. "And so in Frank galloped, your knight in shining armor."

"He's been very kind. And so have you."

He leaned closer. "And tell me. What's that on your finger?"

Her gold wedding band. Charlotte had forgotten to remove it. After all these years, it had become a part of her, invisible. She tugged the ring off her finger and dropped it into her purse.

"Once upon a time, there was a girl," she said. "She didn't know what she wanted. Or rather she knew what she wanted but was afraid to admit it. And then one day . . ."

"She wasn't afraid anymore," Ed said. "She made her decision and held on for dear life."

"Yes."

He contemplated her. "I will tell you another secret," Ed said, but then Frank materialized next to them, the girls at his side.

"How are you two hitting it off?" he said. "I told you she was a peach, Ed, didn't I?"

"That you did. And that she is." Ed gave Charlotte's knee a fatherly pat and stood. "Join me below in the salon, boychick. There's a business matter I'd like to discuss in private."

Frank groaned. "Ye gods, Ed. I'm on my vacation. Let's wait till this evening at least. I'll drive out to the house. Don't ask me to abandon these three beautiful ladies on such a beautiful day."

"Cindy will keep them company," Ed said. "Cindy! Come play with the new kids!"

Ed waved to his niece, who stood off by herself, leaning far out over the railing and gazing at the water.

"Ed, please," Frank said. It was unmistakable this time, the pinch between his eyebrows, a pucker as when the fabric is too thin and the thread too tight. "We can talk later, as much as you want."

"We'll be just fine," Charlotte said. She didn't understand why he was so reluctant to leave her and the girls alone for a few minutes. "Really, we will."

Still Frank hesitated. But he could see her puzzling.

"All right, Ed," he said finally. "Down the hatch we go. Your wish is my command."

Frank and Ed went below deck. Ed's nephews helped Leo pack up the buffet. Cindy floated over, trailing a finger along the rail and swaying to a song it seemed only she could hear.

"What's that?" Cindy asked.

"This?" Charlotte said. "My camera."

"Do you want to take my picture? Ed's friends always take my picture."

Cindy was indeed striking, with her blue eyes and heart-shaped face. "All right," Charlotte said. "Are they photographers? Ed's friends?"

"Yes."

Charlotte waited until Cindy turned her head to gaze back out over the water and then snapped the photo. The slant of Cindy's chin, the blond braids beginning to fray, a dreamy expression that made her face seem ever so slightly out of focus.

"Do you know how to play Down Down Baby?" Rosemary asked Cindy. "It's hard to learn, but we can teach you."

Cindy didn't seem to hear. "I'm looking for her," she said.

"For who?" Rosemary said.

"The ghost."

Rosemary was immediately transfixed. "What ghost?"

"The girl," Cindy said. "She went for a swim in the middle of the night, when everyone else on the boat was in bed. We were all asleep."

"It was *this* boat?" Rosemary said.

"The summer before last. Yes. She went for a swim and never came back." Cindy giggled. "Down, down, baby."

Joan pressed against Charlotte. Unlike her sister, she didn't enjoy ghost stories. Neither did Charlotte, and certainly not this one.

"Let's talk about something else, shall we?" Charlotte said. "Let's make a list of our favorite boats from books and movies."

But Rosemary would not be deterred. "Who was she? The ghost?"

"A cocktail waitress at the Stardust," Cindy said. "That's what she told everyone. But we knew she was lying. She was a dirty little liar. That's what Ed said."

The splinter of uneasiness that had worked its way under Charlotte's skin began to ache. Surely none of this was true. Surely this was just a story that Cindy had invented to frighten the girls.

Cindy put a finger to her lips. Shhh. "You have to promise," she told Rosemary. "To keep the secret. You know what happens if you can't keep secrets."

"That's enough," Charlotte said, more sharply than she'd intended. She pulled Rosemary closer.

Cindy regarded Charlotte placidly. "Okay."

"But I want to hear more about the ghost," Rosemary said. "Don't you, Joan?"

"No," Joan said.

"I saw her once," Cindy said. "The ghost. She's beautiful now. Like a flower after it dies. She's peaceful. She thinks she's dreaming. She thinks someday she'll wake up."

"Mommy," Rosemary said, "I can feel your heart beating."

Cindy's attention drifted back to Rosemary. She crooked a finger at her. "Come with me," she said. "Let's go look for her together."

Frank was still below deck. Leo and the nephews were out of sight, on the far side of the cabin, nowhere near. Cindy reached for Rosemary's hand, and Rosemary reached automatically to take it, and just as automatically Charlotte seized Cindy's wrist, yanking it roughly away from Rosemary.

The girls stared at Charlotte, shocked.

Cindy stared at Charlotte's hand on her wrist. "Wow," she said.

Charlotte tightened her grip. "Go away. Do you understand? Leave us alone."

For the first time, Cindy really looked at Charlotte, really seemed to register her. Cindy's expression—no anger, no surprise, no *anything*—chilled Charlotte. She remembered the stray dog, when she was a child, that bit two neighborhood children. Before her father chased it off with a rake, the dog had approached Charlotte, too. Moving slowly, calmly, with what seemed the utmost indifference.

"You're going to be sorry," Cindy said.

"Do you understand?" Charlotte said. "Leave us alone."

And then the deck shuddered beneath Charlotte's feet. Ed had returned to the bridge and started the engines. Charlotte dropped Cindy's wrist, and Cindy spun away with a laugh, her plaid skirt flaring.

The blood rushed back into Charlotte's body as Frank walked toward her and the girls, smiling.

28

Guidry knew that Ed had no pressing business to discuss below deck. He was just tugging Guidry's strings, making him dance, having what he, Ed, called fun. Guidry couldn't cause a scene. For his sake and Charlotte's both. She and the girls would be fine for five minutes. Leo was up there with them. He wouldn't let Cindy get out of hand.

"Scotch?" Ed poured without waiting for an answer. They were down in what Ed called the salon. Guidry had seen cathouses with a more subdued use of brass and red velvet.

"Where's the fire, Ed?" Guidry said. "Don't say you've had a change of heart about sending me to Vietnam."

Who, me? Ed waved away the mere suggestion. He settled into a stuffed leather wing chair and put up his feet.

"Boychick," Ed said, "this is your masterpiece. How'd you do it? You should see how she looks at you. She thinks you're the cat's meow. Don't sweat, I won't blow it for you."

"You just want to see me squirm a little," Guidry said.

"Just a little, sure."

"I still need her, remember. I'm not in Saigon yet."

"Don't sweat. The kids are on their best behavior. You like their getups? That was my idea. I knew you'd get a kick out of it."

Guidry listened to the slap and mumble of water against the hull. He listened to Ray Bolger snoring on the other side of the wall. Guidry couldn't hear what was happening up on deck. Anything at all, he knew, could be happening up on deck.

He lifted his glass and admired how the light filtered through the scotch. Don't rush. If he tried to rush, Ed would slow it down and make him pay.

Ed lit a cigar. "So. Our dear Charlotte. You really dig her, don't you?"

"Dig her?" Guidry said. "What do you mean?"

"Frank Guidry, of all people. I wouldn't believe it if I hadn't seen it with my own eyes."

There was no safe way to play this. Guidry could

hold his bluff and pray. He could come clean and pray. Ed might decide it was a weakness he couldn't afford: Guidry's feelings for Charlotte. Ed might decide it was a weakness he couldn't afford: Guidry sticking to a weak bluff.

Guidry shrugged. "Sure, I dig her," he said, "but what does it matter?"

What does it matter? He asked himself the same question. What did it matter if he might want to spend his life with Charlotte and the girls? What did it matter if he'd lost his goddamn mind? Tomorrow he'd be on a plane to Vietnam or he'd be dead. Either way he would never see Charlotte and the girls again.

Ed kept working away at his cigar. The first match burned down, so he lit a second one. He nodded, satisfied with Guidry's answer.

"Ray was supposed to sing for half an hour," Ed said. "That goggle-eyed bean-eater. He's not getting his money, I can promise you that."

"Let's toss him in the lake," Guidry said. "Make him swim home."

"Come by the house tonight. Nine o'clock or so. I'll have what you need for tomorrow. You want me to send Leo for you?"

"I remember the way."

"C'mon." Ed stood. "Back to the party."

Charlotte and the girls were safe and sound. It had never been in doubt, Guidry told himself. Ed raised anchor, and they headed back to port. Guidry had to prove to the satisfaction of Rosemary and Joan that he remembered the game they'd taught him, every word and every handclap.

Sweet, sweet, baby,
I'll never let you go,
Shimmy, shimmy cocoa pop,
Shimmy, shimmy pow.

Charlotte sat by herself, watching them, watching Guidry. Dusk falling, the lights of the marina twinkling. In the fading glow, Charlotte seemed to be fading, too, just a figment of his imagination, and that thought—she wasn't real, none of this was real—filled Guidry with a dread unlike any he'd ever known. Unlike any he'd known for a long, long time. He'd lost his mind. He'd fallen from grace. Until Charlotte and the girls came along, nothing in heaven or earth had been able to move him.

Guidry rode up front with Leo so that Charlotte and the girls could stretch out in the backseat of the Rolls. Rosemary and Joan slept all the way to the Hacienda. Charlotte did, too, curled in the far corner, her head resting against the window. Images flickered

and flared on the glass behind her, headlights and bill-
boards and a forked tongue of lightning far off across
the desert. It was as if Guidry could see the dreams
passing through her mind, projected up onto a movie
screen.

He couldn't go to Los Angeles with her and the
girls. The idea was too impossible to even entertain.
Carlos would find Guidry, anywhere in the country,
only a matter of time. That was if Ed didn't kill him
first, when Guidry said, *No thanks, Ed, I've changed
my mind about Vietnam, sorry for any inconvenience.*

"Leo." The backseat was a mile away, the tires on
the pavement a noisy hum, but Guidry kept his voice
soft anyway. Leo, absorbed by thoughts of his own,
didn't hear him the first time. "Leo."

"Yes, sir?" Leo said.

"I could use some good advice, Leo," Guidry said.

"As could we all, sir."

Guidry couldn't go to Los Angeles with Charlotte
and the girls. But what if they came with him to Vietnam? Guidry would have to convince Ed. Wasn't that
an even more impossible, and dangerous, idea?

"A man finds himself in a dark wood," Guidry
said. "And then he finds himself in a different, even
darker wood. He becomes exasperated with the hand
of fate."

"Quite understandable," Leo said.

"It's Milton, isn't it? Where Lucifer falls from grace? I never read Milton. I never really read Dante either. Just enough to fake it."

"'Awake, arise, or be for ever fall'n.'"

"Is that Milton? Don't show off, Leo. With that accent of yours, it's not a fair fight."

Leo nodded in pleasant agreement.

"I know the knack to a happy life, Leo," Guidry said. "So that should make every decision an easy one, should it not? I've never had any struggle before."

Leo didn't ask Guidry to explain the knack to a happy life. He didn't even raise a wry eyebrow. He seemed to grasp the point that Guidry was making. Guidry supposed that if Ed had detected his feelings for Charlotte, Leo had probably detected them, too.

"Say something, Leo."

Nope. Nothing. Not a single twitch of the Clark Gable mustache. Guidry gave up. But then Leo sighed.

"With every decision we create a new future," Leo said. "We destroy all other futures."

"That's heavy, Leo," Guidry said.

"Is it?"

"It sounds heavy, at least. With the accent."

Leo raised that wry eyebrow and pulled the Rolls up to the hotel entrance. Guidry reached over the seat to touch Charlotte's knee, but she was already sitting up. She hadn't been sleeping after all.

"Here we are," he said.

"Yes," she said.

No one had much of an appetite after the feast on Ed's boat, so they skipped dinner and watched the go-karts instead. Noisy insects, oily little exoskeletons, scuttling around the track. Guidry, Charlotte, and Joan watched—Rosemary pined to be out there, her fingers clutching the chain-link and steering each driver around the turn. Guidry smiled, but Charlotte hadn't noticed. After the go-karts, Guidry had a drink at the bar while Charlotte supervised baths and prayers, tucked the girls in.

Upstairs, his room, Guidry put a hand on Charlotte's waist and drew her close for a kiss. But she slipped away before he could get properly started.

"What's wrong?" he said.

She crossed to the window. Her back to him, her troubled face in profile. How had he missed it before now? On the boat, in the car. Frank Wainwright had missed it. Guidry, if he'd been himself, if he hadn't lost his goddamn mind, would have seen this coming from a mile away.

"Feeling all right?" he said. "Too much dessert earlier?"

"Frank," she said.

What had Cindy said to her on the boat? God only knew. God only knew what damage Guidry would now have to repair.

He walked over, caressed Charlotte's shoulder. "What is it?"

She turned to him finally. "Is there something you're keeping from me, Frank?"

He looked into her eyes. Tell her everything. Everything. Guidry had to fight the impulse. Tell her everything and beg her to believe that he'd changed, that he was changing, that he might change, just give him half a chance.

She'd be moved by his honesty and throw her arms around his neck, just like the actresses did in the movies, a swirl of perfume and violins. Sure, just like that. *Oh, Frank, you only needed a good woman to save you, didn't you?*

"Am I keeping something from you?" he said. "Of course not."

"It's Ed," Charlotte said. "Maybe I'm being silly, but it just seems . . . I don't know. I've seen you with him, Frank, and something just isn't quite . . . right."

"Well . . ."

"His niece, Cindy, told us a story about a woman who drowned. A woman on Ed's boat, a cocktail waitress at the Stardust. Or the woman claimed to be a cocktail waitress. Cindy made it seem as if Ed . . . I thought at first it was just a silly ghost story, but now I'm not sure."

J. Edgar Hoover's undercover girl. Guidry silently cursed Cindy. "That's why I didn't want to leave you alone with Cindy," he said. "I should have been honest from the beginning. It's why I didn't want to go to Lake Mead in the first place."

"Why?" Charlotte said.

"Ed does everything he can for her. She's his sister's only kid. He's paid for half a dozen different private schools. Cindy gets things mixed up in her head. She's a little . . . mixed up. You figured that out."

They were the right lyrics, but Guidry could tell that he was botching the melody. Charlotte's eyes searched his. You had to put your heart into deception, you had to give it everything you had. But Guidry didn't want to be doing this, he didn't want to lie to her, ever again.

She nodded, though. "I could see that, yes."

"Cindy read something in the papers," he said. "Or she saw something at the movies. Nobody drowned. She sat next to a cocktail waitress from the Stardust on the bus one day. That's how her mind works. Nobody drowned, not on Ed's boat."

"Who is he, Frank?" she said.

"Ed?"

"Who is he really?"

Put your fucking heart into this, Guidry warned himself, and do it now. Do it now or everything ends now.

"Look," Guidry said. "I admit it, Ed's no choirboy. That's why I didn't want you to meet him. Nothing illegal, but he does business with some characters. He has to, now and then. It's Las Vegas, after all."

"I have *children*, Frank," she said. "I have two daughters. Do you understand?"

"I'd never do anything to put the girls in any kind of danger. Never. I swear on my life. And we're done with Ed now. We're done with Cindy. All right?"

She took a deep breath and let it out slowly. She nodded again. She believed him. Guidry felt sick to his stomach with shame. If he really loved her, he'd turn around and walk out the door. If she really knew him, she'd walk out the door and run.

The thought of losing her, though, losing the girls—he truly couldn't bear it.

"I love you," he said.

She sighed. "Frank."

"It's crazy. You don't have to explain that to me. We've known each other hardly a week. But . . ."

Guidry had taught himself to drive when he was

ten years old. Sunday mornings, while his father slept off the Saturday-night bender. The truck was a rattletrap Ford, with a push-button starter and the gearshift down on the floor. Guidry bouncing along the parish back roads, palms sweating on the steering wheel and eyes watering because he was afraid to blink. Don't forget to check the mirror. Don't forget to check the other mirror. Aware of every thought and movement. Every movement requiring, first, a thought.

He remembered that feeling now. Don't forget to breathe.

"I'm not a kid anymore," he said. "I can tell what's fake and what's real. I think I can. You can tell it, too, can't you?"

She said nothing but let him take her hand and press it against his cheek.

"I didn't rub a lamp and wish for this," he said. "But now what can I do? I want to be with you and the girls, for the long haul. I just can't imagine it, my life, any other way."

"Frank . . ."

"Ed offered me a job overseas," Guidry said. "In Asia, in Vietnam. I have to go see him about it in a minute. It's a legitimate opportunity, no funny business. I want you to come with me. You and the girls."

"Come with you?" she said, startled. "To Asia?"

"Come with me. Vietnam is a beautiful country. Think of the pictures you'll take. Shadows you won't find anywhere else. I can't turn down the job. But just for a year or two, and then we'll go wherever we want."

She stared at him, trying to decide if he was serious.

Guidry needed that first yes again. He needed the chance that she'd given him back in Santa Maria, when he first offered the ride to Los Angeles.

"Just think it over before you decide," he said. "Will you do that? That's all I'm asking. Think it over before you decide. The girls can learn a new language. We'll all learn a new language. You said you wanted to see the world. Let's see it together."

"Frank," she said. "I'm not even divorced yet."

"That doesn't matter."

"It does. I left Oklahoma so that I could make a new life for myself, for the girls. I have to do that on my own. I *want* to do that on my own."

"You can. You will. We don't have to get married. That doesn't matter either. All that matters is I'm with you and you're with me. I love you. I love the girls."

"You're not listening to me, Frank."

"I am," he said. "Please. I don't know what the hell's happened to me. My life made sense to me before I met you. Now . . . it's like I bumped into you and the girls and something inside of me tumbled off a shelf. No. It's like all of me fell off the shelf and broke to pieces on the floor. I don't . . ."

Words were failing him. When in Guidry's life had that ever happened?

She turned back to the window, away from him again. He couldn't tell if she was looking out at the lights of the go-kart track or at her own reflection in the glass.

"I'm so thankful that I met you, Frank," she said. "You've no idea. I think *I* must have rubbed a lamp and wished for you, wished for this week we've had together. I just didn't realize it."

"Do you love me?" he said.

"I can't come with you, Frank."

"We'll make a life together. Any kind of life you want."

He gripped her slender arm so tightly that he could feel her pulse beating. He'd made a point of it, his entire life, of never wanting anything he didn't already hold in the palm of his hand. Of never wanting anything he wouldn't mind letting go.

Not now. Not now.

"Please," he said. "I'll be back in an hour, and we can talk about it. Just think about it. Give me a chance."

"Oh, Frank."

"We love each other. Nothing else matters."

He pressed his lips against hers. After a moment she kissed him back.

"Just think about it," he said. "Yes?"

She nodded again. "Yes," she said.

29

Searchlight was an hour south, on the way to Bullhead City. Barone had been through it on his way
up to Las Vegas. He'd passed right by the El Condor.

Moe Dalitz's meat had names. Joey, the driver, the
talker, the younger of the two, the dumber of the two,
thick neck striped with razor burn. He was the one
who'd put his arm around Barone back at the Hacienda.
Shelley, in the passenger seat, not a talker, snapping his
gum and cracking the knuckles on his right hand, one
by one. A former boxer, by the look of his chewed-up
ears. He didn't seem too bright himself.

I could use a guy like you around here. What Dalitz
had said to Barone, but it wasn't true. Dalitz and
Sam Giancana had a couple of guys almost as good as
Barone. But instead Dalitz had sent Joey Won't Shut

Up and Shelley the Broken-Down Palooka to pick up Barone and babysit him.

Did that mean something? Was Dalitz sending Barone a message? Was he telling Barone one thing and wanting him to do another? Barone didn't know. Not his line of work. Moe Dalitz, Carlos, Seraphine. They disguised every move. They told the truth with a lie and a lie with the truth. They arranged the dominoes and let some chump knock them over.

Barone could feel the fever building, brewing. Like it had back in New Mexico. His head would be steady for a long stretch, and then without any warning he'd be out to sea, bobbing around. Jumping through time, back in the Quarter as the old colored man played "'Round Midnight."

The ditch where he'd left the kid was on the other side of Bullhead City. Theodore, don't call me Ted, don't call me Teddy. Maybe the cops had found his body by now. Just some colored kid, who cares? The cops wouldn't go to any trouble for him.

Maybe after he took care of Guidry, Barone would forget about New Orleans. He didn't know where he would go, what he would do. His mind traveled to a place covered with snow, the air cold and sweet. Alaska, maybe.

"Your hear me?"

Barone came back from Alaska. "What?"

"I said here we are," Joey Won't Shut Up said.

Barone walked into the El Condor. His head was steady again for the time being, the clouds gone and the sky bright. Joey came inside with him. Shelley stayed in the car to watch the parking lot. In case Barone tried to sneak out of the hotel and give them the slip.

Joey talked to the manager and came back with Barone's key. The ratty little room had a bed, a chair, a dresser. Barone didn't see anything that he could use against Joey. The TV antenna ears, maybe. The glass ashtray. On a good day, he'd take Joey nine times out of ten, even Joey with a piece and Barone without one. But it wasn't a good day for Barone, and nine times out of ten wasn't good enough odds anyway.

If it's a fair fight, Barone learned early on, you've screwed up somewhere.

He took a seat on the edge of the bed. Joey took a seat in the chair. Barone stood back up. So did Joey.

"I'm getting a drink," Barone said.

"Whatever you say, Mr. Barone," Joey said.

The bar was dim and almost empty. They sat on the rail. Barone picked a spot by the jiggers and shakers, the spoons and the strainer, a bin full of ice. He ordered a double rye and Coca-Cola on the rocks for himself, one for Joey, too.

"Thank you," Joey said. "Now, that's the brotherly spirit."

"You have to sit on my lap?" Barone said.

Joey smirked. He scraped his stool an inch closer. "I'm just doing my job, Mr. Barone."

"Call me Paul."

"I got a brother named Paul," Joey said. "He lives back east, Providence, works construction. You think I'm a load, you should see Paulie. I'm the runt of the family."

"Who tipped your boss?" Barone said. "You have any idea? You weren't tailing me last night. I would have made you."

Joey smirked. Barone didn't make him nervous. Why would he? Joey was one of Moe Dalitz's guys. You hit one of Moe Dalitz's guys, you're hitting Moe himself, and then watch out. Nobody would be so foolish. That's what Joey believed. Barone understood that it was more complicated than that. He understood better than anyone.

"Paulie played right tackle at Notre Dame," Joey said. "You should have seen him play. When he hit the defensive line, it'd blow up like you threw a hand grenade at it. Boom. Could have played in the pros. Everybody said so."

It was driving Barone up the wall. Nobody knew

that he'd tracked Guidry to the Hacienda. Just Stan Contini. Just Seraphine if Stan had talked to her. So how then . . . ?

Seraphine.

But she wouldn't want to gum up the works. She wanted Barone to finish Guidry. She *needed* him to finish Guidry. Seraphine was on the hook for all this, the same as Barone.

Somebody had tipped Moe Dalitz, though. Somebody . . . Fuck, Barone saw it now, he started to pick apart the knot. Go all the way back to Houston. How did Guidry get past Remy, that first night at the hotel bar? Because someone had tipped him. Guidry had known that Remy was waiting for him.

Seraphine. She'd tipped Guidry in Houston. She was gumming it up for Barone in Vegas. Or it was whoever owned that green Rolls.

Joey pointed his swizzle stick at Barone's wrapped-up right hand, his bad hand. "What happened to your mitt there?"

"It was in the wrong place at the wrong time," Barone said.

"Hurt much?"

"Only when my heart beats."

"I got another brother, Gary, he works for Ray up in Boston," Joey said. "You ever heard of him? Gary

Ganza. He's the brains of the family. He's on his way up. Gary Ganza. Watch the marquee. His name'll be up in lights one of these days."

Barone waited until Joey leaned and reached for a handful of peanuts. He gave the barstool a nudge with his knee. Joey was almost as big as the mark back in Houston—bigger, even—but give me a lever and I can move the world.

Joey caught himself just in time, before he toppled over. Slapping the bar top, though, spilling peanuts, cussing. The bartender had seen it before. He shot Joey a dirty look and moved away to smoke in peace.

"You're wet already, Joey?" Barone said. "After only one drink?"

Joey wasn't grinning now. He bent over and glared down. "Something's wrong with the goddamn stool."

"Better write a letter to your congressman."

"Screw you," Joey said.

"I've heard of a Gary who works for Patriarca," Barone said. The lacquered cherrywood handle of the ice pick was curved, shaped like an hourglass. The wood cold in Barone's left fist, because the bartender had left the pick lying right next to the bin. "What's the last name again?"

Joey finished giving the leg of his stool what for. "Ganza. What did you hear about Gary?"

"I don't want to tell tales out of school," Barone said. "C'mon. Spill."

Barone put his right arm around Joey's shoulders, and Joey leaned in to listen, and Barone brought up his left hand and jammed the five-inch needle through Joey's earhole. So quick and clean, in and out, that Joey didn't realize for a second that he was dead. His lashes fluttering, his lips puckering. And then he slumped. Barone, ready, caught him before he could slide off the stool. Not a drop of blood. The angle had to be just right, but that was the beauty of an ice pick through the brain.

Now the tough part. Barone ducked under Joey's arm and lifted him to his feet. The runt of the family, hard to believe. Barone staggered, dug in, held up. The dead weighed more than the living. It was a fact.

"C'mon, buddy," Barone said. "You've had enough to drink. Let's put you to bed."

Barone left a five on the bar. When the bartender glanced over, Barone gave him the Moe Dalitz shrug, shoulder up around his ear. Hey, what can you do?

He lugged his blacked-out pal from the bar. Slow work. Heave. Ho. Barone started to sweat, his legs shaking. Past the blackjack tables. Nobody paid any attention to him and Joey. Down the hallway. Good thing the El Condor was such a runt itself, the entire joint not much bigger than the lobby of the Dunes or the Stardust. If Barone had to lug Joey through the Dunes or the Stardust, he'd never make it.

The room, finally. Barone unlocked the door and dumped Joey on the bed. He tried Joey in a couple of different positions, arms and legs here and there, with the pillow and without, before he decided on an arrangement that looked right, looked natural, like a guy flopping off a bender.

He took Joey's piece, the .45. A dribble of blood now, curling out of Joey's ear and down his cheek, along his jaw. Barone found Joey's handkerchief in the breast pocket of his sport coat. He dabbed the blood clean and then folded the handkerchief back up, tucked it away.

In Belgium when a shell burst close by, the concussion sucked you out of your body and then shoved you back inside, wrong side up. Barone's fever was more gentle than that, more like the universe breathing you in and out, in and out, but the same general sickening sensation. Barone needed to puke. He went into the bathroom and bent over the bowl. Nothing came up. The sweat poured off him. But he just needed to wait a minute. It would pass.

Seraphine. Was she the one who'd tipped Guidry in Houston? Who'd gummed up Barone in Vegas?

He would find out. You could count on it. After Barone took care of Guidry, he was going to hop the first flight back to New Orleans, kick in the door of Seraphine's house on Audubon Park, and do to her for pleasure all the things that over the years she'd had him do for business.

Shelley the Broken-Down Palooka had the car window open, his arm resting on the frame. He saw Barone and tried to figure it. Barone alone, but not running away. Barone alone, walking toward him with a calm, friendly expression. Barone saying, "Better come inside, Joey is puking up his breakfast. Must be some kind of bug."

By the time Shelley started fumbling for the piece in his holster, Barone was already there, and it was too late.

30

When Charlotte said that she'd consider going with him to Vietnam, that she'd give him a chance to convince her, the relief Guidry felt was such sweet thunder—the sky breaking open and the rain raking across parched fields. But he enjoyed the moment for exactly that long: a moment. By the time the elevator dropped him to the lobby and the doors rattled open, his stomach was clenched, his mouth dry.

First the hard part, now the harder part. Here we go.

He walked across the parking lot. Cold tonight, the wind slashing. What would Ed say when Guidry asked if he could bring Charlotte and the girls along to Saigon? Ed might say yes. He might shrug and say, *Why the hell not?* Because Ed was, let's be honest, certifiably cuckoo. He might think it was a gas—Guidry in Saigon with June Cleaver and the two little Beaverettes. As long as Guidry did the job that Ed wanted him to do, as long as Guidry did it well. *Sure, boychick, why the hell not?* Ed would want to hear all the amusing details. He'd tune in every week.

Driving, Guidry prepared his case. *Ed, I'll do the job you want me to do. I'll do it well.*

Charlotte and the girls would be an advantage in Vietnam, not a vulnerability. Consider the angles. Guidry needed to make friends in high places. A lot of the Americans in Saigon—the lieutenant colonels and brigadier generals, the embassy officers and economic advisers, the procurers and suppliers—a lot of those men would bring along their own wives and kids. They'd trust a fellow family man. Cookouts and dinner-dances and sunbathing by the hotel swimming pool. *Say, Jim, have you and Susie found a reliable babysitter yet?*

Don't you see, Ed?

Ed might see, if he let Guidry get that far. If Ed didn't just laugh and shoot Guidry before he even got started.

But why worry? The time for that had passed. Guidry's history was already written. He thought about what Leo had said: *With every decision we create a new future. We destroy all other futures.* Guidry had made his decision. He'd destroyed all futures but this one.

He turned off the highway and followed the winding drive to Ed's house. The night couldn't make up its mind. Black or bright? For a hundred yards, Guidry couldn't see an inch past the reach of his headlights, but then the moon would punch free of the clouds. The saguaro rearing up, the red rock walls about to topple down on him.

He kept his window open. Freezing his ass off, but he didn't want to start sweating.

Ed's glass house was dark. In one far window, Guidry caught what might have been the tip of a cigarette glowing.

The front door had a heavy brass knocker that Guidry hadn't noticed the first time. It was the mournful face of a gargoyle, eyes closed. When Guidry lifted the face to knock, he found a second face underneath. The same gargoyle, but grinning now, eyes open, staring back at him.

After a long minute, Leo opened the door. He'd traded his black Savile Row suit for a sport shirt and faded blue jeans and a pair of leather huaraches.

"Sorry," Guidry said. "I was looking for my old pal Leo."

Leo's eyes twinkled. "Good evening, sir. Mr. Zingel is in the library. If you'll follow me."

They passed through the dark and empty living room. Through the dark and empty dining room. Not a sound, just their footsteps' *tap-tap-tap* on the marble and the wind booming against the plate glass. Out over the desert, the moon blinked on, the moon blinked off. Guidry wished that Cindy and her friends were here, splashing in the pool or lounging on the zebra-skin rug. Ed's lost boys and girls gave him the creeps, but this deserted house was worse.

"Where's the gang tonight, Leo?" he said.

"Mr. Zingel sent them to the pictures in town," Leo said.

A light at the end of the tunnel, the golden frolic of a fireplace, Ed's library. Ed sat behind a big oak desk. Guidry took one of the club chairs in front of it. There wasn't much on the desk. A telephone, a box of cigars, a manila envelope stuffed thick. Ed's gun.

"Romantic, Ed," Guidry said, "and I appreciate the effort, but turn on a lamp for God's sake, will you?"

"I do my best deliberating in the dark," Ed said.

The moon blinked on. Two walls of the library were nothing but glass.

Guidry nodded. "That's better," he said. "Thank you."

"Anything for you, boychick."

"You're still deliberating?"

"Not about this. Not about you." Ed glanced at his watch. "I made up my mind minutes ago."

Leo brought Guidry a glass of scotch, neat. Ed pointed to the manila envelope.

"The paperwork that'll get you onto Nellis, out of Nellis, into Vietnam," Ed said. "It's all on the up-and-up, more or less. You toil in middle management for a company that has an army contract. Rain-suit parkas and combat trousers, lightweight, Limited Procurement Order 8901. Fletcher and Sons Fabric and Apparel, Holyoke, Massachusetts. It's a real company, a real contract. I might even turn a profit."

"You know, I've always wanted to get into pants."

"You're hitching a ride with a fine pilot and degenerate gambler by the name of Colonel Butch Tolliver. His bird flies tomorrow evening at seven sharp, a transport Cargomaster. I'm still working on a passport. Give me a few weeks. You won't need one right away, since you're flying into Tan Son Nhut. That's the air base. Nguyen's greased all the necessary wheels. So for the time being, you're still Frank Guidry. Can you remember that?"

"I'll do my best," Guidry said.

"Leo, run downstairs and get us a bottle of the good stuff, will you?" Ed said. "The '46 Macallan. We're celebrating. Grab yourself a glass, too."

Ed gave the manila envelope a flick of his finger. It spun across the polished wood to Guidry's side of the desk. Guidry didn't reach for it.

"What are you waiting for, boychick?" Ed said. "There's no surprise twist. The surprise twist is that there's no surprise twist. You're going to have a long and fruitful life. We're going to have a long and fruitful partnership."

"I've a favor to ask, Ed."

Ed had been about to clip the end off a cigar. He put down the cutter. He put down the cigar. "Another favor, you mean."

"You've already done a lot for me," Guidry said. "Nobody understands that better than I do."

"It appears not," Ed said, "or you wouldn't be asking for another favor. Do you have any idea what I've sacrificed for you? The money and the goodwill I'm leaving on the table? Guess how much you're worth to Carlos."

"So you've made the discreet inquiry."

"Of course I have. Don't sound so shocked."

"I'm not shocked."

"You would've done the same thing, boychick, if you'd been in my place. I hope so, anyway."

Guidry drank his scotch, all of it, one long swallow. "I want to take Charlotte and her daughters with me to Vietnam."

The moon blinked off. The room went dark again. Guidry couldn't make out Ed's expression. The wind outside paused to gather itself and then charged again, yowling at the glass.

"You've got some balls," Ed said. "I'll say that for you."

"Let's look at the advantages," Guidry said.

"What's the expression you always use? 'Ye gods.' That's it. Mind if I borrow it?"

"I've thought it through, Ed. I'll do the job you want me to do. I'll do it well. This won't change anything."

Hearing the words out loud, Guidry knew that his argument was doomed. He'd known it all along and just refused to admit it. Balls were well and good, but a man who put those balls on the block for a woman and two kids he'd met a week ago? Who in the world would ever have faith in that man's judgment again?

"Ye gods," Ed said.

"Ed . . ."

"All right. I can arrange it."

Guidry's momentum had almost carried him into the next sentence. *Ed, just listen to me, they'll trust a family man even more than they'll trust a single . . .*

"What?" Guidry said.

"I've picked my horse, boychick. Now I want to see him run. You'll pay off for me or you won't. Besides, who am I to stand in the way of true love?"

What?

But then Ed was shifting in his chair, his smile was flashing from the darkness, his hand was resting on the gun.

"Just one condition," Ed said. "I keep one of the little girls for myself. Your choice, I don't care which one."

Guidry tried to smile back. "Hilarious, Ed," he said.

"Is it?" Ed said. "It's a good deal, I think. You still come out ahead. We can flip a coin if you want. What are their names again?"

A log in the fireplace burst into brilliant confetti. The moon blinked on. Ed roared with laughter. "You should see your face, boychick."

"Goddamn it, Ed."

"Am I a monster?" Ed said. "Is that what you think of me? I'm disappointed. I'm flattered."

"Goddamn you."

Ed picked his cigar back up and clipped the end. "I've already arranged it. Charlotte, the kids. All four of you are on that flight tomorrow."

"You already . . ."

"I knew you'd want to take them along," Ed said. "Well, I gave it even odds. Everything you'll need is in the envelope. Go ahead, take it."

Ed noticed that Leo was still lingering in the doorway.

"Did I just imagine it, Leo," he said, "or did I ask you to run downstairs and get that bottle of '46 Macallan so we can celebrate?"

Guidry picked up the manila envelope. He wanted to climb over the desk and give the big bastard a hug. "Goddamn you, Ed."

"I was in love once," Ed said. "I bet you didn't know that. Long ago, but I remember what it feels like. Love doesn't last, but that doesn't mean it wasn't ever there."

"I don't know if it's love," Guidry said. "I don't know what it is."

"Just don't come crying to me. When you get bored and want to ship the wife and kids back stateside. By the way, you're staying here tonight. You'll be safer."

"Safer?"

"I'll send Leo for the ladies. Give them a call. Let them know he's on the way." Ed looked over again. "Leo! Wake up, for God's sake!"

Leo still hadn't moved from the doorway. Guidry had only half a second to wonder why, half a second to wonder why Leo had a gun in his hand, and then time jerked forward, jumped ahead, Leo's arm already raised and the trigger already pulled, the earsplitting rip of blue fire leaping toward Ed and Ed's head snapping back, a puff of blood.

Leo.

Leo.

Leo, who knew how much Guidry was worth to Carlos, dead or alive.

Guidry had been shot at before, plenty of times during the war, so he didn't freeze when Leo turned and pointed the gun at him. He dove for the desk. Oak and heavy, between him and the doorway. He felt and then heard, thump and crack, the second bullet miss him by inches. The glass wall behind the chair where he'd been sitting frosted over.

All Leo had to do was take a few steps to his left. Guidry was in a corner, nowhere to hide. Ed, one last favor before he died, had managed to grab for his gun and knock it to the carpet. But it was too far away, on the wrong side of the desk.

Leo. Making his big move. Take out Ed, cash in Guidry. Ed, if his brains hadn't been blown loose, would have been impressed.

"Come out," Leo said.

"Leo. Let's discuss this."

What was Leo waiting for? He hadn't spotted Ed's gun yet. He thought Guidry might have it.

"Come out," Leo said.

The moon blinked off. He who hesitates. Guidry

scrambled for Ed's gun, and blue fire blazed, and out of nowhere a girl screamed. A scream of blistering, bloodthirsty fury.

The shot missed, Guidry wasn't dead. He didn't think so. He came up and saw some kind of demon thrashing around on Leo's back. Cindy, digging her fingers into Leo's face, like she was trying to peel the skin off his skull.

Leo spun, looking for a clean shot over his shoulder. They lurched together across the library, and Leo fired, and Cindy's head snapped back. Still she hung on to him. Leo spun again and flung her off, into the window already frosted by the bullet. The glass shattered. Cindy and all the winking shards spilled onto the black lava rocks outside.

Leo turned toward Guidry, and Guidry shot him in the chest. Leo dropped his gun and went down on one knee. He shook with laughter. *Ha! Ha!* That's what it looked like. Guidry shot him again. Leo tipped over. He blew one last dark bubble of blood.

Cindy was dead, too. Ed was dead. Guidry allowed himself three deep breaths. One, two, three. That was it, all he could afford, no more. He made sure he had his car keys. He made sure he had the manila envelope.

He walked through the house and out the door. He didn't hear or see anybody else. Either Cindy had returned alone from the movies or the other kids had fled when they heard the gunshots.

One last deep breath, for the road. Guidry got into his car and started the engine.

31

It was clear now to Charlotte that Frank was hiding something from her. Hiding everything, perhaps. About Ed, about himself. But a different realization—he wasn't listening to her, he'd stopped listening to her— made her heart grow even heavier.

"I left Oklahoma so that I could make a new life for myself and the girls," she said. "I have to do that on my own. I *want* to do that on my own."

"Just think about it," he said. "Give me a chance. We love each other. Nothing else matters."

He kissed her. She kissed him back.

"Will you think about it?" he said. "Yes?"

Charlotte nodded. "Yes."

She did love him, she supposed. But at this point in her life, so much else mattered, too. So much else mattered more. He would have understood that, if only he'd been listening.

"Good-bye, Frank," she said.

"I'll be back in an hour or so."

The door closed behind him. Charlotte took a seat on the bed to wait. The cream-colored chenille spread was patterned with rosebuds. She counted them one by one. When she reached fifty, when she'd given Frank enough time to take the elevator down and walk to his car, when she was sure that he wouldn't return for forgotten car keys or wallet, she stood and crossed the hall.

She left the light in her room off—the glow from the miniature-golf course would have to do—and slid open the dresser drawers as quietly as possible.

The girls would be indignant. They always insisted on packing their own suitcases and placed great importance on what went where, in which order, exactly. But Charlotte didn't want to wake them yet, not until everything was ready. Rosemary would have too many questions. Charlotte would have to stop and explain to her why they were leaving now, why Frank wasn't coming with them, why they needed to hurry, hurry, hurry. Charlotte had only an hour until Frank returned. She didn't want to say good-bye to him twice.

Get in the cab, girls, hurry, hurry, hurry. I'll explain everything once we're on the bus.

Was there a late-evening bus to Los Angeles? Yes, surely there was. If not, Charlotte would cross that bridge when she came to it.

Would the girls ask why Frank hadn't said good-bye to them? Oh, yes, surely they would. Charlotte had no idea yet what she'd tell them. She'd cross that bridge later, too.

One of Joan's shoes was missing. Charlotte got down on her knees and felt around beneath the bed. The dog padded over and pressed his cold nose against the side of her neck.

"Don't worry," she whispered to him. "I haven't forgotten you."

The dog flopped down next to her and heaved a skeptical sigh.

"They won't keep you off the bus," she told him. "I won't let them."

Charlotte felt . . . good. Bright-edged and clear-headed and optimistic. It was only a bit more than a week ago that she'd sat numb and exhausted at the dining-room table as Dooley carved the Sunday roast. Only a bit more than a week ago that the prospect of yet another day of this—her life, in her skin—had made her want to curl into a ball and never move again.

Now, even though she knew that there were trials yet to come, she couldn't wait for tomorrow. She couldn't wait to see what it might bring.

Joan's missing shoe finally revealed itself, wedged between the wastebasket and a leg of the desk. Climbing to her feet, Charlotte saw an envelope on the desk. She'd almost missed it in the dim light. Inside the envelope were the prints from the roll of film she'd entrusted to Gigi.

Charlotte shuffled through the stack. The shot from the miniature-golf course had turned out rather nice, though not quite the way she'd expected. The shutter had lagged a bit, spilling the shadows from the windmill onto Frank and the girls. But the extra split second had given Rosemary's pirouette an extra inch of lift and thrown Joan's golf ball into stark white relief and caught Frank at the very beginning of a smile.

She stuffed the photos into her purse and finished packing. She checked to make sure that the girls were still asleep. Their day at the lake had knocked the stuffing out of them, and they hadn't stirred. It would be a struggle to wake and dress them, but Charlotte had time.

Back across the hall in Frank's room, she found a pen and a sheet of hotel stationery. She didn't know what to put in the note. What more was there to say? Already he was beginning to transform in her mind, changing from a real person to a fond memory. A memory that would grow perhaps even fonder over time, but also less real.

She considered giving the photo to him, the one from the miniature-golf course. It was the best of the batch, though, so she decided to keep it for herself.

When she opened the door to leave, she was surprised to find a man standing there. He'd been about to knock, she assumed, though his arms were at his sides.

"Oh," she said. "Hello."

"I'm with the hotel," the man said.

"Is there a problem?"

"Back inside."

Her sudden panicked thought: a fire, the girls, why had she not heard the alarm? She had to go to them, she had to go to them *now*. "My daughters. I need to—"

"Back inside," the man said. He took a step forward, and Charlotte had to take a step backward and before she realized what was happening, the man had closed the door behind him, he'd locked it.

He was chalky, sweating, a fringe of dark hair damp and jagged against his forehead. His suit looked as if he'd slept in it.

He didn't work for the hotel. His eyes moved around the room. His right hand was bandaged, from the wrist to the tips of the fingers. She hadn't noticed that before. In his left hand, he held a gun. Where had the gun come from? She hadn't noticed it either.

She felt dizzy. Maybe, maybe this man did work for the hotel. Hotel security. Maybe . . .

"Where is he?" the man said.

"This isn't my room," Charlotte said.

"Where is he?"

"He's not here. He went to visit a friend."

"Sit down. The bed."

If she screamed, the girls might wake. They might come running. They knew where she was. Every night when she'd tucked them in, she'd made sure that they understood. *I'm just across the hall. I'll be back by ten. If you need anything, anything at all, come and get me.*

If she screamed and the man fired his gun at her, the girls would hear the shot and come running. He would shoot them, too.

The girls, the girls, the girls. Charlotte's brain stammered and stalled. The girls, the girls, the girls—she could think of nothing else. Whatever happened, whatever she did or did not do, whatever this man did or did not do to her, she had to keep him away from Rosemary and Joan.

She'd been so stupid. This was about Frank. No, it was about the man she'd thought was Frank. How could she have been so stupid? Her hands were shaking. She clenched them and pressed her fists flat against the chenille bedspread, the patterned rosebuds.

"When will he be back?" the man said.

"I'm not sure," she said. "In about forty-five minutes, I think."

The man peeked into the bathroom, into the closet. He pulled the drapes shut. "I'm not going to hurt you."

His voice, quiet and conversational, should have calmed her. It didn't. He pulled the chair away from the desk and took a seat by the door. He used his bandaged hand to swab the sweat from his temple, his forehead.

He was Frank's age. Shorter, slighter, just . . . ordinary. That was really the only way Charlotte could think to describe him. If not for the pallor, he might have been just any one of a dozen men—clerks and waiters and fellow guests—she'd encountered at the hotel. Eyes, a nose, a mouth. She waited for him to blink as he looked around the room one more time, but he didn't.

He crossed his legs. He draped the arm with the bandaged hand over the back of the chair. He rested the gun on his knee, the barrel angled casually at a spot a few feet to her left.

He wasn't nervous. Why was he sweating? He wasn't drunk either.

"You understand what happens if you give me any trouble?" he said.

She forced herself to ignore the gun. She concentrated on the nodding toe of his black oxford. The girls, the girls, the girls. What if Rosemary had one of her nightmares and could not be consoled? Joan knew what to do. Let's go get Mommy. What if Joan woke with a tummyache? Rosemary knew what to do. Let's go get Mommy. She's just across the hall.

A soft, tentative knock on the door. Any minute now. The man would turn. Charlotte would scream as loud as she could. *Run!* She'd throw herself at the man and grab for his gun and keep screaming. *Run!*

Would they? Would the girls run? Almost every decision that Rosemary and Joan made together required much discussion. How many times had she come across them whispering, their heads together, deliberating like a pair of lawyers in the courtroom? Charlotte's scream might blast them into action, or it might freeze them in place.

She wouldn't live long enough to find out which. She would die without knowing if they were safe or not.

"You understand what happens if you give me any trouble?" the man said again.

She looked up at him. "Let me go," she said. "Please. I'm leaving. I've already packed my bags. Whatever it is, whatever you want with Frank or with Ed, I don't have anything to do with it. I . . . I don't care."

"I'm not going to hurt you." But the man said it only after a pause, as if he were an actor prodded from off-stage to deliver a line required of him.

"Please," she said. "Let me go."

His shoulders sagged. His eyes softened. What was happening to him? One time Charlotte had taken a chocolate cake from the oven too soon, an early poor effort, and watched it slump in on itself before her eyes.

The man managed to steady himself. He straightened back up. He didn't drop the gun.

"Ted?" he said.

"No," she said. "His name is Ed. I don't know his last name. He's Frank's friend."

A shiver rippled through the man. Rippled away. Color, a little, returned to his cheeks and his lips.

"You're ill," Charlotte said. "You have a fever."

"I've been worse," he said.

"My name is Charlotte. What's your name?"

She knew that it was hopeless. He looked at her the same way he looked at the goosenecked lamp on the desk or the glass ashtray on the nightstand or the blank wall behind her.

"If anyone asks me," she said, "I'll swear that I never saw you."

"Shut up," he said.

"Would you like me to bring you a glass of water?"

What could she do? The girls, the girls, the girls. The knock on the door, any second now. What would happen when Frank returned?

"Where are your kids?" he said.

Now the shiver rippled through *her*. He could read her mind. No. She remembered that she'd told him about the girls, even before he entered the room. So stupid. She'd been so stupid from the beginning.

"I said where are your kids?"

"Downstairs," Charlotte said. "In the nursery."

"The nursery's closed."

He didn't know if the nursery was closed or not. But Charlotte realized it too late. He caught her initial hesitation.

"Are they next door?" he said. "Across the hall?"

"What happened to your hand? I have aspirin in my purse." Anything to change the subject. "Is Frank Wainwright his real name? He told me that he sold insurance in New York. I'm so stupid."

The man uncrossed his legs and planted his black oxfords on the carpet. He braced his elbow against the back of the chair but managed to lift himself only a few inches before he sank down again. Charlotte thought he might set his gun on the floor or the dresser, so that he could use his good hand to pull himself up. He didn't, though, and when he tried a second time to stand, he succeeded.

"Toss it here," he said.

"What?" she said.

"The aspirin."

She unsnapped her purse. The stack of photos, an emery board, a box of matches, her compact and lipstick, a room key attached to a diamond-shaped plastic tag. Nothing that Charlotte could use as a weapon. A stick of gum. Rosemary's beloved Rickshaw Racer, a snap-together toy from a box of Rice Krinkles.

"Toss it here," he said.

He caught the bottle between his bandaged hand and his chest. He unscrewed the lid with his teeth. He shook tablets into his mouth and chewed them.

"I can bring you a glass of water," he said.

"Let's go see your kids."

He might have said something else, too, but Charlotte didn't hear it. For a moment she went deaf. Just a thin, whining buzz in her ears, growing louder and louder, the steam pressure building and building. How long, after your heart had stopped beating, could you stay alive?

"No," she said.

"Take me to your room," he said. "We're going to wait for Frank there."

"We can wait here."

"Don't you want to be with your kids?"

He was going to murder her and the girls. Charlotte knew that without a doubt. She could *see* it. Could see the gleam of porcelain and tile and mirrored glass. Rosemary's lifeless body in the bathtub. Joan's lifeless body nestled against her. Two peas in a pod. The plastic shower curtain torn from its rings. Charlotte's own lifeless body on the floor. The sink faucet running and a man's hand cupping the water.

Charlotte saw exactly what the man with the gun saw. It was as if the two of them stood side by side at a window, gazing out together at the future they would share.

"Get up," he said.

"No," Charlotte said.

He lifted the gun and pointed it at her. She panicked. She came apart at the seams. The girls, the girls, the girls. And yet, at the same time, something more powerful than panic held her still, calmed her mind, emptied it of every fear, every dread, every distraction.

Let him shoot her. The girls would hear the gunshot, but so would the other people in this wing of the hotel. Someone would call the front desk, the police. The man would have to flee. He knew that. That was why he didn't want to shoot her. He wanted to take her across the hall and keep everything quiet. He expected Charlotte to keep the girls quiet for him. *Shhh,* he expected her to tell them. *It's all right, he's not going to hurt us.*

"Get up now," he said.

She knew that he would shoot her. She didn't care. Charlotte saw him for what he was: a weak man, powerless to move her as long as she refused to budge.

And she could do that. She had not a doubt in her mind.

"How did you hurt your hand?" she said.

"Get up or else," he said. "I won't tell you again."

"Do you have someone?"

"Do I have someone?"

"A wife. A girlfriend. Someone who can take care of your hand."

He was unsteady on his feet. Sweating, shivering. She watched as it began to happen again—the sag, the swoon, his fever bursting into fresh bloom. He watched, too. They stood side by side at their window and looked into the future together. His eyes glazing, his knees buckling, the gun slipping from his grasp and thudding to the carpet.

"You're very ill," she said. "Don't you think you should sit down again?"

He set the gun on the dresser. And then he was across the room, two startlingly swift strides—he was standing above her, he had his hand around her throat, he'd shoved her backward onto the bed. The weight of him astonished her. A thousand crushing pounds falling from the sky. She couldn't breathe. She tried to twist away, but that made it worse. Her throat. The steady crushing strength of his fingers astonished her. He'd pinned her shoulders. She couldn't breathe and she couldn't move. Her vision started to warp and pulse.

"Shit," he said. His voice in her ear. She smelled the aspirin on his breath. She smelled the sweet, rotten tang of the dirty bandage. His sweat dripped down and stung her eyes. "Shit."

Because he'd begun to float. That's what it felt like. Like he was lifting slowly away from her, all that weight, ounce by ounce, flakes of ashes scattered by the breeze. He struggled to hold on. He shivered, his eyes glazed.

She could move one arm now, just a little. What was she searching for? She didn't know. His gun, tucked into his waistband. No. He'd left the gun on the dresser. He was too smart.

Ounce by ounce, flake by flake, he lifted away, the pressure on her throat easing. The fever had taken him again. But not far enough, too slowly. She still couldn't breathe.

Her searching hand was trapped now—tangled in a pocket, the pocket of his suit coat. She touched a smooth wooden handle. She touched a steel shaft attached to the handle, slender as a needle. The sharp tip pricked the pad of her index finger.

She gripped the wooden handle, and then with the rest of the life left in her she thrust the ice pick into his side. Into his stomach? His thigh? Between his ribs? She didn't know. She didn't know if he even felt it. His breathing quickened slightly, but that might have been the fever and nothing else.

And then she felt his grip on her neck go slack. He slid off her, turning to recline languidly on his side, head resting on his arm. She didn't know if he was alive or dead. He might have been a man just waking from a nap, about to open his eyes and yawn, if not for the dark stain spreading out from beneath his belly.

She rolled off the bed and stumbled to her feet. Her throat was on fire. She had to learn how to breathe again. In, out. *She* was alive. She was fairly sure of that.

She found her purse and closed the door of Frank's room behind her. At some point, soon, all this would overwhelm her. Whatever black magic that Charlotte was using to keep away the panic, the fear, the horror—soon it would vanish with a thunderclap, and in the flood that came afterward she'd be lost for hours, for days, she'd not be able to remember her own name or put one foot in front of the other.

Soon, but not yet.

32

Guidry forced himself to drive the limit. Steady Eddie, sticking to his lane and signaling well in advance of every turn. He forced his mind to slow down, too. Take your time. Look at the big picture. Don't miss anything.

Ed's house was in the middle of nowhere. Good. No nosy neighbors, no visitors dropping by for a chat or a cup of sugar. Cindy's friends wouldn't call the cops. Those kids had been around, they understood how the world worked. If they hadn't bolted already, they would scatter when they sniffed the shit they were in.

So Guidry had time. Ed's housekeeper wouldn't report to work and find the bodies until tomorrow morning. Or maybe Ed didn't employ a housekeeper.

Maybe it was Leo who'd mopped the floors and scrubbed the toilets and fished the golden hair of youth out of the drains. And that indignity was why he'd turned on Ed and made his grab for the brass ring.

Guidry didn't take it personally. Leo saw his chance and jumped. But Guidry needed to know if Leo had negotiated a price for him in advance. He hoped Leo had been acting on impulse when he pulled the trigger, because if not . . .

Had Leo talked to someone about Guidry? Did he spill the beans that Guidry was at the Hacienda? A good-faith gesture, proof that Leo had the golden goose in hand?

No. Leo wouldn't do that. Giving up Guidry's whereabouts would've made him disposable. Leo wouldn't have cut himself out of his own deal. Guidry hoped not.

He checked the speedometer. The needle had begun to creep. Easy, now. He'd be at the Hacienda in ten minutes. He'd have Charlotte and the girls packed up in twenty. He'd have them in the car and the car back on the road and the road singing beneath the tires all before the blood on the floor of Ed's library had stopped steaming.

They had to get out of Vegas. Not too far out of Vegas. A motel in one of the little dried-out desert towns that littered Highway 90 like molted snake skins, a safe place where they could wait out the day.

A day was all they needed. Because Ed might be dead, but Colonel Butch Tolliver, degenerate gambler, was still alive. His plane would still fly out of Nellis tomorrow evening at seven o'clock, with Guidry and Charlotte and the girls aboard.

Why wouldn't it? Colonel Butch had been paid up front, Guidry assumed, and wasn't waiting for Ed to give the go-ahead. Ed would have used a cutout to make the arrangements. Probably Colonel Butch didn't even know from where in heaven his bread was falling.

Guidry glanced at the manila envelope in the seat next to him. The paperwork was clean an hour ago. With luck it would remain that way.

You're staying here tonight. You'll be safer.

Ed's last words. Guidry hadn't pondered them until now. What did they mean? Maybe that Seraphine had tracked Guidry to the Hacienda. Maybe that Guidry's time, if he didn't turn the car around right now, was already up.

He didn't turn the car around. The girls would be asleep already. It was almost ten-thirty. Guidry would carry them to the car, one on each hip, the way he'd carried them that first night in Flagstaff. He could still feel the dense warmth of them, Rosemary's soft cheek against his rough one, Joan's breath on his neck. He could still see Charlotte, at the top of the steps, smiling down at him.

Guidry remembered the first time she smiled at him. He remembered the first time he made her laugh. The diner in Santa Maria, Pat Boone on the jukebox, not long after Guidry had launched his devious scheme. The laugh started in her eyes, and in that first spark he caught a glimpse of her from beginning to end, her past and present and future, the little girl she'd been and the old woman that one day she'd become.

This is going to work, he remembered thinking. I hope this works.

What kind of father would he be? What kind of husband? A lousy one, Guidry had to admit, let's be honest. He knew nothing about being a father and a husband. But he planned to give it everything he had, everything. That was a price he was prepared to pay.

And who could say? Maybe twenty or thirty or forty years from now, Guidry would look back at the man he'd once been, that sharp-dressed fella sitting in the Carousel Bar at the Hotel Monteleone in New Orleans, and barely recognize him, just some old acquaintance whose name he could no longer recall.

The southern end of Las Vegas Boulevard. The runway lights of McCarran just ahead. Across the street reared the Hacienda's neon cowboy on his bucking bronco, waving hello, good-bye, hello, good-bye. Guidry parked as far from the sign as he could get, in the darkest, most deserted corner of the lot.

You're staying here tonight. You'll be safer.

Guidry realized that he had it wrong. Those hadn't been Ed's last words. Ed's last words had been, *Leo! Wake up, for God's sake!*

The girls had left their Disney book in the backseat. True-life adventures of the creatures who lurked and maneuvered in darkness. *Secrets of the Hidden World.*

He stashed Ed's gun in the glove box and went straight up to Charlotte's room. He knocked lightly. How the hell was he going to sell her this late-night, last-minute dash?

He knocked again. To calm his nerves, he picked out a place for them to live in Saigon. A cream-colored town house with tall, arched windows and wrought-iron balconies, on a cobbled lane shaded by palms. He didn't know if the streets were cobbled in Saigon, and his imaginary town house bore a suspicious resemblance to one on Esplanade Avenue in New Orleans. But Indochina had been a French colony, had it not? So maybe.

A garden in back where the girls could read and play and spread out a blanket for picnics, with a little bubbling fountain and the bougainvillea spilling over the stone wall like foam over the lip of a beer mug.

He tried the knob. Unlocked. Guidry didn't turn it. As long as he didn't open the door and step inside, as long as he didn't switch on the light and see with his own eyes the empty beds, the naked hangers, the missing suitcases, he could continue to pretend that Charlotte and the girls were still here.

But he knew they were gone. Of course they were gone. That last kiss. *Good-bye, Frank.* Guidry had known right then what was happening, but he'd just refused to believe it. Of course Charlotte was saying good-bye. She was too smart to stick around, to trust a man like him a second time. It was one of the reasons he'd fallen for her in the first place.

Though maybe Rosemary hadn't been able to sleep and the three of them had trekked down to the café for cookies and warm milk. Maybe they were on their way back to the room right this minute. . . .

Oh, the power of self-deception. What superhuman strength, what feats of derring-do.

He opened the door, switched on the light. Beds empty, hangers naked, suitcases missing. Of course Charlotte and the girls were gone. Of course.

Guidry thought he'd prepared himself for the pain. No. Not even close. He'd expected a blow, a blast, a ripping, and a tearing. Hunker down, weather the storm, let it pass. Instead the pain inside him was like a dark tide, rising inch by inch, with nothing to contain it but the far edge of his life on earth.

He didn't bother going back to his own room. He could buy a new toothbrush. If Charlotte had left him a note, he didn't want to read it.

In the hotel lobby, a bellhop noticed Guidry.

"Mr. Wainwright," the bellhop said. "I wondered where you were. I loaded the ladies into a cab to the bus depot, half an hour ago. They were in some rush. You better . . ."

And then the bellhop put two and two together. Oops. He realized that poor Mr. Wainwright had been abandoned.

"Oh, jeez, Mr. Wainwright," he said, "I just figured . . ."

"Don't worry, Johnny, I'm meeting them there." Guidry gave the poor kid a reassuring smile. "Life couldn't be peachier."

Guidry walked across the parking lot. Made it all the way to his car with the smile on his face, the tide of pain rising, rising.

"Frank."

From the shadows emerged a man, his face so white it seemed to glow. A ghost. Maybe Cindy had been right about the afterlife after all.

"You've got me confused with someone else, friend," Guidry said.

The ghost stopped ten feet away and lifted a gun. Guidry felt relief, not fear. Charlotte and the girls were safe. They'd escaped Guidry in the nick of time. Only he and he alone, right now, was going to die. Any grievance that Guidry might have had against God and the universe was instantly forgiven.

"Car," the ghost said.

Guidry didn't understand. "What?"

"The car."

"You want the car?" Guidry said. "Help yourself."

"Get in. You drive."

Now Guidry got it. Somewhere out in the desert, a hole had been dug for him, his grave awaited. Well, forgive him if he declined to make his killer's job easier.

"Forget it," Guidry said. "I'm not going anywhere."

The ghost moved slowly around to the passenger side. A breath, a step. A breath, a step. At first Guidry thought he was missing his right hand, but no, the hand was just slipped between the buttons of his suit coat. The ghost was hugging himself, bent over like he had a stomachache, but he kept the gun on Guidry.

"You work for Carlos?" Guidry said.

"What do you think?"

"Who killed you?"

"What?"

"You look like a ghost."

The ghost managed to get the passenger door open. The dome light clicked on and lit him up. He looked worse than any ghost. Guidry doubted there was a drop of blood left in him.

"Are you Paul Barone?" Guidry said.

"What do you think? Get in."

In the confines of the car, Guidry might be able to wrestle the gun away from him. Or might be able to get to Ed's gun in the glove box. What, though, was the point?

"I told you," Guidry said. "I'm not driving you anywhere."

"New Orleans," Barone said.

"What?"

"Get in. You drive."

"You want me to drive you to New Orleans?" Guidry said.

Barone wasn't making any sense. He tried to climb into the car but slipped and fell to one knee. When he tried to pull himself up, he slipped again and dropped the gun. He stayed down on his knee this time, head bowed, like he was praying.

Guidry came around to the other side of the car. He kicked the gun away. He saw that the bottom half of Barone's shirt was soaked with blood, the front flaps of his suit coat soaked, too, his trousers soaked all the way to the crotch.

He really was missing a hand. That's what Guidry thought at first—a bloody stump hooked onto the door handle. But then he realized that the stump was a hand wrapped in a bloody bandage, fingers with bloody fingernails poking out the top.

Barone didn't look up at Guidry. His breathing sounded like a dead leaf scraping down the sidewalk when a breeze blew.

"I'm going to kill her," Barone said.

Guidry considered again how close to the fire he'd dragged Charlotte and the girls. It was unforgivable. He was unforgivable.

"Too late," he said. "You're out of luck."

"She tipped you," Barone said.

Guidry crouched so that he could hear him better. But he kept his distance. If this was Barone, or someone like Barone, he might have a last sting left in his tail.

"What did you say?" Guidry said.

"She tipped you in Houston," Barone said. "She tipped you here."

"Who?"

"She knew what she was doing. Bitch. All along."

Guidry realized that Barone had to be talking about Seraphine. The guy was off his rocker. "Seraphine never said a word to me," Guidry said. "Not here, not in Houston."

"I'm going to kill her," Barone said.

"You're not going to make it out of this parking lot," Guidry said.

Barone seemed to know it. Head hanging lower and lower, breath barely scraping along. "Carlos will find you," he said. "He always does."

"Long may he search," Guidry said.

"If he can't find you, he'll go after her. He knows how to hurt you now."

Seraphine had been trying to kill Guidry for the past week and a half. He lacked much sympathy for her.

"Seraphine's not my problem," Guidry said. "I'll be just fine."

"Not her," Barone said.

"Who then?"

Finally Barone turned his head to regard Guidry. Stick a few gallons of blood back into him and he'd look like half the guys Guidry had served with overseas. He'd look like half the guys in New Orleans. Just another one of Carlos's boys. Guidry had probably bumped shoulders with him a dozen times.

"The woman," Barone said. "Her kids. Carlos knows how to hurt you now."

For a second, Guidry's lungs wouldn't fill. His heart wouldn't pump. He could feel all the machinery inside him seize, the belts shredding and the gears grinding.

Charlotte. The girls.

Barone had tailed Guidry to the Hacienda. He'd seen Charlotte and the girls. Which meant that he'd probably told Carlos about Charlotte and the girls.

"Carlos can't hurt me," Guidry said.

"You know he doesn't like to lose," Barone said. Not a warning, not a threat. Just a fact so plain and obvious to both of them that it hardly needed to be said. "Help me up."

"The woman's nothing to me."

"Help me up," Barone said. "Get in the car. You drive. New Orleans."

"Carlos will never find them," Guidry said. "He doesn't know her name. You don't know her name. They'll be fine."

Barone didn't answer. Dead, finally. He let go of the door handle, one bloody finger at a time, and sank to the pavement.

That night Guidry stayed in Henderson, half an hour south of Las Vegas, at a motel attached to a bowling alley. Guidry's room shared a wall with the bowling alley. He lay in bed, listening to the *whunk* of the ball hitting the lane and then a couple of seconds later the sharp ceramic clatter of flying pins. *Whunk! Crash!* Over and over again.

That wasn't what kept him awake till the wee hours, though, the *whunk* and the *crash*. What kept him awake was the stretch of silence in between, the anticipation, the wait for the other shoe to drop.

Whunk.

Charlotte and the girls would be fine. Carlos had no way to track them down. Sure, he'd send someone out to the Hacienda to nose around. But all the employees there assumed that Charlotte's last name was Wainwright.

Crash!

Whunk.

The bellman knew that Charlotte had taken a cab to the bus depot. The cashier at the bus depot might remember Charlotte, too, might remember the attractive lady with the two well-behaved little girls who'd bought a ticket on the late bus to Los Angeles.

Crash!

Whunk.

But so what? Charlotte was a needle and Los Angeles was the biggest haystack on the West Coast. Though it was possible that someone might recognize Charlotte at both the bus depot in Las Vegas *and* the bus depot in downtown L.A., and then . . .

Crash!

Sleep came. Dreams came. A dream strange in that there was nothing too strange about it. Guidry was back at the Monteleone, talking to old Mackey Pagano again. The same conversation they'd already had.

I'm in a bind, Frankie. I might be in a real bind.

I'm sorry, Mack.

A new dream bled into the old one. Guidry was a kid again, fifteen years old. He knew exactly how old because he stood on the sagging porch of the shitty little house in St. Amant saying good-bye to Annette. She was eleven years old when he left home for New Orleans. Two months later, Christmas Eve, their father got drunker than usual, felt meaner than usual, and beat her to death with the fireplace poker. Normally their father used the fireplace poker on Guidry, but Guidry was no longer around—he'd hightailed it to the big city and saved himself.

Why you gotta go, Frick?

Sorry, Frack. I'll send for you when I have a big, fancy house.

Guidry had returned to visit that moment every single day for the past twenty-two years. What would he give, to turn back the clock and live it out differently? He hoped the dream might let him, but it wasn't that kind of dream.

So long, Frick.

So long, baby.

Guidry killed the next day—Tuesday, departure day—without too much trouble. He slept late. He went next door to the bowling alley for a hamburger and a couple of beers. *Whunk. Crash!* He read the morning paper. The hue and cry about the assassination continued: *Find the truth!* Carlos, in New Orleans, raged. At the Warren Commission, at Guidry.

At six o'clock the cab dropped Guidry at Nellis. He handed the corporal at the gate his pass. The pass looked official. Maybe it was. The corporal picked up his phone. He said a few words that Guidry couldn't make out. He put down the phone and wrote something in his log. He wrote and he wrote. If a couple of MPs were lying in wait to arrest Guidry, now was the time for them to pop out of the cake.

The corporal finished writing and handed the pass back to Guidry. "You know where you're going, sir?" he said.

"I'm thumbing a ride with Colonel Tolliver tonight," Guidry said. "Know where I can find him?"

"Try the BOQ. Bachelor Officer Quarters, straight ahead, last building on the left."

"Thanks."

Guidry slipped the pass back into his pocket. Once he walked through that gate, once he climbed aboard the plane and it lifted off the tarmac, he'd be a free man.

Would Carlos go after Charlotte and the girls? Would he find them and kill them? Would he do worse than that? Would he make them pay for Guidry's sins?

Guidry didn't know. He'd never have to know. In Vietnam, thousands of miles away, he would be a free man again. He could choose to believe whatever he wanted to believe.

The corporal had better things to do than watch Guidry stand there. "Is there a problem, sir?" he said.

Guidry thought about the question. He shook his head. "No."

33

They approached from the west, dropping out of the bright blue empty and into the clouds. Just a few frivolous puffs at first and then more serious stuff, layer on top of layer, so dense and soggy that the plane seemed to labor, a dull knife trying to saw through waxed gray canvas.

Vietnam was supposed to be even hotter and more humid than New Orleans. That's what Guidry had heard somewhere. He relished the return to hot and humid. The desert, with air too thin and too dry to sustain meaningful life, had almost killed him. He was glad to be back in his natural habitat.

Falling, falling, the landing gear clanking into place. Out of the clouds, a lush tropical patchwork below, the streams and swamps and canals a silvery stitchwork in the flat afternoon light.

Guidry considered stopping off for a quick bite first. But the muffuletta from Central Grocery or the muffuletta from Frank's? The gumbo from Bozo's in Mid-City or the gumbo from Uglesich's? Or the gumbo from . . . Ye gods, whose gumbo? Guidry would never be able to choose, the decision would cripple him. He picked up his car and drove straight to The Famous Door on Bourbon.

It was too early for any Dixieland, but a few years ago the club's owner had squeezed in a kitchen and turned the back room into an invitation-only social club. The Spot, he called it. Reprobates and street rats only, thank you very much. On Wednesdays, when the owner's wife made her legendary braciole with tomato gravy, the joint jumped. Carlos, a champion eater in a town of champion eaters, wouldn't have missed his Wednesday braciole if the whole Quarter had been on fire.

He was sitting at his usual table, Seraphine on his right and Frenchy Brouillette on his left, Frenchy yammering away and keeping Carlos entertained while he ate. No bodyguard. Carlos almost never used one, not around town. What was the point? Take a crack at Carlos in New Orleans and you'd hit the ground before he did.

Frenchy spotted Guidry first. Frenchy almost fell off

his chair. Seraphine, who'd just taken a drag from her cigarette, held the smoke for a moment and then exhaled through her nostrils. That was her almost falling off her chair. She wore a demure little sweater dress, seafoam green, with a gathered waist and pleated skirt. A white cardigan draped over her shoulders, hair with spit-curled bangs and a ponytail in back, a headband that matched the dress. She looked like she was ready to integrate an Alabama high school in 1954.

Carlos glanced up but kept eating. "Frenchy," he said.

"What?" Frenchy said. "Oh."

Frenchy scrammed. Guidry sat down across from Carlos.

"You want a plate?" Carlos said.

"No thanks." Guidry liked the braciole at The Spot just fine, but he'd never grasped the general hysteria. Maybe it tasted better if you were Italian. "I'll take the rest of Frenchy's wine, if you don't think he'll mind."

"Take it," Carlos said.

Seraphine looked at Guidry without looking at him, tenser than he'd ever seen her before. She was wondering what he'd say about her, to try to save his own skin.

Barone claimed that she'd tipped him. Guidry had thought it over during the flight from Vegas. He'd recalled the last conversation he had with Seraphine. From the phone box at the filling station on La Porte, back in Houston, right after he dumped the Eldorado in the ship channel.

You'll spend the night at the Rice?

The slip that got him thinking. Why is she asking that? She knows I'm spending the night at the Rice.

Except it hadn't been a slip. Seraphine never slipped. She knew the fertile soil of Guidry's suspicious mind. She'd planted the seed of doubt with purpose. She'd saved his life. Maybe she'd saved his life in Vegas, too, and he hadn't even realized it.

Carlos stabbed and shoveled and chewed. The heavy linen napkin tucked into his collar wasn't just for show. "You suppose to be dead, Frank," he said.

"Don't I know it," Guidry said.

"You like one of them cats," Carlos said. "With the five lives."

"Nine."

"Don't count on it."

By now everyone in the room was trying not to gawk. Even the owner's wife, chopping garlic in the kitchen, was peeping out through the pickup window. Guidry liked to think that people would be telling this story, however it ended, for years to come.

He walked right in.

No he didn't.

Sat right down across from Carlos.

No. And you saw it all?

I was right there.

Carlos mopped up the last of the tomato gravy with a crust of French bread. Seraphine still hadn't said a word. She lit a fresh cigarette, the flame of the match not quite as steady as it might have been.

"So what you want, Frank?" Carlos said. "Why you here?"

Guidry reached for the bottle of red and topped up his glass. "I want to make a deal."

"All right."

"You back off me and I'll back off you," Guidry said. "Tit for tat, quid pro quo."

Carlos smiled. He only smiled when he was feeling murderous. "You gonna back off me?" he said. "You a real comedian, Frank. I forgot that about you."

"Back off me or I'll go to the feds," Guidry said. "I'll tell them what I know, and I'll tell them everything Barone told me before he croaked. Oh, baby, Barone told tales that curled my hair. I'll tell the feds and the newspapers and Earl Warren, too, if he'll lend me an ear. I bet he will. And just so we're good and goddamn clear, Uncle, I never would have ratted you out, not if you hadn't tried to cut my string first."

It was a good thing Carlos had already finished his dinner, or he might have choked on it. Guidry watched as the bags under his eyes grew darker and darker. Good. Guidry wanted him mad as hell. He wanted Carlos so mad that he forgot about everyone in the world but Guidry.

Seraphine was staring openly at Guidry now. Disbelief. He turned to face her.

"Was it your idea, darlin'?" he asked her. "To toss dear old Frank Guidry in the trash? Well, the hell with you, too. Because once I spread the gospel, you won't spend the rest of your life in Leavenworth or Guatemala like Uncle here. You'll swing low, swing high, sweet Seraphine."

Can you believe it?

You were there? Really there?

Right there, baby. Couldn't hear what they was saying, but you could feel it. Know what I mean? The whole joint, everyone's nerves about to fry.

"Do we have a deal?" Guidry asked Carlos.

Carlos yanked the napkin out of his collar. He looked down at the napkin to see if maybe he could use it to strangle Guidry, right then and there.

"Do we have a deal or don't we?" Guidry said.

"Yeah." Carlos smiled. He stood and tossed the napkin onto the table and walked out. Someone else might have missed the glance he gave Seraphine, might have missed the subtle acknowledgment that she returned, a subtle dip of the head. But Guidry was waiting for it.

Once Carlos was gone, Seraphine took out her compact and applied a fresh coat of lipstick. "Thank you," she said.

"I owed you one," he said. "Yes? Maybe more than one."

"I didn't agree with the decision."

"But you didn't fight for me either. Don't worry. I wouldn't fight for me either."

"What are you doing, Frank?" she said, her voice almost too quiet to hear. And lo, could it be? A damp shine along the soft pink under-edge of her eyelid, an actual tear beginning to well? Probably not, but a man could dream.

"You know what I'm doing," he said.

"*Why* are you doing it?" she said.

"It's just a matter of time. I'm a realist. Carlos will get me. You'll get me. This way I make it quick and easy for you and you'll make it quick and easy for me."

She didn't believe it. But neither could she fathom any other reason to explain what he was doing. For the first time in their long partnership, friendship, relationship, she couldn't fathom *him*. He'd surprised her with unexpected depths, secrets of the hidden world.

If he told Seraphine he'd decided to trade his life for Charlotte and the girls, she'd be absolutely baffled. She'd gape at him like he was a complete stranger.

"You'll make it quick and easy for me," Guidry said again. "Yes? I want to stress that part."

"You're a fool."

"Promise me," Guidry said. "One last good deed for an old pal."

"You're a fool," she said.

"How much time do you need to set it up? A couple of hours?"

He thought she might refuse to answer. But then she snapped her compact shut and put it back into her purse and said, "Yes."

Guidry stood. "All right. I feel like a walk in the park. You know the levee behind the zoo? Nice view of the river, secluded, a good spot for peaceful rumination. I must have told you about it a dozen times. You guessed that's where I would go."

Her composure, if ever it had really fled, returned. She paid the check. "Good-bye, *mon cher,*" she said, and walked out without looking back.

He followed the streetcar line Uptown and left his car parked across from Loyola. The Sacred Heart of

Jesus statue out front beseeched him, arms raised high, begging Guidry to . . . what? Stay the course? Turn tail and flee?

The park was always eerie as a winter twilight approached. Not many people around, the oaks shrouded with Spanish moss, the shadows lunging across the path for one another, twining and embracing. Guidry regretted that he'd never actually seen any of Charlotte's photos. It was funny, wasn't it? She'd have a picture of his shadow, strung across that redbrick sidewalk in Flagstaff, but not one of him.

The zoo was already closed for the day. Guidry crossed River Drive and climbed to the top of the levee. Not another soul in sight. He found a comfortable patch of grass and spread out the ugly houndstooth sport coat he'd purchased in New Mexico.

Another regret: He hadn't stopped by his apartment to change into his own clothes. But which suit? As with the gumbo, it would have been an impossible choice. He just hoped that the *Times-Picayune* didn't run a photo of him in this getup. His reputation would never recover.

He took a seat on the sport coat. The drive from the Quarter had taken him twenty minutes, the walk through the park another half an hour. If Seraphine's man had any sense, he'd drive up Walnut to the cul-de-sac and spare himself the hike.

Guidry wasn't afraid of dying. Well, he was terrified of dying. But more terrified of dying badly. So many of the people who crossed Carlos died just so. In this matter, though, Guidry trusted Seraphine. Quick and easy was in her best interest almost as much as it was in his.

It really was a nice view of the river. The water rippling, the merry lights of the barges and the towboats.

Your life was supposed to flash before your eyes right before you died, was it not? Time slowing and stretching and one last stroll through the daisies. Guidry wouldn't mind. Oh, the redheads, the brunettes, the blondes. Or maybe you had to pack light for the afterlife, and the last memory in your head, when the works shut down, was the only one you were allowed to keep for the rest of eternity. If you were lucky, if you knew what was coming, you got to choose your memory. Guidry liked that idea better.

After a few minutes, he heard the footsteps behind him.

He closed his eyes and waited.

2003

Epilogue

The thing is, she loves her life. Even days like today, when her son refuses to acknowledge her existence at breakfast (Rosemary won't let him spend spring break in Hana with his dad and Sporty Spice; Rosemary refuses to call her ex-husband's girlfriend by her real name; Rosemary won't stop being *such a hater, Mom, Jesus*). Even days like today, when her daughter declares on the way to school that college is a scam, a Ponzi scheme, a something-something of late-stage capitalism (*Sweetheart, you're going to college if I have to drag you there with my bare hands*). Even days like today, when every writer she met pitched mismatched partners teaming up to solve a murder or pull off a heist or open a day-care center.

Rosemary loves her life! She has two healthy, smart, kind, occasionally wonderful, always challenging, never dull children. She's a vice president of production at a major studio (how many women in Hollywood can say *that?*). She has real friends, the sort who would help you chop up a body and bury it in lime, no questions asked. She's forty-six but looks mid-late thirties, thanks to genetically blessed skin and a lifelong aversion to beaches and cigarettes. Mid-late thirties is still ancient by industry standards, but whatever. She ran a half marathon last year. Her ex is a good father and not a bad guy.

She's a cliché. In so many ways, yes. But who isn't? At least Rosemary picked a cliché that she's happy to inhabit.

"You don't have to marry him," Joan is saying. "It's a first date. Have drinks. See what you think. He's your type."

Joan must be driving through the canyon. Her voice cuts out, warbles. Rosemary gets the gist. Joan fell in love in medical school and has been with her girlfriend ever since, almost half her life. She fears that Rosemary will never find her soul mate, that she'll grow old and die alone.

"Guess who's starting his own production company and wants me to run it," Rosemary says.

"I have no idea," Joan says.

"He's a huge, huge star."

"I have no idea."

Rosemary loves how stubbornly oblivious Joan has remained to any- and everything Hollywood. Joan grew up in L.A., she lives in L.A., her sister works for a studio, her mother spent twenty-five years working in the publicity departments of various studios. And yet there is an excellent chance that if Nicole Kidman walked into Joan's exam room, Joan would say, "Oh, I like your accent, are you from Australia?"

"I love what I do now," Rosemary says. "But a change would be fun. But a change would be risky. In Hollywood you only get a second act if you're under forty. I'm too old to fall down the stairs."

"So stay where you are," Joan says.

"Or you could say, 'No, Rosemary, of course you're not too old. Of course you won't fall down the stairs.'"

"I'm almost there. Are you almost here?"

"Joan."

"What."

"Do you think we'd be friends if we weren't sisters?"

"No."

Another thing that Rosemary loves about Joan. She is not one to mince words. Neither, Rosemary supposes, is she.

At the cemetery they walk up the path arm in arm, the way they used to do as little girls coming home from school. Rosemary has brought daisies and larkspur, Joan gladiolus. Rosemary also has a ticket stub from her last movie, a rom-com that performed better than expected. She tucks it in among the larkspur. Their mother saw every single one of Rosemary's movies. At the end, in the hospital, she read every script. And she gave Rosemary notes, you bet she did.

Joan leaves behind a small photo of a beaming African-American girl, seven or eight years old. Every time their mother saw Joan, she would ask, "Whose life did you save today, chickadee?" If Joan had saved a life, or two, their mother would want to hear all the details.

"Do you know what Mom told me once?" Rosemary says. She glances at Joan. Joan is crying, quietly and without expression. One of her many talents. "She probably told you, too."

"What."

"That when she was young, she wanted to be a photographer. A real photographer, I mean. Like, I don't know, Annie Leibovitz."

"I know that," Joan says.

"I just said that you probably did."

"We have all those boxes of photos in storage. We need to go through them at some point."

"Every single industry thing I go to," Rosemary says, "someone comes up and says, 'Oh, I worked with your mother at Warners.' 'Oh, I worked with your mother at Paramount.' 'She was always the smartest one in the room.' 'She was always the toughest one in the room.'"

A tear rolls down Joan's cheek and catches in the corner of her mouth. Rosemary takes a pocket pack of tissues from her purse. She keeps a couple of tissues for herself before she hands the pack to Joan. Rosemary never cries at work or at home. Only when she's here, with Joan.

"Can you believe she's been gone four years already?" Rosemary says.

Joan considers.

"It's a rhetorical question, Joan."

Joan blows her nose. "I had a dream about Lucky the other night."

Their old dog, their faithful companion all the way through elementary school and junior high.

"Do you remember . . . I can't remember if I remember," Joan says. "There was a motel, and maybe Mom had to sneak Lucky in because no dogs were allowed?"

Rosemary's memory from that time in her life is hazy. The trip from Oklahoma to California is mostly a blur. It's the same for Joan, they've compared notes. Rosemary remembers the Grand Canyon and the hotel in Las Vegas. Joan remembers a boat ride across a lake and a man who did card tricks for them. She remembers, or claims she remembers, meeting the scarecrow from *The Wizard of Oz*. Sure, Joan, sure.

Neither of them remembers the car wreck that stranded them in New Mexico. Rosemary remembers the Good Samaritan who gave them a ride to Las Vegas. What was his name? And what the fuck, by the way, was their mom thinking, hitching a ride to California with some strange guy? It was a more trusting time, Rosemary supposes. Hollywood hadn't yet produced dozens of thrillers about mismatched serial killers who partner up to murder helpless hitchhikers.

Rosemary wants to say the Good Samaritan's name was Pat Boone, but she knows of course that can't be right. He had a nice smile, she's pretty sure.

"Do you know what I really remember?" Rosemary says. "That one day."

Joan blows her nose and smiles. "Yes."

It's Rosemary's first real memory from California, the most intact and fully developed. They'd been staying with Aunt Marguerite for only a month or two, her little bungalow on Idaho, five blocks from the ocean. Their dad and their uncle, their dad's older brother, came out from Oklahoma to visit. Their dad took Rosemary and Joan to the pier, and they rode the carousel.

When they returned to the house, their mom and their uncle were still sitting in the front room. Their mom on the sofa, their uncle in the chair with the scarlet-and-cream striped satin. Rosemary and Joan, in the hall, watched through the arched doorway. Their mother and their uncle didn't hear the girls come in. Their dad was still outside. Parking the car maybe?

"Charlie, I'm going to warn you one more time." Their uncle's face had turned the color of the chair, scarlet and cream both. "I'll get Dooley the best lawyer money can buy. The two best lawyers. If you and the girls don't come home with us right this minute, I promise you'll be in for the fight of your life."

Their mom. Oh, their mom. Cool and collected, smiling pleasantly. She might have been chatting with a girlfriend about which particular shade of eye shadow looked best on her.

"Well, then," their mom said, "I suppose I'd better be ready."

A mist has begun to fall. The June gloom in Santa Monica. Rosemary blows her nose, too.

"She was a force of nature," Rosemary says.

"It doesn't feel like she's been gone four years," Joan says. "But it also feels like forever."

"Yes."

"I don't want to forget her."

"Don't be stupid, Joan," Rosemary says.

"Okay," Joan says.

Acknowledgments

It's my great good fortune to have an agent, Shane Salerno, who cares ferociously about his clients and labors passionately on their behalf. He's always been there for me, day or night, with the right answer or the right question. I'm indebted to Don Winslow, Steve Hamilton, and Meg Gardiner for steering me Shane's way.

My editor, Emily Krump, is not only scary smart and talented but also an absolute pleasure to work with. I'm grateful to my publisher, the amazing Liate Stehlik, and to Lynn Grady, Carla Parker, Danielle Bartlett, Maureen Sugden, Kaitlin Harri, and Julia Elliott. There are so many terrific people at William Morrow and HarperCollins. Many of them I'm not acquainted with personally, but I know how much they do for me and their support is deeply appreciated.

I'd like to thank my friends and family. I don't deserve them. A few require special mention this time around: Ellen Berney, Sarah Klingenberg, Lauren Klingenberg, Thomas Cooney, Bud Elder, Ellen Knight, Chris Hoekstra, Trish Daly, Bob Bledsoe, Misa Shuford, Alexis Persico, and Elizabeth Fleming (and all the Diefenderfers, who provide a welcoming place for me to write every day).

The best part about being a crime writer is that you become part of the crime-writing community. I want to thank all the writers, readers, reviewers, bloggers, marketers, and booksellers who have been such an invaluable source of encouragement and advice.

This book belongs to my wife, Christine—as do they all, as will they all.

About the Author

Lou Berney is the author of three previous novels, *Gutshot Straight, Whiplash River,* and the multiple prize–winning *The Long and Faraway Gone.* His short fiction has appeared in publications such as *The New Yorker, Ploughshares,* and the *Pushcart Prize* anthology. He lives in Oklahoma City, Oklahoma.

THE NEW LUXURY IN READING

We hope you enjoyed reading
our new, comfortable print size and found it
an experience you would like to repeat.

Well – you're in luck!

HarperLuxe offers the finest in fiction and
nonfiction books in this same larger print size and
paperback format. Light and easy to read, HarperLuxe
paperbacks are for book lovers who want to see
what they are reading without the strain.

For a full listing of titles and
new releases to come, please visit our website:

www.HarperLuxe.com

Prescriptions for *Heart to Start*

"Although I have coached athletes to Olympic gold medals, I'm using *Heart to Start* as my training guide to help my own father get in shape and live a healthier life. Prevention is for all of us."

ALBERTO SALAZAR, *Three-time New York City Marathon winner, 1982 Boston Marathon winner, cardiac arrest survivor*

"*Heart to Start* is a must read. Cardiologist Jamie Beckerman leverages his wealth of personal and professional experience to develop a tangible and obtainable platform for health and longevity. For the patient grappling with heart disease or the care provider looking to better serve his or her patients, *Heart to Start* passionately demystifies the 'exercise health halo' and reminds us that we were all born to move, both in sickness and in health."

AARON BAGGISH, M.D., *Cardiologist, Massachusetts General Hospital; Co-Medical Director, Boston Marathon*

"With inactivity more dangerous for your heart than smoking, Dr. Beckerman's book is vital to those looking to get their heart in shape. Not only does he show you that it's within your power to prevent America's #1 killer, but he also provides step-by-step instructions on how to incorporate moving more into your life."

MICHAEL SMITH, M.D., *Chief Medical Editor, WebMD*

"Physicians, get out your prescription pads and prescribe this book to every one of your heart patients. This encouraging, common sense and easy-to-read book deserves to be in the hands of all freshly-diagnosed heart patients and those who love them."

CAROLYN THOMAS, *Heart attack survivor and patient advocate, www.myheartsisters.org*

"Dr Beckerman brings a fitness plan for life straight from his heart. *Heart to Start* is an easy-to-follow guide to a heartfelt and fitness-filled life."

DAVE WATT, *Executive Director, American Medical Athletic Association and American Running Association*

"Heart problems or even being at risk can sometimes make people frightened or less confident. But don't let these feelings keep you from becoming active. *Heart to Start* is your step-by-step guide for returning safely to physical activity, exercise training, and finally a 5K race. It's time to get inspired and get going!"

"*Heart to Start* is a realistic and enthusiastic prescription that will not only bring years to your life, but more importantly, life to your years."

"The turn to health often begins with a spark, a reason, a goal. *Heart to Start* provides that nudge, and with readable prose and real-world human stories, Dr. Beckerman also provides the most valuable treatment in all of Medicine – knowledge."

"Dr. Beckerman does what I wish every doctor would do – not just tell us what to do and why to do it, but motivate us to WANT to get our bodies moving. Not to burn a calorie or two here and there, but for something deeper – to live a long and vibrant life. Dr. Beckerman has the warmth of a close friend, the you-can-do-it encouragement of a good coach, and the scientific savvy of a doctor who lives what he loves. Just as he says, with this great line from his book: Prepare to be moved."

"What makes *Heart to Start* special is not just its easy explanatory style, or the evidence-backed, fad-less, common sense advice it delivers – it's the fact that Jamie Beckerman really cares. His bedside manner jumps off the page, puts its arm around you, and gently motivates you toward a healthier lifestyle."

HEART TO START

The Eight Week Exercise Prescription
to Live Longer, Beat Heart Disease,
and Run Your Best Race

JAMES BECKERMAN, M.D.

Providence Heart and Vascular Institute
Portland, Oregon

Copyright © 2015 by James Beckerman, M.D.

Providence Heart and Vascular Institute
9205 SW Barnes Road
Portland, OR 97225
(503) 216-2088
hearttostart@providence.org

Cover designed by Liana Moisescu
Book designed by The Book Makers, www.thebookmakers.com
Illustrations designed by Arif
Photo Image: Providence Health & Services

Printed in the United States of America

10 9 8 7 6 5 4 3 2 1

ISBN 978-0-9907146-0-6
ISBN (ebook) 978-0-9907146-1-3

In memory of Gerald Lyell Fatka (1939-1998)

And for every individual and family impacted by heart disease

Promise Yourself

To be so strong that nothing can disturb your peace of mind.

To talk health, happiness, and prosperity to every person you meet.

To make all your friends feel that there is something worthwhile in them.

To look at the sunny side of everything and make your optimism come true.

To think only of the best, to work only for the best and to expect only the best.

To be just as enthusiastic about the success of others as you are about your own.

To forget the mistakes of the past and press on to the greater achievements of the future.

To wear a cheerful expression at all times and give a smile to every living creature you meet.

To give so much time to improving yourself that you have no time to criticize others.

To be too large for worry, too noble for anger, too strong for fear, and too happy to permit the presence of trouble.

To think well of yourself and to proclaim this fact to the world, not in loud word, but in great deeds.

To live in the faith that the whole world is on your side, so long as you are true to the best that is in you.

— Christian D. Larson, 1912
Adopted as the Optimist Creed in 1922

Contents

COOL DOWN

Foreword

"What's your legacy?"

That's the last thing I remember thinking as I was rolled into the operating room. But it all started a few years before that, long before the day of my first surgery, when our two daughters were very young. I started having a recurring problem I couldn't explain.

I enjoyed exercising and even competed in races. I felt really good. But in the middle of one race, my heart rate started jumping all over the place: rising at 160, 170, 180, and then 200 before dropping down to 70. Then back up to 220, and way down to 30. I started to falter, and then had what I guess you could call a whiteout. I lost my senses, literally, and fell to the ground.

The medics at the race chalked it up to overexertion, dehydration, and poor nutrition. And my primary care physician at the time couldn't find any reason to disagree, but as a precaution, he referred me to a cardiologist. That decision might have saved my life.

The cardiologist, not finding anything obviously wrong, also agreed that the cause of my symptoms was most likely overexertion. However, he sent me for an echocardiogram – an ultrasound of the heart – and it told a different story. I had what's called a bicuspid aortic valve. Normally, the exit valve of the heart has three cusps that open and close to help pump blood through the heart, but I was born with only two, so my heart was working overtime. But the cardiologist thought everything else looked fine and that the diagnosis of overexertion at the event was likely correct.

But as time went on, the episodes of racing heart rates and fatigue became more frequent, occurring at odd times. I would run thirteen miles one day with no problem. The next day I couldn't make it a mile. And then I started experiencing the episodes when I was just sitting on an airplane or watching television, or worst of all, driving my car.

This went on for almost two years, without any clarity about what was happening to me. The symptoms began to get worse, and so did my frustration. Every time I had one of these "episodes" I honestly thought I was going to die. I swear my body was speaking to me. We just didn't know what it was saying.

I fortunately made my way to a team of doctors that were able to get to the bottom of things. Not only did I have a bicuspid aortic valve, but I also learned that the episodes I was experiencing were due to atrial fibrillation, an irregular and sometimes very rapid heart rhythm. And on top of that, I had an aneurysm of my aortic root that was on the verge of rupturing. That could mean instant death.

Maybe my body was telling me something after all.

No sooner did we begin discussing my aneurysm when a heart surgeon walked in my room. He sat down and said, "You

don't just *need* this surgery. You need this surgery *now*." After the
shock wore off, I realized that death was knocking on my door.
Was I scared? Yes. More like complete terror.

So we got things moving. One thing I will never forget is that
the surgeon told my wife and me that he would never leave my
side until he knew I was in the clear. No matter what happened.
That was quite a promise, I knew, but it sure made my wife feel
better.

"What's your legacy?"

It was one of the last things I was asked as I was being rolled
into surgery. How would my two young daughters remember me
if I didn't live through surgery?

I didn't have an answer – and that upset me. I knew I was a
good dad, but had I really left any footprints in the sands of time
for them to follow? Did I engrain any "message" in their impres-
sionable minds? My answer was no. It was my darkest moment,
and one of the last I remember as I went under the knife.

The surgery was supposed to take about four hours, but my
body didn't want to cooperate. My doctors called it the perfect
storm. Nothing fit. Nothing worked. My bicuspid aortic valve
had to go, and was replaced by a valve from a pig. My aortic root
was cut out and replaced with a Dacron graft. They cut tiny slices
in one of my heart chambers to correct my atrial fibrillation. I
was a mess. This four-hour procedure ended up taking fifteen
grueling hours. My surgeon worked on me for all fifteen hours,
and when I was wheeled into the Intensive Care Unit to begin
my recovery, he was still there.

A nurse told my wife that I might be waking up soon, so she
came in to see me. And as if on cue, the moment she walked in,
I flat lined. My heart stopped. As my wife Kerri watched, my
doctor tore the wires from my chest, opened me up, climbed on

top of me and began manually massaging my heart. The man had every right to be home sleeping, and there he was – literally straddling me – keeping my heart pumping with his own two hands. He was keeping his promise.

Kerri was on the verge of losing it, as were my parents. The nurses brought them in to speak to me, to share any last words with me.

They told me to fight.

They told me to stay strong.

And they told me they loved me.

Back in surgery, they performed an emergency coronary artery bypass to correct the problem, and then sent me back into recovery. I would love to say that the drama ended there. That I recovered, ran some races, and everything was hunky-dory. But I wasn't so lucky.

Recovery is always going to be hard, and mine was hard on both of us. I couldn't lie flat in a bed, so I slept in our recliner in the living room. Kerri, afraid to leave my side, slept on the floor next to me. She was getting no sleep, and I could see it. So I finally told her to call some friends and get out of the house. I jokingly promised not to die while she was gone. "Oh," I added. "Just bring me back some Kung Pao shrimp."

Man, I was ready for some good food.

She came home with the Kung Pao shrimp, and I happily devoured them. And that's when it hit me. Apparently, when you get a blood transfusion, you can temporarily inherit the allergies of the donor. And, against all odds, my donor just happened to be allergic to both shellfish and peanuts. Not to mention Kung Pao shrimp.

I had a life-threatening allergic reaction and I soon went into atrial flutter – another racing heart rhythm. And back to the hospital I went. When your heart goes into atrial flutter, your blood can pool and clot. And clots, as you may know, can sometimes lead to strokes.

After another week in the hospital, and a few shocks to my now burned chest, my doctors confirmed that my heart rhythm was back to normal, that everything looked good, and that I could go home.

On Father's Day, we decided to celebrate with a Thanksgiving meal of our own. Turkey, stuffing, sports – the works. I may have even had a beer in my hand. It was going to be a good day. We had a lot to celebrate.

But suddenly, it was as though a curtain had dropped in front of me. Everything went black. I could talk, but I couldn't see. Then my left side starting tingling, and I began losing feeling in my face.

I was having a stroke.

But we had my surgeon's personal phone number, and we called it. He talked me through everything I was going to be experiencing, step-by-step. Again, he kept his promise. It was a minor stroke, thankfully. What they call a transient ischemic attack, or TIA. But there was something about it – after my initial diagnosis, my valve replacement, my cardiac arrest, my emergent bypass surgery, the atrial flutter, and the shocks to my chest – that finally flipped a switch inside of me. Enough was enough. I looked at Kerri and said, "This is it. I'm done being sick. I'm done having symptoms. I'm finished."

She nodded supportively, with no idea what I was about to say next.

"I'm signing up for an Ironman triathlon."

Let's just say that her next words are best left out of print. I told her I would talk to my doctor about it. She helpfully suggested that I start with a psychiatrist. To be fair, she was right. I mean, here I was seemingly barely able to survive a meal without some sort of catastrophe, and I was proposing to sign up for the most challenging race in the world?

Maybe I *was* crazy.

But I thought back to my darkest day and knew that it was time to start creating my legacy for my girls. I stuck to my guns. I surrounded myself with great people who helped me train, and we formed a group we called Ironheart Racing. My goal was to teach my kids that with focus and determination, you can accomplish amazing things. The Ironheart logo is appropriately a pig with wings – symbolic of both my new heart valve and overcoming the seemingly impossible.

One year and one month after my surgery, I made it to the starting line. Just 2.4 miles of swimming, 112 miles of biking, and 26.2 miles of running to go. My swim went well, but during the bike ride, I lost a pedal about eighty miles into it, and I was forced to ride the last thirty miles with one leg pushing. When I finally got to the final transition, they had to literally pick me up off of my bike while still in the crouch position. They stood me upright, changed my shoes, and said, "Okay. Go run a marathon."

The Ironman course was littered with competitors who didn't make it. Exhaustion or injury, all understandable. But that wasn't going to be me. I was not giving up on this. As I was nearing the end of the run, with my wife now at my side, it was clear that I was not going to finish under the 17-hour time limit. Kerri started seeing officials packing up tables and booths along the course. She ran ahead to the finish line and pleaded with them.

"Please," she cried. "You don't know what my husband has been through. You are not going to pack up this finish line until he crosses it!" And they didn't. I crossed the finish line to the sound of the construction trucks beeping as they tore down the finish line bleachers. My two daughters, Maya and Madeline, were there along with my parents, friends, and a few construction workers.

Mission accomplished. A few years later, I took on Ironman again. It was "Part 2" of the legacy for my girls. This time, the goal was to teach them that if you fall short of your goals, regroup, reassess, refocus and try again. This time at Ironman Florida in 2010, I finished three hours faster and beat the cutoff time. Once again, my kids were there at the finish line cheering me on.

The final chapter in what had become a legacy quest came to pass in 2012. "Do what you love" was the message. I grew to love the sport of triathlon, and wanted Maya and Maddy to know that they should never stop following their own passions in life. Ironman Arizona was the target. But this time would be different.

By now, The Ironheart Racing Team had grown into one of the largest virtual teams in the world. With athletes in 46 states and 14 countries, we decided to convince a few of them to join us on this journey. Eight cardiac athletes set out to race that day in the hot desert. Some of us made it to the finish line, and others did not. For me, success was once again seeing my beautiful kids cheering and yelling as I completed the race. Regardless of how we finished, we all enjoyed the journey.

This is really my message to you. Enjoy this journey. Live your passion. Surround yourself with people you trust and love. Challenge yourself. Use this book to find the starting line to the rest of your life, no matter what your own personal race might be. Because somewhere along the road, I know you will find the answer to your own question.

What's *your* legacy?

David Watkins
Founder, Ironheart Foundation
www.ironheartfoundation.org

WARM UP

1.

Do You Have the Heart to Start?

"I think my dad is having a heart attack."

My pulse shot up. I started to sweat. My girlfriend shook me awake. I sat up and stared at her for a second, still trying to bring her words into focus as I remembered where I was. I looked around at the walls of our little cabin on the shores of Lake Okoboji in northwest Iowa, three days into a family vacation with my new girlfriend, her sisters, her mom, and her father, Jerry. Stacie and I had been dating for only four months.

We burst out of the cabin into the warm, sticky summer night and flew barefoot down the path towards Cabin 3G, which overlooks the grassy lawn at the lake's edge where we had been playing Frisbee just a few hours earlier. We rushed breathlessly into the bedroom and found Jerry lying on his back. Stacie's mother and three older sisters were huddled around him in shock. Stacie's oldest sister had already begun mouth-to-mouth resuscitation. She turned and looked at me. I leaped onto the bed, placed my hands on his bare chest, and started to perform compressions. I will never forget the cool moistness of his skin, and the way his ribcage bent slightly under the pressure of my hands.

I was a third year medical student on summer vacation. We had recently taken a class in basic CPR as preparation for clinical rotations. Our instructor estimated that more than 95% of cardiac arrest victims die before reaching a hospital. And a victim's chances of survival are reduced by 10% for each minute that passes without an electric shock bringing the fibrillating heart back into normal rhythm.

We stayed in our positions for nearly an hour as we waited for the paramedics to arrive. I can't remember anyone speaking. All I heard was the strain of our own ragged breathing and the creaking of the bed underneath our combined weight. I then sat in the ambulance by Jerry's side as we raced toward the small local health center. I knew that he was already dead. Even so, I made him two promises that night in the final moments before we arrived at the emergency room.

Both promises changed my life. The first promise is why I wrote this book. As a third year medical student, I was unable to save my future father-in-law's life as his family watched him die. I think about him every single day. He is with me every time I make rounds in the hospital. He is with me each time I meet a new patient in clinic. He is with me whenever I deliver news, good or bad, to patients or their families. Because on that June night seventeen years ago, in the back of an ambulance racing through the streets of Lake Okoboji, Iowa, I promised Jerry that I would devote my career to preventing heart disease from tearing other families apart, and helping survivors put their lives back together again.

Jerry was born in Cedar Rapids, Iowa to a union laborer and a mother who stayed at home to raise him and his five brothers. He served overseas in the Air Force before going back to school. He and his wife Carol raised four daughters together. He was active in his church and he was president of his local Optimist's Club. Jerry was diagnosed with coronary artery disease in his late forties. He underwent open-heart surgery, and his perspective was never the same. His life was transformed at a young age to an uncertain future of pillboxes, medication side effects, and a possible lifetime of angioplasties, stents, and even more surgery. He felt transformed from a seemingly healthy young man to a cardiac patient, literally overnight. Years after surgery, in the months leading up to our trip to Lake Okoboji, he was experiencing chest pains. But he had resolved never to go under the knife again.

You may know someone like Jerry. Or you might see some of him in yourself.

Heart disease can present itself silently with the gradual accumulation of risk factors like diabetes, high cholesterol, and hypertension, or it can appear suddenly and without warning – with symptoms like chest pains, shortness of breath or fatigue, or even a heart attack. And sometimes we are born with heart disease, only to learn about it through screenings or when symptoms strike.

While we do not always have the ability to change our own destiny, much of our overall heart disease risk is within our control. By addressing high blood pressure, abnormal cholesterol, diabetes, obesity, and tobacco, we can cut our risk of heart disease by 80%. Medications can help us along, but lifestyle changes are king. We know this because a few decades ago, medical researchers started to study the health patterns and lifestyles of members of a small community in Framingham, Massachusetts. Their discoveries from studying multiple generations have identified the associations between heart disease and its various risk factors. You can calculate the heart disease risk for you or your loved ones online by going to *http://tools.cardiosource.org/ASCVD-Risk-Estimator/*. Take a second and try it. Cardiologists use calculators like these every day to help guide recommendations regarding lifestyle changes and even medical treatments.

But primary prevention is only part of the conversation. You may already know that despite our best efforts, one out of two men and one out of three women in the United States develop coronary artery disease. Heart disease is the number one cause of death, not only in developed countries, but also throughout the entire world. So in a very real sense, we are all at risk. Heart disease impacts almost everyone, once you consider your spouse, your parents and your kids.

Or maybe even you.

So our mission is to put this risk into perspective. In this book, I will share with you the evidence, insight, and a concrete sustainable plan that is research-proven to add years to your life. This is a book about exercise, and I guarantee that it will move you to run your best race, whatever it may be. Because in the words of *Chicago Tribune* columnist Mary Schmich (best known for her "Wear Sunscreen" essay), "the race is long and, in the end, it's only with yourself."

Who can benefit? Anyone. Everyone. Because prevention is for everyone, especially everyone with heart disease. Exercise is the treatment of choice. Our health care system treats people aggressively with medications, but lapses in sharing lifestyle interventions to help you improve your quality of life and perhaps most importantly, your perspective. I believe that exercise is the least prescribed and most effective heart treatment – and until now, we have been leaving it off the table.

REALITY CHECK-UP

This program is not intended to make you lose weight. There are hundreds of books to help you with that. I even wrote one of them. But that's not our goal right now. You will find no recipes, no meal plans, and definitely no fads or fictions. There are many valuable approaches to a heart-healthier diet, from Mediterranean to vegan and everywhere in between, and there are excellent resources available that explore their relative merits. But first and foremost, the key feature of any healthy lifestyle change is sustainability. As a physician, my goal is to write effective prescriptions that are realistic to fill. Advice is not useful if you are unable to follow it. I want to promote a long-term change in your lifestyle, not break you down or yell at you. Our goal here is much greater, and I need you to feel good about yourself to get there.

This book is also not a substitute for your doctor's advice. I recommend that you speak with your doctor before performing any of the exercises detailed in the chapters that follow. And if you have heart disease, you need to discuss exercise specific to your medical history with your own health care team. To that end, this book is not meant to replace a hospital-based cardiac rehabilitation program. If your doctor prescribes it, do it. I will tell you why, and also give you the tools to continue it at home so that your results are long-term.

My hope is that this program will extend the partnership between you and your health care providers by helping make their exercise prescriptions more complete and concrete. For whatever reason, physicians do not counsel their patients to exercise as much as we should. By sharing this resource with your own doctor and submitting the Heart to Start program for your doctor's approval, I am hoping to turn more physicians into exercise-prescribing "cardiactivists" by witnessing the impact of physical activity on their own patients' health.

PREVENTION IS FOR EVERYONE

We tend to focus our prevention efforts on people who view *themselves* as generally healthy, rather than also tailoring our message toward people who are at serious risk or who have already experienced heart disease. We preach to the healthy about how not to get sick – but the people who live with a diagnosis are overloaded with medications and memories of uncomfortable procedures rather than freed up to use their own feet and forks. Prevention should be for everyone. We cannot leave anyone out, especially since most of us will be impacted by heart disease in one form or another during our lives.

Years ago as a college student, I studied anthropology and learned about the concept of the "liminal state." The word liminal comes from the Latin word *limin,* which means "threshold" – it is commonly used in anthropology circles to describe the cultural practice of having young men or women leave their community or tribe to complete their transformation to adulthood. The liminal period is a time of transition.

As a father of two young boys, I am no stranger to transitions as I experience and observe periods of growth and embrace my kids as they change. Any parent would agree – this is one of the joys and fascinations of having children. But the liminal state of wellness as it shifts toward illness is another story. It seems like the world is divided into two groups – the "healthy" and the "sick." The healthy people enjoy a positive perspective and benefit from preventive care. They focus on lifestyle changes rather than on medications, surgeries, or other invasive procedures. The healthy group receives notices about screening colonoscopies, health fairs, Zumba classes, and low-calorie dessert recipes. They are counseled to be optimistic.

But people who have already been diagnosed with a medical condition or who have accumulated risk factors along the way are approached more tentatively – like outsiders to their own health care. Where is the inspiration for them? Where is the motivation to keep them moving forward? Sometimes I feel like our wellness movement is in denial that illness and suffering are even out there. But by the time we reach our forties, many of us have already crossed over into that "outsider" group in one form or another. It could be as seemingly harmless as a diagnosis of high blood pressure or as powerful as a heart attack. And I guarantee that everyone who has been prescribed a medication for the first time or who has received an abnormal test result is affected by it. It makes us feel different. It makes us feel older. And it makes us feel vulnerable.

Take it from my patient, Matt. Matt and I met because of our shared passions about bouncing back from heart disease. My passion is professional – but Matt's is very personal. When he was in his thirties, Matt was diagnosed with an abnormal heart valve. Heart valves are like the doors and windows of the heart – now imagine if your front door wouldn't open or close the way it should. Heart valve abnormalities are some of the most common forms of congenital heart disease, and many people born with one will require open-heart surgery to replace it at some point in their lives. But as Matt learned, sometimes the future is now.

MATT, 44 YEARS OLD

I always thought I was invincible. I have fallen off a motorcycle going eighty with no helmet and stood up until the ambulance arrived. I was a wrestler, a boxer. I was a bouncer to pay for my college education. I always thought nothing could stop me.

But as my wife and I hugged in tears as they wheeled me into the operating room, I realized this *could* stop me.

I lost vision one day in my right eye for ten minutes. I didn't even have a primary care doctor at the time. I quickly found one and had things checked out, and they determined I had a bicuspid aortic valve – which I was born with, but never knew until I lost my sight. The theory was that a piece of calcium broke off the valve, and hit the blood supply to my brain. They said that when I'm sixty or seventy I would need a new heart valve. When I heard that I figured I was good for another twenty years. I did four or five marathons after that. And I decided last year that I should go back for an annual physical (six years post vision loss) – just a few weeks after doing a twenty-mile trail run. She listened to my heart, and sent me back to the cardiologist.

"You need a new heart valve right now."

I was at a work meeting when I received this news and my partner said I looked white as a ghost. Fear, anger, everything comes into play. You ask yourself, "Why me? How did I get stuck with a bad valve?" But everybody's got their own DNA. I exercise six days a week. I eat well. I have never smoked. I'm the youngest of six kids, single mom…I learned early on that you just have to pound through stuff. I have been doing that my whole life. I always pound through things.

Somebody told me after surgery, "Just walk." So I walked.

And then I ran. Six weeks after surgery I ran a 5K. Six months post I ran a half marathon on my favorite trail. And on the one-year anniversary of my surgery, I'm going to run the same twenty-mile trail run I did before surgery.

Now that I'm through it, I think to myself sometimes…this *didn't* stop me.

And it doesn't need to stop you. Everyone's journey toward better health is profoundly personal and unique, but my underlying message to you is surprisingly simple and applies to nearly everyone. Physical activity is the single most important lifestyle intervention you will make to change your own life. And Matt will be the first to tell you that you don't need to do a twenty-mile trail run to do it, let alone an Ironman. But the stories that you will read from my own patients and from people like you will help you realize that anything is possible, no matter what your experience might have been so far. But it may take a change in perspective.

My goal is to change your perspective.

WHAT TO EXPECT

This is the story of exercise – as prevention and as *intervention* for people who are concerned about heart disease, and especially those who already have it. The most important part of that story is your own personal experience and what you can do today. So in the next chapter I will take you through an easy self-assessment, which will give you new insight about everything from your own level of musculoskeletal fitness to your actual risk of dying over the next five years. And you won't even have to change into gym clothes.

And then we will find your aerobic exercise starting line by walking you through a six-minute fitness test that will guide you toward better health over the next ten years. We will use the results of both of these tests as benchmarks that you can return to later on so that you can quantify your own progress. We will then delve deeper into the link between exercise and heart disease by exploring the impact of fitness on your cardiac risk factors. Learning more about your own risk is the best way to overcome it.

Next we will take the diet industry to task where it comes to using exercise as a health tool. Diet books as well as the media have done a poor job of defining the appropriate role of exercise and activity in a healthy life. They create tension, false expectations, and mislead us when we are most vulnerable by distorting the truth and presenting extremes as commonplace. I will share some of my own experiences with exercise that have surprised me, and will also address concerns that there can indeed be too much of a good thing.

Prepare to be moved. I have asked my patients as well as others who have completed our cardiac rehabilitation program and 5K training program to share their boots-on-the-ground perspectives on using exercise and activity to reduce their risk, recover from heart disease, rebuild after surgery, and restore their faith. Their generous statements are interspersed throughout the text, and they will teach you not only how they crossed their own personal finish lines, but also how they got the heart to start in the first place.

The final chapters are action-packed. We will give a reboot to traditional cardiac rehabilitation, explore the surprising history of exercise and activity recommendations for people with heart disease, and provide useful evidence to support the benefit of structured exercise programs as treatments as well as preventive measures. And what if you don't live near a hospital with a cardiac rehabilitation program? No problem. Home-based exercise works just as well, and I'll tell you why.

And then I'll show you how – with exercise prescriptions personalized to your specific level of fitness. They combine aerobic (cardiorespiratory) and resistance (musculoskeletal) routines to help you live your heart-healthiest life. They will also challenge you to incorporate more activity into your everyday living. And after just eight weeks, you will begin to recognize how far you have already come. And then you will move even further. At least five kilometers further, because I'm going to train you to complete a 5K race. Yes. You.

PLAY SMART

Just one last thing. Thank you. Because by reading this book and taking these physical and figurative steps to improve your health, you are also paying forward good health to others. When it comes to prevention, you can never start too early. That is why our team at the Providence Heart and Vascular Institute launched Play Smart Youth Heart Screenings a few years ago. Check us out at *www.playsmartgetscreened.org*. Our goal is to identify asymptomatic heart conditions in young people to prevent sudden cardiac arrest and to provide opportunities for treatment to ultimately keep kids safe and active. Our screening program is quick and painless. It is also free. In addition to checking blood pressure, we perform a simple cardiac test called an electrocardiogram. You may have had one yourself. Electrocardiograms can identify heart conditions in young people that can put them at risk on the basketball court, the football field, and in the classroom – or may cause them trouble later in life. We have screened thousands of kids and have identified dozens with heart conditions.

SPENCER, 17 YEARS OLD

It is said that life can change in an instant. But until you are faced with that, you never realize how true it is. One evening during a basketball practice in my high school gym, I began to feel dizzy as I ran down the court. I called a time-out and put my hands on my knees…and later woke up confused and scared in a hospital. I had suffered a sudden cardiac arrest.

Without warning, my heart stopped, and I was clinically dead for almost eight minutes before being rescued by an automated external defibrillator. I was a sixteen-year-old multi-sport athlete fighting for my life, but so grateful to those who helped me survive, and so happy to have the chance to see my family again.

But would I be able to play sports again? Would I have a normal, healthy life? Could this happen to me again? As my family and I worked through months of testing to determine what caused my sudden cardiac arrest, it was very possible that I could never be active again. The thought of that was hard to understand or accept. But after working with my doctors, I am lucky enough to be able to play sports. Although I have limitations, I am fortunate to have a plan that allows me to be active and compete. That active spirit has helped me to heal, and offered me a new platform for personal growth.

You shouldn't have to face your own mortality at such a young age. When you are sixteen years old, your identity is more about what you do. Because of my experience, my faith, my family, my heroes, and my friends, I have learned that my identity is more about who I am, how I believe, and how I act – and not what sports I play.

There isn't a day that goes by that I don't think about what happened to me, or touch that amazing little bump under my skin where my implanted defibrillator sits. As scary as it sometimes still is, I know that I am blessed. I'm one of the few lucky ones. I hope that by sharing my own story of survival, I can motivate others to accept that life, even though perhaps different from before, can be happy, healthy, and active!

And that is where you come in. Our screening program is and will always be free for our kids and their families, thanks to you. One hundred percent of your book purchase will go directly to support Play Smart Youth Heart Screenings. Every single penny will help screen a child. By reading this book and improving your own health through exercise, you will help make exercise safer for kids in our communities. You may even save a life. And maybe your own in the process. We thank you for your support, and your family and friends thank you for investing in your own health. We all have a stake in this game.

I told you earlier that I made two promises to Jerry in the back of the ambulance on that hot summer night in Lake Okoboji. You are about to experience the first promise. The Heart to Start program will turn your setbacks into opportunities. You will give your diagnosis a direction by creating movement and momentum in the rest of your life. You will be inspired to move toward better health for you and your family.

But the second promise will have to wait. Stick with me and I'll tell you before we're done.

2.

You May Want to
Stand Up for This

Are you sitting down? I'd like you to join me in a little experiment that is going to give you some insight into your health – it may even surprise you.

Stand up. That's right. I want you to sit down on the floor and then stand up again, using the minimum support you need. Your goal is to sit and then rise again without having your hands, elbows, or knees touch the floor, and without using your hands or arms to support yourself on your knees or legs. You are allowed to cross your legs if you like. Take your time. Think you have what it takes? Go for it. Right now.

Not so easy, right? Now let's try it again. But this time you are going to give yourself a score. Let's start with a maximum possible score of five points for sitting down. For each support you use to sit down – that means touching your hand, arm, knee, or side of your leg on the floor – subtract one point. Subtract another point if you place your hand on your knee. If you lose your balance while sitting down, subtract half a point.

Unhappy with your score? That's all right – try it again.

Now let's tally your score for standing up. Like before, start with five points and subtract one point for each support you use – hand, arm, knee, or side of leg – to stand up. Subtract another point if you need to place your hand on your knee. If you lose your balance while standing up, subtract another half a point.

Now let's add up your best scores. If you were able to sit down and then stand up without using any supports at all, you would have ten points total. How do you think you did? Write down your scores – you will need them later.

SITTING	STANDING	TOTAL

Congratulations! You just performed a sitting-rising test (SRT), one of the simplest yet most accurate ways to quickly assess your musculoskeletal fitness. The ability to sit down and stand up is a major predictor of your functional capacity and your core fitness – and maybe more surprisingly – how long you will live. A recent study examined the SRT in over 2000 adults ages fifty to eighty. Scores were graded in four categories as indicated below. Write your score next to the appropriate category.

CATEGORY	YOUR SCORE
0 – 3	
3.5 – 5.5	
6 – 7.5	
8 – 10	

The researchers found that your SRT score predicts long-term survival. In fact, there was a *three year* shorter life expectancy among participants in the lowest score category as compared to those in the highest score category. People scoring 0-3 were five to six times more likely to die in the next six years as compared to those scoring 8-10. And with each improvement in score category – for example, the difference between scoring a 4 and scoring a 7 – there was a twenty-one percent reduction in death from all causes.

So what does this all mean for you? The SRT is a quick and easy way to help locate *your* starting line on this journey toward understanding the role that fitness can play in your life. And regardless of your fitness level today, improving it is your greatest opportunity to reduce your risk moving forward as well as to treat heart problems if they occur.

Are you still sitting down?

HEART DISEASE IS A SITTING DISEASE

It is high time for an uprising. We have known for years that regular exercise can prevent and treat heart disease – just thirty minutes a day is an ideal dose for many people. But that is just part of the story. Recent research has highlighted the fact that how you spend the *other* twenty-three-and-a-half hours of the day matters too. And it may matter even more. This comes as a disappointment to those of us who spend a half hour in the gym and then feel like we can justify spending the rest of the day sitting behind a desk or in our easy chair. Being active is a lifestyle, not just an appointment in your Outlook calendar.

This was beautifully demonstrated in an Australian study of nearly a quarter of a million people over a five-year period, in which researchers examined the relationship between sitting and survival. Take a minute and think about how many hours a day *you* spend in a chair. Add up the time you spend eating meals, sitting in your car during your two-way commute, and working behind your desk. And don't forget about all those hours you might spend curled up in front of the television, behind your tablet or computer, or even reading a book. Be honest, and let's see where you sit.

	MEALS	COMMUTE	WORK	SCREENS	READING
Hours					

Are you spending half the day sitting down? Lots of people do. Researchers found that if you spend more than eleven hours a day in a chair, you are forty percent more likely to die in the next five years than someone who sits for just six or seven hours. Remember, that is even when you take into account your planned physical activity – even if you make a point of exercising thirty minutes a day. The takeaway is that in addition to scheduling exercise during our busy days, we also benefit greatly from incorporating activity into the rest of our lives. And it's not always easy.

But let's find the silver lining. The good news is that you have a real opportunity to do something that will *reduce* your likelihood of dying in the next five years by up to forty percent – just by getting up on your feet. Let's put this into perspective. Most heart medications that cardiologists prescribe, like statins for lowering cholesterol or blood thinners to prevent blood clots, reduce the risk of death or heart attack by up to thirty percent – if you are lucky. Despite their effectiveness, medications can also be associated with side effects, not to mention money out of your pocket. Standing up is free, and side effects are pretty uncommon. It's not a substitute for other treatments, but it sure is easy to hold down.

The link between sedentary lifestyles and heart disease is so strong that some researchers have gone so far as to suggest that sitting is an independent risk factor for developing coronary artery disease, like smoking, high blood pressure, or diabetes. Some people hear these statistics but understandably feel overwhelmed by recommendations to stand up an additional six hours a day. But thankfully, here is yet another example of how smaller lifestyle changes can have a real health impact.

One study of nearly 125,000 American men and women over a fourteen-year period used some stricter cut-offs to demonstrate that small changes in standing really do matter. These researchers compared the impact of sitting more than six hours versus less than three hours a day, and found that women sitting more than six hours were thirty-four percent more likely to die, and that men sitting fewer than three hours were seventeen percent more likely to survive. This was independent of body weight. Another study estimated that if people were to reduce sitting to fewer than three hours a day, they could expect to add two years to their lives.

What would two more years mean to you? Two more years with your family and friends? Two more years to watch your children grow? Two more years to travel, to experience new things, to enjoy the people you love? People undergo major surgery and intense medical treatments every day just for the possibility of two more years. Their possibility is your opportunity.

Standing up is like any health intervention – there is a dose response. Some is good. More is better. And in this case, everything counts. And don't worry – you can still keep your Barcalounger. This was demonstrated nicely in a study of 17,000 Canadians who were followed for twelve years. They kept it simple and reported their sitting *qualitatively* rather than quantitatively – they reported sitting almost none of the time, one fourth of the time, half of the time, three fourths of the time, or almost all of the time. Regardless of smoking status, body weight, and other physical activity, more sitting was associated with earlier death from all causes, and from heart disease specifically. Full-time sitters were fifty-four percent more likely to die than the least sedentary.

But can you exercise your way out of a sedentary lifestyle? Lots of us try to. But the data would suggest that while you would expect regular exercise to be beneficial in a more sedentary group, it actually takes a surprising amount of exercise to make up for the time you spend on your seat.

Put another way, if you spend half your time in a chair and do not exercise regularly, you are at similar risk as a person who sits all day, except for when he goes to the gym. Being sedentary reduces the beneficial effects of exercise – and that's true for any amount of time you spend in a chair. There is something about the very act (or the "inact") of sitting that's literally killing us. Let's explore why. And later we will brainstorm some ways to stay on our feet.

BORN TO WALK

Even when our muscles are not called upon to run, jump, or just help us stand up, they continue to play a constant role in our health. They are more than just engines that make us move. Muscles also lay down new tracks that impact what direction our health will take. And the path we will follow is guided by inflammation.

As you may know, heart disease is the end game of an inflammatory process that results in cholesterol plaque forming in the walls of our coronary arteries. The more plaque you have, the more likely you are to develop exertional symptoms like chest pain or shortness of breath as the plaque obstructs the flow of blood and oxygen to hungry heart muscle. And with more inflammation, you are also more likely to experience a heart attack when the plaque ruptures and a blood clot forms that can completely obstruct blood flow. This is not a random process. It requires microscopic damage to blood vessel walls to create the perfect storm. Inflammation is that perfect storm. And the more you have, the more likely you are to develop coronary artery disease, and the more likely you are to have a heart attack.

Here is where your muscles play a role, regardless of how you are using them. Active muscles turn on genes that produce anti-inflammatory proteins and anti-oxidants, which protect your blood vessels from damage. Healthier blood vessels are less likely to develop the blockages that can result in chest pains or heart attacks. Active muscles also produce proteins that help us to process the sugars and fats that can cause blood vessels to run amok. That is why more active people experience better control of diabetes and elevated cholesterol. Active muscles lead to a happier metabolism, and in turn, happier blood vessels.

But it is not realistic to be moving, or even standing, all the time. That's why I'm going to let you in on a little secret. There are three times of the day when you can get the biggest bang for your standing buck by getting on your feet and moving around. Scientists have proven that the twenty minutes after your three daily meals – breakfast, lunch, and dinner – are truly the "golden hour." Here stands your opportunity to make, or break down, the process of putting down cholesterol plaque. Doctors call the period just after eating the postprandial state. Studies indicate that a postprandial state marked by elevated blood levels of sugar and fats is a predictor of future heart attacks. Higher levels of sugar and fats put stress on your blood vessels, trigger inflammation and dysfunction of the blood vessel walls, and even increase your risk of developing blood clots.

This does not just apply to diabetics. Even if you have never had a problem with blood sugar, small spikes after meals can still increase your risk of heart disease over time. But the good news is that we can break this cycle by moving our bodies right after we eat, or even between meals throughout the day. Interrupting prolonged periods of sitting with low to moderate intensity walking lowers blood sugar and triglyceride levels after meals. It only requires about ten minutes to get your juices flowing in the right direction and your muscles producing the proteins that help to curb the postprandial inflammation that puts you at risk.

All this research into the effects of sedentary lifestyles on our health begs the question – how did we get so sedentary in the first place? There is a lot of armchair quarterbacking going on to try to explain it. We blame our cars and long commutes, the expansion of cities and the dawn of suburbs, and even what we do for a living. A fascinating study using data from the United States Bureau of Labor Statistics (bean counters who count the bean counters) looked at the correlation between the number of jobs requiring at least moderate intensity physical activity over the past fifty years and the changes in men's average body weight over the same period of time. Researchers found that in the early 1960's, about half of jobs involved some serious physical activity, whereas less than twenty percent do today. They used this data to estimate that the average modern man burns about 142 fewer calories a day than his grandfather. That reduction in calories, explained only by changes in the workforce, would predict an average weight gain from a baseline of 169 pounds in the 1960's to about 197 pounds today. It turns out that this labor model works pretty well – the average weight of American men in the mid-2000's was 202 pounds.

We also can't forget about the impact of television, personal computers, tablets, and especially smart phones. Screen time of any type increases the amount of time we spend sitting. I personally did a lot of field research in this area (i.e., television) as a teenager, and I can assure you that the correlation is real. For many people, limiting television or other screen time to fewer hours per day is a concrete way to ultimately spend more time on their feet. The impact on life expectancy is significant. Compared to people who do not watch television, individuals who spend six hours a day in front of the television will ultimately have 4.8 fewer years to do it. Studies suggest that every single hour of television you watch after the age of twenty-five (phew) reduces your life expectancy by twenty-two minutes. Not to mention the impact of watching all those commercials – let's not even go there. To put this into proper perspective, consider the assertion that smoking one cigarette cuts eleven minutes off your life. That's scary for sure. Especially when you consider that smoking a cigarette has the same health impact of watching a half hour of television.

10 WAYS TO GET UP AND STAY UP

1. Stand while speaking on the phone.
2. Take a ten-minute walk after dinner every evening.
3. Set a reminder every hour to get on your feet.
4. Get off the couch during commercials.
5. Encourage walking meetings at your workplace.

6. Wear comfortable shoes.
7. Use a pedometer, tracker, or app to set a daily goal.
8. Invest in a standing desk.
9. Meet in person rather than by phone or email.
10. And stop looking for a good parking space!

Take a minute – or ten – to stand up for your health. Even as you fill your exercise prescription, please do not ignore how you approach your every day behaviors. Working out a half hour a day and then sitting the rest is like eating a steady diet of bacon cheeseburgers and washing them down with some cholesterol lowering medication.

Don't shoot yourself in the feet. Stand on them instead.

Find Your Starting Line
in the Next Six Minutes

Every Wednesday night throughout the rainy Oregon winter, I walk out of the hospital into the blustery evening, remove my white coat, and replace it with a coach's whistle. Because it's track time. This weekly workout tradition started a couple years ago, when a group of us at the Providence Heart and Vascular Institute trained a team of hospital employees and former patients to finish their first 5K race. They were of all ages, all backgrounds, and all ranges of experience with regular exercise. Not to mention that one of us had a pacemaker, and another had experienced a heart attack a few years earlier. Some hadn't gone for a run in over twenty years, but everyone was hoping to kick-start a healthier new year.

For three months we met in the early evening at a running track in downtown Portland. If you have ever spent much time in Oregon during the winter (or spring, or fall), you can imagine that the weather conditions were less than optimal. Sideways rain, freezing fog, and darkness kept us company every Wednesday night – not to mention rush hour traffic in our efforts to get there on time.

But our team showed up every single week. And we got the job done, together. When we first got started, some of our runners had a tough time completing even just a few circuits around the track. But after a few months, everyone was warmed up and ready to go. And on a chilly February Saturday morning, we *ran* our first race together, now officially called the Heart to Start 5K. Since then, we continue to train together – and in a hundred pages, you can join our team. Think of this book as your coach.

KATIE, 58 YEARS OLD

I realized that I was turning into my parents.

I work in an office five days a week, sitting in a chair, with no source of exercise during the day. I'll be honest – I was getting soft. Very soft. When my annual blood tests came back, my doctor took one look at me and told me I was pre-diabetic! I needed to get my blood sugar back to normal, my blood pressure was steadily climbing year by year, and my cholesterol numbers were heading into the high range.

I didn't want to be static in life. I wanted to be back white water rafting, riding my bike, and playing with my grandchildren...like a kid again. The opportunity came to train with the Heart to Start team to run a 5K. It was hard. Trying to run two minutes seemed like it lasted for five! I thought about quitting more than once, but having a team that was working towards the same goal gave me the strength to continue. When I crossed the finish line with my husband and friends at our 5K it felt great! I'm now training to run a 10K – it seems like a goal that is attainable.

This year my doctor was so happy to see that my test results are now in the normal range for my cholesterol, blood pressure and sugar levels! No need to consider taking medication to improve any risk factors.

Working with a group that will lift you up and help you along makes the small steps connect together and become larger steps toward major accomplishments. Find a team and keep your momentum moving forward.

Famed writer and surgeon Atul Gawande, M.D. published an article in *The New Yorker* called "Personal Best," in which he explored the idea that doctors, much like athletes or singers, could benefit from coaching throughout their careers to maintain or even improve their skill set. But let's take it one step further. Could you benefit from a coach? I sure could sometimes. Gawande writes:

> *The concept of a coach is slippery. Coaches are not teachers, but they teach. They're not your boss—in professional tennis, golf, and skating, the athlete hires and fires the coach—but they can be bossy. They don't even have to be good at the sport. The famous Olympic gymnastics coach Bela Karolyi couldn't do a split if his life depended on it. Mainly, they observe, they judge, and they guide.*

And sometimes we run. People talk about health care provider shortages all the time, but I think that what we really might need is more coaches. Doctors can be both.

Whether I am seeing patients on the track or in the examination room, I believe that it is essential to help them develop some insight as to where they are today. And like every transformative journey, this one begins with a single step. Every adventure begins at the starting line. Starting points are more than just a fixed position – they establish direction and speed towards achieving goals. Your doctor measures your cholesterol, checks your blood pressure, and even gets you on a scale. Each of these data points provides you both with a snapshot that begins to tell a story which may even help you assess your future risk. But I would argue that your level of fitness is possibly your most important vital sign. The problem is that our health care system does not prioritize it or quantify it – and therefore misses an important chance to get you started on an essential journey.

So let's help you find *your* starting line.

You can break down fitness into two different components. The first is musculoskeletal fitness. That is what the Sitting-Rising Test measures. It is the combination of strength, flexibility, and balance. Musculoskeletal fitness is what makes one person able to perform the downward dog in yoga class while the rest of us fall flat on our faces. It is why some people trip and break their hip while others have no problem running down the stairs. Musculoskeletal fitness will let you play on the floor with your grandchildren, carry a bag of groceries in one hand while fumbling for your keys as you walk up the front steps, and it might even give you abs. Your exercise prescription in Chapter 6 will help improve your musculoskeletal fitness with resistance training, and you will get the opportunity to prove it by repeating your Sitting-Rising Test after eight weeks and literally measuring the benefit, point by point.

The second component is cardiorespiratory fitness – also known as aerobic fitness. Aerobic fitness allows you to move quickly and for longer distances. Your cardiorespiratory system is what controls how high your heart rate will go when you exert yourself and how hard you will be breathing when you get there. In Chapter 2 we focused on the importance of getting up on our feet. And now we are going to learn how to use them. Let's explore the link between aerobic fitness and heart disease, and realize that our greatest risk factor is also our greatest opportunity.

It's time to put on your shoes.

TAKE SIX

This is not a race. I repeat – this is not a race.

But it is a test.

It is called the Six Minute Walk Test – also known as the 6MWT. Developed in the 1960's and proven to be both reliable and prognostic, the 6MWT is a quick, easy way to assess what is called your functional capacity – another way of describing your cardiorespiratory fitness starting line. All you need is some space and a stopwatch. And as with any type of fitness assessment, it is vital to make sure that you are a safe candidate to participate. If you have had a heart attack or have been diagnosed with unstable angina in the past month, you aren't yet ready to dig in to this. And if your resting heart rate or blood pressure is not under good control (heart rate greater than 100, blood pressure greater than 170/100), please talk to your doctor about getting your numbers on track before you get *on* the track.

The purpose of the 6MWT is to establish how far you can comfortably walk during a six-minute time trial. For some readers this will be difficult, and for others it might seem easier. But the purpose of this test is not to beat your neighbor – it is to determine your baseline exercise capacity right now to get you thinking about where you want to end up. The first thing you will need is a space to walk. Ideally, a 100-foot segment of a straight hallway is the place to do it. Or you can choose a 100-foot straightaway outside. Make sure that it is flat and away from traffic. Alternatively, you can walk around a high school or college track near you. Whichever you choose, decide upon a location that you will be able to access again so that you can repeat this test eight weeks from today. Do not use a treadmill – the goal is to set your own pace rather than having the equipment set it for you.

GEARING UP FOR THE 6MWT

> Stopwatch
> Comfortable clothing and shoes
> Two items to use as turnaround points
> Borg Scale
> 100-foot hallway, sidewalk, or track
> BONUS: friend or family member

If you plan to perform your 6MWT in a corridor or on a sidewalk and will be walking back and forth, place a small item at either end so that you know where to reverse direction. Consider bringing three additional items to mark the halfway point and the quarter/three-quarters distances to help you tally your partial laps at the end of the test.

The goal of the 6MWT is to walk as far and as fast as you can during a six-minute interval. You will walk back and forth if you are in a hallway or on a sidewalk, and will walk continuously if you are on a track. You may get out of breath or become tired. You can slow down anytime you want. You can stop and rest if you need to. But resume walking again as soon as you can. If you are walking back and forth, pivot quickly around the markers and continue back the other direction without stopping.

Ready to get started? There is just one more thing you need. It's called the Borg Scale of Perceived Exertion. It is a way to rate your level of shortness of breath or fatigue during exercise – doctors use it during exercise stress tests or when performing the 6MWT in the office. The scale starts at 6 and ends at 20 – the idea is that if you multiply your Borg Scale number by 10, the product should approximate your heart rate at that level of exertion. You will record your Borg Scale score after performing the 6MWT.

BORG SCALE

6	No exertion at all	13	Somewhat hard
7		14	
7.5	Extremely light	15	Hard
8		16	
9	Very light	17	Very hard
10		18	
11	Light	19	Extremely hard
12		20	Maximal exertion

You should stop the test if you have any of the following symptoms: chest pain, intolerable shortness of breath, leg cramps, dizziness or unsteadiness, sweating, or getting pale or ashen in appearance. And as always, you should discuss this activity with your health care provider beforehand to make sure it is safe for you.

If you feel that you can manage all of this on your own, go for it. But a 6MWT Buddy can help you keep track of your time and distance so that you can concentrate on walking. Consider finding a family member, friend, or coworker to join you. Have them read the next section.

WANTED: 6MWT BUDDY

Thanks for helping! Studies show that people with heart disease have a lower risk of future heart attacks if they have good social supports – so you are already making an impact just by reading this paragraph. Fitness is also a family (or friend) affair, and you can play an essential role today. Your support will help your relative, friend, or coworker achieve new goals and improve heart health – and you might also get inspired too. Your job is to help supervise the Six Minute Walk Test, keep track of time and distance (or number of laps), and most importantly, make sure that your friend or family member is doing all right. And when you are finished, consider taking the test yourself.

THE 6MWT SCRIPT

1:00   "You have five minutes to go."
2:00   "You have four minutes to go."
3:00   "You are halfway done."
4:00   "You have only two minutes left."
5:00   "You have only one minute to go."

5:45   "In a moment I'm going to tell you to stop."
6:00   "Stop."

You will both stand at the starting line together. When your friend/family starts walking, start the stopwatch and stay where you are. And remember, it is your job to keep track of both time and distance, so try not to get distracted. You will need to stick with this script while you are measuring time. Studies have shown that encouragement can impact the results of the test – so no cheating! If the person stops to take a rest, no problem. And if the person stops walking before time is up and cannot continue, stop the test and record your findings. When the test is over, record the person's total distance, time elapsed (if finished before the six minutes were up), and the Borg Scale score.

Date	
Time Elapsed	
Borg Scale	
Distance	

So now what do you do with your results? There are reference tables, charts, and graphs that describe the normal values for various groups of people. But as you might guess, there is a lot of variation that can be attributed to age, sex, weight, and height (those long legs will make you walk further!). That is why it can be misleading to score yourself in comparison to other people. If you have coronary artery disease, recent surgery, or chronic lung disease, that may impact your score as well.

But despite this variability, we know that people who walk further generally do better. One study analyzed 6MWT results in over 500 people with known coronary artery disease and then recorded future cardiovascular events like death, heart attack, and heart failure during the following eight years. Researchers found that people in the lowest 25th percentile of 6MWT distance had four times the rate of cardiac events as those in the highest 25th percentile. Every additional increase of 100 meters was associated with a 30% lower risk of cardiac events.

But here's the important thing – this is not a competition with anyone else. This is just the first step on your own journey. And your goal is to fill your fitness prescription so that you can improve your endurance and ultimately lower your risk. Keep your score somewhere safe, and complete your eight-week exercise prescription before you try it again. You will surprise yourself.

FORESTS AND TREES

Earlier, you had the opportunity to go online and estimate your cardiovascular risk by using a calculator developed by the American Heart Association and American College of Cardiology. That risk assessment considers traditional risk factors that can be easily measured, like cholesterol and blood pressure, but focuses less on behaviors, like dietary choices or exercise. This calculator, as well as previous iterations developed by the Framingham Heart Study and other organizations, encourages you to "know your numbers" and emphasizes the role of medications as interventions to bring down blood pressure and optimize lipids. But the elephant in the room is always exercise. We don't measure it. We usually don't even ask you about it. And as a result, we don't have a complete picture.

Risk factors never exist in a vacuum. People who engage in some unhealthy behaviors are more likely to engage in others. But the opposite is also true. Not only does exercising regularly improve your blood pressure and cholesterol numbers, which will improve your estimated risk, but it also helps to lower your risk by changing other behaviors. People who exercise tend to smoke less and eat healthier. Exercise creates a health halo that impacts other areas of your life – this effect helps make regular exercise the single most effective intervention in reducing heart disease risk.

Put another way, being out of shape can be your single greatest risk factor. Worse than smoking. Worse than diabetes. And definitely a bigger deal than bad genes. This has been demonstrated in multiple populations of people, from those nice folks in Framingham to dockworkers in San Francisco to Harvard graduates. Turns out it matters less who you are and more what you do.

When we think about risk, there is the possibility of getting so focused on our individual risk factors that we sometimes miss the big picture. Don't get me wrong. I prescribe cholesterol medication and blood pressure drugs just as much as the next cardiologist. But blood tests are no substitute for the person sitting across from you in the examination room. We need to rethink our approach to reducing heart disease risk by recognizing that people are more than just the sum of their laboratory tests.

Although physicians sometimes prescribe exercise as a means to impact traditional risk factors for heart disease, it also benefits you even when it stands alone, regardless of your numbers. One study of lifestyle interventions intended to reduce cholesterol found that regardless of cholesterol level, being more active was associated with a 50% lower risk of dying from heart disease. In this study, physical activity was defined as walking for thirty minutes, four or five times per week.

And there is more good news, especially for the millions of us who focus on one number above all others – our weight. Research has confirmed that physical fitness is even more important than body weight in impacting risk of heart disease. In one study of over 14,000 men during an eleven-year follow-up period, maintaining or improving fitness was associated with a lower risk of death from heart disease and stroke regardless of *any* changes in body weight. These researchers focused on units of increased fitness called METs – metabolic equivalent of task. A MET is a physiological measure of the intensity of a particular activity. The greater the METs, the more intense the activity. In this study, every increase in MET was associated with a 19% lower risk of heart disease and stroke-related death, irrespective of losing or even gaining weight. Here is a case where smaller changes yield big results – and for once, we are not talking about the scale.

Fitness researcher Steven Blair famously commented, "It's not the obesity, it's the fitness." But you unfortunately won't read that in any diet book. It's true that weight loss can be a valuable means to a meaningful end – better health. But the real weight loss secret is that losing weight is not necessarily the be-all end-all prescription for everyone. Because you will become healthier by becoming more fit – even if you never lose a single pound. We are so hardwired to measure our success by a number on a scale that we lose perspective on the overarching goal – not to mention the process. In the next chapter, we will take a quick step backward into the wild world of weight loss, and realize that we have been selling mixed messages all along.

4.

What Your Diet Book
Isn't Telling You

They say it takes one to know one. In 2011, I wrote a book called *The Flex Diet*. My goal was to break away from the lopsided, rigid dietary approaches I saw my patients getting frustrated by, and instead emphasized the idea that being flexible and making small changes can help you lose weight safely and comfortably while reducing your risk of heart disease and maintaining your sanity. *The Flex Diet* encourages a balanced, sustainable lifestyle with more plants (although I still believe in the occasional burger), less processed food, and few if any absolute restrictions. Turns out it works. People lose weight in a healthy way and can keep it off because small, gradual changes can be accommodated into almost anyone's lifestyle.

But why a diet book? Early in my practice as a cardiologist, I realized that an impressive arsenal of stents, surgeries, and medications were no substitute for something far less complex but much more important – the right message. Historically, doctors present their patients with rigid guidelines about what works and what doesn't, and people are expected to twist and contort their lives to fit them – as uncomfortable as it might be. I thought it could be interesting to turn that relationship around, and create a message that by definition would be flexible and made to fit into my patient's lives. Flexibility creates a template for success by allowing people to define the process that makes sense for them.

While *The Flex Diet* includes chapters on exercise and increasing activity, it focuses more on food and drink. I knew that in order to get to my patients' hearts, I needed to go through their stomachs first. The reality is that many people make lifestyle choices based upon the promise of weight loss. And given that the majority of sustainable weight loss is achieved through diet rather than exercise (more on that in a minute), that is how I structured my approach.

After the book was published, I traveled throughout the country meeting readers. But to be honest, the best part was always coming back home to my family and taking care of my patients. The true test of any health message isn't what happens in an auditorium or on a television show, but rather what goes down face-to-face in the examination room, in the ER, or in the intensive care unit. That's where health care happens in real life. And with that perspective, it became clearer that doctors and diet book authors alike (including me) have been selling exercise short – and for reasons different from what you might expect. Mixed messages from the diet industry are getting in the way of your health, and maybe your weight loss too. Let's shed some light and create some heat.

THE PURPOSE OF EXERCISE IS *NOT* TO BURN CALORIES

Whether you are sitting at home trying to get motivated or sitting in a hospital bed looking forward to your recovery, exercise occupies a unique space in your mind. You are already probably familiar with the concept of a heart-healthier diet. It is just a question of extremes. Less processed food, fewer simple sugars, and smaller portions of meat. More plants, and more healthy fats. You might have tried your hand at being vegan, or maybe you are more the "I'll have skim milk with my coffee" type. Either way, you already get the idea that putting healthier things in your body will help you heal and will reduce your risk moving forward.

But when we think about the role that exercise will play in our transformation, we tend to leave the holistic behind and instead turn our thoughts toward particle physics and calorimetry with the false promises of websites that promise rock hard abs and DVD sets that claim to shred our belly fat, confuse our muscles, and possibly drive us insane. We are conditioned to think that it is all about the calories. It is easy to start viewing your body as a machine that requires fuel for the sole purpose of consuming it. You begin to view exercise as a mathematical inevitability or obligation – purely as a way to burn calories.

Because we know that if we burn calories, we will lose weight. Right?

Except that when it doesn't work out that way. There is a simple reason why diet books tend to gloss over exercise even as they provide disturbingly minute details about *how* much of *which* foods you should eat *when*. Sure, exercise gets its own little chapter – maybe a short workout plan for lip service back towards the appendix, which no one ever reads anyway. But even as exercise is short-changed, it is made clear to you that the purpose of it is to burn those nasty calories away.

But the problem is that for you and the majority of people you know, exercise is not a weight loss panacea. You may have already experienced it. I have seen it from two perspectives – as a doctor and as a patient who tries to fill my own prescription. In the examination room, I like to take an exercise history. I think of it as an extra vital sign. And there seems to be a common thread among patients who have gone on a weight-loss diet and also started an exercise program. People quit diets that are not sustainable. It's that simple. And it makes sense. If a food plan is rigid and unpleasant, no one will be able to stick with it beyond a few weeks – despite that fact that these calorie-restricted programs will help most people lose some weight in the short term. Success in weight loss does not guarantee that you will continue a diet. But if you talk to people about why they no longer exercise, you may hear a very different tune.

"I exercised every day, but I didn't lose any weight. It didn't work."

It didn't work because of the way we define success. When many people take on weight loss, they approach it in a compartmentalized way. That is to say, they either make drastic changes in their diets or they start exercising more consistently and more intensely. That is why we see spikes in gym memberships every January. And the pattern is pretty predictable. The person goes to the gym for a few weeks, doesn't see any significant reduction on the scale, and then is discouraged. The exercise experiment is considered a failure, and the work of burning calories is reduced to a weight loss technique with a negative reputation.

It is not that people are necessarily wrong about the impact of exercise in weight loss. For many people, it honestly *doesn't* work very well. In general, the role of diet is far greater – approximately 80% of weight loss is related to diet, and only about 20% is related to exercise. It turns out that exercise is more effective for weight maintenance and holding steady rather than trimming down in the first place.

For a very different perspective, talk to anyone training for an endurance event like a half-marathon. They amp up their mileage and speed while training, but are often surprised that even while burning an incredible number of calories, they do not lose a commensurate number of pounds. I have experienced this myself, especially when training for a longer race. After months of increasing my distance, I end up at the same weight where I started. That whole "3500 calories equal a pound" adage falls apart in real life. But it's not that the scientists were wrong in the physics laboratory. It's just that people are not research subjects. And we don't live inside a lab. When we go for a run or hit the gym, we get hungry. And we eat.

And there is absolutely nothing wrong with that.

Anyone participating in an exercise program will be expected to have a larger appetite and will tend to consume a similar number of calories as they just burned on the treadmill or on the track. Or sometimes more. Our bodies did not evolve to lose weight – they evolved to maintain it, even under extreme circumstances. So any attempt at weight loss that focuses primarily on exercise to burn calories will tend to come up pretty short, unless there is a similar concentration on calorie restriction.

At the end of the day, even though exercise does burn calories, most people should not rely upon it to help them lose weight.

There is a lot more to exercise than just weight loss. Let's stop selling it short. It is time to redefine success.

THE CHEESECAKE STANDS ALONE

I remember watching a television show a few years ago about introducing healthier foods into school lunch programs and vending machines – a fantastic goal. To illustrate his point, the host explained the relative merits of two different snacks. But rather than focus on their nutritional value, the host instead showed students the track behind their school. The message was that if the kids ate the healthier option, they would only need to go around the track a few times to "burn it off," whereas if they ate the less healthy snack, they would have to exercise for a longer period of time to somehow counteract it and become calorie-neutral.

Is this how we should be thinking about exercise? As a way to undo poor dietary choices? As a punishment?

This comes up sometimes when my family goes out to dinner. My kids are big fans of The Cheesecake Factory for a special night out. If you ever find yourself eating there, you may witness a fascinating moment that occurs hundreds of times a night – at every Cheesecake Factory across the country. After devouring your jumbo salad, pasta dish, or burger, your friendly server comes casually by the table, and without skipping a beat, asks the question that you might have feared all along.

"Are you ready for some cheesecake?"

You stare at your plate. You steal a glance at your dining companions to determine their own strategy. And in a split second, you make some quick calculations. If you enjoy that slice of cheesecake right now, all you need to do tomorrow is wake up an hour early and sweat it out on the treadmill. You will burn the calories off and be right back where you started. It's perfect math, and what could go wrong?

But here's the thing.

The cheesecake always wins.

Understandably, you may find it pretty difficult to get yourself out of bed at 5:00 AM while nursing that food hangover. You might just press the snooze button a couple of times. And when you do wake up, you remember everything you need to do. The lunches you need to pack. The conference call that you can't miss. Or you just lie there in bed, thinking about your plans for the day. And you don't make it to the treadmill.

We talk a lot about the benefits of resistance exercise. But this is a completely different type of resistance. When we create tension in our lives, we view the opposing forces only as they relate to their opposite. A slice of cheesecake is no longer a special dessert to enjoy with your family at a favorite restaurant – it's a calorie bomb that requires a deactivation strategy. And a good sweat on the treadmill, a fitness class, or a brisk walk with your dog turns into a self-inflicted punishment that you "deserve" for the horrible mistakes you made the night before at the dinner table. It sounds miserable, but that's how we roll. While it may be convenient to think that you can arrange a perfectly matched tug of war in your calorie balance by adding one treadmill workout for every slice of cheesecake, it never works out that way. One side wins. And it's not your health – mental *or* physical.

Let's get away from viewing diet and exercise as a Yin and Yang, and instead take more of a Zen approach. Each should be valued independent of the other. A slice of cheesecake every once in a while is okay. And when you order it, you should enjoy every last bit of it. And when you do exercise, take a moment to experience the increased flow of blood into your working muscles, the exhilaration of an increase in your heart rate, the purity of movement. Push and pull, but without resistance. Without adding to the tension already present in your life.

YOU CAN HAVE TOO MUCH OF A GOOD THING

Every week, millions of overweight Americans gather around their televisions to watch a handful of overweight Americans be insulted, humiliated, and driven to the point of mental and physical breakdown. This is reality, and this is reality television. The original concept of reality television was to allow the audience to become a voyeur into the social interactions among a diverse group of people placed into an extraordinary circumstance. Whether or not you liked it, there was an assumption that the people were safe and that just off camera there were some responsible adults around just in case things got out of hand.

Weight loss reality television has gotten out of hand. Not only because of the yo-yo results that it achieves, not only because it mixes motivation and ridicule, but also because it misrepresents entertainment as health care by highlighting the oversight of medical professionals in its program. While it is encouraging that a reality television show could potentially contribute to the national dialogue about obesity and health, the reality is that it is taking away more than it is actually adding to the conversation.

WEIGHT LOSS REALITY SHOW NON-REALITIES

> Physicians believe that it is safe to lose a significant amount of weight (i.e. much more than two pounds) every week.

> Trainers believe that it is safe to exercise four to six hours a day, to the point of crying, passing out, or vomiting.

> Nutritionists believe that the purpose of exercise is to lose weight, and place less emphasis on the role of a healthy diet.

I'm happy to say that I do not know any health care providers in the real world who subscribe to these practices. Not only are these takeaways not sustainable in the longer term, but there are also legitimate scientific concerns that they negatively impact health, not to mention weight loss. Consider the role of your metabolism. Metabolism is your engine – it determines the rate at which you burn calories, whether at rest or in motion. But here's the thing – this engine works more quickly or more slowly depending on how much work it needs to do. That means that a heavier person has a faster metabolism than a lighter person. Therefore, as you lose weight, your metabolism actually slows. Doctors call this metabolic adaptation. That's why people plateau during weight loss attempts if they continue to maintain the same diet and exercise behaviors even after losing an initial amount of weight. In order to promote further weight loss with a slowing metabolism, you need to change what you are doing. In effect, your diet needs to go on a diet.

But here is the problem. If you lose weight too quickly, your metabolism slows too quickly as well. As you lose both muscle and fat, exercising to excess doesn't help speed up your metabolism accordingly. Researchers have actually studied the impact of reality television weight loss on metabolism. After six weeks, show participants had lost 13% of their body weight, and after thirty weeks, they had lost nearly 40% of their original weight. Sounds impressive. But after six weeks on such an aggressive program, their metabolisms had slowed by 244 more calories a day than would have been expected. And at thirty weeks, their metabolisms had slowed by 504 more calories a day than expected based on their weight. This slowing in metabolism is the equivalent of no longer burning off a whole meal's worth of calories. That's like feeding someone an extra meal a day. When excessive exercise is compared to weight loss surgery, with a focus on metabolism and comparable weight loss, people who exercise to extremes have a significantly greater metabolism slow-down. So unless they continue to exercise four to six hours a day in perpetuity, they are almost guaranteed to regain a good portion of the weight that they have just lost. We need to change the stakes to help our biggest losers become winners in the end, but exercise bulimia is not a healthy approach to make this happen.

So even once you rationalize the fact that for many people, exercise plays only a small role in weight loss, the question inevitably comes up: "How much is too much?" This has been an area of intense research over the past few years, as more weekend warriors have dipped their toes in triathlons or made a move to run a marathon. Understandably, there is a lot of passion among athletes who enjoy endurance events. Most endurance athletes would agree that the goal of participating in an endurance event or exercising in excess of an hour a day goes beyond just health. It becomes more of an individual search for performance or goal achievement that belongs on a bucket list rather than on a prescription pad. Some of the people profiled throughout this book have pursued endurance sports as a way of redefining themselves and regaining control over their bodies, using sports to defend against the hits that self-esteem commonly takes following a diagnosis of heart disease. But these types of events are not for everyone. All of us have different goals, and we should feel comfortable pursuing them. But even if you never run a single race, you can still be inspired by the course that others may take, and use it to fuel your own journey.

ANTHONY, 56 YEARS OLD

It took me about six weeks of chest pain until the angiogram confirmed I had four totally blocked arteries. I wasn't even allowed to leave the hospital before undergoing open-heart surgery. I was forty-eight, never smoked, worked out regularly – a pretty big guy but not seen as someone with a weight problem. In fact, nobody believed it was my heart. That is why it took so long to get to the diagnosis. I had to have quadruple bypass surgery.

After the surgery my world was rocked. I had heart disease. I was slowly recovering both physically and emotionally when I found out that two of my bypasses had failed and they had to go back in and use stents – exactly what they *didn't* want to do in the first place. So now, my confidence was at an all time low. I tried to get back into working out, but again, when your confidence is so low that every muscle ache feels like another heart problem, I found myself questioning everything I did physically.

Slowly, it got better. As my confidence increased I challenged myself more. I slowly moved from a lot of road biking to a lot of running. I liked the challenge of doing something that I really did not have the body for. I liked how I felt so good after finishing a run that I didn't even think of myself with heart disease. At age fifty-four, I ran my first half marathon. One year later, I completed my first marathon. It took a while for me to believe that a diagnosis of heart disease did not mean that I was not able to go after what I really wanted to accomplish. In fact, in some ways, it made me go after it much harder and made it even more fulfilling. I not only got through the twenty-six miles but also years of self-doubt of what I really could do regardless of my diagnosis.

People who exercise more than what you could call the "Minimum Effective Dose" are looking for something else that exercise can offer – from inspiration to competition to fulfillment, and for some – even weight loss. And despite the research that suggests that a lifetime of endurance sports may actually *contribute* to some types of heart disease in select people, there are also some cardiologists out there who have their doubts. The reality here is that we all come from different places of bias, which tends to impact how we interpret any data that comes our way. But for the purposes of the Heart to Start program and your own personal experiences – whether you are recovering from heart disease or trying to prevent it – my only bias is to help you do exactly what you need to do to accomplish your goals. That is why your exercise prescription should be measured, realistic, and without side effects.

But that is not to say that we should not be inspired by other people's experiences, even if they are different from our own. Sometimes those differences are the most inspiring part. Whether you are watching the Olympics or are standing at the starting line of your local 5K race, athletes at every level of performance and ability amaze us. We marvel at their successes and their challenges. We imagine the very different paths they have taken to arrive at the same finish line. They motivate us. They help us realize that there is always something new that we can achieve too. That is why it is so valuable to listen to their stories. Put yourself in their places and see what can be possible in your own journey.

Because if the sky is the limit, it is time to start looking up.

5.

Cardiac Reboot

I stared straight ahead, walking quickly but not so fast that it would sense that I was starting to panic. Stealing a glance out of the corner of my eye, I caught the shaggy blur dancing at the margins of my peripheral vision. I tightened my jaw and concentrated on the steady rhythm of my feet and their crunch on the gravel road. I tried to focus on the sunlight and gentle headwind on my bearded face. I smelled the soil of farmland on all sides of me.

And then I felt it. Just a little bit of fleeting pressure at the back of my right ankle. It didn't break skin, thanks to the thick heel of my hiking boot. But I still couldn't help arching my shoulders and clenching my fists, preparing myself for what might come next. As if it would have made a difference. I had always heard that you should never look an angry dog in the eye. But just then, I turned my head slightly to get a better sense of what I was up against. And it growled.

This was the third stray dog I had met along the Camino de Santiago, and even though I was afraid, I felt that if I just continued on my path it would eventually leave me alone. It was a long path. I had begun the walk seventeen days earlier near Roncesvalles, a short bus trip northeast of Pamplona, nestled comfortably at the border between Spain and France. And for the next five hundred miles, I hiked through plains, mountains, and wine country, through unseasonal February sun and drenching March rain mixed with snow, spending nights in churches, hostels, and bars – like thousands of pilgrims before me.

The Way of St. James is a pilgrimage with centuries of history, and has been walked as a penance, a religious rebirth, a spiritual journey, and as an adventure. For me, it was all four. In all, it took me twenty-seven days and three stray dogs to reach my destination – Santiago de Compostela in northwest Spain. But as I reflect on this journey, the road was most definitely the goal. Nearly twenty years later, I can summarize the swings in temperature, the blisters on my feet, and the sheer exhaustion I felt every single day with one word.

Ultreya.

Ultreya means "onward." Now imagine hiking through a small village in the Rioja country in northern Spain. You have a paper map that tells you that your next stop for the night is anywhere from three to five hours away. You take a sip of water from your canteen. And then you hear it. A farmer looks up at you from his shed. A small group of children interrupt their soccer game on a field. A bartender leaves his post and walks out onto the dirt road.

"Ultreya."

Everywhere I walked, from the first days to the final push, I heard the most perfect word I have ever known from people who

I will never know. Their encouragement gave me momentum, and their confidence in me pushed me forward. They reminded me that no matter where your Camino might be, there will always be stray dogs nipping at your heels. But there will also be complete strangers who want you to succeed.

ULTREYA

During medical school, I became interested in the idea of physicians as activists. I learned about the organization International Physicians for the Prevention of Nuclear War, and realized that its founder was a cardiologist whose office was just a few blocks away from my apartment. Dr. Bernard Lown won the Nobel Peace Prize in 1985 for his efforts in involving physicians to raise public awareness of the human consequences of nuclear war. His medical career has been equally inspiring. He is the inventor of the defibrillator and cardioverter, and introduced the drug lidocaine into medical practice, used for decades to help control dangerous heart rhythms. But possibly his most interesting contribution involved something far simpler, which has had an incredibly far-reaching impact.

A chair.

I sat with Professor Lown in his office on Longwood Avenue in Brookline, Massachusetts as he told me the story of how he used to care for cardiac patients in the early 1950's. Until that point, patients with heart attacks were confined to strict bed rest for four to six weeks. Even sitting in a chair was not permitted. Patients were fed by nurses and forced to use bedpans – they even required assistance to shift their position in bed. But Dr. Lown and his mentor, Dr. Samuel Levine, theorized that patients would recover more quickly if they spent more time in a sitting position rather than lying in bed. During a five month period, Lown recruited eighty-one patients to participate in this "intervention" – a strangely progressive treatment for its time – in which patients were placed in a chair for thirty to sixty minutes a day for one week, and then remained in a chair for the majority of their waking hours during the rest of their hospitalization.

And their patients did well. Dr. Levine, more of a traditionalist, believed that the benefit was due to simple physics. Levine opined that gravity caused blood to pool in the legs of a seated person rather than settle into the bases of the lungs of the bedbound, thus helping seated patients breathe more comfortably. Also, more blood in the legs might hypothetically mean less blood moving through the heart, so the recently damaged heart would get some rest. But Dr. Lown felt differently as he recognized the lasting impact of just sixty minutes in a chair. How could sitting just an hour a day result in a benefit that would last the other twenty-three?

Dr. Lown was very familiar with the idea of the liminal state, which we explored earlier. Having a heart attack or undergoing open-heart surgery can be a psychological trauma for many people that ravages their sense of control over their lives. Dr. Lown writes in his memoir, *The Lost Art of Healing,*

> *The ominous implication was reinforced by the physician's insistence on complete bed rest, proscribing all activity, even to prohibiting movement in bed. The patient was left to the mercy of forces over which he or she had no control. By contrast, patients managed in a chair did not consider themselves hopelessly ill. After all, in our*

culture the act of dying takes place in bed,
so there was some sense of safety in being
out of it.

Dr. Lown and Dr. Levine presented their research findings to a group of physicians in Atlantic City in early 1951, and never could have known back then that their study would revolutionize the care of patients with heart disease. Their research was a precursor to the modern concept of cardiac rehabilitation, in which we encourage our patients to move more than they believe they can, to try harder than they think they should, and to recover with the confidence and self-esteem that we know they deserve. We owe so much to Dr. Lown and the other cardiologists, nurses, and exercise physiologists who have forged this path for the rest of us to follow, so that we might all walk a little more briskly, pushed onward by their whispers of "Ultreya" on the trail.

GOT REHAB?

Cardiac rehabilitation is an under-prescribed yet very effective treatment for people with heart disease. In this section, we will explore the essentials of cardiac rehabilitation and the evidence that supports it. Depending on your own health history, you may even be a candidate or might have completed a program yourself. Unfortunately, this can be a situation where if you do not bring it up, it is possible that no one else will.

For unclear reasons, only about 20-30% of eligible heart patients are even referred to cardiac rehabilitation – and of those, only about 40% participate. It is bad medicine to withhold a life-saving treatment, and many physicians are selling their patients short. Whether it is for lack of awareness or lack of availability, cardiac rehabilitation referral rates leave a lot to be desired. What makes this even more surprising is that it is actually covered by most insurance providers for many cardiac conditions, including a recent heart attack (within the past year), coronary artery bypass graft surgery (CABG), stable angina, heart valve repair or replacement, congestive heart failure, and coronary stenting. Medical evidence supports its use for even broader indications, like congenital heart disease, pulmonary hypertension, peripheral vascular disease, and even diabetes mellitus. It is the best medication that you will never find in a television commercial, and its only side effect is a better quality of life.

The primary component of cardiac rehabilitation is exercise. Participants typically attend sessions three times a week for eight to twelve weeks with the goal of developing and filling an individualized exercise prescription. Exercise sessions are generally monitored by a nurse or exercise physiologist as well as an electrocardiogram (ECG). Participants are hooked up to an ECG machine while on the treadmill or elliptical machine so that heart rate and ECG tracings may be recorded and interpreted. The second component of cardiac rehabilitation is risk factor education. This may include educational programming designed to address smoking cessation, diabetes management, nutritional counseling and weight management, and even treatment of hypertension and elevated cholesterol. The final aspect of cardiac rehabilitation is identifying and addressing the various psychosocial effects of heart disease or heart surgery. As you may already know, upwards of 20% of people develop depression or anger following a heart attack or heart surgery, and many people experience anxiety or fear about returning to their normal quality of life. Depression can be associated with a significant increase in cardiac complications, and cardiac rehabilitation can confront it directly.

Cardiac rehabilitation was initially designed to be performed in phases. Phase I was introduced in the 1960's – it occurred in the hospital after a medical event, and it included "armchair medicine," some walking, and assessment of one's ability to perform activities of daily living. Phase II is the outpatient program above which occurs in a medical setting, which was not available until the 1970's. Phase III is an outpatient program that you and your health care provider can carry out in the clinic or at home. Phase IV is the long-term maintenance program, designed to motivate and continue the benefits of the medically supervised second phase. Phase IV is the rest of your life. This book gives you the tools to create a Phase IV cardiac rehabilitation program in collaboration with your own physician. Whether or not you have heart disease today, this program will lower the risk of you experiencing it tomorrow.

Earlier in our discussion of fitness and heart disease, we emphasized the research demonstrating the effectiveness of exercise as prevention. But an exercise prescription is just as beneficial as an *intervention* – as an actual treatment for people who already have a heart disease diagnosis. Many people will avoid exercise after a cardiac event because they believe that it is too late for it to make a difference – like a smoker who has already developed lung disease. But they couldn't be more mistaken. The science could not be stronger in its support of a fitness intervention – whether prescribed in the form of cardiac rehabilitation or in a structured exercise program like Heart to Start. The benefits of exercise rival any medication you might have already been prescribed. Studies suggest that cardiac rehabilitation is associated with a 17% lower risk of heart attack at one year, and a 20% lower risk of dying – with a 25% decreased risk of dying specifically from heart disease. And among depressed patients, one study identified a 75%

reduction in the risk of dying in those who participated in cardiac rehabilitation.

JOHN, 75 YEARS OLD

I had my heart attack (they called it "the widow maker") on my 73rd birthday. I was shown the cardiac rehabilitation manual upon discharge but didn't sign up. But during a subsequent checkup, after I had been doing my own rehab, and had lost thirty pounds and was feeling great, the doctor still recommended I consider the rehab program in addition to my walking program. I did it and loved the results. The staff was unbelievable. Creating a personal program for each of us, being monitored constantly, being encouraged to maximize our efforts by the great staff, all made it something I actually looked forward to twice a week. I have since continued my own exercise program, walking two miles every day with two of my neighbors, keeping me inspired physically and mentally. And thanks to the coaching from my wife, I have now lost *forty* pounds and have really changed the way I eat (I can't believe I do not crave cheeseburgers anymore). I believe my heart attack was a blessing. It gave me a second chance to take better care of myself.

The benefits of cardiac rehabilitation and structured exercise have been demonstrated in both women and men, and among the young, middle-aged, and elderly. It doesn't matter who you are – because what you do has a similar impact. Exercise will strengthen and lengthen your life. So are *you* a candidate? If you have stable angina, heart failure, a recent heart attack, coronary stenting, coronary artery bypass graft surgery, or surgical valve repair or replacement, you should absolutely talk to your doctor about cardiac rehabilitation resources in your area. And if you are more interested in prevention, you have still come to the right place.

LOW RISK, HIGH REWARD

It is understandable that people feel a little wary about beginning an exercise program shortly after experiencing a cardiac event. But it is generally very safe. Even so, it is essential to assess your own risk of complications with your doctor's help before getting on that treadmill. That is why the American Heart Association came up with four categories of risk so that you can see where you belong – whether that's in the gym or maybe back at your doctor's office for a check-up.

CLASS A	Healthy	"No" risk
CLASS B	Stable, known heart disease	Low risk
CLASS C	Multiple heart attacks, Cardiac arrest, Symptomatic heart failure Abnormal stress test	Moderate / High risk
CLASS D	Unstable	No exercise

Cardiac rehabilitation is generally intended for people in Class B or C, and the Heart to Start program is most appropriate for people in Class A or B. It all comes down to safety and supervision. Even though exercise is safe for the majority of people, putting your heart under any stress at all does increase the risk of cardiac complications for a small minority of people. The American Heart Association has estimated that one cardiac event occurs for every 60,000 to 80,000 hours of supervised exercise. Whereas exercise lowers overall cardiovascular risk – especially in the longer term – the associated elevations in heart rate and blood pressure do briefly increase the risk of a cardiac event during and immediately after the actual workout. This is true even for healthy people without a known history of heart disease. If a person's risk of having a cardiac event is one in a million in any given moment, that risk may increase to three in a million after exercise or after having sex. Those are pretty good numbers to hang your heart on for all the known benefits.

Safety is always an important consideration because supervision will also vary depending on the model of cardiac rehabilitation you might be considering. Traditional rehabilitation takes place in a modified fitness center or gym, often located in a hospital or medical center. A team of exercise physiologists and nurses supervises participants, with a physician medical director typically overseeing the operations.

But the limited availability of these hospital-based programs has led to some alternative approaches, including home-based programs. A rigorous review of a dozen studies of home-based cardiac rehabilitation programs found that they are *as effective* as hospital-based programs in improving exercise capacity and reducing cardiac risk factors, heart attacks, and death. Participation rates for home programs are high – 72% at six months and 41% at four years – because exercising at home is convenient for most people, especially those who might find it more difficult to travel regularly to and from a hospital-based program. People have doubled their level of physical activity in home-based programs, and studies have also found similar success in lifestyle changes like stopping smoking, improving blood pressure and cholesterol, and addressing symptoms of depression and anxiety.

So it's time to take charge of your own treatment without adding a single medication to your pillbox. Call your primary care doctor or cardiologist. Go to the website of the American Association of Cardiovascular and Pulmonary Rehabilitation (*www.aacvpr.org*) to learn more about cardiac rehabilitation and the resources available in your own area. The link will take you to a searchable database so that you can locate programs close to where you live and see if you qualify.

After training in an outpatient cardiac rehabilitation program for eight to twelve weeks, participants have improved their exercise tolerance and are hopefully addressing their risk factors for future cardiac events while feeling more confident about the future. But one of the challenges that all of us face after our initial attempt at changing behavior is what to do next – what to do when no one is watching over us. It can be so hard to continue a healthy lifestyle when it's just us, back at home, face-to-face with a treadmill masquerading as a coat hanger, or back at the Cheesecake Factory, face-to-face with you-know-what. It is time to take your rehab on the road. Because if there is one thing I learned while walking the Camino de Santiago so many years ago, it is that the road *is* the goal.

WORK OUT

6.

The Heart to Start
Exercise Prescription

This prescription is your potential, and this journey has been about living up to it. We initially set the stage by proving that fitness is your greatest opportunity to reduce your risk of heart disease as well as treat it. You stood up, sat down, and got up again with the Sitting-Rising Test to get some insight into your core. And then you walked as far as you could for the Six Minute Walk Test, establishing a baseline level of speed, balance, and endurance. Along the way, we have been joined by people like you, who have shared their own stories. Stories of fear and pain. Stories of frustration and almost giving up. And ultimately stories of effort, determination, and triumph.

Their stories are your stories. And it is time to see what can happen next. Right now you have the power and the opportunity to write the next chapter for yourself. I hope you will make this prescription a part of your life for the next eight weeks. If you fill it in earnest, I believe that you will keep coming back for refills because I know that it will change your quality of life. And science says that it will help you live longer too.

This Heart to Start prescription really has three parts. The main component is a structured exercise program that is tailored to you from the outset. If this is the only part of the prescription you participate in, you should achieve a significant benefit. Studies of exercise "rehabilitation" by itself suggest an associated 28% reduction in death. It is hard to say that about any other prescription I write. The second part is risk factor education. Programs that combine exercise and education are associated with a 38% reduced risk of having a heart attack, and risk factor education on its own is associated with a 13% reduced risk of dying. The last part is mind-body health. Self-acceptance and a little bit of introspection will help you stay focused and motivated to think positively about your future. Combining exercise and mind-body health lowers both cardiac risk and emotional stress more than just exercise alone. So let's get moving.

VO 2 THE MAX

Motivation requires the perfect combination of appreciation and achievement. I want you to enjoy what you are doing, feel challenged by it, but also be empowered to succeed. So that's why I need your help to make this prescription perfect for *you*. Remember the Six Minute Walk Test? That was a quick and dirty way for you to establish a baseline and also give you a starting point to come back to eight weeks from now to assess your progress. But in order to create your personalized exercise prescription, you need to determine where and how fast you are going to move. It is time to determine your VO_2 Max. This is your fitness vital sign.

$$V = \text{Volume}$$
$$O_2 = \text{Oxygen}$$
$$\text{Max} = \text{Maximum}$$

Also called your maximum aerobic capacity or maximal oxygen consumption, your VO_2 Max is the maximum volume of oxygen that your body can use in a given period of time while you exercise. It is the ultimate measurement of your physical fitness. Cross-country skiers have some of the highest in the business, but don't even come close to the ultimate in endurance athletes – sled dogs! And we all have something in common – we can improve our VO_2 Max with practice. Sled dogs call it fun. Athletes call it training. We call it a little bit of both.

Formal exercise testing is performed in an exercise physiology laboratory with treadmills and oxygen masks – or your doctor can estimate your VO_2 Max by doing an exercise test similar to the Six Minute Walk Test. But now there is an even easier way to estimate your VO_2 Max without leaving your living room. All you need is a computer or a smart phone.

The Cardiac Exercise Research Group (CERG) at the Norwegian University of Science and Technology measured the VO_2 Max of 4600 people ages 20 to 90, and determined the average VO_2 Max at every age. They then used some additional information, including the people's reported exercise frequency, intensity, and time as well as measurements of their waistline and resting pulse, and came up with a formula that not only estimates VO_2 Max, but also correlates it with the typical age of healthy people with that same VO_2 Max. So in a sense, you not only can estimate your level of fitness using this formula, but you can also determine your "fitness age." For example, a 55-year-old woman might learn that her fitness age is closer to 40, suggesting she is in great shape, or it could be estimated at 75, which means that with some training she might be able to bring down her "fitness age" as she becomes more active.

You can measure your resting pulse by placing the tips of your index and second fingers on your wrist below your thumb at the base of your hand. Press gently, and carefully feel for your pulse. Count it for fifteen seconds, and multiply by four to get your heart rate per minute.

You probably already know your waistline in inches, but the calculator requires you to know it in centimeters. Here is a quick table to help you along. Multiply your waist in inches by 2.54 to make the conversion yourself.

INCHES	CENTIMETERS
30	76.2
31	78.7
32	81.3
33	83.8
34	86.4
35	88.9
36	91.4
37	94.0
38	96.5
39	99.1
40	101.6
41	104.1
42	106.7
43	109.2

INCHES	CENTIMETERS
44	111.8
45	114.3
46	116.8
47	119.4
48	121.9
49	124.5

Now let's take your data and estimate your VO_2 Max. You have two choices. If you have an iPhone, download a free application called VO_2Cal and take it from there. Or just head on over to *www.worldfitnesslevel.org* to access the CERG website for its free online calculator.

You now have three fitness data points to work from, so let's put them all in one place. Go back to your Sitting-Rising Test to collect your score and your Six Minute Walk Test to remember your distance so you can record them both here. You can use them as a basis of comparison after you complete the Heart to Start training program. Think of your Six Minute Walk Test as an indicator of where you are right now, and your VO_2 Max as establishing a game plan for where you are going to go. Your VO_2 Max will guide your exercise prescription for the next eight weeks.

SRT	6MWT	VO$_2$MAX

Let's learn more about your exercise prescription by identifying its essential components – Frequency, Intensity, and Timing.

FREQUENCY

Heart to Start is an eight-week training program. By the end of the eight weeks, you will be exercising every single day. If you need to (or want to) miss a day here or there – whether for a reason ("I had to work an extra shift") or an excuse ("I slept through my alarm again"), it's not the end of the world. This is a process, not a punishment. And I consider every single day a success, no matter how many you exercise in a row. But let's start by thinking big. Because your goals are big, aren't they? Lofty goals deserve daily attention. We will achieve them by being active nearly every day without holding ourselves to something unrealistic. If you are on the road or recovering from the flu, I have your back. But if it's a television show or a rainy day that is holding you back, then there is a lower chance that you are going to move forward. Make the decision right now to move forward.

We will break your training program down into two parts. The aerobic training brings the greatest benefits to your heart, so you will be moving it with an aerobic workout four days a week. Studies show that we require three to five days a week of moderate aerobic exercise to achieve a significant benefit. The American Heart Association and the American College of Sports Medicine each recommend a minimum of 150 minutes per week. You will exceed that by the end of eight weeks.

While it is true that riding your bike, climbing stairs, or using a rowing machine would provide a solid aerobic work-out, we want to keep things low-tech and low-impact so that you can keep it simple, do your workout anywhere, and minimize your risk of injury. The saying is true – you have to walk before you learn to run. And running will come later! But be patient. Studies tell us that walking is as powerful as more vigorous exercise like running for preventing cardiovascular events and treating heart disease. So you are in good company. That is why the HEART training program is a structured walking experience.

The first two weeks will look like this, with walks four times a week:

WEEKS 1 – 2

SU	M	T	W	TH	F	SA
HEART		HEART		HEART		HEART

The START resistance regimen is the second part of Heart to Start. Previously, people with heart disease or even people trying to prevent it were encouraged to primarily engage in aerobic activities, often to the exclusion of performing resistance exercise. But it turns out that most of your important daily activities require muscle strength – from opening car doors to carrying grocery bags (or even your children or grandchildren). Being independent means becoming stronger. And becoming stronger creates more confidence and a better quality of life, including a lower risk of depression or fatigue. Finally, resistance exercise is associated with lower blood sugar, a better cholesterol profile, and even lower blood pressure.

SHOULD YOU WAIT ON WEIGHTS?

Talk to your doctor before doing strength exercises if you have any of the following cardiac conditions:

> Unstable angina
> Uncontrolled high blood pressure
> Symptomatic congestive heart failure

> Severe valvular stenosis or regurgitation
> Hypertrophic cardiomyopathy
> Sternal complications as a result of surgery

START training will help you increase your strength and endurance with exercises using your own body weight as well as dumbbells. Start yourself at a lower weight than you think you might need. People with little or no experience with weights might start between two and five pounds, and those with more experience or bigger frames might start between five and ten. You always have the option of sizing up to a heavier set as you proceed through the program. Some people may initially feel awkward or uncomfortable lifting weights – or even going to buy them in a sports store. But in your regular life you are constantly lifting and pushing and pulling, so you need to replicate that in your training environment to achieve the greatest benefit. And to be honest, it's fun. The START workouts are introduced in Week 3 on Mondays, Wednesdays, and Fridays, and each exercise is accompanied by a detailed description and a diagram for your reference.

WEEKS 3 – 8

SU	M	T	W	TH	F	SA
HEART	START	HEART	START	HEART	START	HEART

During this phase of the program, you will also add intervals to your HEART workouts to add variety and improve your efficiency. Studies suggest that we burn more calories and improve our VO_2 Max when we change our speed intermittently as we train. This brings us to intensity.

INTENSITY

Citius, Altius, Fortius. These are the Latin words for "Faster, Higher, Stronger" – the motto of the Olympic Games. These words will also apply to you during the next eight weeks, as we will use the symbolism of the Olympic rings to guide your progress. The five interlocking rings, colored blue, yellow, black, green, and red, were chosen to represent the national flags of all the countries involved in the Olympics when the Olympic flag was designed over a hundred years ago. We will use these colors to represent your own abilities at the beginning of this program. There are five different categories of VO_2 Max – each one is assigned to a different color. Find your own and follow your color week to week. If you find that your track doesn't seem right for you – either a little too easy or too difficult – you are encouraged to move to a different color to find the best fit. I recommend you do this in your first week so that you don't lose momentum later on.

Blue	< 34
Yellow	34 – 37
Black	37 – 43
Green	43 – 46
Red	> 46

Each week you will be provided with a HEART chart that provides a suggested walking distance. An approximate time of completion for walking at a brisk pace is given for your reference. The fitter you are, the faster you should plan to move. You may find it more convenient to perform these workouts on a treadmill or at a track. However, you can do them anywhere as long as you can reliably estimate the distance you are walking. Here is a sample HEART chart from Week 1 that will help you find your starting line.

WEEK 1

VO₂ MAX	MILES	TIME	% MPHR
Blue	1	20	60
Yellow	1.5	30	65
Black	2	40	70
Green	2.5	43	70
Red	3	45	70

The final column of the chart is your goal heart rate during exercise, represented as a percentage of your Maximal Predicted Heart Rate (MPHR). While you do not have to wear a heart rate monitor to succeed at this program, you might actually find it helpful to use your heart rate as a measurable indicator of your effort. The harder you are working, the higher your heart rate will typically go. And as the weeks progress, you will target a higher heart rate as you improve your level of fitness and increase your effort. The Heart to Start program intends to push you to a range of 60% to 75% of your MPHR.

Your MPHR is most accurately estimated using a research-derived formula in which MPHR = (211 − 0.64 x your age). This formula was developed by the same team that created the VO_2 Max calculator you used earlier. It replaces the better-known, but less reliable estimation of MPHR as (220 – your age). You can find your own estimated MPHR on the next page, along with the percentages that you will see throughout the eight-week program. Refer to this chart week to week to find your goal heart rate.

Keep in mind that the MPHR is just an estimate. Every individual's actual MPHR is unique. And some people are on medications that may impact how high their heart rates can go. My recommendation is to use your heart rate as just a guide, and not as a judge of how hard you are working. How you feel matters most.

AGE	MPHR	60%	65%	70%	75%
30	192	115	125	134	144
31	191	115	124	134	143
32	190	114	124	133	143
33	190	114	124	133	143
34	189	113	123	132	142
35	188	113	122	132	141
36	188	113	122	132	141
37	187	112	122	131	140
38	187	112	122	131	140
39	186	112	121	130	140
40	185	111	120	130	139
41	185	111	120	130	139
42	184	110	120	129	138
43	183	110	119	128	137
44	183	110	119	128	137
45	182	109	118	127	137
46	182	109	118	127	137

AGE	MPHR	60%	65%	70%	75%
47	181	109	118	127	136
48	180	108	117	126	135
49	180	108	117	126	135
50	179	107	116	125	134
51	178	107	116	125	134
52	178	107	116	125	134
53	177	106	115	124	133
54	176	106	114	123	132
55	176	106	114	123	132
56	175	105	114	123	131
57	175	105	114	123	131
58	174	104	113	122	131
59	173	104	112	121	130
60	173	104	112	121	130
61	172	103	112	120	129
62	171	103	111	120	128
63	171	103	111	120	128
64	170	102	111	119	128
65	169	101	110	118	127
66	169	101	110	118	127
67	168	101	109	118	126
68	167	100	109	117	125
69	167	100	109	117	125
70	166	100	108	116	125
71	166	100	108	116	125
72	165	99	107	116	124

AGE	MPHR	60%	65%	70%	75%
73	164	98	107	115	123
74	164	98	107	115	123
75	163	98	106	114	122
76	162	97	105	113	122
77	162	97	105	113	122
78	161	97	105	113	121
79	160	96	104	112	120
80	160	96	104	112	120
81	159	95	103	111	119
82	159	95	103	111	119
83	158	95	103	111	119
84	157	94	102	110	118
85	157	94	102	110	118
86	156	94	101	109	117
87	155	93	101	109	116
88	155	93	101	109	116
89	154	92	100	108	116

Finally, we can't talk about workout intensity without introducing the concept of intervals. Exercise physiologists have determined that people burn calories more efficiently by varying the intensity of exercise throughout a given workout. These are called intervals, and we will add them to your HEART training in the third week of the program. Rather than maintain the same pace for the entire duration of your walk, you will add short bursts of a faster pace at regular intervals of time. During weeks three through five, this will occur for just one minute out of every ten, and during weeks six through eight, we will increase the intensity by increasing the frequency of intervals to one minute out of every five. Studies suggest that you can achieve similar vascular health but improved fitness (as estimated by VO_2 Max) by combining a steady pace with higher intensity intervals as compared to maintaining the same pace throughout your entire workout. The variety will also keep things interesting and fun, and keep you focused on what you are doing. The best workouts happen when you are engaged in the process.

TIMING

The length of your HEART workouts is based upon your initial estimated VO_2 Max and the specific week of the program. Each week you will use the corresponding HEART chart that indicates which workout you should do depending upon your starting fitness level. The times listed in the HEART charts are estimated if you are walking on a track and are focusing on the specific distance, and will be even more accurate if you are doing your walks on a treadmill where you can set the time and distance.

Structure your workouts in the most convenient way for you. I do not believe that there is any significant advantage to exercising in the morning versus the afternoon or evening. But I do believe that if you are committed to working out at the same time each day, it will be easier to incorporate it into your daily schedule and you will be less likely to "forget" to exercise. Once you add a five-minute walk at a casual pace to the beginning and the end for a warm-up and cool-down, you are looking at a total duration of between a half hour to an hour of HEART training, four days a week. The START workouts are shorter. Each lasts less than a half hour.

THE FINE PRINT

Like any athlete, you do not want to get injured. So I suggest that you run this or any exercise program by your health care provider before getting started.

If you have had a recent cardiac event, consider cardiac rehabilitation first.

If you have a history of heart disease and are using this program as a kick starter toward better heart health and improved fitness, please touch base with your doctor to make sure that you are both on the same page.

If you experience chest pain, breathing problems, dizziness, muscle pains, joint paints, or balance problems, please stop what you are doing and let your doctor know. And if you experience muscle or joint pains during the weight-bearing exercises, don't be a hero. Take a break and let yourself heal. You're in this for the long term.

START RESISTANCE PROGRAM

The START resistance program beginning in the third week is straightforward and comprehensive. There are twelve exercises involved, and it shouldn't take you longer than thirty minutes to complete two sets of twelve repetitions of each one. We will focus on your shoulders, back, biceps, and triceps, and will spend some additional time working on your core. The key is not to rush during the exercises themselves, but also move briskly from one to the next. Do them in the order in which they are presented, and after your first full set of the twelve exercises, start over from the beginning for another go-around.

GET STARTED

Push Ups

One Arm Dumbbell Shoulder Press

Shoulder Shrugs

Dumbbell Raise

Flat Bench Leg Raises

Lateral Dumbbell Raises

Arnold Press

Rear Deltoid Row Dumbbell

Supermans

Front Raises

Dumbbell Upright Row

Side Plank

PUSH UPS

1. Lie face down on the floor with your feet together and rise onto your toes. Keep your knees on the floor if you need to.

2. Place your hands shoulder width apart on either side of your chest.

3. Draw your abs in.

4. Inhale as you raise your body up until your arms are straight.

5. Exhale out as you lower your body back to the floor.

ONE ARM DUMBBELL SHOULDER PRESS

1. Stand with your feet shoulder width apart, back straight and abs drawn in.

2. Grasp a dumbbell in your hand and lift it with a bent elbow to your shoulder height to start.

3. Lift the dumbbell straight up until your arm is fully extended overhead.

4. Lower slowly and return to starting position.

5. Repeat and then switch sides.

SHOULDER SHRUGS

1. Stand with your feet shoulder width apart.

2. Hold a dumbbell in each hand, with your arms at your sides.

3. Lower your shoulders.

4. With your arms straight, raise both shoulders up towards your ears.

5. Hold the upright position for a moment and then lower slowly.

DUMBBELL RAISE

1. Stand with your feet shoulder width apart and a slight bend in your knees.

2. Grasp a dumbbell in each hand, in front of your thighs.

3. Draw your abs in.

4. Raise the dumbbells up on either side of your ribs in a rowing motion by bending your elbows and moving them outwards.

5. Lower to starting position.

FLAT BENCH LEG RAISES

1. Lie on the floor with your hands under your hips supporting your back.

2. With your feet together, raise your straight legs up a few inches off the floor. This is your starting position.

3. Keep your legs straight and raise your legs to about ninety degrees with your hips.

4. Pause at the top and lower your legs slowly back to the starting position.

LATERAL DUMBBELL RAISES

1. Grasp a dumbbell in each hand, palms facing inward towards your body with the dumbbells at your sides.

2. Stand with your feet shoulder width apart, draw your abs in and bend your knees slightly.

3. Raise your arms up until they are in line with your shoulders; your palms should face the floor.

4. Hold the position for a moment, and then slowly lower your arms to the starting position.

ARNOLD PRESS

1. Sit on a chair or bench, feet pointed forward with your abs drawn in.

2. Grasp a dumbbell in each hand with your palms facing towards your body.

3. Bend your elbows to ninety degrees and raise both your arms to the starting point in line with your shoulders.

4. Slowly raise the dumbbells up while rotating your forearms so that your palms now face forward.

5. Bring the dumbbells closer together.

6. Slowly lower the dumbbells to the starting position at your shoulders.

REAR DELTOID ROW DUMBBELL

1. Place your right foot on the floor, and rest your left knee and hand on a flat bench or chair.

2. Keeping your back flat, reach down and pick up the dumbbell with your right hand.

3. Raise your right arm, while bending and bringing your elbow back as far as you can.

4. Pause at the top for a moment and then lower the dumbbell slowly to the starting position.

5. Switch arms by doing the opposite positioning.

SUPERMANS

1. Lie on the floor, flat on your stomach with your arms stretched out in front of you...like Superman!
2. Raise your arms and legs off the floor and hold this position for two seconds.
3. Return to the starting position.

FRONT RAISES

1. Stand with your feet shoulder width apart, abs drawn in and knees slightly bent.

2. Grasp a dumbbell in your left hand, with your palm facing your body.

3. Start with the dumbbell at waist height.

4. Raise your left arm, keeping your elbow slightly bent and your arm straight, in line with your shoulder.

5. Pause for a moment and slowly lower your arm to back to the starting position at your waist.

6. Repeat with your right arm.

DUMBBELL UPRIGHT ROW

1. Grasp a dumbbell in each hand with your palms facing your body and hold them in front of your thighs. They should be touching.

2. Starting with the dumbbells at your thighs, slowly raise them up towards your shoulders by bending your elbows.

3. Pause at the top.

4. Lower the dumbbells slowly.

SIDE PLANK

1. Lie on the floor on your side with your legs straight and your forearm perpendicular to your body in front of you.

2. Drawing your abs in, slowly raise yourself up so you are balanced on your feet and your forearm.

3. Hold this position for thirty seconds and slowly return back to the starting position.

4. Repeat on other side one time to complete the set.

WEEK 1

Your HEART workout begins on a Sunday, and continues every other day through Saturday.

SU	M	T	W	TH	F	SA
HEART		HEART		HEART		HEART

Now use your VO$_2$ Max to choose the right workout for you. Remember to take a five-minute slow warm-up walk at the beginning and at the end to cool down.

VO$_2$ MAX	MILES	TIME	% MPHR
Blue	1	20	60
Yellow	1.5	30	65
Black	2	40	70
Green	2.5	43	70
Red	3	45	70

WEEK 2

Your second week maintains a similar schedule.

SU	M	T	W	TH	F	SA
HEART		HEART		HEART		HEART

But take it up a notch. Each workout is longer by about five minutes.

VO₂ MAX	MILES	TIME	% MPHR
Blue	1.25	25	60
Yellow	1.75	35	65
Black	2.25	45	70
Green	2.75	47	70
Red	3.25	49	70

By the end of these two weeks you will be in a rhythm and will have gained enough momentum to introduce some variety in the upcoming weeks as we introduce the START resistance workouts on Mondays, Wednesdays, and Fridays.

WEEK 3

During Week 3 you will begin the START resistance workouts on Monday, Wednesday, and Friday.

SU	M	T	W	TH	F	SA
HEART 10	START 2/12	HEART 10	START 2/12	HEART 10	START 2/12	HEART 10

Remember, this week we also introduce ten-minute intervals on your HEART days (the "10" is your friendly reminder). In the tenth minute of each ten-minute segment of your workout, push yourself to walk a little bit faster for one minute before returning back to your regular pace. On your START days, plan on doing two sets of twelve repetitions ("2/12") of each exercise.

VO₂ MAX	MILES	TIME	% MPHR
Blue	1.25	23	60
Yellow	1.75	32	65
Black	2.25	42	70
Green	3	51	70
Red	3.5	53	70

WEEK 4

During Week 4 you stick to the same schedule as last week.

SU	M	T	W	TH	F	SA
HEART 10	START 2/12	HEART 10	START 2/12	HEART 10	START 2/12	HEART 10

Push yourself during your intervals, and concentrate on doing your resistance exercises slowly. Mindful, purposeful movements are associated with a lower risk of injury – and greater muscle development.

VO$_2$ MAX	MILES	TIME	% MPHR
Blue	1.5	30	60
Yellow	2	37	65
Black	2.5	46	70
Green	3	48	70
Red	3.5	49	70

WEEK 5

This is your final week of ten-minute intervals during HEART workouts and two sets during your START workouts – we will dial them both up next week!

SU	M	T	W	TH	F	SA
HEART 10	START 2/12	HEART 10	START 2/12	HEART 10	START 2/12	HEART 10

VO₂ MAX	MILES	TIME	% MPHR
Blue	1.5	30	60
Yellow	2	37	65
Black	2.75	51	70
Green	3.25	52	70
Red	3.75	53	70

WEEK 6

During Weeks 6, 7, and 8 you will double the frequency of your HEART intervals from once every ten minutes to once every five minutes. You will also add a third set to your START training.

SU	M	T	W	TH	F	SA
HEART 5	START 3/12	HEART 5	START 3/12	HEART 5	START 3/12	HEART 5

VO₂ MAX	MILES	TIME	% MPHR
Blue	1.5	26	65
Yellow	2	34	70
Black	2.75	47	70
Green	3.25	49	75
Red	3.75	50	75

WEEK 7

Same intervals, same number of sets. But slightly longer workouts.

SU	M	T	W	TH	F	SA
HEART 5	START 3/12	HEART 5	START 3/12	HEART 5	START 3/12	HEART 5

Plan on speeding up this week and pushing yourself a little harder during your five-minute intervals. If you aren't comfortable maintaining your speed (some of you will be doing a light jog), then focus on your heart rate. The most important component to being successful is putting in the time.

VO$_2$ MAX	MILES	TIME	% MPHR
Blue	1.75	30	65
Yellow	2.25	38	70
Black	2.75	47	70
Green	3.5	56	75
Red	4	53	75

WEEK 8

Your HEART workouts sped up in Week 6, got a bit longer in Week 7, and now level out in Week 8 to give you a maintenance aerobic regimen that you can stick with or build upon in the future.

SU	M	T	W	TH	F	SA
HEART 5	START 3/12	HEART 5	START 3/12	HEART 5	START 3/12	HEART 5

VO$_2$ MAX	MILES	TIME	% MPHR
Blue	1.75	30	65
Yellow	2.25	38	70
Black	3	51	70
Green	3.75	56	75
Red	4	53	75

After Week 8, it's time to take a breath and see how far you have come. Remember the Sitting-Rising Test and the Six Minute Walk Test? Remember estimating your VO$_2$ Max? Before moving onward, take a few moments and try again. The past eight weeks have really made an impact.

	SRT	6MWT	VO$_2$ MAX
Before			
After			

COOL DOWN

7

What Would a Healthy Person Do?

Earlier in our journey, you had the opportunity to estimate your risk of having a cardiovascular event in the next ten years. The organizations that created this calculator use a 7.5% cut-off to help categorize individuals as higher risk – some of them might be candidates to take cholesterol-lowering medications to further reduce their risk of future heart problems. But if you are currently recovering from a heart attack, a stent, or heart surgery, these types of risk scores, calculators, and probabilities have possibly lost their meaning. Because you may have already experienced "risk" first hand.

Patients frequently ask their doctors about risk. They want to know their own personal percentages and probabilities down to the smallest detail. That makes sense. Information can be empowering, and assigning a number can sometimes bring abstract ideas into focus. They can motivate us to change our behavior.

But I also think that it is important to remind ourselves that we can choose to interpret risk in a different way.

Because there is no such thing as a 7.5% heart attack.

Even though your estimated risk of a heart attack, stroke, or even dying from heart disease might be greater than 7.5% – or perhaps lower depending on your risk factors – your actual personal reality is either 0% or 100%. Let's put it another way. The risk of being in an airplane crash is exceedingly low – far less than 1%. But for the unfortunate people on a plane that crashes, their reality is 100%. Despite this very low probability, airlines use checklists upon checklists to account for any level of systematic or human error in order to ensure the safety of their passengers.

No matter how unlikely an event may seem, we have to prepare for any and every possibility. Because if it happens to you, it is very, very real. And if it happens to you, you are no longer a statistic. We need to prepare for the 100%. That is why we wear seatbelts. That is why we wear bicycle helmets. And that is why we need to move our bodies and feed them with respect. Risk is more than just a number. Understanding it will impact how you live.

While the first part of traditional cardiac rehabilitation programs includes an exercise prescription, the second part focuses on risk factor education. It is vital to consider your exercise in the context of each of your modifiable risk factors for heart disease. In Chapter 1, we estimated that 80% of your overall risk is under your control. And amazingly, your exercise prescription is the unifying intervention that brings your risk factors down together in a very real way. Rather than think purely in terms of traditional cardiac risk factors like high blood pressure, blood sugar, and cholesterol, let's focus on how you want to live your life.

SUSTAINABILITY, REDEFINED

More fiber. More healthy fats. More vegetables.

Less sugar. Less salt. Less meat. No trans fats.

That's a heart-healthy diet. It's also brain-healthy and reduces your risk of cancer. Sure, you can break it down even further or add labels like Mediterranean, vegetarian, vegan, or even vegan no-oil. But remember, restrictive does not necessarily mean realistic, or even enjoyable for some people. Try to think about your diet like a sculptor might view a piece of stone. The initial strikes of the chisel make the greatest impact. They change the shape, introduce new angles, and begin to create the intended image. But as the process moves forward, each incremental change has a smaller absolute impact even though it adds to the final product. While small changes are necessary to refine, it is the larger, *first* steps which initially commit you to your goal. That is why as long as you follow the general principles of a healthy diet, the details can be flexible and can adapt to your lifestyle.

We also should recognize that research in this area constantly generates new approaches, but is limited by its own design. It is easier to demonstrate how paradigm shifts in diet can be healthier (i.e. a Mediterranean diet versus a typical Western diet) but it is more difficult to prove how best to use your chisel to create the details. Is a vegan no-oil diet truly better than a mostly plant-based, low carbohydrate diet? We really don't know. But we are realizing that the benefits of diet on the risk of chronic diseases occur long-term. For example, while eating less salt today may lower your blood pressure next week, it really takes years for a lower blood pressure to reduce your overall cardiovascular risk. The same goes for lower blood sugar, cholesterol, or even body weight. While diet can impact so many of these secondary endpoints rather quickly, which can help to inspire or reinforce change, it takes years to prevent heart attacks or cancer. That means that the largest changes you make *today* that you can stick with *tomorrow* will have the greatest impact *next year.* If a particular dietary approach does not appear sustainable to you, it ultimately matters less if it might be potentially more effective.

Exercise is an amazing tool to help make your heart-healthier diet sustainable. We previously noted that the purpose of exercise is not to lose weight. In fact, many people maintain a similar weight as they exercise, particularly if they are training for an endurance event or begin a more vigorous exercise program. Burning more calories drives you to eat more too. But not all calories are the same. Exercising regularly will influence the types of calories you eat and will direct you subconsciously toward a heart-healthier diet.

Neuroscientists call the ability to accomplish tasks and achieve goals "self-efficacy." And it appears to be contagious. Self-efficacy in one area of your life may carry over into other areas. Regular exercise impacts your mood, motivation, and willpower so that you make changes in other parts of your life, like diet, with relatively less effort. Exercise not only trains your muscles and your heart. It trains your brain. Scientists have postulated that a neurocognitive connection exists between diet and exercise, so much so that they have suggested beginning any diet program with regular exercise even before attempting to change what you are eating. Consider tackling the first couple weeks of your Heart to Start training before attempting any changes in your diet.

REVERSAL OF MISFORTUNE

If the single greatest risk factor for heart disease is low fitness and a sedentary lifestyle, smoking cigarettes comes in at a close second. And unfortunately, exercising and quitting smoking are each challenging lifestyle changes for many people to make. But they both have amazing short and long-term effects on your overall risk. I have seen many patients who continue to rationalize smoking because they feel that the damage is already done. They do not believe that stopping will reduce their future risk in any serious way. But the good news is that even after putting down cigarettes for a few days, your body begins to heal. Your blood pressure comes down. Your blood vessel walls become healthier. And once you have quit for good, your heart disease risk comes down to rival a never-smoker's after one to two years. That is a serious reversal of risk that is completely yours to control.

But to be fair, stopping smoking is extremely difficult, with success rates at one year less than five percent for many people who really are giving it an honest try. That is why you need all the advantages you can find to set yourself up for a greater chance for success. Pills, patches, and even therapy have been demonstrated to increase the likelihood of a good outcome, but many people do not realize the added value of a good workout.

Exercise has been examined as a treatment to help smokers stop the habit. And while nothing is guaranteed, exercise is definitely another option in your toolbox. Studies suggest that even a shorter bout of exercise – from a few minutes of resistance training to walking a mile – can reduce the desire to smoke, reduce the withdrawal symptoms (think irritability and stress), reduce your anticipation of your next cigarette, and increase the actual amount of time before you smoke again. Researchers performed magnetic resonance imaging (MRI) on the brains of smokers, and found that following exercise, there was reduced activity in areas of the brain associated with reward (the caudate nucleus) and attention (parietal lobe, parahippocampal, and fusiform gyrus), which might be expected to be associated with cigarette craving. This is your brain on exercise. If you smoke and are trying to quit, begin your Heart to Start training a few weeks before your quit date for even greater success.

RISK HAS NO ON-OFF SWITCH

As health care providers, we are sometimes limited by the tests that we recommend. Cholesterol. Blood pressure. Blood sugar. Large population-based research studies tell us that people with certain numbers generally have a lower risk of developing heart disease as well as other chronic diseases. But how does that affect you as an individual? Should you be living your life to make a laboratory test look a certain way?

Yes and no. It all comes down to the idea of endpoints. Ultimately, the purpose of living a heart-healthy life is to reduce your risk of heart disease. That makes sense to all of us. But it would be difficult to know at any given moment if you were making the right choices, or if you might benefit from medication in some situations. Researchers from the Framingham Heart Study and other population-based studies have recognized that variables like blood pressure, cholesterol, blood sugar, and body weight have strong associations with future risk. So we end up targeting those as secondary endpoints because our primary endpoint – the heart disease risk itself – is a bit more elusive and takes longer to measure.

But those secondary endpoints can be limiting, especially when we establish what might seem to be somewhat arbitrary cut-offs that frame our goals as doctors or as patients. Is a blood pressure of 141/91 really all that different from a blood pressure of 139/89? The first is abnormal by standard definitions. The second is normal. But for any given individual, each probably confers a similar risk level. But what about a blood pressure of 139/89 versus a blood pressure of 120/80? We believe that the lower pressure is healthier, even though both are in the normal range. You can imagine a similar situation when considering your blood sugar, cholesterol numbers, and in some situations, your weight. Our biology exists on a continuum, even though we think about it in terms of cut-offs. It is time to rethink our risk as a moving target. Risk is relative, which means that we can always do a little bit better. We always have an opportunity to reinvent ourselves.

Rather than just encourage you to learn your numbers and target a specific goal, like triglycerides below 150, or blood pressure less than 140/90, consider your risk level instead as something that you can always improve upon or optimize as you go. Go back to your risk calculator and input your own data. And once you have estimated your risk, play with the calculator and make some changes in the variables – you will realize that you can still lower your risk even if you are in the "normal" categories for blood pressure or cholesterol just by making changes in your diet, incorporating the Heart to Start program, or having an honest discussion with your doctor about your medications. While not always the case, a higher dose will sometimes achieve a greater reward.

WHAT WOULD A HEALTHY PERSON DO?

Every January, it seems that there is a new line of products for sale to usher in a "New Year, New You." But I don't think there's anything wrong with the Old You. We expect ourselves to flip a switch and become some turbocharged, super motivated, highly evolved version of ourselves, without flaws or insecurities, like a Superman transformed from years of struggling as Clark Kent. That is a lot of pressure, and it is also not very realistic. We should never stop celebrating who we already are, but we should also *start* celebrating what we are capable of. Even as we hope to rebrand ourselves as healthier individuals, we are still hopefully the same people beneath it all as when we started.

I ask my patients to ask themselves a simple question as they work through this transition: "What would a healthy person do?" There seem to be two types of people – those who want to "be" something, and those who want to "do" something. The diet industry and late-night infomercials thrive on the first group. By purchasing a set of DVD's, a piece of exercise equipment, or a new blender, you can pretend that you have already accomplished your goals. The act of buying the book or shopping in the healthier supermarket aisle satisfies our desire to "be" that healthier person without actually doing all that much. And in most cases, we do not follow through.

But it turns out that if you focus on "doing" the healthier thing, you *become* the person that you have been looking for. So ask yourself as you walk towards the elevator and see the stairwell just down the hall, "What would a healthy person do?" Ask yourself when you are placing your order at Starbucks, "What would a healthy person do?" And ask yourself when you lie in bed, fighting the impulse to press that snooze button for the third time as you anticipate your morning workout, "What would a healthy person do?"

Because "healthy" doesn't have to be an identity crisis. It is not something you inherently "are" as the result of some gift of character or impeccable motivation. *Healthy is what you do.* While it is sometimes easier to focus on your workout or diet as checkboxes on a shopping list for some recipe for success, it often comes down to those little decisions you make throughout the day. And it is these choices that impact how you will see yourself. You can follow the Heart to Start program to a tee, but if you do not encourage yourself to make healthier choices day to day, you can end up experiencing life feeling like an unhealthy person who once followed an eight-week exercise program. Lots of people have been there. But I believe you deserve more than that.

Let's be honest. All of us have some limitations and have what I like to call "creative differences" on a genetic level. Some of us will develop heart disease despite our best efforts to "do" or "be" someone different. But at the same time, that is no reason to deprive ourselves of the opportunity to be the healthiest version of ourselves that we can be. That part is purely up to us. If you ask yourself, "What would a healthy person do?" enough times, and if you start to answer the question honestly, you will come to realize that the question starts to change. It becomes, "What would *I* do?"

Because you have *become* the healthier person.

8.

You Will Run Again

In 2014, I worked in the medical tent at the finish line of the Boston Marathon, and remembered standing at the starting line twenty years earlier.

I was a senior in college. I was never an athlete. My roommates and I would jog along the Charles River once in a while, but I doubt I ever ran more than five miles before that April 18th Patriot's Day in 1994. But I was younger, more impulsive, and had a higher threshold for pain – and I did it on a dare.

My friend and I caught a ride to the starting point in Hopkinton, Massachusetts early that Monday morning, wearing garbage bags over our t-shirts to keep off the morning chill. We huddled with hundreds of other runners in the Back of the Pack – who, like us, hadn't qualified to wear an official bib number, but still wanted to be part of the greatest race in the world.

And so we ran. And walked. And ran some more. Countless spectators cheered us on, and thanks to their encouragement and the inspiration of everyone around us, we crossed the finish line on Boylston Street many hours later and immeasurably happier. For most people, running the Boston Marathon is the pinnacle of their running career. But for me, it was only the beginning. The joy of just being there, alone in my physical struggle, but surrounded by the selflessness of spectators and the community of athletes around me, inspired me to continue to pursue running and exercising throughout my life and as part of my career. I may never actually qualify for the Boston Marathon, but it will always be my greatest race.

I will never forget one particular runner on the course. He was in his sixties, and had the wiry frame and freckled neck of someone who had done this race before. Despite a forty-year age gap, we ran alongside one another for the better part of the marathon. He must have noticed that I was having a rough time of it, and he started talking to me. I wasn't in much of a position to hold a conversation. I remember him telling me not to limit my focus to just the path ahead, but rather to look around so that I could take it all in. The bikers on the sidewalk, cheering with both arms sky-high, black fringe of their leather jackets blowing in the wind. The college students from Wellesley, Boston University, and Boston College along the route, slapping five with runners as they passed by. And the runners. All the runners, representing every shape and size and color, moving in sync like a single organism through the Boston city streets.

The marathoner-muse encouraged me, "Run in place. Let the road rise up to meet *you*." A little bit Old Irish Blessing, with some *Zen and the Art of Motorcycle Maintenance* thrown in for good measure. Do your part and the miles will pass you by. You will ultimately get where you need to go. And while it is true that you can never predict what lies around the corner, you do control how well you trained and how you will feel when you face those inevitable obstacles.

Even the fastest runners in the world have to climb Heartbreak Hill.

The Heart to Start training program reduces your cardiovascular risk and improves your quality of life. But sometimes that is not enough. Because sometimes you just need to go for a run to prove to yourself that on *this* road you are never alone.

I am going to train you to run your next race. Because I know that once you are out there on the course, whether you are running, walking, or doing some combination like I did back in Boston so many years ago, you will realize that this road was *always* the goal. And that even after you complete the course, there truly is no finish line.

H2S 5K

The H2S 5K (Heart to Start 5K) is a twelve-week interval-training program that you can begin after you have completed Week 8 of the Heart to Start program, and it will place you comfortably at the finish line of any 5K race in the country. But the first step is signing up. Committing yourself to a race is more than just spending money on the entry fee. It is a statement to the world outside of you that you deserve to be there. Find a local 5K in your area and sign up.

Now tell someone about it. Your spouse, your kids, your co-workers. Share it on Facebook. Tweet it. Tell the world and use the hashtag #hearttostart so that I will be able to cheer you on. Because I want you *all in*. Research shows that involving other people in your challenge will make you pursue it with more confidence and perseverance.

JUDY, 57 YEARS OLD

I am a librarian and I have read many articles about the benefits of exercise but it was still hard to get myself out the door to work out. Nonetheless, on what seemed to be the rainiest night of the year, there I was at the track. I reminded myself that speed did not matter as much as tenacity.

As time went on, my teammates and I got to know each other. We would cheer each other on as we moved around the track. The group support was so crucial for me. Skipping a workout would have been so easy, but the workouts with my group were so collegial and fun that I did not want to miss one unless I absolutely could not make it.

Signing up for the 5K was my first fitness goal ever. It is not as if I had never exercised before in my life, but this was the first time that I received some good coaching and direction that matched my fitness level. After we completed the 5K, my group and I all had a feeling of "What next?" so we created a Heart to Start Facebook page so that we could continue to support each other and post photos of other races that we complete. Sometimes smaller groups meet up to work out. The ongoing support has been very important to me. The support helped me keep my fitness goals – especially my goal to do one 5K a month for six months. The Heart to Start group has been life changing for me and I am participating again, but this time my goal is to complete the 10K!

You have already probably figured out that motivation is sometimes hard to come by. It is all too common to maintain a healthy behavior for the length of time it takes you to get to the end of a book or DVD program. The more important question, to me, seems to be what you will do next. A key part of this is setting realistic goals that are achievable and that provide motivation – that is how you maintain momentum. In the end, it is your accomplishments that will provide motivation, which will give you the momentum you need to move forward. We will achieve those goals by creating a S.M.A.R.T. plan. Specific. Measurable. Accountable. Realistic. Time-based.

SPECIFIC

Just because an overarching goal is long-term does not mean that it cannot be broken down into specifics. In health care we call these secondary endpoints. For example, if our goal is to reduce your risk of a heart attack, we might target a secondary endpoint like cholesterol, blood sugar, blood pressure, or body weight. By becoming more specific about those targets, we ultimately address the big picture. The goal of an exercise program is obviously to exercise, but it is also a very specific way to achieve your greater goals – live longer and beat heart disease. And by training for a 5K you break down your exercise goal into something even more specific, more achievable, and definitely more motivating.

MEASURABLE

In your doctor's office, you think about health using terms like blood pressure, weight, cholesterol, and blood sugar. They are easy to check, and easy to repeat six months later. They help you and your health care provider identify successes as well as areas that may require further effort. And when you are training – on the track, on the road, or even on your treadmill – we can also measure your progress. By time. By distance. And also just by showing up so that you check off your training session on your calendar.

ACCOUNTABLE

Before you ever take that first step, you need to believe that you can do it. The goal of this program has been to bring medicine and motivation together into a prescription that can move you forward. That starts and ends with you. Even once you get started, following through can be difficult. That's why cardiac rehabilitation is so effective – it provides you with a team of supporters that not only want you to succeed, but are also counting on you to try. The truth is that it's hard for all of us sometimes to stay on track. That's why accountability is key. Pick a person in your life that you are accountable to – a spouse or partner, a child, a parent or sibling, a friend, or even your doctor. Or tell the world on social media. Share what you are doing. Write it down. Place it on your calendar. Stick a note on your bathroom mirror. And please keep me posted on Twitter or Facebook with the hashtag #hearttostart. Because if you decide to run this race and you put in the time, I believe that you can win. And more importantly, I am counting on you to try.

REALISTIC

The goal is to succeed. That sounds obvious, but how many times have you set yourself up to fail by inadvertently biting off more than you could chew? In an effort to make our dreams a reality, we sometimes forget that we are human, too. We have our challenges, and we have our limitations. That is okay. But that is also why it is essential to set yourself up for success by identifying a goal that you can reasonably expect to accomplish. Base your dreams in your reality. That is how process meets success.

People participating in any training program need to feel comfortable with their goals and recognize that they are achievable with good information and coaching support. There is a reason why we are not starting our training in Hopkinton, Massachusetts – although I would not be surprised if you end up there someday too! While a marathon can be a lot to get your mind and legs around, a 5K race is the perfect dose of motivation medicine that I know you can hold down. I have trained so many people like you and marvel at your progress, week by week. My favorite part of race day is just beyond the finish line – when runners ask where they can sign up for their next race. There is no better motivation than accomplishing an attainable goal.

TIME-BASED

I believe that every training program should have a natural start and finish. It is easier to view a longer-term goal by breaking it down, week by week. Visualizing your progress as you go puts your training into perspective. As you move through this twelve-week program you will be motivated by what you have already done, and by how your training evolves as you get closer to race day.

Interval training has been shown to improve your cardiovascular fitness and make you burn calories more efficiently – that is why we started you off during Week 3 through Week 5 of your HEART training program with ten-minute speed intervals and then increased the frequency to five minutes in Week 6 though Week 8. We will use a similar philosophy here by mixing running and walking throughout your training.

The H2S 5K training program breaks it down for you, week-by-week and day-by-day. As with your previous eight-week Heart to Start training program, we continue to emphasize resistance training on Mondays, Wednesdays, and Fridays. Your 5K training will happen on the other four days of the week.

You do not need to consult any charts, calculate a VO2 Max, or even measure your heart rate during these workouts. But you do need a watch to time your intervals. Each week will challenge you with a new interval workout on your "5K" days, summarized in the training column below. Let's take a look at Week 1 as an example.

1R/2W X 5

"R" stands for "Run." "W" stands for "Walk." The "1" and "2" indicate the number of minutes for each activity. Think of each "1R/2W" as a single set of 5K training intervals. Now multiply that set by the number of repetitions that follows – in this case, "x 5." Translation? During Week 1, you will run for one minute, and then walk for two minutes. You will repeat this pattern for a total of five repetitions. So in your first week of H2S 5K, your 5K training only takes fifteen minutes. And in Week 12, you will be training for nearly thirty minutes. Make sure you start and cool down with a five-minute walk.

While these 5K training sessions are generally shorter than your HEART workouts during the initial eight-week program, keep in mind that "R" stands for "Run!" Your goal is to up the ante and work on creating a definite distinction between your running and walking speeds. If you do not feel that you can run, that's totally okay! But I do want you to move faster during the running parts of the intervals. Move your arms, and push yourself to a higher level of exertion (remember the Borg Scale?) to achieve the results you are looking for.

So let's get S.M.A.R.T. Identify your race, and count backwards twelve weeks to find your starting line. Week 1 is right around the corner!

H2S 5K TRAINING PROGRAM WEEKS 1-12

W	TRAINING	SU	M	T	W	TH	F	SA
1	1R/2W x 5	5K	START	5K	START	5K	START	5K
2	1.5R/2W x 5	5K	START	5K	START	5K	START	5K
3	2R/1.5W x 5	5K	START	5K	START	5K	START	5K
4	2.5R/1.5W x 5	5K	START	5K	START	5K	START	5K
5	3R/1W x 5	5K	START	5K	START	5K	START	5K
6	3.5R/0.5W x 5	5K	START	5K	START	5K	START	5K
7	4R/0.5W x 5	5K	START	5K	START	5K	START	5K
8	5R/1W x 4	5K	START	5K	START	5K	START	5K
9	6R/0.5W x 4	5K	START	5K	START	5K	START	5K
10	7R/0.5W x 4	5K	START	5K	START	5K	START	5K
11	8R/0.5W x 4	5K	START	5K	START	5K	START	5K
12	9R/0.5W x 3	5K	START	5K	START	5K	START	5K

As you move through the H2S 5K program, I want to hear from you to know how you are progressing. Social media works wonders. Become part of our Facebook group at *www.facebook.com/hearttostart* and share your stories. Please join me at *www.facebook.com/drjamesbeckerman* or on Twitter at *@jamesbeckerman.* Use the hashtag *#hearttostart* so that other runners can find you and learn from your experiences.

You will quickly learn that the athletic community is as intimately supportive as it is universal. We all experienced that in the aftermath of the tragedies at the Boston Marathon in 2013. Following the attack, the President spoke to the people of Boston. He told them – he told all of us – "You will run again." I believe those words, and I know that their truth exists on so many levels and in so many areas of our lives. Sometimes it feels like the world is holding us back or pushing us places we don't want to go. There are so many things that we cannot control. Reality can be so harsh, so brutal sometimes. It can attack our greatest institutions, and it can damage our own resolve. Every day, we fight to return to a new normal. And somehow, sport can help us in ways that nothing else can to smooth our scars, whether they run on a city street or run down the center of your own chest. Sport helps us heal. Even if we have never run before, we *all* can run again.

Looking forward to meeting you someday in Boston.

Acknowledgments

This is a book about journeys. Hopefully it has made yours a little bit easier. Thank you for enriching mine.

For me, this Camino began on June 30, 1998 in an ambulance in Lake Okoboji, Iowa. It chased me through internal medicine residency training in Boston and cardiology fellowship in Palo Alto, before thankfully bringing me to the Providence Heart and Vascular Institute in Portland, Oregon in 2006.

I am indebted to the support of my colleagues and the leadership of our health care system for their faith in this project and their commitment to our patients.

Thank you to Dr. Daniel Oseran and Jennifer Zelensky for their mentorship and patience, and their unswerving ability to turn passion into programs that serve our community.

I am, as always, inspired by the kindness, compassion, and professionalism of my partners, and I hope that this book can be a tool to help their patients, as they have given so much to help mine.

Thank you to my colleagues and friends Lisa Helderop and Laura Klink for being the soul behind our Heart to Start training team, every week, regardless of the forecast.

Thank you to my friends Dr. Jon Duke, Dr. Chuck Fox, and Dr. Wen Shen for their helpful feedback and interest in bringing this project to the patient community.

Thank you to my parents, Alan and Natalie, and my brother Jon for their love and friendship.

I told you earlier that in the back of the ambulance on that tragic night in Lake Okoboji, Iowa, I made two promises to Jerry. You have already helped make the first one true by helping me share the messages in this book. The second promise I made to him was that his daughter would never be alone. Stacie and I have been married for over thirteen years, and we have two wonderful sons, Jack and Henry. This book is inspired by my patients and is dedicated to my father-in-law. But it wouldn't have been possible without my family's love. I thank them from the bottom of my heart.

Ultreya.

Appendix I:
The HEART Charts

WEEK 1

VO$_2$ MAX	MILES	TIME	% MPHR
Blue	1	20	60
Yellow	1.5	30	65
Black	2	40	70
Green	2.5	43	70
Red	3	45	70

WEEK 2

VO$_2$ MAX	MILES	TIME	% MPHR
Blue	1.25	25	60
Yellow	1.75	35	65
Black	2.25	45	70
Green	2.75	47	70
Red	3.25	49	70

WEEK 3

VO₂ MAX	MILES	TIME	% MPHR
Blue	1.25	23	60
Yellow	1.75	32	65
Black	2.25	42	70
Green	3	51	70
Red	3.5	53	70

WEEK 4

VO₂ MAX	MILES	TIME	% MPHR
Blue	1.5	30	60
Yellow	2	37	65
Black	2.5	46	70
Green	3	48	70
Red	3.5	49	70

WEEK 5

VO₂ MAX	MILES	TIME	% MPHR
Blue	1.5	30	60
Yellow	2	37	65
Black	2.75	51	70
Green	3.25	52	70
Red	3.75	53	70

WEEK 6

VO₂ MAX	MILES	TIME	% MPHR
Blue	1.5	26	65
Yellow	2	34	70
Black	2.75	47	70
Green	3.25	49	75
Red	3.75	50	75

WEEK 7

VO₂ MAX	MILES	TIME	% MPHR
Blue	1.75	30	65
Yellow	2.25	38	70
Black	2.75	47	70
Green	3.5	56	75
Red	4	53	75

WEEK 8

VO₂ MAX	MILES	TIME	% MPHR
Blue	1.75	30	65
Yellow	2.25	38	70
Black	3	51	70
Green	3.75	56	75
Red	4	53	75

Appendix II: H2S 5K Training Program

W	TRAINING	SU	M	T	W	TH	F	SA
1	1R/2W x 5	5K	START	5K	START	5K	START	5K
2	1.5R/2W x 5	5K	START	5K	START	5K	START	5K
3	2R/1.5W x 5	5K	START	5K	START	5K	START	5K
4	2.5R/1.5W x 5	5K	START	5K	START	5K	START	5K
5	3R/1W x 5	5K	START	5K	START	5K	START	5K
6	3.5R/0.5W x 5	5K	START	5K	START	5K	START	5K
7	4R/0.5W x 5	5K	START	5K	START	5K	START	5K
8	5R/1W x 4	5K	START	5K	START	5K	START	5K
9	6R/0.5W x 4	5K	START	5K	START	5K	START	5K
10	7R/0.5W x 4	5K	START	5K	START	5K	START	5K
11	8R/0.5W x 4	5K	START	5K	START	5K	START	5K
12	9R/0.5W x 3	5K	START	5K	START	5K	START	5K

References

Adamopoulos S, Parissis J, Karatzas D, et al. Physical training modulates proinflammatory cytokines and the soluble Fas/soluble Fas ligand system in patients with chronic heart failure. J Am Coll Cardiol 2002; 39:653.

Adams KJ, Barnard KL, Swank AM, Mann E, Kushnick MR, Denny DM. Combined high-intensity strength and aerobic training in diverse phase II cardiac rehabilitation patients. J Cardiopulm Rehabil.1999; 19(4):209–215.

Adams J, Cline MJ, Hubbard M, McCullough T, Hartman J. A new paradigm for post–cardiac event resistance exercise guidelines. Am J Cardiol. 2006;97(2):281–286.

Ades PA. Cardiac rehabilitation and secondary prevention of coronary heart disease. N Engl J Med 2001; 345:892.

Ades PA, Grunvald MH. Cardiopulmonary exercise testing before and after conditioning in older coronary patients. Am Heart J 1990; 120:585.

Ades PA, Savage PD, Toth MJ, et al. High-calorie-expenditure exercise: a new approach to cardiac rehabilitation for overweight coronary patients. Circulation 2009; 119:2671.

Ades PA. Cardiac rehabilitation and secondary prevention of coronary heart disease. N Engl J Med 2001; 345:892.

Ades PA, Pashkow FJ, Fletcher G, et al. A controlled trial of cardiac rehabilitation in the home setting using electrocardiographic and voice transtelephonic monitoring. Am Heart J 2000; 139:543.

Ades PA, Waldmann ML, Meyer WL, et al. Skeletal muscle and cardiovascular adaptations to exercise conditioning in older coronary patients. Circulation 1996; 94:323.

Agency for Healthcare Research and Quality (AHRQ) Technology Assessment Program. Randomized trials of secondary prevention programs in coronary artery disease: a systematic review, Rockville, Maryland 2005.

American College of Sports Medicine ACSM's Guidelines for Exercise Testing and Prescription. 6th ed. Philadelphia: Lippincott Williams & Wilkins; 2000.

American Association of Cardiovascular and Pulmonary Rehabilitation Guidelines for Cardiac Rehabilitation and Secondary Prevention Programs. 4th ed. Champaign, IL: Human Kinetics; 2004.

American College of Sports Medicine. ACSM's Guidelines for Exercise Testing and Prescription, Eighth edition, Wolters Kluwer/Lippincott Williams Wilkins, Philadelphia 2010.

American College of Sports Medicine. ACSM's Resource Manual for Guidelines for Exercise Testing and Prescription, Wolters Kluwer/Lippincott Williams & Wilkins, Philadelphia 2010.

Annesi JJ. Supported Exercise Improves Controlled Eating and Weight through Its Effects on Psychosocial Factors: Extending a Systematic Research Program Toward Treatment Development. Perm J. 2012 Winter; 16(1):7–18.

Applegate WB, Miller ST, Elam JT, et al. Nonpharmacologic intervention to reduce blood pressure in older patients with mild hypertension. Arch Intern Med 1992; 152:1162.

Ardern CI, Katzmarzyk PT, Janssen I, Church TS, Blair SN.Revised Adult Treatment Panel III guidelines and cardiovascular disease mortality in men attending a preventive medical clinic. Circulation. 2005 Sep 6;112(10):1478-85. Epub 2005 Aug 29.

Arena R, Myers J, Williams MA, et al. Assessment of functional capacity in clinical and research settings: a scientific statement from the American Heart Association Committee on Exercise, Rehabilitation, and Prevention of the Council on Clinical Cardiology and the Council on Cardiovascular Nursing. Circulation 2007; 116:329.

Arena R, Williams M, Forman DE, et al. Increasing referral and participation rates to outpatient cardiac rehabilitation: the valuable role of healthcare professionals in the inpatient and home health settings: a science advisory from the American Heart Association. Circulation 2012; 125:1321.

Aspenes ST et al. Peak oxygen uptake and cardiovascular risk factors in 4631 healthy women and men. Med Sci Sports Exerc. 2011 Aug; 43(8):1465-73.

ATS Statement: Guidelines for the Six-Minute Walk Test Am J Respir Crit Care Med Vol 166. pp 111–117, 2002 DOI: 10.1164/ rccm.166/1/111.

Balady GJ, Ades PA, Comoss P, et al. Core components of cardiac rehabilitation/secondary prevention programs: A statement for healthcare professionals from the American Heart Association and the American Association of Cardiovascular and Pulmonary Rehabilitation Writing Group. Circulation 2000; 102:1069.

Balady GJ, Williams MA, Ades PA, et al. Core components of cardiac rehabilitation/secondary prevention programs: 2007 update: a scientific statement from the American Heart Association Exercise, Cardiac Rehabilitation, and Prevention Committee, the Council on Clinical Cardiology; the Councils on Cardiovascular Nursing, Epidemiology and Prevention, and Nutrition, Physical Activity, and Metabolism; and the American Association of Cardiovascular and Pulmonary Rehabilitation. Circulation 2007; 115:2675.

Balady GJ, Arena R, Sietsema K, et al. Clinician's Guide to cardiopulmonary exercise testing in adults: a scientific statement from the American Heart Association. Circulation 2010; 122:191.

Balady GJ, Ades PA, Bittner VA, et al. Referral, enrollment, and delivery of cardiac rehabilitation/secondary prevention programs at clinical centers and beyond: a presidential advisory from the American Heart Association. Circulation 2011; 124:2951.

Balke B. A simple field test for the assessment of physical fitness. CARI Report 1963; 63:18.

Beatty AL, Schiller NB, Whooley MA. Six-minute walk test as a prognostic tool in stable coronary heart disease: data from the heart and soul study. Arch Intern Med 2012; 172:1096.

Beckie TM, Beckstead JW, Kip K, Fletcher G. Physiological and exercise capacity improvements in women completing cardiac rehabilitation. J Cardiopulm Rehabil Prev 2013; 33:16.

Belardinelli R, Georgiou D, Scocco V, et al. Low intensity exercise training in patients with chronic heart failure. J Am Coll Cardiol 1995; 26:975.

Belardinelli R, Georgiou D, Cianci G, et al. Exercise training improves left ventricular diastolic filling in patients with dilated cardiomyopathy. Clinical and prognostic implications. Circulation 1995; 91:2775.

Belardinelli R, Georgiou D, Cianci G, Purcaro A. Effects of exercise training on left ventricular filling at rest and during exercise in patients with ischemic cardiomyopathy and severe left ventricular systolic dysfunction. Am Heart J 1996; 132:61.

Belardinelli R, Georgiou D, Purcaro A. Low dose dobutamine echocardiography predicts improvement in functional capacity after exercise training in patients with ischemic cardiomyopathy: prognostic implication. J Am Coll Cardiol 1998; 31:1027.

Belardinelli R, Georgiou D, Ginzton L, et al. Effects of moderate exercise training on thallium uptake and contractile response to low-dose dobutamine of dysfunctional myocardium in patients with ischemic cardiomyopathy. Circulation 1998; 97:553.

Belardinelli R, Georgiou D, Cianci G, Purcaro A. Randomized, controlled trial of long-term moderate exercise training in chronic heart failure: effects on functional capacity, quality of life, and clinical outcome. Circulation 1999; 99:1173.

Beniamini Y. Effects of high-intensity strength training on quality-of-life parameters in cardiac rehabilitation patients. Am J Cardiol. 1997;80(7):841–846.

Berent R, von Duvillard SP, Crouse SF, Sinzinger H, Green JS, Schmid P. Resistance training dose response in combined endurance-resistance training in patients with cardiovascular disease: a randomized trial. Arch Phys Med Rehabil. 2011 Oct; 92(10):1527-33.

Berkman LF, Blumenthal J, Burg M, et al. Effects of treating depression and low perceived social support on clinical events after myocardial infarction: the Enhancing Recovery in Coronary Heart Disease Patients (ENRICHD) Randomized Trial. JAMA 2003; 289:3106.

Bethell H, Lewin R, Dalal H. Cardiac rehabilitation in the United Kingdom. Heart 2009; 95:271.

Bey L, Hamilton MT. Suppression of skeletal muscle lipoprotein lipase activity during physical inactivity: a molecular reason to maintain daily low-intensity activity. J Physiol. 2003; 551(Pt 2):673–682

Blanchard CM, Reid RD, Morrin LI, et al. Demographic and clinical determinants of moderate to vigorous physical activity during home-based cardiac rehabilitation: the home-based determinants of exercise (HOME) study. J Cardiopulm Rehabil Prev 2010; 30:240.

Blumenthal JA, Sherwood A, Babyak MA, et al. Effects of exercise and stress management training on markers of cardiovascular risk in patients with ischemic heart disease: a randomized controlled trial. JAMA 2005; 293:1626.

Bittner V, Sanderson B, Breland J, Adams C, Schuman C. Assessing functional capacity as an outcome in cardiac rehabilitation: role of the 6 minute walk test. Clinical Exercise Physiology 2000.

Boesch C, Myers J, Habersaat A, et al. Maintenance of exercise capacity and physical activity patterns 2 years after cardiac rehabilitation. J Cardiopulm Rehabil 2005; 25:14.

Borg, G. Physical performance and perceived exertion. Gleerup, Lund, Sweden 1962.

Borg G.A. Psychophysical bases of perceived exertion. Medicine and Science in Sports and Exercise. 1982; 14:377-381.

Borghouts LB, Keizer HA. Exercise and insulin sensitivity: a review. Int J Sports Med 2000; 21:1.

Braith RW, Welsch MA, Feigenbaum MS, et al. Neuroendocrine activation in heart failure is modified by endurance exercise training. J Am Coll Cardiol 1999; 34:1170.

Byrne M, Doherty S, Murphy AW, et al. The CHARMS Study: cardiac patients' experiences of sexual problems following cardiac rehabilitation. Eur J Cardiovasc Nurs. 2013 Feb 6. [Epub ahead of print]

Caulin-Glaser T, Maciejewski PK, Snow R, et al. Depressive symptoms and sex affect completion rates and clinical outcomes in cardiac rehabilitation. Prev Cardiol 2007; 10:15.

Church TS, Thomas DM, Tudor-Locke C, Katzmarzyk PT, Earnest CP, Rodarte RQ, Martin CK, Blair SN, Bouchard C. Trends over 5 decades in U.S. occupation-related physical activity and their associations with obesity. PLoS One 2011; 6(5):e19657.

Clark AM, Hartling L, Vandermeer B, McAlister FA. Meta-analysis: secondary prevention programs for patients with coronary artery disease. Ann Intern Med 2005; 143:659.

Coats AJ, Adamopoulos S, Radaelli A, et al. Controlled trial of physical training in chronic heart failure. Exercise performance, hemodynamics, ventilation, and autonomic function. Circulation 1992; 85:2119.

Cole CR, Blackstone EH, Pashkow FJ, Snader CE, Lauer MS. Heart-rate recovery immediately after exercise as a predictor of mortality. N Engl J Med. 1999 Oct 28; 341(18):1351-7.

Cortés O, Arthur HM. Determinants of referral to cardiac rehabilitation programs in patients with coronary artery disease: a systematic review. Am Heart J 2006; 151:249.

Cottin Y, Cambou JP, Casillas JM, et al. Specific profile and referral bias of rehabilitated patients after an acute coronary syndrome. J Cardiopulm Rehabil 2004; 24:38.

Couillard C, Després JP, Lamarche B, et al. Effects of endurance exercise training on plasma HDL cholesterol levels depend on levels of triglycerides: evidence from men of the Health, Risk Factors, Exercise Training and Genetics (HERITAGE) Family Study. Arterioscler Thromb Vasc Biol 2001; 21:1226.

Dalal HM, Zawada A, Jolly K, et al. Home based versus centre based cardiac rehabilitation: Cochrane systematic review and meta-analysis. BMJ 2010; 340:b5631.

Darcy L. Johannsen, Nicolas D. Knuth, Robert Huizenga, Jennifer C. Rood, Eric Ravussin, & Kevin D. Hall. Metabolic Slowing with Massive Weight Loss despite Preservation of Fat-Free Mass The Journal of Clinical Endocrinology and Metabolism 2012; 10.1210/jc.2012-1444.

Das SK, Roberts SB, McCrory MA, Hsu LK, Shikora SA, Kehayias JJ, Dallal GE, & Saltzman E. Long-term changes in energy expenditure and body composition after massive weight loss induced by gastric bypass surgery. The American Journal of Clinical Nutrition 2003; 78 (1), 22-30.

Davies EJ, Moxham T, Rees K, et al. Exercise based rehabilitation for heart failure. Cochrane Database Syst Rev 2010; CD003331.

Davies EJ, Moxham T, Rees K, et al. Exercise training for systolic heart failure: Cochrane systematic review and meta-analysis. Eur J Heart Fail 2010; 12:706.

de Brito LB, Ricardo DR, de Araújo DS, Ramos PS, Myers J, de Araújo CG. Ability to sit and rise from the floor as a predictor of all-cause mortality. Eur J Prev Cardiol 2012; Dec 13.

DeBusk RF, Haskell WL, Miller NH, et al. Medically directed at-home rehabilitation soon after clinically uncomplicated acute myocardial infarction: a new model for patient care. Am J Cardiol 1985; 55:251.

Dunn AL, Marcus BH, Kampert JB, et al. Reduction in cardiovascular disease risk factors: 6-month results from Project Active. Prev Med 1997; 26:883.

Dunn AL, Garcia ME, Marcus BH, et al. Six-month physical activity and fitness changes in Project Active, a randomized trial. Med Sci Sports Exerc 1998; 30:1076.

Dunn AL, Marcus BH, Kampert JB, et al. Comparison of lifestyle and structured interventions to increase physical activity and cardiorespiratory fitness: a randomized trial. JAMA 1999; 281:327.

Dunstan DW, Kingwell BA, Larsen R, Healy GN, Cerin E, Hamilton MT, Shaw JE, Bertovic DA, Zimmet PZ, Salmon J, Owen N. Breaking up prolonged sitting reduces postprandial glucose and insulin responses. Diabetes Care 2012 May; 35(5):976-83. doi: 10.2337/dc11-1931. Epub 2012 Feb 28.

Edelmann F, Gelbrich G, Düngen HD, et al. Exercise training improves exercise capacity and diastolic function in patients with heart failure with preserved ejection fraction: results of the Ex-DHF (Exercise training in Diastolic Heart Failure) pilot study. J Am Coll Cardiol 2011; 58:1780.

Ewart CK. Psychological effects of resistive weight training: implications for cardiac patients. Med Sci Sports Exercise 1989; 21(6):683–688.

Fletcher BJ, Thiel J, Fletcher GF. Phase II intensive monitored cardiac rehabilitation for coronary artery disease and coronary risk factors--a six-session protocol. Am J Cardiol 1986; 57:751.

Fletcher BJ, Lloyd A, Fletcher GF. Outpatient rehabilitative training in patients with cardiovascular disease: emphasis on training method. Heart Lung 1988; 17:199.

Flynn KE, Piña IL, Whellan DJ, et al. Effects of exercise training on health status in patients with chronic heart failure: HF-ACTION randomized controlled trial. JAMA 2009; 301:1451.

Franklin BA, Bonzheim K, Gordon S, Timmis GC. Safety of medically supervised outpatient cardiac rehabilitation exercise therapy: a 16-year follow-up. Chest 1998; 114:902.

Frengley JD, Sansone GR, Alba A, et al. Influence of age on rehabilitation outcomes and survival in post-acute inpatient cardiac rehabilitation. J Cardiopulm Rehabil Prev 2011; 31:230.

Georgiou D, Chen Y, Appadoo S, et al. Cost-effectiveness analysis of long-term moderate exercise training in chronic heart failure. Am J Cardiol 2001; 87:984.

Giannuzzi P, Temporelli PL, Corrà U, et al. Attenuation of unfavorable remodeling by exercise training in postinfarction patients with left ventricular dysfunction: results of the Exercise in Left Ventricular Dysfunction (ELVD) trial. Circulation 1997; 96:1790.

Giannuzzi P, Temporelli PL, Corrà U, et al. Antiremodeling effect of long-term exercise training in patients with stable chronic heart failure: results of the Exercise in Left Ventricular Dysfunction and Chronic Heart Failure (ELVD-CHF) Trial. Circulation 2003; 108:554.

Giannuzzi P, Temporelli PL, Marchioli R, et al. Global secondary prevention strategies to limit event recurrence after myocardial infarction: results of the GOSPEL study, a multicenter, randomized controlled trial from the Italian Cardiac Rehabilitation Network. Arch Intern Med 2008; 168:2194.

Gilson ND et al. Do walking strategies to increase physical activity reduce reported sitting in workplaces: a randomized control trial. International Journal of Behavioral Nutrition and Physical Activity 2009; 6:43.

Goel K, Lennon RJ, Tilbury RT, et al. Impact of cardiac rehabilitation on mortality and cardiovascular events after percutaneous coronary intervention in the community. Circulation 2011; 123:2344.

Gulati M, Pandey DK, Arnsdorf MF, et al. Exercise capacity and the risk of death in women: the St James Women Take Heart Project. Circulation 2003; 108:1554.

Haennel RG, Quinney HA, Kappagoda CT. Effects of hydraulic circuit training following coronary artery bypass surgery. Med Sci Sports Exerc. 1991; 23(2):158–165.

Hagberg JM, Montain SJ, Martin WH 3rd, Ehsani AA. Effect of exercise training in 60- to 69-year-old persons with essential hypertension. Am J Cardiol 1989; 64:348.

Hambrecht R, Niebauer J, Fiehn E, et al. Physical training in patients with stable chronic heart failure: effects on cardiorespiratory fitness and ultrastructural abnormalities of leg muscles. J Am Coll Cardiol 1995; 25:1239.

Hambrecht R, Fiehn E, Weigl C, et al. Regular physical exercise corrects endothelial dysfunction and improves exercise capacity in patients with chronic heart failure. Circulation 1998; 98:2709.

Hambrecht R, Gielen S, Linke A, et al. Effects of exercise training on left ventricular function and peripheral resistance in patients with chronic heart failure: A randomized trial. JAMA 2000; 283:3095.

Hambrecht R, Hilbrich L, Erbs S, et al. Correction of endothelial dysfunction in chronic heart failure: additional effects of exercise training and oral L-arginine supplementation. J Am Coll Cardiol 2000; 35:706.

Hambrecht R, Wolf A, Gielen S, et al. Effect of exercise on coronary endothelial function in patients with coronary artery disease. N Engl J Med 2000; 342:454.

Hambrecht R, Walther C, Möbius-Winkler S, et al. Percutaneous coronary angioplasty compared with exercise training in patients with stable coronary artery disease: a randomized trial. Circulation 2004; 109:1371.

Hammill BG, Curtis LH, Schulman KA, Whellan DJ. Relationship between cardiac rehabilitation and long-term risks of death and myocardial infarction among elderly Medicare beneficiaries. Circulation 2010; 121:63.

Haykowsky M, Scott J, Esch B, et al. A meta-analysis of the effects of exercise training on left ventricular remodeling following myocardial infarction: start early and go longer for greatest exercise benefits on remodeling. Trials 2011; 12:92.

Haykowsky MJ, Liang Y, Pechter D, et al. A meta-analysis of the effect of exercise training on left ventricular remodeling in heart failure patients: the benefit depends on the type of training performed. J Am Coll Cardiol 2007; 49:2329.

Henriksson J. Effects of physical training on the metabolism of skeletal muscle. Diabetes Care 1992; 15:1701.

Hidde P. van der Ploeg, PhD; Tien Chey, MAppStats; Rosemary J. Korda, PhD; Emily Banks, MBBS, PhD; Adrian Bauman, MBBS, PhD Sitting Time and All-Cause Mortality Risk in 222 497 Australian Adults. Arch Intern Med. 2012; 172(6):494-500

Hurley BF. Effects of resistive training on lipoprotein-lipid profiles: a comparison to aerobic exercise training. Med Sci Sports Exerc. 1989; 21(6):689–693.

Hurley BF, Kokkinos PF. Effects of weight training on risk factors for coronary artery disease. Sports Med. 1987; 4(4):231–238.

Jolliffe JA, Rees K, Taylor RS, et al. Exercise-based rehabilitation for coronary heart disease. Cochrane Database Syst Rev 2001; :CD001800.

Jolly K, Lip GY, Taylor RS, et al. The Birmingham Rehabilitation Uptake Maximisation study (BRUM): a randomised controlled trial comparing home-based with centre-based cardiac rehabilitation. Heart 2009; 95:36.

Jolly MA, Brennan DM, Cho L. Impact of exercise on heart rate recovery. Circulation 2011; 124:1520.

Joseph RJ, Alonso-Alonso M, Bond DS, Pascual-Leone A, Blackburn GL. The neurocognitive connection between physical activity and eating behavior. Obes Rev. 2011 October; 12(10): 800–812.

Katzmarzyk PT, Church TS, Craig CL, Bouchard C. Sitting time and mortality from all causes, cardiovascular disease, and cancer. Med Sci Sports Exerc. 2009 May; 41(5):998-1005.

Katzmarzyk PT, Lee IM. Sedentary behaviour and life expectancy in the USA: a cause-deleted life table analysis. BMJ Open. 2012 Jul 9; 2(4).

Kelemen MH, Stewart KJ, Gillilan RE, Ewart CK, Valenti SA, Manley JD, Kelemen MD. Circuit weight training in cardiac patients. J Am Coll Cardiol. 1986; 7(1):38–42.

Kenney WL, Humphrey RH, Bryant CX, et al. American College of Sports Medicine Guidelines for Exercise Testing and Prescription, 5th ed, Williams & Wilkins, Baltimore 1995.

Kim MK, Tanaka K, Kim MJ, Matsuo T, Ajisaka R. Exercise training-induced changes in heart rate recovery in obese men with metabolic syndrome. Metab Syndr Relat Disord. 2009 Oct; 7(5):469-76.

Kline, GM, Porcari JP, Hintermeister R, Freedson PS, Ward A, McCarron RF, Ross J, Rippe JM. Estimation of VO2max from a one mile track walk, gender, age and body weight. Med Sci Sports Exerc 1987; 19: 253-259.

Kokkinos PF, Choucair W, Graves P, et al. Chronic heart failure and exercise. Am Heart J 2000; 140:21.

Kotseva K, Wood D, De Backer G, et al. Cardiovascular prevention guidelines in daily practice: a comparison of EUROASPIRE I, II, and III surveys in eight European countries. Lancet 2009; 373:929.

King AC, Haskell WL, Young DR, et al. Long-term effects of varying intensities and formats of physical activity on participation rates, fitness, and lipoproteins in men and women aged 50 to 65 years. Circulation 1995; 91:2596.

Kitzman DW, Brubaker PH, Morgan TM, et al. Exercise training in older patients with heart failure and preserved ejection fraction: a randomized, controlled, single-blind trial. Circ Heart Fail 2010; 3:659.

Kitzman DW, Hundley WG, Brubaker PH, et al. A randomized double-blind trial of enalapril in older patients with heart failure and preserved ejection fraction: effects on exercise tolerance and arterial distensibility. Circ Heart Fail 2010; 3:477.

Kugler J, Maskin C, Frishman WH, et al. Regional and systemic metabolic effects of angiotensin-converting enzyme inhibition during exercise in patients with severe heart failure. Circulation 1982; 66:1256.

Kwan G, Balady GJ. Cardiac rehabilitation 2012: advancing the field through emerging science. Circulation 2012; 125:e369.

Latouche C, Jowett JB, Carey AL, Bertovic DA, Owen N, Dunstan DW, Kingwell BA. Effects of Breaking up Prolonged Sitting on Skeletal Muscle Gene Expression. J Appl Physiol. 2012 Dec 27. [Epub ahead of print].

Lavie CJ, Thomas RJ, Squires RW, et al. Exercise training and cardiac rehabilitation in primary and secondary prevention of coronary heart disease. Mayo Clin Proc 2009; 84:373.

Lawler PR, Filion KB, Eisenberg MJ. Efficacy of exercise-based cardiac rehabilitation post-myocardial infarction: a systematic review and meta-analysis of randomized controlled trials. Am Heart J 2011; 162:571.

Lear SA, Spinelli JJ, Linden W, et al. The Extensive Lifestyle Management Intervention (ELMI) after cardiac rehabilitation: a 4-year randomized controlled trial. Am Heart J 2006; 152:333.

Lee D-C, Sui X, Artero EG et al. Long-Term Effects of Changes in Cardiorespiratory Fitness and Body Mass Index on All-Cause and Cardiovascular Disease Mortality in Men: The Aerobics Center Longitudinal Study. Circulation 2011; 124:2483-2490.

Lett HS, Blumenthal JA, Babyak MA, Strauman TJ, Robins C, Sherwood A. Social support and coronary heart disease: epidemiologic evidence and implications for treatment. Psychosom Med. 2005 Nov-Dec; 67(6):869-78.

Levine, SA and Lown B. "Armchair" Treatment of Acute Coronary Thrombosis, Journal of the American Medical Association 148 (April 1952): 1365.

Liu JL, Irvine S, Reid IA, et al. Chronic exercise reduces sympathetic nerve activity in rabbits with pacing-induced heart failure: A role for angiotensin II. Circulation 2000; 102:1854.

Lown, B. *The Lost Art of Healing*, The Ballantine Publishing Group, 1996.

Malin SK, Niemi N, Solomon TP, Haus JM, Kelly KR, Filion J, Rocco M, Kashyap SR, Barkoukis H, Kirwan JP. Exercise training with weight loss and either a high- or low-glycemic index diet reduces metabolic syndrome severity in older adults. Ann Nutr Metab. 2012; 61(2):135-41.

Manson JE, Greenland P, LaCroix AZ, et al. Walking compared with vigorous exercise for the prevention of cardiovascular events in women. N Engl J Med. 2002; 347(10):716–725

Martin BJ, Hauer T, Arena R, et al. Cardiac rehabilitation attendance and outcomes in coronary artery disease patients. Circulation 2012; 126:677.

Mazzini MJ, Stevens GR, Whalen D, et al. Effect of an American Heart Association Get With the Guidelines program-based clinical pathway on referral and enrollment into cardiac rehabilitation after acute myocardial infarction. Am J Cardiol 2008; 101:1084.

McCartney N. Role of resistance training in heart disease. Med Sci Sports Exerc 1988; 30(10 Suppl):S396–S402.

McCartney N, McKelvie RS, Haslam DR, Jones NL. Usefulness of weightlifting training in improving strength and maximal power output in coronary artery disease. Am J Cardiol 1991; 67(11):939–945.

McKelvie RS, Teo KK, McCartney N, et al. Effects of exercise training in patients with congestive heart failure: a critical review. J Am Coll Cardiol 1995; 25:789.

McKelvie RS, Teo KK, Roberts R, et al. Effects of exercise training in patients with heart failure: the Exercise Rehabilitation Trial (EXERT). Am Heart J 2002; 144:23.

Meyer K, Görnandt L, Schwaibold M, et al. Predictors of response to exercise training in severe chronic congestive heart failure. Am J Cardiol 1997; 80:56.

Meyer K, Schwaibold M, Westbrook S, et al. Effects of exercise training and activity restriction on 6-minute walking test performance in patients with chronic heart failure. Am Heart J 1997; 133:447.

Milani RV, Lavie CJ, Cassidy MM. Effects of cardiac rehabilitation and exercise training programs on depression in patients after major coronary events. Am Heart J 1996; 132:726.

Milani RV, Lavie CJ, Mehra MR. Reduction in C-reactive protein through cardiac rehabilitation and exercise training. J Am Coll Cardiol 2004; 43:1056.

Milani RV, Lavie CJ. Impact of cardiac rehabilitation on depression and its associated mortality. Am J Med 2007; 120:799.

Miller NH, Haskell WL, Berra K, DeBusk RF. Home versus group exercise training for increasing functional capacity after myocardial infarction. Circulation 1984; 70:645.

Mosca L, Banka CL, Benjamin EJ, et al. Evidence-based guidelines for cardiovascular disease prevention in women: 2007 update. Circulation 2007; 115:1481.

Myers J, Prakash M, Froelicher V, et al. Exercise capacity and mortality among men referred for exercise testing. N Engl J Med 2002; 346:793.

Nes BM et al. Estimating V·O 2peak from a nonexercise prediction model: the HUNT Study, Norway. Med Sci Sports Exerc 2011 Nov; 43(11):2024-30.

Nes BM et al. Age-predicted maximal heart rate in healthy subjects: The HUNT Fitness Study. Scand J Med Sci Sports 2013 Dec; 23(6):697-704.

Niebauer J, Hambrecht R, Velich T, et al. Attenuated progression of coronary artery disease after 6 years of multifactorial risk intervention: role of physical exercise. Circulation 1997; 96:2534.

Nygaard H, Tomten SE, Høstmark AT. Slow postmeal walking reduces postprandial glycemia in middle-aged women. Appl Physiol Nutr Metab. 2009 Dec; 34(6):1087-92.

Ogawa T, Spina RJ, Martin WH 3rd, et al. Effects of aging, sex, and physical training on cardiovascular responses to exercise. Circulation 1992; 86:494.

Otsuka Y, Takaki H, Okano Y, et al. Exercise training without ventricular remodeling in patients with moderate to severe left ventricular dysfunction early after acute myocardial infarction. Int J Cardiol 2003; 87:237.

O'Connor CM, Whellan DJ, Lee KL, et al. Efficacy and safety of exercise training in patients with chronic heart failure: HF-ACTION randomized controlled trial. JAMA 2009; 301:1439.

O'Keefe JH, Bell DSH Postprandial Hyperglycemia/Hyperlipidemia (Postprandial Dysmetabolism) is a cardiovascular risk factor. American Journal of Cardiology 2007; 100(5):899-904.

Pack QR, Mansour M, Barboza JS, et al. An early appointment to outpatient cardiac rehabilitation at hospital discharge improves attendance at orientation: a randomized, single-blind, controlled trial. Circulation 2013; 127:349.

Paffenbarger RS Jr, Hyde RT, Wing AL, et al. The association of changes in physical-activity level and other lifestyle characteristics with mortality among men. N Engl J Med 1993; 328:538.

Parashar S, Spertus JA, Tang F, et al. Predictors of early and late enrollment in cardiac rehabilitation, among those referred, after acute myocardial infarction. Circulation 2012; 126:1587.

Patel AV, Bernstein L, Deka A, et al. Leisure time spent sitting in relation to total mortality in a prospective cohort of U.S. adults. Am J Epidemiol. 2010; 172(4): 419–429.

Pavy B, Iliou MC, Meurin P, et al. Safety of exercise training for cardiac patients: results of the French registry of complications during cardiac rehabilitation. Arch Intern Med 2006; 166:2329.

Piña IL, Apstein CS, Balady GJ, et al. Exercise and heart failure: A statement from the American Heart Association Committee on exercise, rehabilitation, and prevention. Circulation 2003; 107:1210.

Plowman SA, Smith DL, editors. Exercise Physiology for Health, Fitness, and Performance. Boston: Allyn & Bacon; 1997. p. 134.

Pollock ML, Wilmore JH, editors. Exercise in Health and Disease: Evaluation and Prescription for Prevention and Rehabilitation. Philadelphia: WB Saunders Co; 1990. pp. 486–508.

Powers SK, Howley ET, editors. Exercise Physiology: Theory and Application to Fitness and Performance. 3rd ed. Chicago: Brown and Benchmark Publishers; 1997.

Radzewitz A, Miche E, Herrmann G, et al. Exercise and muscle strength training and their effect on quality of life in patients with chronic heart failure. Eur J Heart Fail 2002; 4:627.

Reddy HK, Weber KT, Janicki JS, McElroy PA. Hemodynamic, ventilatory and metabolic effects of light isometric exercise in patients with chronic heart failure. J Am Coll Cardiol 1988; 12: 353.

Reed SD, Whellan DJ, Li Y, et al. Economic evaluation of the HF-AC-TION (Heart Failure: A Controlled Trial Investigating Outcomes of Exercise Training) randomized controlled trial: an exercise training study of patients with chronic heart failure. Circ Cardiovasc Qual Outcomes 2010; 3:374.

Rees K, Taylor RS, Singh S, et al. Exercise based rehabilitation for heart failure. Cochrane Database Syst Rev 2004:CD003331.

Roveda F, Middlekauff HR, Rondon MU, et al. The effects of exercise training on sympathetic neural activation in advanced heart failure: a randomized controlled trial. J Am Coll Cardiol 2003; 42:854.

Sandvik L, Erikssen J, Thaulow E, et al. Physical fitness as a predictor of mortality among healthy, middle-aged Norwegian men. N Engl J Med 1993; 328:533.

Seki Y, Berggren JR, Houmard JA, Charron MJ. Glucose transporter expression in skeletal muscle of endurance-trained individuals. Med Sci Sports Exerc 2006; 38:1088.

Smart N, Marwick TH. Exercise training for patients with heart failure: a systematic review of factors that improve mortality and morbidity. Am J Med 2004; 116:693.

Smith SC Jr, Benjamin EJ, Bonow RO, et al. AHA/ACCF Secondary Prevention and Risk Reduction Therapy for Patients with Coronary and other Atherosclerotic Vascular Disease: 2011 update: a guideline from the American Heart Association and American College of Cardiology Foundation. Circulation 2011; 124:2458.

Soga Y, Yokoi H, Ando K, et al. Safety of early exercise training after elective coronary stenting in patients with stable coronary artery disease. Eur J Cardiovasc Prev Rehabil 2010; 17:230.

Stewart KJ, Mason M, Kelemen MH. Three-year participation in circuit weight training improves muscular strength and self-efficacy in cardiac patients. J Cardiopulm Rehabil. 1988; (8):292–296.

Suaya JA, Shepard DS, Normand SL, et al. Use of cardiac rehabilitation by Medicare beneficiaries after myocardial infarction or coronary bypass surgery. Circulation 2007; 116:1653.

Suaya JA, Stason WB, Ades PA, et al. Cardiac rehabilitation and survival in older coronary patients. J Am Coll Cardiol 2009; 54:25.

Sullivan MJ, Higginbotham MB, Cobb FR. Exercise training in patients with chronic heart failure delays ventilatory anaerobic threshold and improves submaximal exercise performance. Circulation 1989; 79:324.

Sullivan MJ, Higginbotham MB, Cobb FR. Exercise training in patients with severe left ventricular dysfunction. Hemodynamic and metabolic effects. Circulation 1988; 78:506.

Tavazzi L, Ignone G. Short-term haemodynamic evolution and late follow-up of post-infarct patients with left ventricular dysfunction undergoing a physical training programme. Eur Heart J 1991; 12:657.

Taylor RS, Brown A, Ebrahim S, et al. Exercise-based rehabilitation for patients with coronary heart disease: systematic review and meta-analysis of randomized controlled trials. Am J Med 2004; 116:682.

Thompson PD. Exercise prescription and proscription for patients with coronary artery disease. Circulation 2005; 112:2354.

Thompson PD, Franklin BA, Balady GJ, et al. Exercise and acute cardiovascular events placing the risks into perspective: a scientific statement from the American Heart Association Council on Nutrition, Physical Activity, and Metabolism and the Council on Clinical Cardiology. Circulation 2007; 115:2358.

Thomas RJ, King M, Lui K, et al. AACVPR/ACC/AHA Performance Measures on Cardiac Rehabilitation for Referral to and Delivery of Cardiac Rehabilitation/Secondary Prevention Services. Endorsed by the American College of Chest Physicians, American College of Sports Medicine, American Physical Therapy Association, Canadian Association of Cardiac Rehabilitation, European Association for Cardiovascular Prevention and Rehabilitation, Inter-American Heart Foundation, National Association of Clinical Nurse Specialists, Preventive Cardiovascular Nurses Association, and the Society of Thoracic Surgeons. J Am Coll Cardiol 2007; 50:140.

Tyni-Lenné R, Gordon A, Jansson E, et al. Skeletal muscle endurance training improves peripheral oxidative capacity, exercise tolerance, and health-related quality of life in women with chronic congestive heart failure secondary to either ischemic cardiomyopathy or idiopathic dilated cardiomyopathy. Am J Cardiol 1997; 80:1025.

Van Camp SP, Peterson RA. Cardiovascular complications of outpatient cardiac rehabilitation programs. JAMA 1986; 256:1160.

Van Rensburg KJ, Taylor A, Hodgson T, Benattayallah A. Acute exercise modulates cigarette cravings and brain activation in response to smoking-related images: an fMRI study. Psychopharmacology April 2009; 203(3):589-598.

Varin R, Mulder P, Richard V, et al. Exercise improves flow-mediated vasodilatation of skeletal muscle arteries in rats with chronic heart failure. Role of nitric oxide, prostanoids, and oxidant stress. Circulation 1999; 99:2951.

Veerman JL, Healy GN, Cobiac LJ, Vos T, Winkler EA, Owen N, Dunstan DW. Television viewing time and reduced life expectancy: a life table analysis. Br J Sports Med. 2012 Oct; 46(13):927-30.

Wannamethee SG, Shaper AG, Alberti KG. Physical activity, metabolic factors, and the incidence of coronary heart disease and type 2 diabetes. Arch Intern Med 2000; 160:2108.

Watanabe J; Thamilarasan M; Blackstone EH; Thomas J; Lauer MS Heart Rate Recovery Immediately After Treadmill Exercise and Left Ventricular Systolic Dysfunction as Predictors of Mortality. Circulation. 2001; 104: 1911-1916.

Wenger, NK. Rehabilitation of the patient with coronary heart disease. In: Hurst's The Heart, 11th ed, Fuster V, Alexander RW, O'Rourke RA, (Eds), McGraw-Hill, New York 2004. p.1517-1527.

Wenger NK. Current status of cardiac rehabilitation. J Am Coll Cardiol 2008; 51:1619.

Wenger NK, Froelicher ES, Smith LK, et al. Clinical Practice Guideline No. 17. AHCPR Publication No. 96-0672, U.S. Department of Health and Human Services, Agency for Healthcare Policy and Research, and the National Heart, Lung, and Blood Institute, Rockville, MD 1995.

Whellan DJ, Shaw LK, Bart BA, et al. Cardiac rehabilitation and survival in patients with left ventricular systolic dysfunction. Am Heart J 2001; 142:160.

Wijndaele K, Beunen G, Duvigneaud N, Matton L, Duquet W, Thomis M, Lefevre J, Philippaerts RM. A continuous metabolic syndrome risk score: utility for epidemiological analyses. Diabetes Care. 2006 Oct; 29(10):2329.

Willich SN, Müller-Nordhorn J, Kulig M, et al. Cardiac risk factors, medication, and recurrent clinical events after acute coronary disease; a prospective cohort study. Eur Heart J 2001; 22:307.

Wilson JR, Martin JL, Ferraro N. Impaired skeletal muscle nutritive flow during exercise in patients with congestive heart failure: role of cardiac pump dysfunction as determined by the effect of dobutamine. Am J Cardiol 1984; 53:1308.

Wilson JR, Ferraro N. Effect of the renin-angiotensin system on limb circulation and metabolism during exercise in patients with heart failure. J Am Coll Cardiol 1985; 6:556.

Wilson JR, Martin JL, Ferraro N, Weber KT. Effect of hydralazine on perfusion and metabolism in the leg during upright bicycle exercise in patients with heart failure. Circulation 1983; 68:425.

Wisløff U, Støylen A, Loennechen JP, et al. Superior cardiovascular effect of aerobic interval training versus moderate continuous training in heart failure patients: a randomized study. Circulation 2007; 115:3086.

Walsh JT, Andrews R, Johnson P, et al. Inspiratory muscle endurance in patients with chronic heart failure. Heart 1996; 76:332.

Working Group on Cardiac Rehabilitation & Exercice Physiology and Working Group on Heart Failure of the European Society of Cardiology. Recommendations for exercise training in chronic heart failure patients. Eur Heart J 2001; 22:125.

Wisløff U, Støylen A, Loennechen JP et al. Superior cardiovascular effect of aerobic interval training versus moderate continuous training in heart failure patients: a randomized study. Circulation. 2007 Jun 19; 115(24):3086-94. Epub 2007 Jun 4.

Witt BJ, Jacobsen SJ, Weston SA, et al. Cardiac rehabilitation after myocardial infarction in the community. J Am Coll Cardiol 2004; 44:988.

Wood DA, Kotseva K, Connolly S, et al. Nurse-coordinated multidisciplinary, family-based cardiovascular disease prevention programme (EU-ROACTION) for patients with coronary heart disease and asymptomatic individuals at high risk of cardiovascular disease: a paired, cluster-randomised controlled trial. Lancet 2008; 371:1999.

Zderic TW, Hamilton MT. Physical inactivity amplifies the sensitivity of skeletal muscle to the lipid-induced downregulation of lipoprotein lipase activity. J Appl Physiol. 2006; 100(1): 249–257.

Zschucke E, Heinz A, Ströhle A. Exercise and physical activity in the therapy of substance use disorders. Scientific World Journal. 2012; 2012:901741. Epub 2012 May 3.

Zullo MD, Jackson LW, Whalen CC, Dolansky MA. Evaluation of the recommended core components of cardiac rehabilitation practice: an opportunity for quality improvement. J Cardiopulm Rehabil Prev 2012; 32:32.

About the Author

James Beckerman, M.D., F.A.C.C. is a cardiologist and medical director of the Center for Prevention and Wellness at the Providence Heart and Vascular Institute in Portland, Oregon. He directs the cardiac rehabilitation program at Providence St. Vincent Medical Center and is the founder and medical director of Play Smart Youth Heart Screenings. Dr. Beckerman graduated *summa cum laude* from Harvard College and earned his doctorate from Harvard Medical School. He completed his medical training at the Massachusetts General Hospital and at Stanford Hospital and Clinics. He formerly chaired the Oregon Governor's Council on Physical Fitness and Sports and is the team cardiologist for the Portland Timbers Major League Soccer team. He serves on the clinical advisory boards of WebMD Health Services and *Fitness Magazine*. For information about speaking engagements or bulk purchases, email *hearttostart@providence.org* or find Dr. Beckerman on Twitter *@jamesbeckerman* or on Facebook at *www.facebook.com/drjamesbeckerman*.